The Reluctant Landlady

Bernadette Strachan was born in Fulham, London and now divides her time between Twickenham, Middlesex and Nashville, Tennessee with her husband Matthew and their daughter Niamh. Before becoming an author she ran a voiceover agency working with many household names including Hugh Laurie, Stephen Fry, Johnny Vegas, Mariella Frostrup and Harry Enfield. Bernadette Strachan has written for many publications including *Chat*, *Bella*, *Woman's Own* and *J17*. This is her first novel.

Bernadette Strachan

The Reluctant Landlady

FLAME
Hodder & Stoughton

Copyright © 2004 by StrawnyGawn Words and Music

First published in Great Britain in 2004 by Hodder and Stoughton
A division of Hodder Headline

The right of Bernadette Strachan to be identified as the Author
of the Work has been asserted by her in accordance with the
Copyright, Designs and Patents Act 1988

A Flame Paperback

1 3 5 7 9 10 8 6 4 2

A CIP catalogue record for this title is
available from the British Library

ISBN 0 340 83196 0

Typeset in Sabon by Palimpsest Book Production Limited,
Polmont, Stirlingshire

Printed and bound by
Mackays of Chatham Ltd, Chatham, Kent

Hodder Headline's policy is to use papers that are natural, renewable
and recyclable products and made from wood grown in sustainable
forests. The logging and manufacturing processes are expected to
conform to the environmental regulations of the country of origin

Hodder and Stoughton Ltd
A division of Hodder Headline
338 Euston Road
London NW1 3BH

This book is for
Matthew Strachan

Acknowledgements

Thank you Penny Warnes, Julia Tyrell, Annette Green, Philippa Pride and Sara Kinsella. Thank you very much for helping this book to happen, and for making this author so happy.

Evie Crump was sick of hearing that she had a funny name. Bank cashiers said so. Telephonists said so. The woman in the dry-cleaner's had been saying so for years. Even her dad said so, and he had given it to her.

Just that morning Evie's acting agent, the magnificently monikered Meredith de Winter, had been banging on about it. 'I mean,' she'd wailed down the phone, with a voice steeped in half a century's worth of gin and Silk Cut, 'how am I supposed to find work for an actress named *Evie Crump*? What do you see when you look in the mirror, darling? You see a girl in her twenties with big blue eyes and woefully untidy hair, you do *not* see an EVIE CRUMP!'

In fact, what Evie saw as she squinted into the dressing room's cracked mirror was a threadbare fun-fur badger, whose plastic left eye was hanging by a thread and whose paws smelt faintly of curry. God, she hated this costume. There was certainly no need to ask if her bum looked big in this.

An equally moth-eaten squirrel shuffled agitatedly in and said, 'Mflllurg blllllhmph,' rather angrily.

'Oh, get your mouthpiece in the right place, Simeon,' snapped Evie, and wearily pushed her eye back in.

'Sorry.' The squirrel didn't sound sorry. The grubby mask sported a whimsical woodland smile, but the pretentious, possibly alcoholic drama graduate inside it was furious. As usual. 'I *said*, you missed your cue for the song and if you do that again you're fucking OUT!'

'Oh, no!' Evie clasped her paws to her furry head in horror. 'Don't say that! Don't throw me out into the woods alone! How could I cope without you and all the other neurotic bastard cuddly animals?'

There is always good-natured banter backstage. But this was not good-natured banter. More than once the lovable animals had come off stage and tried to beat each other insensible with the scenery.

'I said all along you were wrong for the part,' yelled the squirrel, delving into a nearby rucksack and extracting a bottle of Jack Daniel's.

'You're spilling it on your padded tummy again,' Evie pointed out calmly. The chief – possibly the only – pleasure of this job was being foul to Simeon.

'Shut your face,' responded Simeon cleverly, swigging noisily from the bottle. 'Have you been studying badgers like I told you? . . . Well, have you?'

Evie scratched her massive fuzzy head with a plastic claw. 'Hmm. Well, I've been tuning into the soaps: *BadgerEnders*, *Badgeration Street*. Does that count?'

Simeon flung down his *papier-mâché* nuts in fury. 'Why won't you take this seriously?'

'Maybe because the script is crap, the costumes are crap and the set is crap.' Evie didn't add that Simeon was crap, but he was. Deeply crap. He made John Inman look like Laurence Olivier.

The big squirrel was shaking with fury. Really, thought Evie, this was too easy. Any minute now he'd come out with his no-place-for-cynicism-in-the-theatre line.

'There is no place for cynicism in the theatre,' he screamed, for once right on cue.

'We're not in a theatre,' Evie pointed out wearily. 'We're in a community hall in the arse end of nowhere, perform-ing anti-sexist, anti-racist, anti-ageist, anti-class-distinction and, unfortunately, anti-any-fun-whatsoever playlets for an audience of bored five-year-olds who, by the looks on their little faces, would rather be having rabies jabs.' She paused. 'Your tail's fallen off again.'

'Oh, fuck fuck fuck FUCK!' squealed Simeon, spinning round and smashing his bottle against the rusty sink just as the head-mistress of the audience put her head round the door.

Taken aback, she rallied quickly and asked tentatively, 'Do you think you could come back onstage? Your friend the mole was half-way through a most delightful dance when he slipped and put his head through a plywood tree. There's blood everywhere and I don't really want the children to hear that kind of language.'

One day this would make a great story to tell over a glass of wine, Evie thought, but today wasn't that day. She could certainly appreciate that anybody glancing into Casualty and spotting a giant squirrel and a giant badger propping up a giant mole, who was bleeding profusely and muttering, 'I turned down *Crimewatch* for this,' would laugh. But not her. Not just now.

'Can't we at least take his head off?' she begged Simeon, as they manoeuvred themselves uneasily into two of those orange plastic chairs that seem specially designed to be uncomfortable.

'And spoil the magic? Are you mad?'

Evie sighed and closed her eyes. Simeon made such declarations without a whisper of irony. Evie had become an actress because she liked acting: it was as simple as that. All this po-faced stuff about truth and beauty left her cold. (If she was honest with herself – and this occasionally happened if the wind was in the right direction – she admitted that she had become an actress because she wanted to be famous. But that sounded shallow and cheap so she didn't admit it too often. It was, of course, blindingly obvious to everyone who knew her.) Simeon had become an actor for altogether more noble reasons, but unfortunately he was an actor first and a sympathetic human being second.

And, apparently, a squirrel third.

'*Crimewatch* wanted me,' whimpered Mole, with a concussed slur. 'I turned them down. I'm a fool, a mad, crazy fool.'

'Ssssh.' Evie stroked his latex head as he slumped against her. She tried to ignore the computerised sign informing her that there were a mere three hours and fourteen minutes to wait as she recalled how Meredith had described this job to her: 'A riot! A romp! You'll love it! All those smiling little faces! Being one of the happy band of a touring company!' The reality was being crammed into the back of a medieval Ford Transit with various rejects from the acting world who kept up their spirits by drinking, bitching, being terribly, terribly serious about their craft, or crying. In her time in the van Evie had indulged in all these activities, except the being terribly, terribly serious. It was quite beyond her how anybody with a functioning irony gland could be sincere about what they were inflicting on defenceless five-year-olds within the area encircled by the M25.

Except, of course, Simeon. She noticed he had ostentatiously opened a copy of *King Lear* and was reading it as far as he could through his ragged eyeholes.

That computerised sign had been optimistic. Four hours had crawled by before they were allowed to fold up the bandaged thespian and stuff him into the back of the van. Evie sat wedged against the window in the front passenger seat as the vehicle reached frightening speeds of up to thirty miles an hour towards London, home, baths and fluffy towels. She was almost obscured by the props they'd had to take in the front to make room for the prostrate mole. Cradling an immense bush, she felt too knackered even to irritate Simeon with the tasteless *double-entendres* for which the situation cried out.

Sums buzzed in her head as she gazed out at the rain-sodden dual-carriageway. These days, she always came back to sums as soon as she was unoccupied. The equation went something like *wages minus rent minus bills minus a little bit of fun equals* . . . She could never do it so that it equalled anything at all. In fact, the answer was usually an offensively large minus figure.

If I don't get some sort of a break soon, thought Evie miserably for the thousandth time, I'll have to get a proper job. The very idea made her break out in a cold sweat. She'd had proper jobs. They'd nearly killed her. She admired commuters heading for the tube in the mornings the way newsreel crowds used to admire Tommies heading for the front. The truth was that Evie couldn't actually *do* anything useful. She had the attention span of a toddler tanked up on E-numbers, and reacted to authority the way pit-bull terriers react to a poke with a sharp stick. Besides, she *had* to make it in acting or her family would queue up to stamp 'Told You So' on her forehead. No, she would never give her mother the satisfaction of gloating over her often-prophesied failure.

But those sums. They couldn't be ignored for ever. She could recycle last year's clothes with a clever needle and thread. She could convince herself that she liked Smash and gravy for dinner. She could even use a smaller wine glass. But the rent . . .

'Do you need me to take you to your door?' asked Simeon, as he did every day.

'Yes. That was the deal, after all,' replied Evie, as she did every day. Muttering bad things about Simeon into the bush helped to pass the rest of the journey until Simeon – again, as usual – braked unnecessarily sharply and snarled, 'Here we are. Your elegant townhouse.'

Evie gave him a long, hard look. 'You really are a twat, aren't you?' she said, then hopped down on to the pavement.

The van roared away, leaving Evie alone outside her elegant townhouse. All twenty-six of its floors shot up into the darkening sky. There was elegant dog shit on the elegant steps, pock-marked with cigarette butts and takeaway wrappers. 'Something is very wrong with my life if I can't even earn enough to keep this place,' mused Evie. It was hard to stab her floor number in the lift until she took off one paw. Then she crossed her uncovered fingers tightly and was rewarded with an ancient hum. She held her breath against the whiff of urine until the eighth floor.

As she put the first of her five keys into the door (security was paramount at Dickens Tower) she allowed herself a tiny reckless daydream: the sound of a deep, warm, male voice calling, 'Evie darling! Is that you? I've missed you!'

Instead the smell of garlic almost felled her, badger suit and all, in the tiny hall, and a male voice yelled, 'Where have you been, you useless sow? Get your arse in here and open this bottle of wine.'

'Oh dear,' exclaimed Bing, her flatmate, when she shuffled into the kitchen. 'I don't have to ask what kind of day you've had.'

Evie slumped into a rickety chair and greedily grabbed the humungous glass of red wine on offer. 'If I just say mole, Casualty, Simeon, nervous breakdown if I don't get a decent part soon, you can fill in the gaps yourself.'

'Wouldn't mind filling that Simeon's gap. He's gorge.' Bing was a golden, glowing, tanned, toned, six-foot-two bundle of promiscuity. He managed the enviable trick of being outrageously homosexual without losing an iota of masculinity, thanks in part to his impressive physique and manly bearing. The only pastime he considered comparable to sex was gazing at his blond self in a mirror, something he was managing to do even as he stirred the Bolognese sauce, thanks to the reflective sheen of the eye-level grill.

'Do you *have* to cook in the nude?' enquired Evie, after her first heady slurp of *vin ordinaire*.

'I like the air to get to my skin. Don't worry. I always wear an apron. My magnificent tool won't get anywhere near your dinner.'

'Do me a favour and don't use the words "tool" and "dinner" in the same sentence. You couldn't fill his gap. Simeon, I mean. I've told you before, he's heterosexual. The sort of bloke who gives straights a bad name.'

'Straight schmaight. I could turn him quicker than a revolving door.' Bing simultaneously blew himself a kiss in the grill and tossed a handful of chopped oregano into the pan. 'Was he shitty to you again, darling? After I shag him I'll punch him for you.'

'What a lovely sentiment. He was making snide remarks about this place.'

'Twat,' said Bing, uncannily. 'This is our little palace. He just doesn't have enough soul to understand.'

Evie smiled over the rim of her glass at her lodger, his buttocks clenching and unclenching in perfect time to the Carpenters' song blaring tinnily out of the radio. Evie loved Bing. He was loyal, funny and decorative, all-pouf but all-man. Damned annoying too, with his nuclear-strength campery and vicious tongue. But he loved Evie right back. When he had moved in, the small, creaking, damp old flat had instantly perked up. The plan had been that Bing would live with her for a reduced rent while helping her tackle the countless home improvements that needed doing.

It had been a good plan. It had only one flaw. They'd been living together for six months now and the sole home improvement was a new glitterball hanging above the sagging three-piece suite. 'Face it,' Bing had said, over the dregs of a bottle late one night, 'I'm too busy having sex to do any DIY and you're too busy being depressed about not having sex to do any DIY. Plus, we're both allergic to manual labour.'

'You're sho right,' she'd slurred, and they'd both cackled, happy just to be together and to be blind drunk and to be the type of people who could rise above their surroundings. Tonight, cold, sober, tired and disillusioned, Evie was finding it difficult to rise above the cracked seventies lino, the windows that had been painted shut by some gormless tenant long ago, and the astonishingly accurate map of India the damp had traced on the kitchen wall. It was hardly a palace, but even these humble surroundings would be out of her reach if she didn't get a break soon. The sigh broke into the warmth of her wine glass and died there.

'It's being so cheerful that keeps you going,' remarked Bing. 'Now, what am I forgetting?' He struck a thoughtful pose in his pinny. 'Oh, yes!' He whirled round and thrust a tomato-smeared wooden spoon at Evie. 'A solicitor called! You've got to call him back!'

'A solicitor?' echoed Evie dumbly. 'Called me?'

'Yes. Yes. The number's by the phone. Quick, it's getting on for six.'

Evie stood up slowly. Why would a solicitor be after her? 'Do you think somebody's going to sue me?' she asked Bing.

'Typical. Always look on the black side.' Bing ushered her into the sitting room where the suite jostled for space with the widescreen TV he insisted on. 'Of course nobody's suing you,' he reassured her, as he handed her the receiver and dialled the number, adding, 'unless they saw your Lady Macbeth in Leamington Spa, that is.'

He returned to his saucepans, muttering distractedly, 'Now, what else was I supposed to remember?' as he tossed handfuls of spaghetti into foaming water.

A few moments later Evie trudged back into the kitchen. 'I . . .'

'Yes?'

'I . . .' She looked shell-shocked.

'Don't make me use violence.' Bing raised the wooden spoon. 'I what, you dozy mare?'

'I've been left something in a will. I've been left something *substantial* in a will. Yes, that's the word he used – substantial.' Evie turned wide eyes to Bing. 'I've been left—'

'I get it, I get it. That's fantastic! What can it be?'

Evie was too busy wondering who had heard her desperate prayers to muse on that. It was substantial, and that was enough for now. There must be a patron saint of stressed-out actresses up there. 'I need a bath,' she announced.

'Make it quick,' said Bing sternly.

Still lost in wonderment, Evie opened the bathroom door and was surprised to discover that it was already warm and steamy, and smelt of her favourite expensive bath foam.

''Allo!' beamed the cherubic dark boy from the bath, where his perfectly coiffed head just cleared the bubbles. 'I eez Raoul.'
From the kitchen Bing shouted, 'Ah, *that*'s what I forgot.'

2

What does one wear to a solicitor's office? Grey Marks & Spencer if you're Evie, fuchsia Paul Smith if you're Bing. Sitting in the antiseptic reception room of Snile and Son, they made an incongruous pair. Evie squeezed Bing's hand. She was glad of his support. He could have been licking marshmallows off Raoul's tummy, but he was here in all his immaculately turned-out glory.

'Miss Crump?' Mr Snile Jr stood at the open door to his office, every inch the part, with his balding domed head and his half-moon spectacles. 'Please, do come through.' *Something substantial* buzzed around Evie's head as she and her companion were ushered through the heavy oak door.

The nearby park was a relief after the staid stuffiness of the office. Evie sat on a bench by the pond while Bing paced to and fro in front of her, scattering the ducks, who were imploring them for bread with a self-confidence that was doomed to go unrewarded. She had the dazed look of one who had been dropped from a helicopter but Bing was crackling with excitement.

'A house!' he exclaimed, for the fiftieth, or hundred and fiftieth, time. 'Out of nowhere, a whole fucking house!' He shoved an intrepid mallard out of his way with the toe of his loafer. 'Doors, windows, walls, the whole shebang!'

'Floors, ceilings . . .' muttered Evie.

'Probably even a roof. You realise what this means? You're rich, babe!'

Evie smiled distantly. 'You're forgetting the conditions, Bing,' she said gently, holding up an envelope. 'I'm certainly not rich.'

'What conditions?' Bing snatched the letter from her. 'I stopped listening after he said some old dear had left you a house.' He peered at the typewritten page.

Evie closed her eyes. Belle O'Brien had been no old dear. Warm, laughing, mischievous and always smelling deliciously of roses with just a hint of gin, she had been a big part of Evie's childhood.

Back in the twenties Evie's grandmother and Belle had sat beside each other on their first day at convent school in Dublin, and they'd sat together on the ferry to England when they were giggling blue-eyed twenty-year-olds.

The two young women had had very different ambitions. Gran had only ever wanted to be a nurse. Marriage and multiple motherhood meant that her qualifications had lain unused. But Belle had never been distracted from her dream: ever since her first trip to a panto when she was not much more than a dot, Belle had known she was an actress. She had made up with looks and vivacity what she lacked in talent, and had tripped prettily across most of the stages in the country. Constantly touring in revues, plays and musicals, she had been careful to keep in touch with her old friend. Her career – never stellar – had waned long before Gran found herself bemused by the freedom that widowhood and a grown family afforded her.

The two old women had plenty of time for each other again and it was the Belle of this period that Evie had got to know. Evie, seven years old, liberally sprinkled with freckles, and with hair that consisted entirely of cowlicks, had been allowed to drape herself with Belle's huge store of old stage costumes, and to plaster herself with the heavy Leichner makeup that was still wrapped in its fragile glamorous packaging.

Belle and Gran had been the only people trusted with Evie's fledgling dream of becoming an actress. They had pronounced it a wonderful idea and had been an enthusiastic audience for countless melodramatic improvisations about princesses, witches, bank robbers, pop stars and Victorian heiresses. These command performances took place at Belle's house in the basement, which Evie remembered as large and dramatically furnished with velvet *chaises-longues*, ostrich feathers and rich dark colours. The three floors above, divided into self-contained flats, were let to lodgers, and sometimes as Gran had held Evie's mittened hand on the walk home she would tut and mutter baffling comments about how they were 'bleeding Belle dry'. Evie had shivered in delight without understanding the meaning.

Then Gran, dear loving, forgetful Gran, with her ever-present handbag and inexplicable devotion to Terry Wogan, had gone and died. Evie's mother had taken offence (an activity for which she could win Olympic medals) because Belle had excused herself from the funeral, explaining that she didn't want to think of her dearest friend and companion in the ground, she wanted to remember her alive and happy. All perfectly sensible, even to a child, but Evie's mother had embarked on one of her marathon huffs and Evie had never seen Belle again. If she was honest, it was a good few years since she had even thought of her.

Until today.

Bing was folding the letter. His shoulders had slumped under the fuchsia linen. 'Hmm. Strange conditions. Funny old bird, was she?'

'She was brilliant,' said Evie simply. 'I think I understand what she was trying to do.'

'That makes one of us. It looks to me as if she's left you something valuable, then tried to make damn sure there was no way you could profit from it.'

Evie reckoned she knew better. 'Listen. There's something I have to do. Are you on tonight?'

'Yes. I'll be giving my all upon the London stage.' Bing was in the chorus of the latest revival of *Joseph*. 'I'll bring a pizza home and we'll mull this over, OK?'

Very much OK. A kiss, a waft of Paco Rabanne, and he was gone.

Evie found the tube station and bought a ticket to Surbiton.

Or, as she liked to think of it, the Gates of Hell. Surbiton was where her parents lived.

Now, don't get the wrong idea about Bridgie and John Crump. Nobody else thought of twenty-five Willowdene Gardens as the threshold of the underworld. Even Evie was slavishly devoted to her pipe-smoking, cardigan-sporting father. It was just that if *you* had grown up as the younger, relentlessly under-achieving daughter of Bridgie Crump, you wouldn't recognise her as the mild-mannered, solid and respectable citizen that everyone else saw: you would know her as an ambassadress of Hades.

'Well, hello, stranger!' yelped Bridgie, passive-aggressively as she opened the door. 'To what do we owe this honour?'

'Hi, Mum. I need to talk to you and Dad about something.'

'About what?' Bridgie gripped the door in alarm, the duster falling from her fingers. 'Work? Money? Is it a man? You're not . . . ?' She glanced in terror at her daughter's stomach.

'Er . . . can I come in?' As Evie performed the comprehensive shoe-scraping and mat-stamping that was a condition of entry to number twenty-five she attempted to reassure her mother. 'Don't panic. It's good. I think.'

'Come on through, then. You've caught me on the hop, so excuse the mess.'

As ever, the house was clean enough for Evie to have taken out her mother's appendix on the *faux*-bamboo coffee table. Forensic scientists would have been hard pressed to prove that humans had ever lived there.

'Tea?' queried Bridgie, with the certainty of the second-generation Irish: not so much a question, more a command. 'Sit yourself down while I see what I have.' The vocabulary and style was all Dublin, handed down from Gran, but the accent was hyper-polished suburbia.

Tea never arrives alone in an Irish house. It is chaperoned by a fondant fancy or a little sandwich. On this strange day Evie found the prospect of a cup of tea and a nice little something rather comforting. Less comforting was the migraine-inducing swirly carpet, the countless bowls of pot-pourri, the mystical flicker of the orange bulb from within the moulded-plastic coal-effect fire. Evie burrowed into the obscenely comfy sofa, taking care not to disarrange the artful cushion display. Bridgie Crump lived her life in desperate pursuit of the posh and an abundance of cushions was very posh. Pot-pourri was off-the-scale posh, hence its presence on every over-polished surface.

'Will you have a sausage roll?' screeched Bridgie, through the louvred saloon doors that led to the kitchen.

'Oooh, no, that's too much, Mum.'

'Ah, go on. It's tiny. You can hardly see it. Look!' Bridgie waved it over the top of the door.

'Go on, then.' Resistance was useless. Bridgie's vocation was to feed everyone under her roof as if they were fresh from a famine. Plumbers, window-cleaners, Jehovah's Witnesses all staggered away from her door, covered with crumbs.

A dent in the armchair nearest the fire signalled the absence of the man of the house. 'Where's Dad?' asked Evie, as her mother steered a delicate course between occasional tables and pouffes, bearing her laden tray.

'Taking a turn in the gardens.'

Noting that the medium-sized patch of grass housing the bins and a sagging washing-line had been promoted to 'the gardens', Evie swiftly translated this information as 'Your father has sneaked out to have a quick puff of his pipe as I am too much of a heartless witch to allow him to smoke it indoors.'

'Now,' said Bridgie comfortably, settling herself down and swinging into action with the teapot, 'what's this important news?'

'*Henry!*' Evie sank to her knees and threw her arms round the fat neck of the elderly black mongrel who had just ambled into the room. She was deaf to her mother's squawks of 'Aw, no, he'll get hairs all over your jumper. There's no need to ruin it even if it *is* cheap.'

'Oh, Henry Henry Henry!' gabbled Evie, who had never found

another male to match him for love and loyalty.

But something was wrong. There was a downcast look in Henry's eye. He seemed subdued, ashamed, almost. 'Henry, what is it?' Evie drew back, panic-stricken, and took a good look at him. 'Oh, dear God, Henry, you're *clean*!'

'As you well know, he's always clean,' snapped Bridgie. 'You could eat your dinner off that dog. He's the cleanest Labrador in Surbiton.'

So Henry had been elevated too. It was possible that some portion of him was Labrador, but it was heavily diluted. He was a mutt, pure and simple. What was more, he was a mutt who had never met soap and water head-on before. In fact, Henry's idiosyncratic perfume had been the catalyst for the Crump pot-pourri collection. Washed, he looked smaller. And deeply apologetic.

Evie had an unwelcome flash of intuition. 'Mum, I hope you haven't . . .' She leapt up to investigate Henry's bed, which was lodged behind the sofa. 'Oh, Mum, you have!' This was cruel beyond even her mother's high standards. She'd washed Henry's jumper, the one he'd slept on since he was a pup. The raggedy old stripy sweater was now folded neatly in his basket like something on the shelves at Gap.

All this could mean only one thing: 'Who's coming to visit?'

'Beth and the twins. And *Marcus*.' She made Marcus sound like the Shah of Persia when in fact he was Evie's dentist brother-in-law. Bridgie worshipped Marcus for his conservative appearance, his effortlessly posh accent and his ability to install her elder daughter in a *4 recep/5 bed/3 bath(1 ensuite)/swmmng pl/extnsve grnds* near Henley. Evie had never got beyond small-talk with Marcus (she found cravats an insuperable hurdle) but she liked him well enough.

'Thanks for the invite.' Evie's skin thinned perceptibly around Bridgie.

'You don't need one,' said Bridgie blithely. 'It's on Sunday. I'm doing beef.'

'Just the traditional roast?' Evie was wary. Her mother had a habit of trying out the recipes in the latest celebrity or TV tie-in cookbook.

'Of course.' Bridgie foisted a teetering plateful on to Evie. 'With just a few roast eggs and a nice thin nettle gravy.'

A deep, merry voice rumbled, 'Can't wait,' from the door-way.

'Dad!' Evie stretched to accept the whiskery kiss he was offering. 'Oh, Dad, it's so good to see you.'

And it was. It was good to see his thick grey hair, his warm blue eyes (so like her own), his quietly amused expression and his general, all-round daddishness. At twenty-seven Evie was a good ten years younger than Beth, and her parents had always been a touch older than other people's. She hadn't noticed it until recently. Her mother's thick Irish hair, only barely tamed by the ever-present perm, now had threads of startling silver. They were both slowing down. Dad looked – or was this just her imagination? – ever so slightly smaller, ever so slightly diminished. These were unwelcome thoughts as she watched him ease himself into his favourite chair and covertly help the pristine Henry to a sausage roll.

'I've got a house!' Characteristically Evie leapt straight in.

When the what-do-you-means had subsided she went on to explain more fully.

Bridgie sniffed meaningfully. 'Huh! Belle! That woman was mad as a hatter. There'll be a drawback. She led my poor mother astray for years.'

'Now now, Bridgie,' began John, in the sort of voice vets use to calm hysterical horses, 'Belle was eccentric but perfectly harmless. And you can hardly call going on the swings at the local rec leading your mother astray.'

'They were over seventy! Anything could have happened!' squealed Bridgie, with full backdated outrage. '*And* she dragged her to that life-drawing class.'

'Hmm. Don't recall much dragging being necessary,' muttered

John, then quelled the flow of accusations: 'She was a good friend to your mum at a time when she was lonely. If she's decided to make this generous bequest to our daughter we should be grateful to her.'

Bridgie looked chastened but, rallying, found another negative point to raise. 'You won't want to live in a big old dump like that. You'll sell it?'

John Crump was beaming. 'Looks like those money worries are over, you lucky girl.' He winked at his little girl. He had long ago stopped endeavouring to help her out financially. One of the many traits Evie had inherited from her mother was a ferocious pride.

'Well, no, not really.' Evie sighed and produced the letter. She smoothed it out on her lap and continued, 'There are conditions.' She ignored Bridgie's snort, and the resulting hail of macaroon crumbs, and read out the letter that Mr Snile Jr had given her, which Belle had written a few weeks before she died. Her Dublin lilt came clearly across the divide.

'*Dear Evie*

'*How very peculiar it is to write a letter that will only be read out after I have perished! But perished I have and it is time to redistribute my possessions. My biggest and most significant possession I leave entirely to you, the granddaughter of my beloved friend. I saw so much of her in you and, perhaps fancifully, I came to see something of myself in you as well. As I got older and a slight (slight, mind!) regret began to creep in about the lack of a family of my own, I loved to have you in the house, and listen to your stories and chatter. Then when you proclaimed that you wanted to be an actress I suddenly realised, "This little person and I are alike." How your gran and I relished those impromptu productions when you played every part. I particularly remember your version of* Romeo and Juliet: *your Juliet told Romeo that he ponged and she was running away to join a disco-dancing team. I could see the love of performing in what you were doing even then, and I could also see some real talent.*

'The years steal people from our lives and I lost touch with you after we lost our mutual dear one. But I heard that you had trained as an actress and I saw you occasionally on my crackly TV, in commercials and walk-ons. But I knew you were struggling, because that's what we actresses do, unless we're stars. Very few of us are lucky enough to be Meryl Streep – or even Claire Sweeney – so I leave you my house as security in the fraught but magical life you have chosen. Think of it as a subsidy, to help you carry on with your dream.

'My dear, I hand you the key to eighteen Kemp Street but I also hand you responsibilities. I bought this house for what now seems small change back in the fifties. I had saved for the future, never trusting in a knight in shining armour. I had a plan. When the work dried up – my slender talent was never going to outlive my dimples – I would have an income from letting the rest of the house.

'And that is how I came to be living here, in my warm basement, with all my lodgers in their flats above me. You may think me a very foolish old biddy, but they are special to me. From the day I first put up a "rooms to let" postcard in the local newsagent I have felt that only the folk who were really meant to live here have approached me.

'So, if you accept ownership of this house, you accept responsibility for the lodgers too. None of them must be turned out and the house must not be sold until the last of them has left entirely of their own accord.

'I realise that their rents are low, so reappraise them if you want to. Try to take their personal situations in to account.

'I am tired now and must put down my pen. I hope that you will accept my bequest. I dearly hope that it will be of use to you.

'Love to you, from wherever I am,

'Belle O'Brien.'

Bridgie opened her mouth, but her husband shot her a look he used only rarely and she shut it again noiselessly. 'She obviously cared about you, Evie,' John said. 'But what do you want to do? Do you feel able to take on a house full of lodgers?'

'Yes.' The certainty in her voice surprised Evie. 'Yes, I do. I don't know why,' she added lamely, 'but I do.'

In reality, she did know why. One hopeful, star-struck, dedicated, slightly nutty actress had reached out to another across the years, across the divide between life and death. It was a vote of confidence from one of her own.

Bridgie could never be quelled for long. 'This will just prolong the acting nonsense,' she proclaimed, returning to a well-worn theme. 'If you sold the house you'd have financial security and you could retrain for something useful, like Beth.'

'I didn't realise she had a degree in Dentist's Wife-ing,' mumbled Evie, folding the letter into her overstuffed suede sack of a handbag.

'As you well know, Beth is a qualified solicitor,' Bridgie said. 'Will you listen to me for once and sell this bloody madwoman's house?'

When are you *going to listen to me?* thought Evie grimly. 'There's a codicil – if that's the right word – to the will. If I don't accept Belle's conditions the house passes to the local housing association, with in-built protection for her tenants.'

'I say good luck to you!' Evie's father stood up. 'And good luck to old Belle too. I'll dig out the sherry and we'll toast you both.'

Bridgie sighed as her husband filled three miniature schooners from the prehistoric bottle of sherry that constituted the major portion of the Crump drinks cabinet. 'John, John, John,' she asked sadly, 'is there no end to your appetites?'

It had taken a while to winkle the information out of Bridgie, but once Evie had ascertained that an invitation to the funeral had arrived and been ignored she was determined to visit Belle's grave.

'I have absolutely no idea where Belle O'Brien is buried,' Bridgie had declared. After some skilful topping up of her schooner she had spilled not only the address of the cemetery but the location of the grave. (Bridgie was an enthusiastic and seasoned snubber: if she was going to ignore somebody she would ignore them with all the necessary information to hand. It was more satisfying than a vague, amateurish snub.)

Another tube station, another emergence, but into the metropolitan clamour of Earl's Court this time. According to Bridgie, Belle had bought her plot decades ago in the Catholic corner of Brompton Cemetery. 'Morbid,' she had said, and sniffed, but Evie considered it canny and sophisticated. Of course a sexy young actress would want to make sure her well-applauded bones rested for ever in a chic part of town. South Kensington was a Frenchified Bohemian area – although any Bohemians who ended up there, these days, were well-heeled ones.

How does a cemetery achieve that stillness? Through the gates, it was as if the hectic traffic on the other side of the wall was now on tiptoe. Evie looked at the plan posted for first-timers like herself and set off purposefully down an asphalt path that shimmered hotly in the June heat. She clutched a crackling, Cellophaned bunch of expensive, dusty pink roses to her chest as she passed weeping angels, open Bibles, mournful draped figures, all in stone. Brompton residents were not folk of restraint. Heroes all, surely – no ordinary mortal with a job, an overdraft and mundane habits could merit such a grand memorial.

In a corner shaded by ancient yews, Evie spied a newish grave. Her pace slowed. She was not 'good' at cemeteries. The infrequency of her pilgrimages to her grandparents' graves was a source of tension between her and her mother. This visit had seemed different: more a thank-you to an old friend than a morbid mission. Now she wasn't so sure. That old friend was decaying beneath a hump of earth. She drew nearer. It really was too hot. The road, with its hurtling cars, buses and buildings full of reassuringly alive people, was far away. Even if she ran.

'But I'm not going to run, for God's sake!' Evie admonished herself for bringing her actress's dramatic sensibility to what was, undoubtedly, the most tranquil scene.

She knelt at the foot of plot 443N. Too recent for a headstone, the grave's only decoration was the dry and exhausted funeral wreaths and bouquets, their parched colours jumping in the dappled shade of the wide, kind yew.

'Hello, Belle.' Crazy to feel self-conscious, but she did. You spend your days dressed as a badger singing nursery rhymes set to rap music, she reminded herself. A little thank-you speech should be a doddle. She coughed and raised her voice. 'Hello.' Well, it was a start. 'It's me, Evie. I'm a bit older than the last time we met.' She hesitated, unsure how to go on. 'I'm sorry you had to die.' God! What a stupid thing to say! Was it socially correct, Evie wondered, to bring up death with a dead person? Was it along the same lines as not mentioning the war to a German? 'This is a lovely spot to . . . lie – rest,' she corrected herself hastily. 'What I really want to say, Belle, is thank you. Thank you from the bottom of my heart. I know why you left me the house and I hope I can live up to it. And don't worry about your lodgers. They'll be safe and secure with me.' Evie leant forward and laid down her roses. Their faded colour made them the perfect match for their withered companions.

'Oh.' There was one other fresh token. A small bunch of lavender, tied clumsily with ribbon of the kind you see looped round thick, shiny pigtails at school gates: navy, with yellow smily faces dotted along it. Evie pushed a clod of earth from the luggage label attached to the lavender. 'I miss you,' she read.

She was shocked into a hot tear. Somebody missed Belle. How beautiful, she thought, to be missed. And then she shuddered: she was a single woman and a struggling actress, just like Belle, but who would miss *her*?

The sun bounced a spark off something at the edge of her vision. Evie turned to see a flash of dark fabric dart behind a tree. The movement was furtive, Evie was sure of that somehow, and she sprang to her feet. 'Hello?' she sang, in a voice she hoped didn't sound too alarmed. The faded fabric appeared again as a girl with a basket raced off between the trees and towering statues.

Perplexed, Evie stared after her. The unsettling anxiety ebbed away with a swishing movement of the branches above her and a refreshing breeze that bathed her in a cool wave. She shut her eyes and revelled in it. The rustle of the watching trees seemed to get louder. The leaves were making music. Evie allowed herself to imagine they were telling her that Belle was pleased.

3

To Evie, North London was a foreign land. Fulham born, she regarded Belsize Park as a forbidding alien landscape out of which erupted huge brutal houses full of, well, North Londoners.

Now she was the owner of one such brutal house.

'Eighteen Kemp Street,' announced Bing unnecessarily, looking up at the three grey-brick storeys that reared uncompromisingly in front of them. 'It's handsome.'

'It's falling down,' Evie corrected him.

They were both right. Belle had eschewed (or been unable to afford) modernising blights such as UPVC windows, replacement front doors, satellite dishes, extensions. So far so *Interiors* magazine, but she had also done without basic repairs. The tall, austerely uniform windows were peeling and rickety, the bricks were sooty, the front door was wantonly allowing a peek at its last three colours. The most recent had been pale blue, a sunny Cornwall shade at odds with the gloomy house around it.

'Good-sized front garden,' said Bing.

Knee-deep in brambles as she hacked her way to the wide steps that led to the front door, Evie snapped, 'What are you, the gay happy estate agent? It's like Borneo. Why is it so neglected when three prats live here practically free?'

'Here's one of the prats now,' Bing mumbled. 'Why don't you ask her?'

Evie wheeled round to face the girl who had silently (damn her) emerged from the front door and stood scowling on the decaying top step, a toddler saddled neatly on her hip. The scowl, Evie would come to know, was not because Evie had called her tenant a prat: it was permanent, like death, taxes and *Coronation Street*.

'You the new landlady?' asked the girl, in a fruity Lancashire accent. She managed to sound both belligerent and uninterested.

'Yes. I'm Evie Crump.' Amazingly the girl's face didn't crack. Evie felt slighted. *Everybody* sniggered at her name. She bounded up the stairs and held out her hand like a good little landlady.

The girl cast an incredulous glance at it and walked past her down the steps. 'I'm Caroline and this is Milly,' she threw over her shoulder, as she braved Borneo to get to the lopsided wrought-iron gate. 'I know I owed the old biddy a week and a half. Don't wet yourself. You'll get it.'

After a pause while they watched her progress down Kemp Street Bing said, 'I *like* her.'

Evie laughed, then rapidly regained her crestfallen demeanour. 'Why was Belle concerned about *her*? She's a right madam.'

'Maybe she improves when you get to know her,' Bing suggested philosophically, and leapt up the steps to join her at the front door. 'Although she'd have to work very hard just to achieve "horrible".' He leant over and pulled the creaking front door shut. 'No, you don't. First time. Use your key, Ms House Owner.'

'Here goes.' Evie flourished it.

'No, hang on.' Ignoring her ladylike 'Oi! Fuck off!' Bing swept her up into his arms as if she was a Victorian invalid. 'Let's do this properly. You open the door and I'll carry you over the threshold. Probably the only time anybody ever will, after all.'

'Thank you.'

'Particularly if you keep buying your jeans at Bhs.'

'Thank you again. Actually, they're 501s.'

'That's even worse. It means that on you they *look* like Bhs.'

'May I open the door, please?'

'Yes. I know I'm a trained dancer with the stamina of a finely honed athlete but I haven't had to carry anything so heavy since I played Jesus in the school pageant and they gave me a real cross.'

Evie refused to give Bing the satisfaction of laughing. She leant over, key in hand, just as the door flew open.

'Oh,' said the unkempt man standing there.

'Oh,' echoed Evie. 'I mean hello. I'm Evie Crump, your new owner. Oh, God – no, I'm your landlady. Sorry, that sounded awful.' Her feet thumped on to the floor as Bing gratefully put her down.

'Yes,' said the second of her new tenants. Evidently riddled with shyness, he seemed to be grasping words at random, regardless of their relevance. 'Quite. Well. Ah. Now.' He was a tall, strawberry-blond man of impressive untidiness. Each item of his clothing – tweed jacket, check shirt, *brogues*, for Heaven's sake – might have been donated by a vastly larger or smaller friend. His soft, educated voice gave him an air of other-worldly, baffled academia. His pale features concertinaed with crimson embarrassment. 'I am so dreadfully sorry,' he gasped, with sudden fluency. 'I've spoiled the start of your honeymoon!'

Evie blinked hard. Bing guffawed heartily. 'I'm not married to *that*,' he whooped ungallantly. 'Look. Let's start again. Evie here is moving in today. She's your new landlady. I'm her friend, Bing, and I am deeply – thank God – gay.'

A visible jolt rippled through the other man at the G-word. Just as if, Bing reminisced later, an electric cock had been stuck up his arse. He recovered and informed them that he was Bernard Briggs.

'But of course you are,' said Bing. 'Now, can we come in?'

Bernard flattened himself against the wall, as if he was expecting a herd of large horned things to rush past him, and in they went.

Evie looked around her at the maroon-painted communal hallway, which was high and spacious with original mouldings, heavy-looking doors and dark-stained floorboards.

Bing closed the door after Bernard, who had fled, and squealed gleefully, 'You own all this!'

'I own the damp. I own the rotting door jambs. Lucky me,

I even own the mouse poo I can see in the corners.'

Bing's wide shoulders sank. 'Cheerful as ever,' he said. 'Have you any idea how much I envy you?'

'You? Envy? Me?' echoed Evie idiotically.

'Yes. I might have natural good looks, unbridled talent and all the sex I can eat, but I don't own a thing. The only security I have is the certain knowledge that *Joseph* closes in six months and it's back to auditions and waiting tables. Whatever happens in your career, you have bricks and mortar in your name. What a fantastic safety-net. How lucky you are. Right!' Bing slapped his hands together in a workmanlike way. 'Lecture over. I'll start bringing the boxes up.'

Evie knew he was right. She was acting like an ungrateful baggage. The unexpected bequest of a house was a godsend, usually only granted to Victorian heroines in Sunday-afternoon serials. So why did she feel so oppressed by the dark, damp air of this house? *Her* house. Why did she feel so daunted by her responsibilities?

Before she had time to formulate anything approaching an answer Bing was staggering back up the steps to join her in the main hall with an overflowing box marked 'clothes'. 'Get the bloody door to the basement open. What have you got in here? Chain-mail?'

Confused, Evie gazed about the gloomy hallway. Which *was* the bloody door to the basement? There were two doors leading off it marked 'A' and 'B' with brass letters that didn't quite match. Presumably flat C was up on the first floor, with D nestling at the very top of the house. She gazed up the stairs to where dust motes danced balletically in the antique air.

'I can't support this many size fourteens indefinitely,' warned Bing, his legs beginning to buckle.

'Sorry,' muttered Evie, and fumbled with the unfamiliar key-ring. She heaved open the sticky door to flat A and stood back to allow Bing to stagger through it.

And fall down the stairs, all eighteen of them. The flight began immediately on the other side of the door. He unearthed some creative swear words Evie had never heard before.

'It's a long time since I was here! I forgot!' wailed Evie, racing down to him and trying to sound contrite and sympathetic, rather than laughing like a chimp. Seeing people fall over was one of her favourite things.

Bing recovered speedily and gazed around him. All the doors in the basement flat were open, so they could see into the two small bedrooms, the ancient bathroom, the poky kitchen and the dim sitting room. The maroon upstairs had evidently been Belle's favourite colour, for variants of it were repeated down here. Nosing gingerly through the doors, Evie saw purple, mauve, lavender, heather and indigo everywhere, gobbling up the scanty light that penetrated the fussy lace curtains. Thankfully, all of Belle's personal possessions had been cleared out by an unknown hand, but playbills, publicity shots and carefully framed reviews still smothered the dark walls. Even the bathroom was a deep purple and contrasted oddly with the state-of-the-art fifties boiler. Evie had to smile. Belle had been an actress to the last: a review of her Juliet in the Palace of Varieties, Totnes, was hung over the cracked cistern.

The kitchen had been similarly Belle-ised. You know what colour it was, and Belle, in some bizarre wartime female version of the *Black and White Minstrel Show*, cavorted in a medley of pictures above the antediluvian fridge and a cooker Mrs Beeton would have chucked out as old-fashioned.

'Come and get a load of this.' Bing sounded awestruck. He was, as ever, ahead of her, and she followed his voice into the sitting room. It was a long room, running the length of the side of the house, and its purple expanse culminated in a large conservatory, which opened out to three steps that led in their turn up to a wide, wild and gloriously green garden, heavy with shrubs and shaded by decorous old trees. The June sun throbbed through the glass.

Evie was amazed. She hadn't remembered a garden. Then she frowned and opened her mouth but Bing was across the room with one *jeté* to put his finger on her lips. 'No! Don't say it! Don't say' – here he adopted a whiny mew – '"but it's purple. And the glass is cracked. And there's lino on the floor. And I can't look after a garden."' He reverted to his normal baritone. 'OK? Don't.'

'I wasn't going to,' said Evie, who had been going to.

Bing shot back up the stairs for more boxes. 'A lick of paint and some Ikea curtains and you won't know the place. Honestly, Crump, what are you going to do without me?'

The answer to that was probably 'Reverse my cirrhosis of the liver and sleep undisturbed by loud yelps of male sexual pleasure.' But there was another. Evie thumped up the stairs, puzzled as to why the idea hadn't occurred to her during the previous night's long orgy of chianti, crying and promising to keep in touch that she and Bing had indulged in.

'Bing!' she shrieked, from the crumbling top step.

'What?' came the ungracious response from the back seat of Bing's ancient rainbow-striped Beetle, where he was trying to stuff knickers back into a burst box. He was never at his best when elbow deep in women's underwear.

'Look at me! I can't talk to your arse,' commanded Evie.

'Hundreds have.' Bing straightened up obediently, a fluorescent G-string in one hand and a pair of seen-better-days big pants in the other. 'Whaddyawant?'

'LIVE WITH ME!' bellowed Evie, bouncing on her trainers with excitement. 'GIVE UP THAT REVOLTING FLAT AND LIVE HERE WITH ME!'

For a moment Bing attempted to look reluctant. But, despite his training, he wasn't much of an actor so he threw the knickers into the air and screeched, 'I THOUGHT YOU'D NEVER FUCK-ING ASK!'

The only person who had exhibited unalloyed joy at Evie's news was her friend Sacha. Extremes of reaction were commonplace with Sacha, however. Although she'd been to drama school with Evie, she had never made any progress in the profession, mainly because her emotions were less restrained than any part called for. A simple trip to Tesco would demand far more of Sacha than Lady Macbeth's 'Out, damned spot' speech. She had been hired only once, for a naturalistic fringe play about a reserved teenager pondering her dull life on an inner city estate. Sacha had played her like a pre-menstrual Maria Callas and had scared the front row of the earnest, right-on audience so much that only half of them braved the second act.

'You'll be so near to me!' Sacha had barked joyfully. 'We can see each other every day.'

'Yes.' Evie had managed a smile. If she had to see Sacha every day she'd end the year in a box. Much as she loved her friend, she had learnt over the years to protect herself from her demands. Sacha was the sort of person who would persuade a reluctant chum to let her 'just pop over and watch a bit of telly, you won't even know I'm there'. That same chum would find themselves still up and awake at three a.m., looking at holiday snaps. Not Sacha's, but her parents'.

So Evie was relieved that today Sacha's inner metronome was clicking slowly. Tinkling New Age music filled Sacha's tiny shop in Camden Market. Calmer Karma was stuffed with New Age trinkets, all designed to promote the serenity and wisdom Sacha liked to think that she, in some measure, enjoyed. Ensnared for ever by Sacha's generosity, sweetness and good old-fashioned big heart, Evie had helped her hand-paint the sign, while noting with an inward smile that Sacha's own karma was anything but calm. Sacha's karma was a bag of cats. When Evie stopped to analyse it, the chaos in Sacha's life radiated outwards in a ripple effect: others copped the right hook of fate while Sacha glided on, unaware of their bruises and self-righteously happy that she had shone a little spiritual light into another life.

'Just go through to the back and pop everything off,' said Sacha, by way of hello.

'Er, why exactly?' asked Evie warily. It wasn't beyond Sacha to have arranged a naked Neighbourhood Watch meeting.

'I want to try out my new skill on you. Go on, go.' Sacha flapped her hands impatiently. 'I'm just showing this customer how to heal herself with this crystal.'

Shivering beneath a thin and none-too-clean sheet on the wallpaper-pasting table that Sacha had reincarnated as a treatment couch, Evie sniffed the air with trepidation. It was impossible to guess which skill Sacha had acquired now, but they usually involved aromatic oils. Evie hated aromatic bloody oils. It was one of the main reasons she hated Camden Market. It was peopled by individuals in tie-dye garments, Caucasian Rasta hairdos and sandals that served only to showcase their grotty feet, and who presumably emptied buckets of ylang-ylang, patchouli, or *eau-de*-old-overcoat over their empty heads each morning. Then they would wander off to set up a stall selling signs of the zodiac made from bent spoons, or ancient Buddhist symbols of good luck made from recycled tampons, to credulous French-exchange students who were wetting themselves because one was certain she could smell a joint.

No, Evie didn't like Camden Market. Kemp Street's proximity to it was no advantage.

Sacha's voice drifted through to the back. 'A blue crystal is best for pains in the groin area,' she was explaining, with the confidence of a girl with a trust fund. Sacha's double-barrelled kin were of the truly, madly, overwhelmingly posh variety that Bridgie could only dream of aspiring to. Evie's mother had been keen to meet her upper-class friend from LAMDA and had been mortally disappointed to encounter Sacha in jeans and jean jacket, looking exactly like her own unmistakably non-posh daughter. Sacha was embarrassed by her family's wealth, but had spent rather a lot of it in setting up Calmer Karma, a business that wavered but would never collapse so long as Daddy's arms were long enough to reach into Daddy's pockets.

'Stones!' declared Sacha, with dramatic emphasis, as she swished back the beaded curtain.

'Stones!' shouted Evie, presuming this to be the trendy new spiritual greeting.

'No.' Sacha looked peeved. 'Stones are what we're doing today. Hot stones,' she elucidated.

'Aromatic oils on hot stones?' asked Evie. A horrible suspicion was growing within her.

'God, where have you been?' chided Sacha, rolling up the sleeves of her shirt. 'I'm going to lay hot stones precisely on the energy points of your body to release your negative flow and realign your *chakras*.'

'How hot?' Evie hugged the thin sheet to her. 'Have you done this before?'

'Not very. And yes.' Even with her back to Evie Sacha was a crap actress. 'But, first, a massage with aromatic oils.'

Surprisingly, Sacha was a skilled, sensitive masseuse, so Evie lay on her front and closed her eyes, marshalling her energy for the moment when she might have to wrestle her friend to the floor and knock a hot stone out of her grasp.

Sacha turned down the lights, lit a few beeswax candles and switched on her whale-sounds CD. Designed to help one relax, these CDs made Evie grit her teeth so much that her fillings trembled.

In her low, soothing treatment voice Sacha cooed huskily, 'I wonder what those magnificent beasts of the ocean are saying to each other?'

'Probably "Can you believe humans buy this crap for fourteen ninety-nine a throw?"'

Evie's massage began with a most unrelaxing slap on her arse, then Sacha reverted to her serene persona and said, 'So tell me about the house and your tenants.'

Eyes shut as Sacha's small, strong hands kneaded at her chubby bits, Evie recounted what she knew languorously. 'I'm down in the basement,' she began, 'with Bing. He's got two days off from the Palladium so he's getting busy with the white paint. Up on the ground floor, in eighteen B, is Caroline Millbank and one-year-old Milly. Milly is gorgeous. Obviously. That's her job. Mind you, her mother must have been scowling when the wind changed 'cos now she's stuck like that. She's very pretty, I think, with china-doll features and long shampoo-advert black hair, but she's got a real problem with people. Probably needs her *chakras* realigned. *Ow!*' Sacha didn't take kindly to Evie's open disbelief. 'That bloody hurt. Anyway, up the stairs to eighteen C and we have the bachelor boy, Bernard. And, before you ask, you wouldn't want him.'

'I wasn't going to.'

'Yes, you were. A rumpled academic type, but not at all romantic. We're not talking *Brideshead Revisited*, although there is something lovable about him. A complete mess – shy, awkward, stooped, and with the sort of dress sense tramps aspire to. Ginger too.'

'There's a lot of tension in your shoulders.'

'That'll be all the talk of hot stones. Right at the top of the house, in eighteen D, is P. Warnes. Haven't seen him – or it could be a her – yet. Don't know a thing about him. Or her. So you might be interested. If it's a him. I'm not suggesting you've gone all lesboidal.'

'Even if it is a him, don't automatically assume I'd be interested,' said Sacha, whose voice sounded as though it was struggling to be gentle and soothing. 'Just because I'm twenty-seven doesn't mean I'm *interested* in every man I hear about. You'll turn me into a cliché.'

'And how do clichés become clichés? By being true.'

'I'm heating the stones now. Just lie there and relax.'

Had there been the teeniest hint of a threat in that gentle suggestion? 'Anyway,' Evie gabbled on, to cover the ominous hiss from a candlelit corner, 'I'm having a little drink-up in the garden so that I can meet them all properly. I've put an invite through all their doors. Seven o'clock tomorrow. You'll pop round, won't you?'

'Oooh, yeah.' Sacha was never knowingly under-drunk. 'Now,

I'm going to place the first stone on your main *chakra*. You'll be suffused by an intense feeling of well-being.'

Much later, when Evie had stopped crying and they'd used up a whole bottle of lanolin, Sacha admitted she'd lost the instructions.

4

No party is too small or too odd to circumvent the traditional pre-party paranoia. And parties don't come any smaller or odder than the one for which Bing was tearing open Twiglet packets on that warm evening.

He had partly tamed the back garden with a scythe and his dancer's shoulders while Evie had been depressing the children of a Rotherhithe junior school with Simeon and their replacement mole. (This one had come to them straight from a sell-out season of Brecht and, according to Simeon, brought 'something so very true and special' to the production. According to Evie, he didn't know all the words of his song and had grabbed her breast as they frolicked in the crêpe-paper glade.)

'That was a quick shower,' commented Bing, as she emerged through the conservatory bearing boxes of wine, clad in her one good dress. It was black. Obviously.

'I didn't have one. I'd rather be hot stoned again than face that boiler. It's older than my mother.'

'And rather better-looking. Is that enough Twiglets?'

The kitchen table, dragged outside and draped with a newly laundered ancient white sheet, was home to an eclectic selection of nibbles. The ubiquitous sausage-on-a-stick was well represented, and its humble seventies compatriot, cheese-and-pineapple-on-a-stick, was putting in an appearance too. There were shallow tubs of dip from the corner shop, surrounded by some carrots, sadly no longer in their prime, which Bing had cut into sticks. There were sufficient Twiglets to satisfy their most ardent admirer.

'What if nobody comes?' Evie blurted out, while she fiddled

with the cheese-and-pineapple combo to create a more pleasing aesthetic effect on a cracked dish.

'We've only invited four people. It's not Mardi Gras. Of course they'll come.'

'Five, actually. Sacha.'

Bing pulled a face, his handsome features contorting into a gurn of annoyance. Evie knew that Bing and Sacha were chemically designed not to get on, that everything Sacha said and everything Sacha did made Bing want to buy a rifle. Evie also knew that Sacha, typically, had no idea of this and considered Bing a buddy. 'Well, *she*'ll definitely come. The Black Death wouldn't keep her indoors when there's a wine-box open somewhere.'

'But if the others don't come we'll just look like three alcoholics floundering in a sea of Twiglets.'

'The others will come. They've only got to walk down some stairs – they don't even have to go out into the street. The most dedicated anti-social party hater could manage that.'

'S'pose.' Evie wished that some of Bing's insouciance would rub off on her. Things mattered so much to her. Did they matter as much to other people? Did they search for signs of their own value in the most banal event the way she did? Certainly Bing looked a model of self-assurance as he opened a warm wine-box and deftly poured two glasses.

'Here you go.' He seemed to have read her mind. 'Confidence in a glass.'

Evie pulled a face, but accepted the offering. 'There's the door!'

'I didn't hear anything.'

She was already sprinting through the purple sitting room. She had definitely heard a knock.

An envelope lay on the top stair, just under the door. 'Ms Crump', it read, in a tiny, tidy hand. Frowning, Evie ripped it open. Inside, there was a cheque and a piece of notepaper headed 'P. Warnes'. 'Here is the rent,' she read. 'Cannot do parties. Thousand apologies.'

'Strange,' said Evie aloud. Footsteps were receding in the hall. She could catch P. Warnes and at least say hello. She got the door open just in time to see the street door slam. She dashed over to it, yanked at the still unfamiliar locks and was rewarded with the sight of the garden gate clanging shut. She raced down the steps, without spilling a drop of her wine (years of experience), and scanned the street. No P. Warnes.

When she got back to the garden Sacha had arrived and so had Bernard. They were chatting. Well, Sacha was chatting. Bernard was trying hard not to look as if he'd rather have his leg down the garbage-disposal unit. The poor man is shyness personified, mused Evie, as she approached them.

'Oh. Ah. Our hostess.' Bernard smiled widely and stuck out his hand with a kind of desperation.

'Hello there, Bernard.' Evie shook it. Bernard's arm was as rigid as a rake.

'Bernard's a Leo,' announced Sacha enthusiastically, 'so he's full of passion and fire. A real big cat!' She punctuated her unlikely analysis with a loud roar and a swipe with a paw-shaped hand. Bernard laughed, or it might have been a cough, and attempted a little growl of his own that sounded like a kitten's fart, and Evie decided she rather liked him.

Then, as so often happens around the shy, silence descended. Bernard's self-consciousness blighted the little group and they were reduced to smiling inanely, raising their glasses and looking about them, until Evie rescued them by saying, far too loudly, 'Look, here's Caroline!'

'Haven't you got any soft drinks?' Evidently Caroline mistrusted formal greetings. 'I can hardly give Milly wine.'

'Oh, Lord, of course not.' Bing squatted before the small visitor. 'Sorry, kiddo. Forgot about you. What would you like?'

Milly mumbled something in Serbo Croat, and then laughed and stuck her finger in Bing's eye. 'Ribena. Toothkind,' her mother translated flatly.

'Right.' Bing was no wiser. 'I'll be two ticks.'

'You made it!' gushed Evie, on hostess automatic pilot.

'It were hardly far,' Caroline pointed out, with disdain. 'Your friend, is he a pouf?'

'Yes.'

'Right.'

Evie could only ponder what that exchange had meant. The girl should ask for a full refund from her charm school. 'Would *you* like some wine?'

'OK.' She said it as if she was doing Evie a huge favour.

Sacha sidled up, her glass to her cheek, and said knowingly, 'You look like a virgin to me.'

'You what?' Caroline's face blackened to match her leggings and T-shirt. 'What are you trying to say? What do you think *she* is? A bloody immaculate conception?' She motioned at Milly's curly dark head. The little one was examining an ant with great gravity.

Unfazed, Sacha ploughed on: 'Oh, I can always tell. You are, aren't you?'

Before Caroline got any more het-up or elected to show them her ruptured hymen, Evie said, 'She means she thinks you're a Virgo, born in September. This is Sacha. She prides herself on being able to spot star signs.'

'Oh.' Only slightly mollified – her default setting was 'disgruntled' – Caroline told them that she was a Gemini. 'And I don't believe in all that astrology rubbish.'

'No, Geminis never do,' said Sacha maddeningly.

Perhaps emboldened by the special-offer Pinot Grigio Bernard ventured an opinion: 'Isn't it fascinating, though, to speculate that the movements of the heavens, by dint of laws discovered centuries ago, could dictate our fate?'

'It's all cock.' Caroline was succinct.

Before Sacha could trot out her defence (and it was a defence that had been trotted out more times than Red Rum), Evie changed the topic. 'P. Warnes,' she stated. 'Tell me about him. Or is it her?'

There were blank looks from the tenants. Evidently Caroline felt no onus to answer so Bernard swallowed and said lamely, 'I don't know. It could be a him. But, then, it might be a her. Or not.'

'You mean you've never seen P. Warnes? The rent book says . . . *it's* been here for two years.'

'Never,' said Bernard apologetically.

Caroline shook her head. 'Mind you,' she said, through a mouthful of Twiglet, 'you hear him all the bloody time. Banging. Tap-dancing. Sort of a trundling noise.'

Evie was alarmed. Particularly by the tap-dancing. She'd never met a tap-dancer she liked. 'What does he do up there?'

'God knows.' Caroline stuck out her glass for a refill. 'Might be summat to do with all the stuff that gets delivered.'

Evie just had to ask: 'What sort of stuff?'

'Just stuff. Big stuff. Small stuff.' Caroline was an unsatisfactory reporter. 'Some medium-sized stuff,' she added, after a little thought.

'The ultra-violet light was disconcerting at first,' said Bernard, 'but one gets used to it.'

'Ultra—' Evie was interrupted by Bing, who had returned bearing two big bottles.

'Toothkind for Mademoiselle Milly!' he roared, making the child clap her hands and squeal. 'Don't stop, I live for applause!'

'Oh. Are you a thespian, er . . . Bing?' Bernard had trouble with the unusual name but he straddled it manfully.

Bing topped up everybody's glass. 'I'm a dancer and singer. I'm swing in *Joseph* just now. That means I cover various small parts on a rota.'

'Getting paid for singing and jumping around! You're lucky,' said Caroline.

'You're right. I am.' Bing raised his glass to her without smiling. 'But I've trained and worked hard to be this lucky.'

The sky dimmed to a pink wash as the awkward little party continued. A surfeit of wine and the lack of any substantial food conspired to make Evie's head hot, and her brain useless.

'A toast!' she said suddenly, interrupting Bernard's remark to Bing that he hadn't been to the theatre since he had taken his mother to an amateur production of *Oklahoma!* in 1987. Four expectant, slightly tipsy faces turned towards her. Milly was engrossed in dropping leaves into her Ribena. 'We're all together here tonight because of one special woman. One very special woman.'

'Don't cry,' hissed Bing, who was familiar with the nuances at every stage of Evie's drunkenness.

'I won't,' she hissed back, as her eyes started to glisten. 'Let's raise our glasses to a friend who has gone but is certainly not forgotten. Belle O'Brien!'

'Belle O'Brien,' echoed the others, raising their plastic glasses solemnly.

Caroline remained mute, staring into her wine.

Evie moved towards her, but Bing, who knew that belligerence surely followed tears, put out a hand to stop her. 'Won't you toast Belle with us?' he asked Caroline gently.

Caroline stuck up her chin. Her face was pink. 'She's gone, isn't she? Dead. Finished. Why should I toast her? She's history. Rotting in the ground.' As the silence thickened around her she reached down to take her daughter's hand. 'Come on, Milly, you should be in your bed, pet.'

As Caroline walked away Evie shook off Bing's restraining arm and said, a little louder and with a little more emotion than was strictly necessary, 'She's not history. She was loved. There's a little note on her grave saying she was missed. Who'll miss somebody like you when you're gone?'

Caroline didn't break her step or turn.

Nobody said anything until Sacha intoned sadly, 'That girl's *chakras* are way out.'

Evie counted to ten and her friend's life was spared yet again. As Sacha interrogated a tipsy Bernard about his spiritual health, she leant against Bing and whined, 'Why did I say that? What kind of landlady am I? That was the worst possible start, wasn't it?'

Bing folded his strong, tanned arms round her. 'Shut up whingeing,' he counselled, kissing the top of her head. 'You can apologise in the morning. She deserved it, if that's any consolation. I think the evening's been a roaring success. I mean, look at Bernard, he put on his best shapeless tweed jacket just for you!'

Evie giggled, then immediately snuggled back into gloom. 'P. Warnes didn't even come.'

'We'll catch him/her/it, don't you worry. In fact, it looks like your mystery tenant is home now.' Bing gestured up to the top windows. A ghostly blue light flickered into the dusk. A faint noise, like a chicken being slapped against a wall, could just be heard over the drone of Sacha telling Bernard about his spleen.

The front-door bell buzzed. 'My date!' Bing dropped Evie and leapt off in the direction of the conservatory.

Too sozzled to be miffed by his desertion, Evie wondered who it could be. It wasn't only the volume of Bing's dates that amazed her, it was the variety. Bing was of the opinion that no man was immune to being turned, that even the most stalwart heterosexual was only a Piña Colada and a wink away from his futon. Evie hoped that this wasn't true but Bing's retinue of admirers was awesome. He was fond of saying, 'The whole world is gay and you know it,' and judging by the taxi-drivers, boxers, policemen, security guards and at least one soap star who had found themselves under his duvet, he might be right.

The man now smiling shyly as he came down the potholed lawn was a case in point. The brand-new and uncomfortable-looking tight leather trousers notwithstanding, Evie would not for one minute have supposed that Mr Snile Jr was gay.

After Bing had whisked off his new solicitor friend to the bright lights of Old Compton Street, Bernard showed signs of wanting to go home.

Evie smiled to herself. Sacha was in full flow and he was going nowhere. His participation from now on would be minimal: he needed only to nod and say, 'Really?' as Sacha stampeded on, enlightening him about Buddhism, the Chinese zodiac, ley lines and how Jesus had actually been a space traveller.

Bernard's eyelids were drooping. Even his ebullient hair was wilting. It was time to save him.

'Right. Shut it, Sash. Let this man get to bed.' It wasn't elegant but it was effective.

Bernard mumbled politely, 'Oh, no, no, I'm fascinated,' then scuttled at warp speed towards the house. 'Goodnight. Thank you so much for a lovely party.'

'Oh dear.' Sacha shook her head regretfully at his rapidly disappearing back.

'Oh dear, indeed,' laughed Evie. Bernard did cut a comic figure in his ancient shabby clothes, racing through her sitting room with his shoelaces undone.

'You noticed it too!' gasped Sacha. 'God, what am I going to do? Not again. This is awful.'

'What is? What are you on about?' Evie rebelled against her years of training in the home of Bridgie Crump and gathered the four corners of the tablecloth into the middle, thereby clearing the table in one economical movement.

'He likes me. He *really* likes me.' Sacha smiled ruefully. 'I'll have to let him down gently.'

Evie stared at her. At last she managed to say, 'Yes, that would be best.'

Bing had done Evie's bedroom first. It still smelt of paint but with the window open, it was bearable. The noises that Londoners find familiar and comforting drifted in on the still air: car doors slamming, partygoers singing and arguing on their way home, the distant beep of a pelican crossing. He had rehung the photos and playbills on the freshened walls so Belle's young laughing face was everywhere. Boxes spewing crumpled clothes, books, makeup, even a teddy, were scattered across the varnished floor-boards. They were a job for tomorrow, Evie decided, Scarlett O'Hara-style, as she launched herself on to the high, rather squeaky brass bed. She shivered. An old eiderdown, splashed with peonies, lay bundled on top of the wardrobe. If she stood on the bed she could reach it. She swung it down, and its cosy weight knocked her flat.

Evie burrowed into it, its scent enveloping her: lavender, lilac, roses, a sweet, mood-enhancing dustiness. 'Goodnight, Belle,' she whispered.

5

The Kidz!OK! bus stopped just long enough for Evie to be spat out of the side door, then roared off. 'Simeon, you're a twat,' said Evie, out of habit, to the empty street. Bing was floating down the steps of number eighteen. 'There you are, you filthy stop-out,' she said, also out of habit.

'Surely you mean "There you are, O highly sexed and attractive person who actually gets to achieve sexual congress instead of just thinking about it"?'

'How was Mr Snile Jr?' enquired Evie.

'Quite a laugh after his eighth Piña Colada. Boringly tearful after his tenth. Luckily, during his ninth I managed to—'

'I so wish I hadn't asked. Break your legs tonight, cherub.' Evie darted up to the hall door.

'Oh, by the way, ring your agent. She said it was urgent.'

Evie was beside the phone in the basement before Bing had got out the last syllable. Like all actors, she would wait for a message to ring her agent the way a dog waits for you to open a can of his dinner: the hunger is undisguised, overwhelming and ever so slightly repulsive.

As Evie stabbed at the digits she glanced at her watch. Damn. Six twenty. Never what a doctor would describe as sober, after six o'clock Meredith had G&T administered intravenously. Please don't give me another lecture about my name, begged Evie silently, as the ringing tone throbbed.

'De Winter Associates. Good evening.' The voice was straight out of pre-war RADA.

'It's Evie, Meredith.'

'Evie?'

43

'Yes, Evie.' Don't make me say my surname.

'I know no Evies. Kindly state your business.'

'Meredith, it's Evie Crump. I'm returning your call. You represent me?'

'And how the fuck am I supposed to represent an actress with a name like that?' She was off. 'I mean, do you *feel* like a fucking Crump, darling? Now, Redgrave, there's a name. Even Dench I could live with. But fuck it all to Hades and back, my dearest darling . . . Crump?'

For Meredith the F-word had been bled of its impact long ago and she studded her sentences with it, whether chatting to old ladies, vicars or others of a famously gentle constitution. Evie's mother still drew a veil over the evening when, backstage at a LAMDA production, Meredith had turned to her and bellowed enthusiastically, in a cut-glass accent, 'That little cunt of yours is a super fucking actress.'

'What was it you wanted, Meredith?' asked Evie calmly.

'God knows.' There was the jangle of a great deal of costume jewellery and the breathy rustle of papers. Meredith's office always had the look of a newly burgled crime scene but she could usually nail what she was after with one of her scarlet talons. 'Ah, yes. Here we are. An audition.'

Evie stood up. 'Really?' she whimpered.

'Hmm. Well, more of a go-see, really. For a commercial.'

Evie sat down. 'Oh. Right.' Go-sees were cattle calls. Hundreds of actors called in by a casting director for one or maybe two parts in an ad. You waited for too long in a room full of other actors specially selected to create maximum insecurity in each other. If the other girls were beautiful, Evie would immediately presume there was no way she was going to get the job and would try to tame her hair with a discreet pat, or tug a too-short skirt over knees she considered root-vegetable-like. If the other girls were plain, she'd be affronted. So, the casting director associated her with this lumpen lot, did he? There was also the danger of seeing a familiar face in the line-up. 'So, what are you up to?'

they would ask each other compulsively, dreading the answer. It was always to be hoped that your latest job trumped theirs. Children's educational theatre, Evie knew, trumped nobody. It was the joker in the acting pack.

'Now, I've sorted all this out with Kidz!OK! They're giving you the day off. How's that going, by the way?' enquired Meredith, with all the sincerity of the Queen asking a flag-waving Brownie if she had come far.

'It's an experience,' said Evie carefully.

'Well, so is a fucking vaginal scrape. Are you *enjoying* it?'

'Of course.' Never look a gift agent in the mouth. Especially not such a foul mouth.

'Good, good.' There was a deafening crash, rather like a shelf of files collapsing. 'Oh, Jesus. Fucking Barry's just pulled a shelf of files down on top of him. Must shoot. 'Bye.'

Evie giggled. What a wonderful mental image. Barry, the office assistant, was even older than the Jurassic Meredith, but had the unlined face of a schoolboy, thanks, he claimed, to the fact that he hadn't been sober since 1963. His mishaps in the office were legendary and Evie had often walked in to discover Meredith, lorgnette jangling and wig askew, attempting to sponge the contents of a tea-tray from his front, or trying to coax him out of a locked cupboard. One reason De Winter Associates Christmas parties were so well attended was that everyone was rabid to see what Barry would get up to. Most clients' favourite anecdote concerned him reciting Shakespeare's sonnets in knickers (not his own) and one sock, but Evie preferred his Christmas 1999 suicide attempt with an empty stapler.

The basement was looking, well, *younger*, decided Evie, as she gazed around her. The sitting room was half white now. She ventured into the kitchen. Still purple, unfortunately. Cheese on toast struck her as a good plan and she tussled with the old-fashioned overhead grill. It shot out at last. There was a piece of paper on it with 'APOLOGISE TO CAROLINE' written on it in Bing's loose scrawl.

Sighing, Evie mentally straightened her shoulders. It had to be done. What if the surly piece slammed the door in her face? I'll take a bottle of wine, she thought. Nobody slams the door in the face of a bottle of wine. She remembered Milly. She should take a little something for her too. What on earth did children like? Despite having twin nephews Evie had little to do with children. She looked desperately around the kitchen. A piece of cheese? A nice sheet of kitchen roll? Ah! The remaining Ribena stood on the worktop. Perfect.

'Who is it?' The voice behind the door of flat B sounded every bit as belligerent as it had the night before.

'Evie.' No response. 'With a peace-offering.'

After a couple of beats the door opened a sliver.

'Hmm. More crap wine.' But the door opened all the way.

Stepping into flat B was like entering the kingdom of the toddler. Hectically coloured toys were strewn all over the floor, a line of tiny dresses and dungarees was visible drying over the bath, and racing through it all, at a speed unlikely for somebody so small on all fours, was Milly.

'She's always laughing, isn't she?' said Evie, crouching down to smile at her.

'I'd laugh if I had no problems,' commented Caroline, preceding Evie into the tiny kitchen. 'Coffee?'

Evie was a touch disappointed not to be offered her own wine, but tried not to show it. 'Blimey!' she exclaimed, looking about her. 'This kitchen's new!'

The fitted whitewood cupboards, integrated appliances and gleaming chrome cooker contrasted strongly with the primitive cooking arrangements downstairs.

'Belle had it put in.' Caroline was not the sort to overwhelm with information, but she added, 'She thought it was better for Milly if I had a decent kitchen.'

While managing without one herself, thought Evie. Once they were seated on the threadbare sofa in the middle of a sea of Fisher Price, she embarked on the speech she'd speedily composed on her way upstairs. 'I want to apologise for being so rude last night. I was a bit nervous about taking responsibility for this house and meeting all of you, and I probably drank rather too much wine because of it. If you didn't want to toast Belle that was entirely up to you.' Evie paused, then added, 'Belle's generosity meant a lot to me and I know how much she cared about her tenants,' because she didn't want this sour girl to get off scot-free. Finally, swallowing hard, she pronounced, 'I'm sorry, Caroline. Can we start again?'

Caroline looked into the middle distance – seemingly her favourite place – and after a loud slurp of instant said, 'S'pose so. Yeah.'

'Great.' Evie produced a false, toothy smile. She had come to the wrong person for effusive proclamations.

A silence, not a comfortable one, hung around them like wet knitting until inspiration struck: 'She's gorgeous, isn't she?' Evie cooed, pointing at Milly.

Indeed Milly did look gorgeous as she chattered eagerly about important toddler business affairs on a toy telephone.

'Yeah. She's everything to me.' Caroline buried her face in her mug, possibly alarmed by her own enthusiasm.

Evie, who viewed life as one big soap opera, was itching to know where Milly's dad was, and why Caroline was bringing her up on her own, but Caroline's tetchy guardedness meant that she had to content herself with peripheral, innocent-sounding queries. Unfortunately this did not go down well.

'Where's your accent from?' asked Evie, and qualified her nosiness with 'I often have to do accents in my work so I'm always fascinated by a new one.'

'Bury.' One-word answers were Caroline's speciality, even if she did trill her R exotically.

'So what made you come to London? I'm sure it's lovely in Bury.' Evie wouldn't have been able to tell Bury from Venice, or a hole in the ground for that matter. To her the rest of Great Britain was just a colourful backdrop for London, possibly populated with morris dancers and lavender-sellers. For all she knew, lions roamed the streets of Bury and the inhabitants' local dish was whalemeat.

'Do you need to know that for your work as well?' Only a little less aggressive than a Fascist dictator with hives, Caroline was not easy to probe.

'No, I'm just interested.' Evie remained genial. 'Are your family still up there?'

'My family are all dead.'

As conversation stoppers go, this was a beaut. Evie crumbled. 'Oh, God. I'm so sorry, Caroline.' No wonder the poor girl didn't want to talk about it.

Caroline made no attempt to lighten the tension, just sat on the edge of the sofa, blowing on her coffee.

Evie fidgeted a moment or two, allowing the raspberry colour in her cheeks to cool, then stood up and said, 'I'd better go down and get myself some dinner. I've got an audition tomorrow.'

'Have you.' Caroline left out the question mark.

Evie backed away. 'So, that's our fresh start, er, started, then! Knock on the door if anything goes wrong with – well, with anything, really. You know, plumbing or . . .' Evie's mind raced. 'Dry rot!' she almost shouted, relieved to have shown herself as the kind of practical person who knew what might go wrong with a property.

'Don't walk on my daughter,' warned Caroline evenly.

Evie wheeled round to see Milly right behind her, holding up her arms expectantly. 'Oooh, are you coming to the door with me?' Evie tried to sound pleased, but she'd never been comfortable around kids. She didn't see the point of them. Hopefully, one day her maternal gland would kick in but right now she found children dull: they didn't drink; they went to bed ludicrously early; their jokes were pitiful. Clasping Milly awkwardly she manhandled her off the ground. Christ, she was heavy! Did she have bricks in her nappy?

She smelt nice, though. And the messy kiss she planted on

Evie's cheek was unexpectedly delightful. Evie grinned at her passenger, who seemed to understand the dynamics of carrying rather better than Evie did and settled comfortably on to her hip like a koala on a eucalyptus tree. 'Here we go, then!' It was a voice Evie had never heard coming out of her own mouth before. It was reminiscent of *Playschool, circa* 1973.

Caroline followed, presumably to ensure that Evie didn't maim her daughter on the short trip to the front door. 'See you, then.'

'Yeah. See you.' Evie passed Milly back to her mother. For the first time the similarity in their looks struck her. There was no similarity in their clothes, though. Caroline was in her drab uniform of faded black jeans and faded black T-shirt, while Milly was a riot of clean, pressed gingham. Her little socks were blindingly white with a gingham trim, and her floppy dark curls were held back with a colourful ribbon. Navy ribbon with yellow smily faces on it.

As the door closed to flat B a number of pennies dropped with quite a clunk.

The brief was 'young, carefree, playful'. When Evie had checked herself in the mirror at home she had been satisfied that white Capri pants and a sky-blue camisole looked young, carefree, playful. Haring through Soho after three-quarters of an hour in a stalled tube, which had had all the sensual pleasure of a sauna in a nineteenth-century asylum, she felt old, careworn, murderous.

She had left home with plenty of time and now she was late. Suddenly, this bummer of a job seemed like a prize. When she had lain in bed last night, it had been just a dog-food commercial. Now that she was late and in danger of losing a crack at it, it had morphed into A DOG-FOOD COMMERCIAL! ON LOCATION! WITH REPEATS!!!

Repeats. To an actor the word is beautiful. A couple of months after a commercial is first aired, the repeats (or fees for transmission) start to roll into their parched bank accounts.

Well, sometimes they roll. More often they trickle. At times they limp. The rewards vary greatly but can be staggering, so that beneath the actors' disdain for 'doing a telly' there is always a twitchy, barely disguised need to know about 'the spondoolicks'. Meredith had been vague on this point and such was that lady's mercurial disposition that it was impossible to guess whether this was a good or bad sign.

Screeching to a sweaty halt outside the Green Room casting suite in Argyll Street, Evie was relieved to find that she was only five minutes late. She smoothed her hair, which had reacted badly to being locked in a nuclear-heat tube train with sundry panic-stricken tourists. It was fizzing, like a cat preparing for a fight. 'Stop it,' she begged, but her hair ignored her.

Thankfully, the waiting room was air-conditioned. Thirty other girls of about her age were tensely arranged around the small white space. Some were a lot prettier, some were downright homely, so there was no clue as to what the advertising agency was after.

Evie gave her name to the receptionist, who had excelled at Indifference and Deep Boredom at reception school, then perched on the arm of an oatmeal sofa. A hasty scan of the room reassured her that she didn't know a soul, thank God, and she leant back in relief.

Then the door opened and in walked Miranda.

Evie knew Miranda. Miranda knew Evie. If Evie had had a rifle in her rucksack instead of her purse, a packet of tampons and some elderly Polos, she would have shot herself in the head rather than talk to Miranda.

But there were no firearms available to her, so their script went along these traditional, inescapable lines.

MIRANDA *(tossing flawless flaxen curls, removing Gucci shades)*: Evie! Oh my God! You look fantastic!

EVIE *(tossing frizzy, bathmat-like auburn curls, taking off Next sunglasses)*: Miranda! It's been ages! Look at you! You look wonderful!

The Reluctant Landlady

MIRANDA: Have you lost weight?

EVIE (*through gritted teeth – aware that she's actually put on seven pounds since their last meeting*): No.

MIRANDA: Are you sure? There's nothing of you.

EVIE: How's your lovely fella?

MIRANDA: We're engaged! (*Flashes a diamond the approximate size of tennis ball.*)

EVIE: Oh, that's marvellous! I'm so happy for you! I knew you two were made for each other.

MIRANDA: How about you and that hunky actor you were seeing? (*whose name I can't be bothered to remember.*)

EVIE: Oh, him. That was just a bit of fun. (*She's had more fun having her bikini line waxed by a beginner.*)

MIRANDA: So. (*Here it comes.*) Are you working?

EVIE: Oh, yes. You?

MIRANDA: Just a little teeny something. (*Pauses before killer punch.*) The new Hugh Grant movie. Three lines. A close-up.

EVIE (*resisting urge to shout, 'I hate you', and knock Miranda's head against the wall*): Brilliant! Well done!

MIRANDA: Well, it's helped me get an agent in LA, so that's something. What are you doing?

EVIE: Touring, you know. A tight little piece of snappy new writing . . . Stoppard.

MIRANDA: My God! Are you serious?

EVIE: Yup. (*Doesn't elucidate that it's Charmaine Stoppard.*) It's a fascinating allegory. (*With fun fur.*)

Evie's name was called before she could dig herself any deeper into that particular hole.

The audition room was a small blank oblong with a chair, execution-style, at one end. Facing it were a lighting rig, a video camera on a tripod and three other chairs supporting three men. One, bearded, bald and trendy of trouser, rose and said wearily, 'I'm Greg, the director. Please sit down and go through your drill for us.'

Obediently Evie arranged herself as neatly, yet casually as

51

possible. Endeavouring to sound young, carefree and playful, she said into the camera, 'I'm Evie Crump, and I'm with Meredith de Winter at Meredith de Winter Associates.'

'Okey-dokey.' Greg had the manner of a man who had been waiting for a bus for the last fourteen years. 'You've seen the script?'

'Ooh dear. No, I haven't.' Evie hated to rock the boat, but she couldn't bluff that.

'Jesus!' Greg looked up at the heavens. Or the polystyrene tiles on the ceiling. 'Give the girl a script, someone, pur-lease.'

His assistant, a sheepish, funky guy, who looked lost without his skateboard, scurried over and handed her a dog-eared, doodled-on script.

Greg droned on: 'Right. You play "Woman". "Man" has already been cast, with Dan here. You stay seated and Dan'll read with you out of shot. OK?'

'Er, oh, yeah.' Evie could have been forgiven for her distracted reply: when Dan rose, smiling, out of the dusky edge of the room his appearance should have been accompanied by a heavenly choir, complete with harps.

Dan was . . . well, handsome didn't cover it. Mills and Boon writers would have thrown down their pens in defeat. He really did have hair as black as a raven's wing, a chiselled manly jaw, eyes like twin chips of sky and a devastating smile. The tautness of his crisp white T-shirt across his chest would have made a nun reconsider.

And he was coming towards her. 'Great name,' he was saying. 'Crump. I like it.'

Evie didn't thank him. She stared at him and might well have sat there in silence until death claimed her if Greg hadn't snapped, '*Can* we get a move on, people, please?'

Afterwards she couldn't remember a word of the script. She had been too busy fantasising about what Dan looked like in the bath to take in her lines.

'We'll let you know. You'd have to be available the twentieth through the twenty-second. It's location. We'll get in touch with your agent if we're interested. Thank you, sweetheart, goodbye.' Greg's hand in the small of her back had propelled her out.

She came to. It was hot on Argyll Street. The Palladium's white frontage loomed in front of her. Bing! Today was a matinée. She'd take refuge in his dressing room.

Surrounded by eight, practically perfect, almost naked, undeniably homosexual male bodies, Evie perched on a Formica table and described Dan in minute detail. 'So I have to, *have to*, HAVE TO get this job, but I think I was lousy,' she finished.

'What's the commercial for?' asked Bing, rearranging his fluorescent-green loincloth.

'Some kind of dog food.'

'Class.'

'Don't knock it, green loincloth boy. I did my sums this morning. Belle kept the rents so low they're hardly worth collecting. I need a break, especially if I want to get started on all the improvements the house needs.'

'Not to mention the shag you're crying out for. I thought you'd had a no-actors rule since the last disaster.'

'I do. But . . .'

'Tremendous strength of character as usual.' Bing put a small red dot in the corner of each eye with a scrubby old Leichner pencil. Then, as if obeying some secret call of the wild, he and his eight fellow chorines jogged out to be back onstage for the big dance number in the second act. Left alone with a smell of feet, jockstraps and makeup Evie ruminated, not for the first time, that it was a funny old way to make a living.

6

They were back in the garden and back on the booze. The sun had long since left them to it and gone to bed, but Evie and Sacha were still sipping wine in the warm air on mismatched kitchen chairs. Their swaying figures were lit by the soft glow of the fairy-lights they'd rigged up outside the conservatory.

'Congratulations,' said Sacha. Again. She'd already congratulated Evie many, many times. They were drinking to celebrate the fact that Evie, against all the odds, had got the commercial. (If she hadn't they would have been drinking to commiserate. They had been known to drink to celebrate possession of a bottle of wine.) 'And he's really, *really* handsome?' prompted Sacha eagerly.

'Honest to God, he was so handsome I almost farted,' Evie assured her gravely.

'Dead shexy?' When she was drunk, the well-spoken Sacha sounded like a lascivious Brownie, or a character from the porn version of *The Famous Five*. 'Are you going to . . . you know?'

'If I get the chance I intend to you-know him until I can you-know him no more.' This *bon mot* set them cackling like deranged fowl. Sacha toppling off her chair tipped them over into full-blown hysteria.

Bing approached them through the scorched undergrowth. 'Blimey! What a lovely vision of modern femininity,' he remarked. 'At a guess I'd say that you two might have had a mouthful or two of *vino*.'

'Oh, Bing!' yelled Sacha, from where she lay in the uncut grass. 'You're gorgeous from this angle. Why aren't you straight?'

'Because I've got too much taste. Up you come.' Bing hoisted her back on to her rickety seat. She slithered down again.

Bing sighed. Both women were laughing now as if the Official Funniest Joke Ever had just been unleashed on them.

'Leave her,' gasped Evie. 'When she gets to this stage she can't stay upright. Oh, Sash!' She was choking again. 'Do you remember the time you—' she was finding it nearly impossible to talk '—launderette . . . Funny hat . . . The leg fell off—'

Incredibly Sacha did remember. A fresh bout of side-splitting commenced, with Sacha kicking her legs in the air and Evie sounding as if she was being strangled by a particularly energetic homicidal maniac.

Bing, exhausted by two shows and a virtuoso snog with the new understudy, stomped back to the house for fresh supplies of wine. When he returned an eerie silence had fallen over the two drunks. He stepped over Sacha and took her seat.

Suddenly Evie asked, in the little-girl voice that she knew Bing disliked, 'Would I be an almighty bitch if I put the rents up?'

'Yes,' burbled Sacha emphatically from the grass, 'you would be an almi'y bish if you put the rentsh up,' and fell asleep.

Bing was more diplomatic. 'Leave things as they are for a while. Let them get used to you. Worried about money, Funnyface?'

'Just for a change.'

They sat in companionable silence, the night air filled with the soft swoosh of distant traffic and the insistent bass line of Sacha's snores. Finally Bing said, 'This house is growing on me.'

'Mmm.' Evie leant back and looked up at it. All the windows were dark, and the outlines of the roof were smudged so that it seemed to melt into the sky.

'It feels kind of secure even though it's practically falling down.' Bing rubbed his face. 'Am I making any sense? It's been a long day.'

'Yeah, you are. I know exactly what you mean. It's solid. It's a . . . refuge.' Evie raised her eyebrows at her vocabulary after a surfeit of wine. Although it was in the middle of murky old Camden, the garden felt like a secret one, with its unrestrained trees and hedges. The only door out to it was through Evie's flat, so there was no danger of meeting a lurking tenant. 'My mum's been on at me about living in a basement. "It'll be damp and it'll be dark and it's the first place burglars go for," but it's cosy. I feel like a little furry animal snuggled down in its nest.'

'Yes,' agreed Bing, 'but I possess testicles so I wouldn't be able to put it quite that way.'

'And it's getting whiter every day, thanks to you.'

Bing sighed. 'Nothing I can do about that cooker, though. It's on its last legs. The fridge might be worth something to an archaeologist. As for the bathroom . . .'

'I know, I know. That's why I mentioned the rents,' said Evie sorrowfully. 'Belle kept them so low that the income will never pay for what needs doing, never mind give me the financial security she meant it to.'

Bing narrowed his eyes. 'That's not the only reason she left it to you. Maybe it's not even the main one.'

'Eh?' Evie squinted at him. His strong features were blunted by the dusty glow from the fairy-lights.

'Well . . .' He seemed unsure whether to embark on meaningful conversation with someone two bottles ahead of him. Evidently he decided to give it a go. 'I didn't know you back when you and Belle and your gran were all hanging out together but I suspect you haven't changed much. You're a nosy cow now and probably you were a nosy cow, albeit a smaller one, back then.'

'Oi, you. I'm too drunk for a character assassi-thingy. I'll cry.'

Bing had seen that before and it wasn't pretty. 'Let's put it another way. You like finding out about people, you like to give advice, you enjoy sorting people out, you're never without a collection of lame ducks.'

Evie snorted.

'Snorteth not, Crump. I'm right. On the rare occasions you have a job, whose dressing room do all the little actresses who've had rows with their boyfriends end up in? How many times do I come home to find some tear-stained idiot who's "having a bit of a difficult time at the moment" taking up the sofa? And what about . . .' Bing pointed at the figure on the ground, whose snores had settled down into a disco mix of snot and gurgles. 'You hold her hand through all her doomed love affairs, all her phases and crises, putting up with a level of sheer nuttiness that would make most people head for the hills. And what about me?' Bing pointed at his chest. 'Can you remember what an unholy mess I was when we met?'

Evie remembered it well. A huge party in a tiny flat. Dozens of thespians, with trained diaphragms, shouting, laughing, drinking and flirting at ear-splitting levels. There was cake on the wall, blood on the floor, and a couple who had never met before were attempting copulation under the coats on the spare-room bed. A fairly typical Edinburgh Fringe wrap party.

That day Bing had been chucked out by his Dutch lover of three years for (whisper it) a woman. He was the wrong side of a bucket of Jack Daniel's and a handful of dodgy speed.

'I was sobbing like a new Miss World and there was a six-foot exclusion zone round me – people were scared my misery was contagious. What did you come up to me and say?'

'You can stay at my place if you like.'

'Exactly.' Bing kissed Evie's forehead. 'You love a challenge. I moved in, cried it all out and a fortnight later I was right as rain. Shagging like the Duracell bunny and thanking God I'd met you.'

'Aw. Really?'

'Yes, really, but don't go all dewy-eyed. I can't do drunken sentimentality just now. I'm sober. What I'm trying to say is that Belle had her own collection of lame ducks. I mean, who else would install a modern kitchen for the likes of Caroline but neglect her own place like Belle did? She knew her little band of misfits would be in safe hands with you.'

'Ho, ho, no. No, sirree.' Evie waved her glass around, slopping some of its contents over Bing's Armani trousers. 'I am *not* getting involved with this bunch.'

'Not even with irresistible raw material like Bernard?' He nudged her.

Evie stuck out her chin. 'Bernard's just fine as he is,' she asserted.

'Right. So you haven't been thinking, If only Bernard smartened himself up a bit he could get himself a girlfriend? Or itching to see inside his flat?'

'Absolutely not,' Evie lied. For an actress she wasn't very good at it. 'I don't even care who or what P. Warnes is.'

As if prompted by a secret signal the ultra-violet light flickered on in the top flat.

'There it is again,' sighed Bing.

'But tonight the noise is more like – like stones in a washing-machine,' commented Evie, with an air of erudition.

As they gazed up, a bare bulb sparked into life on the first floor. 'Our guinea-pig is awake!' hissed Bing. He hollered, 'BERNAAAAAARD!'

'Ssssh! He is *not* our guinea-pig. I'm not interested in him. Shut it!' commanded Evie, but the chrysanthemum-like outline of Bernard was already at the window.

'Er, helloooo?' he ventured, like a pre-war schoolmarm.

'It's us, Bing and Evie! Come and join us!'

Bernard evidently didn't want to, would rather eat his own legs, but Bing's powers of persuasion were irresistible and soon he was sitting between them, having brought down his chair as instructed.

'We want to know all about you, Bernard,' said Bing, without preamble.

'Ooooh.' Bernard winced, but enquired mildly, 'What would you like to know? There isn't much to say about me.'

Evie, who had forgotten her resistance to this idea, didn't feel able to ask the real questions. Why was he so pale? Why was he so inexpert at combing his hair? Why did he dress as if he had run from a burning building (in 1940)? Why was he so fearfully shy with his fellow human beings that he found eye-contact impossible? She decided to ease him in with a straightforward one: 'What do you do for a living?'

Bernard nodded rapidly. 'Ah. Yes. That's easy. I collate statistics.'

There was a respectful pause while Bing and Evie tried to think of something interesting to say about statistics.

'Do you enjoy it?' enquired Evie finally.

'Oh, yes!' Bernard's pallid face lit up. 'The statistic is a marvellous thing. Packed with information. Surprising, yet reassuring.'

'Right.' Bing sounded unconvinced. 'What do you do for *fun*, Bernard?' He leant towards him, sharp incisors gleaming in the moonlight. Bing was the King of Fun. This was his territory.

Bernard's eyebrows met. 'Er . . .' There was no immediate answer.

'What twiddles your knobs? What pushes your buttons?'

Bernard looked blank. If he had any knobs they remained, presumably, untwiddled.

Bing simplified his line of questioning: 'What do you look forward to doing?'

'Going to work,' Bernard said apologetically.

Evie smiled. There was something about Bernard that touched her. He was like some dusty artefact tucked away in a neglected corner of a museum, never admired or even noticed by visitors. Perhaps Bing was right. Maybe Bernard could do with a polish and a shove into the sunlight. 'Don't you have a . . . ladyfriend?'

'Nooooo.' Bernard giggled nervously. 'I'm not much of a ladies' man.'

'Oh, come on.' Evie risked a pat on his arm. Poor Bernard jumped a foot off his chair. 'Six foot tall. Blue eyes.' She scrabbled. 'The ability to interpret statistics. I bet you have to fight them off with a pooey stick.'

Bernard gulped. 'No. No. Honestly. I've never, erm, never

actually, well, you know, never had what you'd call an, erm, relationship. As such.'

Bing and Evie had the same thought at the same instant, as if the fairy-lights had suddenly rearranged themselves to read 'BERNARD IS A VIRGIN'.

'Would you like a relationship? As such?' Evie's tipsiness made her bold.

'Of course he bloody would,' snapped Bing. 'Wouldn't you, Bernard?' he said encouragingly, as if he were asking a confused octogenarian whether he wanted meals on wheels.

'I don't know,' said Bernard mildly. 'You don't miss what you've never had.' He went on, in a rare burst of eloquence, 'Mother used to keep me pretty busy and since she died I've kept myself to myself.'

'Do you miss your mother?' Bing's voice wasn't normally so gentle.

'Every day.' Such sincerity. Such sadness. 'She did everything for me, you see. I was a bit lost after . . . Sometimes I wish she'd shown me how to do things like cooking and so on.'

'Don't you cook?' asked Evie.

'No. She did everything. After she died I had to ask my aunt how many sugars I took.'

It is to Evie and Bing's eternal credit that they didn't so much as snigger. Evie probed, fascinated as an etymologist with a new species: 'But you can boil an egg?' A shake of the flopping hair. 'Cook pasta?' Another shake. 'Make a sandwich?' No. 'Then what on earth do you do for food?'

'I get a very acceptable saveloy and chips from the nice takeaway round the corner.'

Bing, whose body was a temple (quite a popular one), said hopefully, 'But not every night?'

'Oh, yes, every night. With a nice big bottle of pop.'

That explained the ghastly pallor. 'Bernard,' said Evie decisively, 'I'm going away for three nights but when I come home you're coming to me for dinner. OK?'

Bernard nodded, more terrified than grateful.

'And, what's more, you're going to cook it.'

After Bing and Evie had seen Bernard to his door on the oppressively maroon second floor, they sauntered arm in arm back down to the basement. 'You've got the bit between your teeth now, girl,' Bing said. 'It only took half an hour to reel you in, and now you're planning cookery lessons for the poor sod.'

'Not just cookery lessons,' pronounced Evie. 'If ever there was a man in need of a woman, it's Bernard.'

'Oh, please, no. I feel a matchmaking coming on.' Bing disengaged his arm.

'You bet your sweet bippy you do. There'll be another guest at that dinner party. Someone nice-looking, who needs a decent, honest, solvent man. Someone who lives *there*.' Evie gestured at the door to flat B.

'Caroline?' Bing lowered his voice. 'She'd eat him alive.'

'Nonsense. She's soft as butter underneath. All her family are dead so she needs a man to stand by her and help bring up Milly.'

Bing shook his head. 'Does she *really* need a man who can't boil an egg? Who wanks over statistics? Who seems to have been raised in a growbag by a domineering mother who led him to believe that making a cup of coffee required a degree in the black arts?'

'We can work on all that.' Evie waved away such trivia.

'You'll also have to work on the clothes, the hair, the body language. One other thing, I suspect that our friend is not exactly a demon between the sheets.'

'God, can you imagine it?' Evie had to laugh. 'All sorrys and oh dears and him leaning on your hair.'

'What have I done?' mused Bing, looking down at his drunken landlady. 'You've really taken the ball and run with it, haven't you? Goodnight, doll.'

'Night.'

A good hour had passed before, giggling hysterically, they raced outside in their dressing-gowns to retrieve Sacha from the damp grass.

7

Sundays aren't really Sundays any more. High streets are open for business; garden centres are lively with bickering couples; cinemas, garages, estate agents, sex shops and World of Leather are all there for our delight. (Plus the odd church, of course.) However, sit down to a plate of roast beef with all the trimmings and suddenly, magically, Sunday is just like it was when we were children, with delicious aromas creeping round the house and the smiling faces of our loved ones.

Not to mention bone-crushing boredom and a passionate desire to burn the family home to the ground, thought Evie ungratefully, as she sat crucified to the sofa, a three-year-old twin at either side of her and a huge photograph album open on her lap. Bridgie was leaning over her, enthusiastically pointing out the glorious highlights of their latest trip to the timeshare in Normandy. 'There's Daddy with a lobster . . . That's me with a little cat we met . . .' and so on.

Charles and Julius were leaning hotly into Evie, seemingly transfixed by the mundane parade of out-of-focus snaps of their grandmother in unflattering sleeveless dresses. Evie felt more relaxed around them than usual, and put this down to Milly's civilising influence. She was fairly smug that, since her rapprochement with Caroline, she could pick up, feed and even amuse a toddler without causing it any harm.

'Nana's boooootiful,' cooed Charles inaccurately, gazing at a shot of Bridgie in what seemed to be a French high-rise car park, gesticulating in man-made fibres, the top of her head out of shot.

'And you're obviously destined for a lucrative career in PR,

Charles.' Evie gave her tiny nephew a squeeze and wondered for the squillionth time why Beth, who came from a long line of Marys, Johns, Catherines and Roberts, had gone berserk at the font and named her children Charles and Julius. 'We don't want them to have the same name as loads of other kids,' had been her reasoning at the time, but on reflection maybe it was all Marcus's fault. No doubt there was a smattering of Jonquils and Hermiones in his pedigree. When – no, let's make that if – I have children, thought Evie, I'm going to keep the names simple and cute. Honey, maybe, or Molly. Or Daisy. Or . . . Milly.

'I can't stand around like this all day.' Bridgie sounded almost angry, as if the family had nailed her court shoes to the carpet. 'I have to get back to that roast.' She regarded a joint of beef as a wily opponent. She had to show it who was boss with constant basting, poking and slamming of the oven door.

The anticipation of gravy made Evie feel so mellow she was emboldened to ask, 'Any chance of a drink, Mum?'

'Squash?' This was always carefully preserved at room temperature. 'Or Coke?' This was supermarket own-brand cola in a bottle big enough to rent out as a spare room. Decanted, it tasted like warm Brasso.

'I was thinking of something a bit stronger.' A reckless request, but Evie kept hoping that a little French *je ne sais quoi* might creep into Surbiton, as a result of the annual fortnight across the Channel, in the welcome shape of a bottle of wine.

But no. A very small sherry was thrust into her hand. Then the twins were promptly removed, presumably in case their sherry-maddened aunt tried to strangle them.

Beth sat down beside Evie, tucking her espadrilles beneath her. While Evie was admiring her sister's expensively cut trousers, the glass was snatched out of her hand and downed in one. 'You don't drink!' hissed Evie, amazed.

Beth replaced the glass in Evie's still schooner-shaped hand as Bridgie cruised past with a groaning tray of appetisers.

'Finished already?' she yelped. 'Oliver Reed had nothing on you!'

Evie scowled at Beth, who mouthed, 'Sorry.' She was as blonde as Evie was auburn, with a lean, rangy silhouette quite unlike Evie's comfortable curves. She took the sun like a dream and today, her brown shoulders gleaming in a pristine white vest, she might have stepped straight off a yacht. She was elegant, grown-up, with that unmistakable 'rich' look, and it was incredible that Evie had waded through the hormone-heavy swamps of adolescence without developing insane jealousy of such brains and beauty. This was in no way thanks to their mother, whose grasps of child psychology was shaky; she had heaped praise on Beth, along with a running commentary on Evie's shortcomings.

And there were plenty of those.

Even Evie had to acknowledge that the sole achievement of her schooldays was a pregnancy scare. Putting cider in the font at Sunday School hadn't endeared her to authority. When her exam results had slunk out of the envelope her father had been temporarily blinded by the flurry of Gs.

By rights Evie should have resented her high-achieving, good-looking elder sibling. Perhaps the reason she didn't was because Evie had never yearned for academic honours. Or perhaps it was because Beth's looks only seemed to attract the kind of bloke Evie would cross the street to avoid; they were always handsome, always wealthy, always buttock-clenchingly boring. They had culminated in Marcus, who was dark, loaded and loved to talk teeth. In Evie's opinion, dentists were to be avoided, visited only when she was in unbearable pain; Beth had chosen to share her life with one. No matter how many zeros nestled cosily on the end of his salary Evie would never be able to get naked with a man who spent all day with his hands in other people's mouths.

Or perhaps the sisters' relationship had survived because Beth had a level head and kind heart. They were not close – the elder sister was as sensible and organised as the younger was reckless and disorganised – but there was never any uneasiness between them, just a comfortable familiarity. Sometimes, particularly when she was slumped in front of a rerun of *The Waltons*, Evie wished she and Beth understood each other a little better. Beth never seemed all that interested in Evie's acting; Evie couldn't conjure up any curiosity about Beth's picture-perfect housewife's life in deepest Henley. But, then, *The Waltons* wasn't on much, these days.

'Congratulations,' Beth was saying. 'Mum told me all about the house.'

'She doesn't approve.'

'Mum never approves of anything. Don't let that worry you. Are you all moved in?'

Evie brought her up to date, noticing that Beth was absorbed in the story to an unusual degree. Generally she had one eye and one ear on the twins, who could do far more damage than their demure, pastel-clad appearance might suggest.

'And is it full?' Beth asked. 'Do you have enough tenants?'

'Yeah.'

'I'm really, really glad for you, sis. A homeowner!'

Evie shrugged. 'You're a homeowner too, you know.'

'Nooooo.' Beth drew the word out like a fat lady's knicker elastic. '*He* is.' She cocked her head at her husband who, by virtue of his accent and his penis, was being awarded a *large* sherry by Bridgie.

'Same difference.'

'Well . . .' Beth changed the subject by dusting off a Crump family favourite. 'When are you going to bring a bloke home to meet us?'

'Do *not* get me started!' Evie thumped a cushion so hard she woke Henry, who farted and was escorted from the room by a thin-lipped Bridgie.

'I'd been married seven years when I was your age,' Beth said dreamily.

'Don't I know it. I spent your wedding day mummified in

fuchsia taffeta that matched my spots perfectly. And the sash was too tight.'

'Are you *still* moaning about that dress?'

'Yes. And I'll never stop. I'll have it on my gravestone. "Here Lies Evie Crump – Her Sash Was Too Tight."'

Beth sighed. 'For the last time, it was fashionable then. And don't change the subject. Why no men?'

Evie said slowly, 'A sash. Why, for the love of God?'

'You looked lovely. Everyone said so.'

'No,' Evie said adamantly, as if she were giving evidence in a major murder trial. 'All the senile great-uncles said so. Nobody under eighty, with full eyesight, thought I looked lovely. They thought I looked like a rather fancy bag of spanners.'

'Will you please get over it? It was seventeen years ago! I put myself in a Juliet cap and fingerless gloves, if that's any consolation.'

Evie laughed, then gave in and returned to the thorny subject of the opposite sex. 'Look, I'm on the shelf. Past my sell-by date. Not wanted on board. Surplus. Redundant. When Charles and Julius grow up I'll be their eccentric spinster aunt and they won't want to kiss me because I'll take my dentures out to suck boiled sweets.'

'You don't like boiled sweets.'

'OK, I'll take my dentures out to suck . . . chop bones.'

'Come off it, Evie, you're in your prime.'

'If only somebody would tell that to the menfolk of old London Town.'

'God.' Beth sank back and stared wonderingly into the middle distance. 'If I was you, with your youth and all that freedom, I'd be shagging like a rabbit.'

'Eh?' Evie's big sister was not supposed to talk like that. She was respectable. She was reserved. She *never* said 'shagging'. 'You wouldn't.'

'Wouldn't I?' murmured Beth, her face an unreadable mixture of sadness and secrecy. 'Everybody else seems to.'

Evie frowned, then followed Beth's glance to Marcus, who was gamely trying to praise a ham 'n' jam *vol-au-vent* he'd been rash enough to accept. 'I see,' she said, in her best lady-detective voice. 'Trouble in Paradise?'

The look Beth flung her way was uncharacteristically hard. 'Don't talk about things you don't understand,' she said, then stood up and strode out of the room. Evie stared after her with a cartoonish look of bafflement. Not only did Beth never drink and never say 'shagging', she never strode out of rooms either. Something was eating Evie's big sister. Something important.

Marcus was skirting the dining-table and heading for Evie, on the run from a tray of prawn and banana crisps with which Bridgie was menacing the other end of the room. He threw himself down on the sofa and grinned toothily (as befitted a dentist) at his sister-in-law. 'How's it going?'

Evie took a moment to answer. An unwelcome thought buzzed round her head like a trapped bluebottle. *You're having an affair.* 'Fine, fine,' she said eventually.

'Do you think old Henry would help me out with this *vol-au-vent*? Oh, he's been banished, has he?' Marcus was burbling on in the tones you would expect from an ex-Eton head boy, but Evie wasn't listening. She was inspecting him with new eyes. She was looking at him as a man, not as her rather dull brother-in-law.

He was still handsome, she was surprised to note. That touch of grey in his thick black hair was – gulp – sexy. Viewed objectively and not from the perspective of a grumpy younger sister in an ill-fitting sash, Marcus was a very attractive man. His hands were manicured (even if they were straight from a stranger's mouth), he smelt good, he had a wide smile and clear blue eyes, which still held a boyish look of innocence.

But he wasn't innocent. Evie was known for jumping to conclusions – Bing said it was the only exercise she got – but this one was inescapable. Her sister's new bitterness could only stem from some terrible disappointment with her husband. It had to be a betrayal – nothing else would cut that deep.

'Lunch is served!' squawked Bridgie.

'Yum yum!' said Marcus.

His grin made Evie's stomach lurch. Her harmless brother-in-law had turned into an adulterer.

'Come on, come on.' Bridgie wasn't a patient woman. Only Marcus's presence saved Evie from being exhorted to get her fat behind to the table.

Ah, the table. Extended to its full length, it had been primped and tweaked by Bridgie as if it was a Greek bride. The heavy lace tablecloth – only ever seen on Sunday – was practically invisible beneath crocheted doilies, ceramic coasters, table mats depicting improbable scenes of Ye Olde Englande, wedding-present crystal glasses, silver-plated cutlery, a candelabrum worthy of Liberace's campest moment (the candles were lit despite the blazing afternoon sun) and an immense display of roses.

Evie sat between her nephews, opposite Marcus and Beth, who had returned from her brief exile in the hall. She searched her sister's face for signs of tears, but Beth was hard to read as she lunged, spooned and poured with the rest of them. It was always a complex matter to fill your plate from all the Sunday serving dishes, particularly with Bridgie neurotically fretting that the men weren't getting enough meat.

'Peas, Marcus!' she yelled hysterically into his face. 'Evie, give Marcus the peas! Beth, pass Daddy the Yorkshires! THE YORKSHIRES!'

Finally, every plate had a bit of everything on it and John said, almost tetchily for he was only human, 'Perhaps you can sit down now, Bridgie, and take that apron off.'

Bridgie snorted. As if. Her apron-at-the-Sunday-lunch-table routine was one of her favourite parts of the week. The apron was her badge of martyrdom: it reminded them all of how she toiled so that they might eat. Furthermore, it signalled that she might be summoned back into the gaping jaws of the kitchen at any moment and that she would not shirk.

After a few wary proddings with forks to determine that this really was just a roast dinner, with no crazy additions, everyone tucked in. Sighs of contentment rose.

'This is *good*!' declared Marcus.

Bridgie tried to look modest.

Evie wanted to empty the jar of horseradish over his head.

'Evie!' Bridgie's squeal made her jump. 'Don't let Julius rub roast potato into his hair!'

What was it with kids? Why couldn't they just *eat* food? 'Sorry, sorry,' she muttered, dabbing at the squirming child with her napkin.

'I think it suits him.' Beth laughed.

Evie grinned at her. Well, as much as she could see of her behind the floral tribute. She was back in her sister's good books: that was a relief.

'We're going to see you on the box soon, eh?' said John.

'Yes!' squeaked Evie, just as Bridgie said, 'It's only a commercial.' A little deflated, Evie carried on: 'It's for dog food. It'll be shot on location. They're taking me to Dorset on Tuesday. Two nights in a hotel!'

Bridgie turned to Beth. 'How's the extension coming along? Did you decide about the skylight?'

Loyally Beth pretended to find the tablecloth fascinating and John asked Evie, 'When will it be on the screen?'

'I dunno. A few weeks, probably. They'll let me know and then I'll warn you, Dad.'

Marcus leant across the table. 'Will you get a bundle for it? They're jolly lucrative, I hear.'

'Well, they *can* be.'

'Are we talking hundreds? Or thousands? Ten thousand? Less than ten? More than ten?'

Beth cut in: 'What I'd like to know is, when are you getting back to *real* acting, *proper* acting?'

'Who knows?' Evie's tone was light, but she felt crushed. Why was Beth directing her anger at her? It was a little while later, when she was wiping down the twins after a spectacular gravy incident, that it clicked. Beth was attacking her husband's materialism, not Evie's career. It was Beth's way of pointing out that Evie was a trained actress, not someone who chased money in commercials.

Or that was what she hoped it was, anyway.

Evie had two escorts to the station. Her dad linked her arm and Henry ambled along behind her. She leant against John so heavily that he staggered. 'Go easy, girl. The neighbours will think I've been on the sauce!'

Evie loved her father and looked up to him for all sorts of reasons, but principally because he had lived with her mother for over forty years without hiring a steamroller and reversing it over her.

As if reading her thoughts he said, in his mild way, 'Mum was on good form today.'

'Yeah. Did you hear her pointing out your new print over the fireplace to Marcus? She said, "It's a Constable but—"'

They finished Bridgie's line together: '*I don't think it's an original!*'

After they'd stopped laughing John said, 'Smashing lunch, though,' by way of making it up to his absent wife. 'Tell me,' he said, looking at Evie quizzically, 'do you and Beth ever get together anywhere else? I mean, do you only see each other at our house?'

'No. I mean, yes, we only see each other at your place.'

'That's a shame.'

They had reached the station. Henry was nosing about in a drift of litter, licking various disgusting items. Evie hugged her father ferociously. She understood what he was telling her: *Your sister may need you.* 'Don't die!' she blurted into his neck.

'Eh?' John held her at arm's length. 'What's all this?'

'Oh, ignore me. I'm being silly.'

On the train, racketing back to North London, Evie wondered if her father understood how precious he was to her. She suspected he did.

8

'SHUT UP AND GO AWAY!' bellowed Bing, from the top of the crumbling steps.

Evie waded meekly through Borneo. With her hand on the gate, she turned and opened her mouth to speak.

But Bing was too quick for her. 'NO! NO MORE! GET ON THE FUCKING TRAIN AND DON'T THINK ABOUT US UNTIL YOU COME HOME!'

Evie winced at the F-word. Surely, even in North London, it wasn't the done thing to shout it at the top of your lungs like that. But he was right. She had to stop fussing. She had used up a lifetime's supply of question marks that morning. 'You will watch the boiler, won't you?' 'Don't forget to warn everybody about that loose stair carpet, will you?' 'Did you remember to ring a plumber about Caroline's sink?' 'Have we got enough paint to finish the landings?' Never before had Evie noticed her surroundings and fretted about them as she did now. Her old flat had been a showcase of damp, rot, peeling paper and carpet tiles that refused to lie down. She had squatted happily in the middle of it, concerned only about the holy trinity of fridge, bed and telly. Owning a house and having three tenants certainly concentrated the mind. Any minute now she'd be experiencing urges to watch *Changing Rooms* instead of *Judge Judy*. She shuddered.

Evie had never been to Lyme Regis before. She suspected it was overrun by comfortably proportioned elderly ladies in cardis, but no matter. It was all free, it was *location work*. It was a proper job at last, with proper fees. All of which, she thought, with a sigh, would sink into the great stone sponge she had acquired in Kemp Street.

Meredith had given her a first-class (first-class!) train ticket, a twenty-pound note for her cab ride to the Bayside Hotel and a call sheet, detailing the schedule of the production and the names of everybody on it. Through coy and careful questioning Evie had ascertained that Dan Dan the Handsome Man was travelling down later in the day and would meet the rest of the crew at the hotel. As she sat in the dubious comforts of first class (it seemed to be the same as all the other carriages, except for dinky little covers on the lights), Evie was relieved that she would have time to comb her hair, floss her teeth and generally collect herself before he appeared. Bing had said, in the manner of a stern Victorian grandparent, 'Now, young lady, I expect you to return home covered in lovebites. Do not let me down.' But, then, Bing saw sex as the great panacea. There was no problem so knotty that a quick shag couldn't fix it. Or, at least, blot it out for the duration of the aforementioned quick shag.

Evie wasn't so sure. The thought of sex with anyone felt like planning a trip to the moon. Men's bodies (not to mention their minds) were foreign territory. And Evie had lost her passport long ago.

The thought of sex with an *actor* was doubly perturbing. Evie had had her fair share of thespians. Older, wiser actresses always counselled her never to get involved with colleagues. But the atmosphere when men and women were performing together was headier than homemade cider: love affairs blossomed like fungus backstage, and lasted about as long. The unarmoured heart could be very bruised, and Evie's had been kicked to death by one actor in particular.

The name 'Jonathan' had been forbidden within a hundred-yard radius of Evie since last summer when she and a Jonathan had appeared together in a (no fee, costs only, natch) production of *A Midsummer Night's Dream* at a local arts festival.

Jonathan had gazed at Evie as she slapped on the pancake and tugged at her ludicrous wig. He had never met anyone like her before, he said. He had never felt like this before, he said.

Evie *had* felt like this before: she knew she was being drip-fed pure hogwash to facilitate the speedier removal of her knickers.

But Jonathan was persistent. And he was sincere. In fact, he was furious when he realised she doubted him, and punched the wall, like Marlon Brando in *A Streetcar Named Desire*.

So she had relaxed, and much snogging and sex had ensued. Jonathan was the daring type and many times other fairies had walked into the dressing room and discovered them blushing, coughing and rearranging their bits of gauze.

Jonathan was passionate, devoted and committed – and she had never heard from him again after the last-night party.

Sacha and Bing would never forget the Dark Time that had come over the land. Crying, drinking, burping, shouting 'That bastard!' and all before breakfast. 'Shall I ring him?' she would beseech them. If the answer was yes, she would shriek, 'What do you mean? You know I can't ring him! He'll know he's got to me!' If the answer was no, she would shriek, 'But I *have* to speak to him! I can't go on like this!' She had spent long nights under a tear-stained duvet, looking up at the damp on the bedroom ceiling and trying desperately to work out how much, if any, of what he had said he had really meant.

Evie's self-esteem had been felled like an oak by Jonathan's behaviour and it had taken round-the-clock care by Sacha and Bing to get it back up to its normal, admittedly shaky, level.

No, despite the drunken bravado with which she had pledged to Sacha that she would you-know Dan to within an inch of his life, Evie had no intention of making the two-backed monster with another actor. As Bing had pointed out after the Jonathan episode, 'Of course he made you believe he loved you: HE'S AN ACTOR.'

Evie had a plan for Dan. Simple, but – for her – unique. She would *get to know him*. She would *take things slowly*. She would even *have conversations with him*. She might not like him when she took the trouble to find out what he was like. He might have a girlfriend. But he just might be very nice and he just might fancy her and they just might embark on one of those things – oh, what were they called? That's right. A *relationship*.

Some instinctive part of Evie, deep in her innards, knew that one of those was ultimately much more nourishing than a shag. The problem was, she'd never achieved one. Knowing you want one is a start, though, surely?

The Bayside Hotel was quaint but it nestled spectacularly right in the middle of the wide sweep of Lyme Regis Bay. Out front was the famous Cobb, a man-made finger of stone that reached out into the sea: Meryl Streep had stood there, looking all moody in a black hooded cape in *The French Lieutenant's Woman*. Evie liked what she had seen of the town from the window of her (paid-for – oh, bliss!) minicab. Absurdly small and pretty houses hugged steep roads that all dribbled down to the bay, which was lined with fishermen's cottages, fish-and-chip shops and the hotel.

Evie wasn't used to hotels. B&Bs were more her style. She had been hoping for cutting-edge modernist, minimalist, funky chic. She had got Fawlty Towers. Reception was a large, panelled room with a log fire (despite the heat), dotted with 1950s-style arrangements of drooping blooms. There was a high wooden desk with a brass bell on it, standing beside an open leather ledger. The silence was broken only by the ticking of the clock. Which was ten minutes slow.

That bell oppressed Evie. Should she ring it? Or was it a prop? Surely people only dinged brass bells in Agatha Christie dramatisations?

Ding it she must. The abrupt tinkle brought about the almost immediate materialisation of a stout woman through a door marked 'Staff'. 'Yes?' she said, by way of greeting.

'I'm Evie Crump, and I think I've been booked in by Gem Productions,' said Evie hopefully.

'Yes.' The woman glanced officiously at the ledger and said, 'Yes,' again, then 'Yes, yes,' for good measure. 'Sign in, please.'

Evie scribbled her name, and was informed that she was in

room thirty-four, that the shower was 'temperamental' and that she was to dial 101 if she needed any help.

'Right,' Evie said, and added, 'Yes,' in an attempt to ingratiate. She bent down for her bag but a hand was already upon it.

Another member of staff had materialised, presumably through a trap-door. 'Allow me.' The porter was about her age, with a blunt but friendly face, and Evie followed him into the lift.

It's never easy to talk in a lift, is it? Evie adopted the commonplace tactic of looking at the floor numbers as they lit up, as if there might be some surprise waiting there.

The porter preceded her down the narrow wallpapered landing to room thirty-four, and stepped back while she opened the door. It was a small, austere but pretty room, as dated as Reception, but pink and welcoming.

Oh, Gawd, Evie thought, as the porter put down the suitcase and turned to her with a smile. *A tip.* She was bad at tipping. She could never do it casually. Working out how much, when, *if* was a nightmare, riddled with possibly insulting miscalculations.

Resolving to be cool and elegant about it, as befitted an actress on location, she delved into her huge suede sack and, unusually, put her hand straight on to her purse. She extracted a pound coin (Was that enough? Was it too much? Would his children go hungry because of her ignorance and meanness or would he laugh at her for parting with such a massive sum just for carrying her not particularly heavy suitcase up in a lift?), held it out with a big smile and said, 'Thank you very much.'

The porter just looked at it. Oh, God. He was insulted. He was going to tell all the other staff and they would spit in her soup and wipe their willies on her curtains.

But he didn't seem insulted: he was smiling. A big smile that lit up his green eyes. 'We seem to have got off on the wrong foot. My name's Aden. I'm the assistant director.' He reached out and took the coin. 'But thanks very much.'

The door closed behind him. Evie collapsed on to the bed

and buried her face in the pillow. It was dense but not as dense as her.

On the phone Bing had said, 'Was he dressed like a porter?' Unless porters wear jeans and sweatshirts the answer had to be no. Evie looked at her call sheet. There he was. Aden Black, assistant director. Assistant directors are important on shoots. They do all the bits the big important director doesn't want to do, which can mean positioning the actors for lighting, running through the scene with them, checking camera angles, liaising with props people and so on. They work hard and their goodwill is vital to actors if they want to be lit flatteringly, directed sensitively and generally treated more like human beings than cattle.

He looked like a nice man, mused Evie, as she glossed her lips in preparation for the 'Cast and Crew Drink in Reception' as detailed on her call sheet. Not at all the sort of bloke who would mind being mistaken for a porter. She cringed. Even though he's a fucking assistant director. And smeared lip gloss on her chin.

He probably won't have mentioned it to anyone, Evie reassured herself in the lift. As the doors opened on to the hubbub of people laying into the free drinks, the first face she saw, devastatingly, was Dan's. 'Carry your bags, Miss?' he said, in a jaunty Cockney accent and everyone laughed.

Evie must have looked sheepish. Dan swooped on her and hugged her as if he had known her all his life. 'Sorry. Couldn't resist it. Great to see you again, gorgeous,' he said, in a husky whisper that coiled like smoke right into her ear. Then he planted a kiss on her cheek. It was warm and delicious and temporarily robbed Evie of the power of speech. Whatever I do, she thought, I mustn't drink.

Aden handed her a glass of wine with an apologetic smile, and she drained it as if she had spent the last forty days and nights in the desert.

* * *

They were a nice bunch, a great bunch, she decided, as they sat down to dinner in the dining room. But, then, everyone's a great bunch when seen through the distorting curve of a glass. Some tiny voice of reason prevailed when the waiter came round and Evie found herself covering her glass with her hand.

The reason for her self-control was seated next to her. Dan was a template for the kind of man Evie found irresistible. It wasn't just the stunning looks, it was the devilish smile and the racy air. He was confident, outgoing. Worst of all, he made her laugh. He was very dangerous indeed. A quick shag (if one was on offer – there was no real evidence so far) was very, very tempting. But a relationship . . . Imagine a relationship with someone who made you sweat with sexual anticipation *and* made you laugh. Now, that would be worth having. So, 'Mineral water, please,' she told the waiter.

Aden was sitting opposite her across the white linen tablecloth, staring none too happily at a plate of nondescript brown soup. He seemed nice too. A bit quiet, probably happily married. He had that air of settled-downness, with his short brown hair and unremarkable clothes. She was grateful to him for making a joke of the mistaken identity: it wasn't going to affect their working relationship at all.

Dan's clothes and hair were just right. A moss-green linen shirt hanging over well-cut khakis. A David Beckham-style quiffy crop.

What was far from just right was that on the other side of all this funkiness was the makeup girl, Melody. Pretentious name, scoffed Evie to herself, which meant, She's got tits that should be fake but aren't and she's blonde and she's got the legs for that micro-mini she's almost wearing. And – and this was the worst bit – everybody always fancies the makeup girl.

Melody was laughing. A lot. 'What's so funny?' Evie leant over, the wine already in her bloodstream emboldening her.

'Oh, it's him!' said Melody, in a deep brown Welsh accent. 'He's a one. He's got me wetting myself!'

Evie and Dan exchanged the tiniest look and she felt reassured. 'That's nice. I always look for that in a man,' said Evie.

'Oh, anybody can make me laugh. I love laughing. I think the world would be a better place if all the politicians and what-have-you got together and told jokes, don't you?' Melody theorised.

This time Dan's look held the faintest hint of a smirk and Evie knew, just knew, that Melody didn't have a chance. Tits or no tits.

'I don't know that politicians can tell jokes,' said Dan. 'I mean, can you imagine Margaret Thatcher doing stand-up?' He launched into an eerily good impression. 'Knock knock. Who's there? Maggie Thatcher. Maggie Thatcher who? SHUT UP, FUCK OFF, I'M HERE TO CLOSE THE MINES!'

'Or Bill Clinton.' Evie laughed, pleased that Melody was looking puzzled. 'Knock knock. Who's there? *I did not have sexual relations with that woman . . .*'

'Perfect!' Dan sniggered.

'Crap Clinton impression, though,' said Aden.

'Oi, leave her alone.' Thrillingly, Dan had defended Evie's skills. 'I thought Bill Clinton was actually sitting here beside me for a moment. Obviously,' he went on as Evie simpered, 'not *the* Bill Clinton.'

Evie belted him with her napkin. Dan grabbed it and tickled her under the arms. She squealed before she recalled that they were in a hotel dining room. Sure enough, a few heads had swivelled their way. 'Whoops! We're lowering the tone,' she whispered to Dan.

'That's what they expect from actors,' he reminded her.

Evie felt high, breathless. She hadn't expected this kind of easy connection so soon. They'd barely been introduced and they were already on tickling terms. Definitely, definitely no more wine.

'So, what are you working on?' asked Aden, as he tried to deconstruct a complicated meringue in front of him. 'Apart from this I mean.'

'I'm the envy of Judi Dench. I'm in a children's educational piece with a group called Kidz!OK!.' Evie felt secure enough to work her pitiful job up into a funny story.

'That'll be with two exclamation marks, I presume?' said Aden.

'And no doubt a Z?' queried Dan.

'Spot on. If they spent a bit less on exclamation marks and a bit more on costumes I might not have to cross the stage with my arse hanging out of my badger outfit.'

'Not altogether a bad thing,' Dan murmured, so that only Evie could hear.

Evie's cheeks – all four of them – went hot, and she squirmed on the hard chair. That was a signal. A definite signal. She was getting signals from Dan that he fancied her! She was breaking out into exclamation marks herself!

The little aside so diverted her that Aden had to repeat his question. 'What do you think the kids you play to *really* want to see? What would you give them if you had the chance?'

It was a good question, an interesting and thought-provoking one, but Evie wanted to shout, 'Oh, shut your face! Dan's got his hand on my knee!' She managed to say, in a high-pitched voice she wouldn't have recognised as her own, 'Something fun, something lively. They don't need stories with a moral all the time. And something that related to their own experiences.'

Aden nodded thoughtfully.

Dan's hand caressed, then roughly squeezed her thigh.

Evie squeaked but turned it into a cough.

She caught Dan's eye. There was a twinkle in it that could have floodlit Wembley Stadium.

'What's in a meringue?' drawled Melody suspiciously. 'Only I can't eat wheat.'

'Meringues are stuffed full of wheat,' exclaimed Evie evilly.

'They're practically *all* wheat,' warned Dan.

'Don't worry, Melody,' Aden cut in. 'There's no wheat in meringues.'

'But they said—'

'Don't pay any attention. I cook meringues and I never put wheat in them.' Aden threw a rueful look Dan's way.

Something in that look told Evie all she needed to know about his attitude to Dan. He was jealous. However, she was about to find out something she didn't know.

Aden put down his coffee. 'Now, about tomorrow—'

'Aw, come on. The night is still young. Tomorrow can wait,' cajoled Dan.

'I just want to make sure you all know your call times. It's my job.' Aden was unapologetic.

Dan turned to Evie. 'He was just like this at school, you know. Right little swot.'

'You were at school together?' That was a surprise. Evie had presumed they'd met on this production. 'Oh.'

'Yeah. I know it sounds unlikely. Square old me and hunky leading man him, but it's true,' said Aden, with a smile.

'Oh, no, I didn't mean that.' Evie grinned. 'Well, not exactly . . .'

Dan leant back and placed his hands behind his head in a languid gesture. His linen shirt gaped across his chest. His tanned, taut chest. Evie dug her nails into her palms as he said, 'Even then Aden was always looking through a lens.'

'And Dan was always looking in a mirror.' Aden ducked the shard of meringue that came his way. 'Hey! You'll get us chucked out. We're in Lyme Regis, not Soho.'

'All right, all right, Head Boy.' Dan stood up, with an abrupt, clean motion that reminded Evie of a cat. (She had it pretty bad. She was thinking almost entirely in clichés.) 'Why don't we explore the Lyme Regis nightlife? See what the glittering south coast has to offer?'

'If anything,' said Evie. 'Unless you fancy bingo.'

'Two little ducks!' shouted Melody, relieved that they had strayed into her area of expertise. 'Two fat ladies!' She'd been drinking while they'd been chatting.

Aden looked dubious. 'We've all got six a.m. alarm calls.'

'Kelly's eye!' chirruped Melody.

Aden continued, with just a sideways glance at Melody, 'And you two have got to look rested. I'm not sure the makeup department is going to be up to covering under-eye shadows.'

Dan ignored him. He looked into Evie's eyes. 'What do you say? Do you want to paint the town?'

If he'd suggested bathing in tramp vomit he would have got the same answer. 'Yeah!'

'Unlucky for shome – fourteen!' burbled Melody, as she followed them out into Reception.

Aden folded his arms and watched them as they stepped out on to the front. 'You make sure you get enough beauty sleep. Oh, and, Dan,' he said, as the heavy etched-glass door swung shut behind them, 'look after the ladies.'

It was cold. The sea snatched all the warmth out of the night and flung spray back at them. The foaming waves were right up against the promenade. It might have been romantic but for 'Key of the Door – twenty-one!'

The cackling Melody was hanging on to Dan's arm as if she was drowning. Evie walked along beside them. She wanted – no, make that needed – to take Dan's other arm. She was desperate to find out if his olive skin was as smooth as it looked. But she was unsure and hung back, despite the unspoken invitation she had received at the hotel.

Hugging herself against the damp breeze she felt utterly sobered. She supposed she should be glad. It guaranteed that she wouldn't do anything stupid. But – God! More than anything she wanted to do something stupid with Dan. She caught his eye as he helped Melody, who was swaying like a weeble, up some steps. She smiled, the way she'd smiled every time she'd looked at him, and reminded herself that doing something stupid would make a relationship with this man unlikely. And there was something real going on between them, something she didn't want to jeopardise.

Good God, Evie, she exclaimed to herself, you might just be growing up at last.

Painting the town red was going to be difficult. Even light pink was tricky. The pubs split cleanly into two camps. There were the touristy ones, garlanded with lobster pots and staffed by bored local teenagers who had no idea what the soup of the day was, and there were the old-man pubs, smoky, moodily lit and lined with septuagenarians. The two styles of pub had one thing in common: they were all closing.

There were no wine-bars, which Evie found mildly shocking. The restaurants were all turning the 'open' sign to 'closed'. The chip shop was doing a roaring trade, with a promising-looking fight or two blossoming outside it. There wasn't even a bingo hall.

In a dark side-street lined with darkened little cottages, presumably full of snoring Lyme Regis natives, Dan shrugged. 'We might as well—'

'Go back?' Evie finished for him. 'Yeah. Might as well.'

'Shame,' he said quietly.

'Yeah. It is.' Evie blushed and was glad of the lack of a moon.

'Ooooo-er! Me guts are bad.' Melody lacked the poetry of her Welsh forebears but she was certainly informative.

It took both of them to haul her along the sea-front and back to the hotel. Bonding over a drunken makeup artist was unusual but at least it would make a good tale to tell the grandchildren, thought Evie, as they dragged Melody into the lift.

'You get off to bed.' Dan draped the rubbery Melody over his shoulder. 'I'll look after this one.'

'Are you sure?' Evie was relieved not to have to take responsibility for a girl who was threatening to spray-paint her surroundings with bile at any moment. But she was sorry to leave Dan. 'Night, then,' she said, like an awkward fourteen-year-old, and stepped out on the third floor.

'Night, gorgeous.' The lift doors closed, and Evie thought it was safe to scream and do a little dance.

Kemp Street and all its dull, everyday problems seemed a million miles away as she pirouetted into her poky room. 'Night, gorgeous!' she squeaked at the girl in the mirror. Her reflection had the pink-cheeked look of someone who might, just might, be about to embark on a *relationship*.

9

The two elderly ladies in sorbet-coloured nylon cardigans linked arms and peered at the array of cameras, lights and people down on the sand.

'Nah,' said one, wrinkling her nose, 'nobody famous,' and they strolled on.

On the beach Evie yawned. It was early. Very early, for Evie.

'None of that!' chided Aden cheerfully, from where he stood behind a gigantic camera. He looked disgustingly pink and healthy. 'Melody, could you touch up Evie's nose?'

Melody staggered across the sand and, with an effort, lifted a small powder brush to Evie's face. 'I feel dreadful, me,' she groaned, in a voice still redolent of the valleys but several octaves deeper than it had been the night before. 'And I hardly touched a drop, an' all.'

Evie flinched. Melody's breath could have stripped wallpaper. 'Was I, you know,' Melody's new deep tones sank to a whisper, 'embarrassing?'

Depends, thought Evie cruelly. Only if you consider it embarrassing to shout, 'Clickety click, sixty-summat,' very loudly outside a packed chip shop. But Evie had suffered from morning-after amnesia many times and she decided to be generous. Besides, even Melody's magnificent frontage was drooping under the weight of her hangover so she didn't constitute half the threat she had yesterday. 'No, don't worry, you were fine.'

'Really? Oh, ta!' One last blast of dragon breath, and Melody dragged herself back to the throng on the other side of the cameras.

It's a silly experience making a TV commercial, but it's one that needs many people to accomplish. The finished film for Toby Small Dog Food would last only ninety seconds, but huddled together on Lyme Regis beach were two cameramen, two lighting guys, a continuity girl, a makeup girl, a wardrobe mistress, two caterers, a dresser, three runners, two writers, an art director, three PAs, a dog wrangler and the assistant director. Plus, of course, two actors.

Only two players were missing. One was Greg, the director, who was making a heated phone call inside the hotel to the client, the big cheese at Toby Small Dog Food Ltd, who had asked for last-minute changes to the script in the mistaken belief that as his company was handing over a seven-figure sum for the commercial he had some authority over the director. The other was Tootsie, the real star of the production. Tootsie was a West Highland white terrier, a veteran of four commercials, one *EastEnders* and a *Crimewatch* reconstruction. Tootsie was . . . where?

'Where's the dog?' enquired Evie innocently, as they stood around waiting for Greg's return.

'Ssssh!' Aden rounded on her. 'I don't want to start a panic, but it looks like Tootsie has . . . stepped out of her office for a moment.'

Dan found this irresistibly amusing. 'Oh, Aden, we're making a dog-food commercial and *you've lost the dog.*'

'I have not lost the dog,' hissed Aden, his habitual cool slipping.

'Won't look good on your CV.' Dan smirked.

Aden didn't rise to the bait. 'The dog wrangler – yes, snigger, Dan, but that's what she likes to be called – is looking for her. Oh, Jesus. Here's Greg.'

Evie felt for Aden. Greg had the look of a man with a sea-urchin down his pants as he strode across the sand, the sun glinting off his John Lennon glasses. Aden met him half-way and whispered in his ear. A roar echoed around the bay: 'YOU'VE LOST THE FUCKING DOG?'

With the impeccable timing of a true pro, Tootsie rounded a rock and raced, barking joyously, into their midst.

Betty, the wrangler, followed close behind, her face wet with tears. Evie saw Aden take her to one side, listen intently for a moment, then wrap both arms round her. 'Betty,' he said, 'you need a cup of hot sweet tea. I'll send a runner for one.'

Evie scuttled over, avoiding Melody's feeble attentions. 'Why on earth is Betty crying?'

Aden's mouth was twitching, but he was trying hard to look grave. 'She's upset,' he said evenly. 'Apparently Tootsie had a little, er, romantic adventure while she was AWOL.' He couldn't help it, he had to laugh. 'With *that*.' Aden pointed to a breakwater where the filthiest, scruffiest, hairiest mongrel sat nonchalantly licking his balls.

'Ooh, dear.' Evie put her hand over her mouth. 'And Betty's scared that Tootsie might be a single mother? She won't get any maintenance from *him*, will she? That's the Shane McGowan of the dog world.'

Dan, of course, thought the whole thing was hilarious. 'So, the leading lady's run off and had a quick how's-your-father in the sand dunes.' He gave Evie an undeniably saucy look. 'Pity we can't follow her lead.'

Evie was uncertain whether he deserved a slap in the face or a damn good snog for that remark.

Aden said briskly, 'You don't have time. Not even the way you do it, Dan.' He stalked off to find the clapperboard.

'Oooooooh, bitch,' lisped Dan, and minced to his mark.

Evie stood alongside him, holding the sluttish Tootsie's lead.

'Hold hands, you two,' Greg barked. 'You're in love, for God's sake.'

Evie's small hand was dwarfed by Dan's warm sexy mitt. Yes, even his hands were sexy.

Greg was still issuing orders. 'I need you to walk from your mark to past that one. Carefree, please, and happy. Brainlessly, imbecilically happy. Tootsie, I'm assured, will romp alongside you at a steady pace. OK. Roll.'

The crew shut right up and Evie and Dan began to stroll.

'*Cut!*' yelled Greg. 'It's not a fucking Chinese state funeral! *Quicker!* Roll.'

The clapperboard clapped and once again Evie and Dan set off.

'*Cut!*' Greg put his hands to his head. 'I'm sorry, but do you have a train to catch? Are we keeping you?'

'Do you think it's his time of the month?' Dan was quite good at talking out of the side of his mouth.

Evie wasn't so good, but she muttered, 'I suspect it's always his time of the month.'

They covered the thirty-yard stretch ten, twenty, umpteen times. They did it fast, slow, and at every speed in between. Evie's face ached from smiling and her ankles were chafed by the sandals Wardrobe had given her. Dan murmured increasingly violent and imaginative threats against Greg's person.

Lunch was a picnic laid out on the rocks. It was as if the contents of a London deli had come to the seaside. Goat's cheese lolled alongside rocket and Parmesan, and bottles of sparkling water peeked out of ice buckets lodged in the pebbles.

Melody plonked herself down beside Evie. 'I'm feeling a bit better now,' she said. 'The squits have tapered off, anyway.'

'Oh,' said Evie. 'Er, well done.' She was looking around for Dan and wasn't remotely interested in Melody's innards.

'If you're wondering where loverboy is,' said Melody, with just a squeeze of lemon, 'he's over there with Aden. Getting a telling-off, by the looks of it.'

Dan trudged over, baguette in hand and a wickedly school-boyish look on his handsome face. 'Just been ticked off by Head Boy.'

'What for?' Evie might have added, 'Pompous squirt.'

'Flirting with my co-star.' Dan lifted an eyebrow. Just the

one. Evie's vulva lurched. 'It's not good for the production, apparently.'

'Dunno,' Evie mumbled. 'I think it might be.'

They held each other's gaze for a long moment. Then Dan passed his hand over his face in a quick, rough gesture. 'You're dangerous,' he muttered.

Dan reckoned *she* was dangerous! Evie grew an inch right there and then. The atmosphere was dense with sexual excitement. They were still and absolutely quiet, while the crew buzzed around them like flies.

It was a relief when Dan broke the spell. 'Hungry?' he said, and stood up to fetch her a sandwich. Evie watched his ten-out-of-ten bum as he strode away, with the utter confidence that she would see it naked. But not just yet, she thought placidly.

The plot – if you can have a plot ninety seconds long – was simple and cutesy. Loving couple and their adorable dog walk along a beach. The guy produces a metal detector, which promptly detects something. The adorable dog digs it up excitedly and – whaddyaknow? It's a tin of dog food, specially formulated for little fellas like him. The last scene shows the couple huddled cosily together by a campfire on the beach, sharing a chicken leg. At their feet the dog is tucking into a bowl of Toby.

Aaaah.

To achieve the requisite light, airy, carefree mood on film, Greg behaved like an African tyrant. 'No! *No!* You people are cretins!' was one of his gentler instructions to the crew. 'Look *happy!*' he bellowed into Evie's face. 'You remember happy, don't you?' In common with a lot of actresses, Evie's most accomplished performance was managing not to look as if she loathed her director.

Aden dashed about, doing his best to second-guess situations and keep Greg calm. An impossible task. Greg was an advertising archetype. He was talented, creative, original but he lacked the courage to risk his neck in the big bad world of TV or movies so he had reached his late forties and found himself filming an ode to the joys of dog food. Two costly divorces ensured that he had to stay where the money was. All of this made him angry. And Greg liked to use what little power he had accumulated to spread that anger around.

His tantrums and abusive outbursts made Evie smile inwardly. Do your worst, she thought. I grew up with the master – Bridgie Crump.

A downpour, in complete contradiction to the weather forecast, scattered the crew. Dan, Evie and Aden all scarpered to a broken-down bathing-hut. No windows, no doors, but if they huddled together they were out of the driving rain.

'Thank you, God.' Aden sighed. 'The sand will be wet. Continuity will be shot to hell.'

'Did Wardrobe bring a fresh set of clothes for us? We're drenched.' Evie shook her hair, scattering droplets over the two men.

'They'd bloody better have.' Aden glanced down at Evie's T-shirt. Something flickered across his face.

Evie's eyes followed his. Her nipples were standing out like doorknobs through the thin damp material.

'I'd better, erm, get off and find the wardrobe mistress,' he said, and rushed out into the deluge.

Evie thought Aden's embarrassment was sweet.

Dan was not embarrassed at all. 'God,' he said slowly, focusing his mesmeric eyes on hers, 'you look soooo horny.'

He didn't touch her. He didn't speak. There was no sound except the rain. An overwhelmingly sexy situation. Yet, despite the tingle in her tummy, Evie felt disappointed. 'Horny' was definitely a horny word, but it was also impersonal. Did she just look horny because her nips were hard enough to hang an overcoat on or did Dan find *her* sexy?

His next utterance made her heart leap and blew away any

disappointment. 'What would you say to dinner one night when we get back to London?'

'I'd say yes, please, and thank you very much.'

Tootsie was required to do take after take of the digging scene before Greg was satisfied that she had given her all. This delayed matters greatly because she had to be washed, groomed and titivated after each dig: the damp sand clung to her rough white coat.

Evie sat on a rock, hugging her knees. She wasn't needed for this scene. Dan's legs were in shot, so he had to stand by while Tootsie went at it.

Melody was perched beside her, evidently recovered. She lit a cigarette. 'I'm giving up,' she announced, as all smokers feel they should these days. 'I only have the odd one when I'm stressed.'

Evie was examining a tin of Toby. 'What does "specially formulated for small dogs" mean?' she wondered aloud.

'Well, there's less of it, but it's the same price as a big tin,' Melody pointed out shrewdly, 'and it's cut into little pieces so that little doggies' mouths can chew 'em.'

'Seems a bit dubious. Dogs are so greedy they just wolf everything down.' Evie pointed at the label and squealed with derision. 'For God's sake, get this! "*With added pasta shapes*". Why would a dog suddenly fancy pasta?'

'An Italian dog might,' reasoned Melody.

'Our dog, Henry, eats anything, up to and including snot. He really doesn't need pasta to tempt him to his bowl,' Evie went on.

'Yeuw.' Melody wrinkled her little nose. Talk of squits was apparently acceptable but snot-eating dogs was going too far. After a showy Bette Davis exhalation of smoke, she changed the subject. 'You and Dan seem to be getting on all right.'

'He's easy to work with.' The new relationship-friendly Evie was noncommittal around makeup girls, an infamous source of on-set goss.

'That's all there is to it?' Melody would make a crap private detective. Her nonchalant air made it obvious that she was desperate to know more. 'You look pretty cosy to me.'

'I don't have the time or energy to get cosy with anyone right now,' lied Evie, in the time-honoured tradition of actresses. *Hello!* is always full of such errant bullshite: a late-thirties actress pictured in her light-filled (borrowed) London flat, spouting on about independence and finding herself and not having room in her life just now for a man. Could this be the same woman hunched over the bubbly in the local wine-bar with two meno-pausal friends, spitting nails because Roger, Adam or Maximilian hasn't returned her late-night tearful phone calls? It could.

'Right.' Melody sounded unconvinced, but Evie was spared any further snooping by Greg's pained shout: '*Where is that little cunt with the makeup when you need her?*'

Melody scrambled to her feet and stamped out her cigarette in the sand. 'I'd watch him. He's a right one.' This was thrown over her shoulder as she scrambled towards Greg.

She fancies him rotten, thought Evie smugly. She fully intended to watch Dan. From very close up.

She fished out her mobile to read her messages. There was one from Bing: 'Just checking in to see that you're OK. Hope it's going well. Don't worry about us. We're fine now that the fire brigade's got the flames under control. Love you!' Evie frowned. He hadn't mentioned the boiler – had something happened? She shook herself. Why would a young man in the prime of his life mention the boiler? Why was a young woman in the prime of her life and in the midst of a wonderful flirtation with Mr Sex thinking about the boiler?

There was another message from Sacha: 'V. BAD DAY. AURA COLOUR OF SICK. HAV U DUN DAN?'

Evie, who was so cack-handed she couldn't open a tin of sar-dines without a paramedic on standby, was nimble-fingered when it came to texting. 'NO. AM WAITING 'COS HE CD BE MR BIG.'

Sacha replied to this in a flash: '!!!!! YR AURA MUST BE LIKE PICCADILLY CIRCUS.'

There was no answer to that. Evie switched off the phone, hoping she hadn't interrupted a hot stones session and sent some poor incense-burning Bohemian to Casualty.

The night shoot went smoothly. Although tired from a day that had started with illicit sex and included fourteen baths, Tootsie behaved impeccably. Evie didn't find leaning back in Dan's arms too strenuous. About ten p.m., Greg said, 'That's it, people. I'm satisfied,' and went straight to a waiting chauffeur-driven car. He was going back to London, as befitted a VIP. The rest of them had another night in the hotel.

Or, more accurately, the hotel bar. The twenty-strong crew practically filled the small, panelled room. A runner, who had been as indolent as a sloth all day, became animated and efficient now that he had the job of keeping them all supplied with drinks.

'Sparkling mineral water, please.' This was becoming a mantra for Evie.

Dan rolled his eyes. 'I had you down as a drinker,' he said, with a touch of disappointment.

Evie pulled a face she hoped was mysterious.

Wrap parties are always wild. However short the shoot, there's always an air of release, of being demobbed, of – to be frank – let's-get-drunk-and-snog-somebody. The careful application of mineral water meant that Evie was comfortably settled in a big leather wing chair at the edge of the action, and not go-go dancing on the bar top in her bra. Like Melody.

'Top marks for enthusiasm. Technique needs work, though,' Evie murmured in Dan's ear, as Melody slipped in a puddle of beer and did an unplanned splits. Dan was perched on the arm of her chair in a pleasingly proprietorial way. He had changed into a crisp blue bowling shirt that accentuated his Paul Newman eyes. Evie was looking forward to presenting him to Bing. He'd be so impressed: a boyfriend who *dressed well*.

The elderly barmaid looked on the verge of tears. She had never had to serve during an impromptu *Stars In Their Eyes* before. The wardrobe mistress was yelling, 'Tonight, Matthew, I'm going to be Cher,' with a handful of bedraggled ostrich feathers stuck on her head.

'Tonight, Matthew,' said Aden, from where he sat on the other arm of Evie's chair, 'I'm going to get completely pissed because I'm so glad this shoot's over. Greg nearly made me rethink my career. Thank you, you two,' he clinked glasses with Dan and Evie, 'for being so professional and so *nice*, for making it easy, in fact.'

'Aw.' Evie felt warmed. It was good to be thanked, especially when you've been yelled at and abused by the Gregs and Simeons of this world. 'You're too nice to make it as a director, Aden. You'd better go for some bastard lessons.'

Aden was a touch *rosé* as he went off to warn the runner that cider and liqueurs don't mix.

'He's a nice guy, my friend,' mused Dan. '*Too* nice.'

Evie risked a flippant, 'You're nice too.'

'Boy, have you got me wrong!' Dan laughed at her stricken face. 'Joke,' he enunciated carefully. 'If you weren't on mineral water you'd have laughed at that.' He pulled her to her feet. 'Come on. Betty the dog wrangler's being Posh Spice. This we've got to see.'

The crowd had thinned out, and only the hardened party animals – plus Evie, who had drunk enough Evian to refloat the *Titanic* – were still in the bar. Dan hadn't left her side all night. Evie had heard snatches of the gossip that was rolling like a wave around the room: she felt smug at having her name linked with his.

She felt even more smug that he was holding her hand behind her back where no one could see it.

Aden move unsteadily across the room to say goodnight. 'Cabs to the station at nine sharp. Don't be late or we go without you.' His authority was somewhat undermined by the fact that he couldn't focus on them.

'Yessir!' barked Dan, saluting and pinching Evie's bum at the same instant.

Evie yelped. Aden put his head on one side and shook it disapprovingly.

'Oh, go to bed, you Puritan.' Dan gave him a shove in the direction of the lift. He turned to Evie and said, 'He's got us all wrong. We couldn't be more innocent, could we?'

Evie opened one eye. During the night elves had apparently superglued it shut. The morning sun was blinding, careering in off the sea. Her limbs were heavy, as if pressed like wild flowers beneath a great weight. Moving was difficult. And why would she want to move anyway? she reasoned. Far simpler to lie here and die.

Where had the evening gone wrong? It had been all happy faces, laughter, jokes, the odd sizzling glance from Dan.

Ah. She remembered where the evening had gone wrong. At the exact moment the runner had popped up behind the bar and shouted, 'I've found some tequila!'

Only vague snatches of the intervening hours were coming through on Evie's scrambled reception. Snapshots of varying horror tumbled through her mind. She saw herself with the salt in her hand. She saw herself ram a piece of lime into her mouth and throw back the shot of tequila. She heard the drunken berks around her cheer as if she had pulled off a tricky manoeuvre on a unicycle. She heard herself say, 'No, one's enough for me, thanks,' then saw herself throw back another shot. And another. She saw Dan's flushed face yelling with delight as she tossed down a fourth.

Dan. Oh, Dan! Evie winced. Her forehead hurt.

Another unwelcome batch of images filtered through. Had that really been her leading a staggering conga line in and out of the toilets? Yes, it had. It had also been her dinging the brass bell dementedly and shouting, 'Cooeee! Mrs Hotel Ladeeeee!'

Evie went hot as she recalled how Dan had shut her up by

kissing her full on the lips. That part of the night was in very sharp focus indeed. The warm intrusion of his tongue, her enthusiastic response. If she'd had the strength to pull the covers over her head she would have as she remembered how the others had silently cleared a path for them. It had been that predictable.

How had she undressed? The details were sketchy. Perhaps her mind wasn't letting her remember because the truth would drive her insane. Evie pleated her brain in the effort to conjure up the sequence of events once they had got upstairs. (There was a flashback involving Dan's zip and the lift that she would have to return to when she felt stronger.) Please, please God, she hadn't done a striptease? Please let her have hidden the safety-pin that was holding her bra strap together. What knickers had she been wearing? Uh-oh. A *thong*. Please, please, most of all, God, please don't let Dan have seen her from the back in her thong with the lights full on. He would have thought he was in Florida with so much orange peel on show.

Evie groaned. And then . . . then they had had sex. Her determination had drifted off over the bay on a raft of tequila fumes.

The kisses were clear enough, burned on her mind. She squirmed with a mixture of pleasure and agony as she remembered them. The light, fluttering ones on the small of her back. The hot ones at the top of her thighs. The brazen hungry ones on her mouth. 'Oh, Dan,' she whimpered miserably, as she relived how he had looked, how he had *felt* when he was on top of her, pushing himself deeper and deeper into her with every ragged breath. It should all have been so special. She should have felt every electric moment to the full, but she had been in a drunken fog.

And it had crippled the 'relationship' before it had begun. The relationship that never was. *Another* one.

Too hung-over to cry, Evie lay desolate until another recollection, a distinctly more welcome one, started to develop.

She could remember, hazily at first and then more clearly, that at one point in their sweaty glorious tussle, she had pushed him back on to the pillows and straddled him. Silencing him with a finger to his lips, she had said wildly that this hadn't been meant to happen.

'Oh, yes, it was.' His voice had been heavy with lust and he had reached up to her, but she had roughly pushed him down again.

'No, no, it wasn't! We were just getting to know each other, but we've gone too far too quickly. It's ruined everything.'

Now it was time for Dan to take the upper hand. He flipped her effortlessly on to her back, raised himself on one elbow and gazed down at her. Cupping her chin in one hand (with surprising tenderness for a man who had been bouncing her off the walls a moment ago), he stared straight into her troubled eyes. 'Listen to me,' he began gravely, 'I'm not a great one for speeches so I'll only say this once. This is incredibly special. I've respected you since the moment we met and I'll always respect you. Tonight just *had* to happen, we both know that. We'll still go out in London for that dinner I promised you. I have a feeling that you and I are going to mean a lot to each other. Now shut up,' he kissed her, 'and let me fuck you.'

Evie sighed. Thank God she had dragged *that* episode out of her sputtering memory banks. She ran through it a couple more times, neurotically double-checking the important bits.

Special: tick.

Respect: tick.

Dinner: tick.

Going to mean a lot to each other: tick tick tick tick *tick*!

So their mad scramble to get naked hadn't ruined things. She felt absurdly grateful to Dan for taking time out from their manic rutting to put her mind at rest. It had been as if he knew what she was thinking. In a way it made it a little less deflating that he wasn't there beside her now . . .

She was looking forward to that dinner.

If she lived that long. Groaning with exertion she turned her clanging head to peer at the clock radio. It was just coming up to half-past minicab.

Borneo was looking a little less wild. A scythe dumped on the gravel was testament to Bing's hard work while she'd been away. When she opened the front door his labours were even more apparent: the hallway was bright, brilliant white. She peered up the staircase. He'd finished right up to the top floor. What a man!

Still moving like an OAP under water – tequila hangovers were the worst – Evie fumbled to open the door to her flat as if it was the first time she'd ever attempted it. She was interrupted by a jaunty knock at the front door.

A postman in shorts stood beaming at her – she felt so fragile that the glow of his teeth hurt her eyes. 'Yes?'

'Package for P. Warnes.' He consulted his clipboard. 'Two packages, actually. Not getting a reply. Can you sign for them, sweetheart?'

'Er, yeah.' Decisions weren't Evie's *forte* right now. 'S'pose so.' She scribbled something that might have been her name on his chit.

'Right.' He danced down the steps and returned much more slowly with an immense package about three feet square. 'Don't know what's in here but it's a dead weight.' Sweating (but still smiling), he let it down on to the parquet and turned to go.

'Hang on! You said there were two packages.'

'What am I like?' asked the postman rhetorically. 'Here you go.' He extracted from his pocket a teeny-weeny package, about the size of a ring box, and placed it incongruously on top of its huge counterpart.

Evie stared at them. What were they? What did P. Warnes

plan to do with them up in his fluorescent lair? She shook the small box tentatively. No sound, and it was light enough to be empty. She shoved the huge box. It was heavy enough to contain an anvil. It occurred to her that getting it up the stairs would mean a lot of noise. If she kept her wits about her she might get a peek at her elusive tenant.

Wits, however, were in short supply as she stumbled down the stairs to the basement. Evie looked around at the over-flowing washing basket, the sink full of mucky dishes, the pile of unopened mail, and decided the best thing to do was go straight to bed.

Those little men with their hammers were still doing their damnedest in her head. Her limbs felt as if they'd been through a mangle. The pillows and the duvet on her bed beckoned to her like sirens. They had never looked so plump and alluring. She drew the curtains and sighed with anticipation as she pulled back the bedclothes.

A knocking, loud and urgent, echoed through the flat. Evie almost managed to ignore it, but it was too dramatic. Growling, she paced the hall, unable to work out where the noise was coming from.

The conservatory! Suddenly alarmed, Evie looked about wildly for something to protect herself with. In films vulnerable women always had a revolver stashed in the bedside table, or they picked up a natty-looking poker. All Evie could lay her hands on was the telephone directory. Well, it was heavy.

She crept through the gloom of the sitting room. Bing had left the curtains drawn. It occurred to her that one of his victims or conquests might have been locked out during sexual game-playing, then forgotten. She hoped she wasn't about to confront Mr Snile Jr in his birthday suit.

The knocking was frenetic now. It's a mad tramp, decided Evie, with panic-stricken certainty. Holding up the phone book menacingly, she swished back the curtain with a flourish.

It was Sacha, grinning like the village idiot.

'Jesus!' Evie unlocked the glass door with bad grace. 'I thought you were a burglar!'

'Do burglars knock?'

'What are you doing round the back?'

'I was trying to make your life easier. You'd have had to climb the stairs to let me in if I'd come round the front.'

'Well . . .' Evie couldn't carry on being a grouch in the face of such thoughtful reasoning, but she threw in for good measure, 'You can't do anything like a normal person, can you?'

'I've shut the shop. I want to hear all about Dan.'

The little men in Evie's head took up heavier hammers. 'Oh, not now, Sash.'

'No, now. *Now!*' Sacha's greed for lurid romantic detail made her forget her manners. 'I mean it. I'm not going anywhere.'

Evie folded her arms resolutely. 'Fine. Don't go anywhere. I'm off to bed.'

Sacha tailed her, crouched and wheedling. 'Please, pleeeease. I'll sit on the end of the bed. You won't even know I'm there.'

It was not Sacha's style to sit on the end of anything, and soon they were tucked up together with the duvet up to their chins.

'This is cosy!' squeaked Sacha.

'No, this is fucking annoying and deeply bizarre. It is *not* cosy.' Evie wondered how Sacha, with all her dippiness, always got the better of her. 'You're hogging the bed clothes.'

'Sorry.' Sacha snuggled down. 'Now, tell me all about Mr Big.'

'I didn't say he was Mr Big.'

'You did!'

'I said he might be.' It was a weak point but it had to be made.

Sacha badgered her until Evie gave in and told the story of the last few days. She found she was enjoying reliving all the saucy exchanges and smouldering eye-contact. Sacha was an excellent audience, shivering with delight when Dan said, 'Goodnight, gorgeous,' and gasping when he pinched her bum. She made

Evie repeat the asking-her-out-to-dinner bit twice, with explicit instructions to phrase and pitch it *exactly* as he had.

It was only when they came to the tequila moment that Evie ran out of steam.

'Go on!' Sacha prodded her under the duvet. 'And then?'

And then . . . Evie had been strenuously avoiding And Then all the way home. 'And then I ruined it,' she whispered.

'*No!*' Sacha sat bolt upright. 'How? You didn't do your Davina McCall impression, did you?'

'What? I don't do a Davina McCall impression.' Sacha's mind regularly made leaps that left Evie wrong-footed and spluttering. 'Shut up, Sash, and I'll tell you. I slept with him.'

Now it was Sacha's turn to look bewildered. 'Why would that ruin it? Oh, my God!' Her voice dropped. 'He couldn't, er, rise to the occasion?'

'Believe me, that was not a problem,' said Evie nostalgically.

'So it was just crap? Were you inhibited?'

'If only.' Evie's cheeks burned. 'No, the sex was brilliant. Athletic, even. We did it three times. I think.'

'Oooh.' Sacha looked envious. 'That's more sex than I've had since Christmas.' She thought for a moment. 'Christmas before last. But how did that ruin it?'

'You know exactly how. Now it's just an opportunistic shag when it looked like it was going to *be* something.'

'It can still be something!' insisted Sacha, with all the fervour of a Deep South preacher. 'See how your dinner date goes.'

'You think he'll ring?' Evie gulped. This was the question she'd been too wary to examine until now. 'Now that he's got what he wanted?'

'But he really liked you. It wasn't just about sex. You've got to have more confidence in yourself than that.'

'And he *did* mention dinner again.' Excitedly Evie acted out the redeeming feature of the night, when Dan had reiterated his intention to see her in London.

'So,' she was coming to the finale, 'he got me like this.' Evie sat up in her elderly winceyette pyjamas, pinned Sacha down and stared into her eyes. 'And he went on about how it was special and he would always respect me and how it just had to happen. Then he said – oh, Sash, it was brilliant – he said that we'd still go out for dinner, and that, oooh, he had a feeling he and I were going to *mean a lot to each other*!' They both squealed like drunken mice. '*Then* he did this.' Evie held Sacha down by her shoulders and imitated Dan's rich deep voice. '"Shut up and let me fuck you."'

From the doorway Bing said calmly, 'How long has this been going on, girls?'

No matter how many times they explained it away Bing would always enjoy making references to 'your lesbian afternoon'.

Sacha was upset by his airy refusal to listen to their explanation of the compromising position in which he'd found them. Evie knew he was just after a reaction, but Sacha found it impossible to stay cool in the face of his muttered 'What you girls do in your own time is your own business,' and 'Must be getting hot in that closet.' With tears in her eyes, she stood in the kitchen with her hands on her hips shouting, 'I am not a lesbian! I am a heterosexual!'

'Whatever.' Bing poured out three cups of tea. 'Get that down you. You'll need to get your strength back.'

Evie sniggered but Sacha threw up her arms in frustration. 'We weren't doing anything!' Her eyes were wild. 'Even if I *was* a lesbian I'd hardly fancy Evie!'

'Hey, hey.' Evie straightened up, insulted. 'What's that supposed to mean?'

'Oh, you know what I'm saying,' snapped Sacha.

'Yes. You're saying that if you were a lesbian you wouldn't fancy me. Thanks a bunch.'

Cornered, Sacha stammered, 'Well, maybe I would. I mean, there's nothing really wrong with you.'

'Gee, thanks.'

Bing, blowing on his Lapsang Souchong was loving every

minute. 'Ladies, ladies, you were getting on *so* well a little while ago.'

'*Will you drop it?*' screamed Sacha, driven over the edge by Bing's languid devilry. '*I am not a lesbian!*'

'Are you implying,' Bing asked, 'that there's something wrong with being homosexual?'

Sacha opened, then closed her mouth. She prided herself on extreme political correctness. She collapsed into a rickety chair.

Evie was full of admiration. Bing had managed something that usually took two bottles of Jack Daniel's to achieve: Sacha had nothing to say.

Caroline was bumping the buggy down step by step. Milly was jiggling about like a jumping bean.

'Let me help you.' Evie put her foot on the steps.

''S all right. Don't need any help.'

'OK.' Evie took her foot off the steps. 'What do you think of the new paint on the walls?'

''S all right,' Caroline repeated herself, pushing Milly to the gate.

'You still on for Friday night? . . . The dinner party?' Evie prompted, seeing her blank look.

'Oh. Yeah.'

'I'm having a cooker delivered later in honour of it.' Evie was acutely aware that she talked too much when she was around Caroline. 'Belle's old one was a health hazard. Don't want to give everyone food poisoning.'

Caroline paused before she stepped out into the street. 'The white does look good, Eve,' she said, in an incongruously defiant tone. 'Like the house is waking up after a long sleep.' The gate banged shut behind her.

'Hasserung?' Sacha had used the phrase so much in the past two days that now, to Evie's ears, it sounded like one nonsensical word.

'No.' Evie braced herself for the spirited defence of Dan that always followed.

'Well, he's busy. He's probably going out early, leaving your number at home, and getting back too late to disturb you. That's a *good* sign – he's thoughtful. Are you sure you gave him the right number? I've heard you mix up the three and the nine before. Did he mention anything about going abroad?'

They were sitting in their new favourite café, and Evie knew Sacha meant well, but she wanted to drown her friend in a sack. 'Look,' she said, in a small, blunt voice, 'Dan is not going to call. It's been two whole days.'

'It's *only* been two days,' corrected Sacha, with the certainty of the unhinged. 'He said he would, didn't he? He *made a point* of saying it. And you told me yourself he sounded sincere.'

Bing joined them, setting down a chipped mug of strong tea. 'He's an actor,' he explained patiently. 'He's been carefully trained to sound sincere.'

Evie sometimes wished that Bing would turn down his honest-o-meter. 'Anyway, I don't care whether he rings or not. His loss!'

Sacha clinked mugs with Evie and said, 'Yeah!' in a right-on kind of way, then added, 'I bet he's working out where to take you before he calls, anyway.'

Bing put down his tea. 'Ladies, allow me to introduce a note of reality. Dan is a sexually attractive man, fully aware of his appeal. He spots our Evie here and is delighted that there's going to be an attractive bint on this job with him. She obviously fancies him right back but is keeping her distance. But aforementioned bint gets sloshed and Dan moves in for the kill. A wonderful slice of sex happens. In the middle of this sex the girl gets jumpy, pulls the I-bet-you-think-I'm-a-tart-now move on him. He reassures her because he does not want the sex to stop. The next morning he's out of there so fast you'd think his Nikes were greased. That is how the Dans of this world operate.' With an air of finality, like a hanging judge, he ended, 'He will not ring.'

Evie looked wounded.

'So why did her bother to ask her out to dinner?' Sacha demanded. 'He must have wanted to or why would he say it?'

'Have you two just landed from the Planet of No Men? He asked her out to dinner because he guessed that that was what she wanted to hear. And he was right, wasn't he? This guy is *good*.'

Evie slumped, beaten down by the ring of veracity of Bing's unvarnished rendering of events. 'So he's really not going to ring?'

Before Sacha could leap in with her sanitised world-view Bing said, 'You know what? It doesn't matter. You were dead right when you said it was his loss. He'd have the time of his life with you if he did go out with you. That's not what he wants, though, and that's his choice. He doesn't *have* to be your boyfriend if he doesn't want to be.' Bing reached over and took one of Evie's hands. 'You haven't come out of the deal so badly, have you? You had two days of flirting and getting your bum pinched, all rounded off nicely with some sex courtesy of a superstud. Better than a poke in the eye.'

Evie had warmed up. 'You're right,' she said, and almost meant it.

'She's still owed a dinner.' Sacha was like a stubborn parrot. 'He promised to take her out to dinner.'

Bing ran a hand over his face. 'For God's sake, the man was trying to get his leg over. He'd have promised her a cure for cancer if he thought it would open her knees. He didn't sign a contract – *I the undersigned promise to take you somewhere posh and feed you*. There was no swearing on the Bible. Give the guy a break.'

'He said he'd take her out to dinner.'

Bing stared at Sacha in a way that a human being with thinner skin would correctly interpret as dangerous. 'This isn't helping Evie,' he said, through gritted perfect teeth.

Evie reckoned it was time to lighten the mood. The handwritten signs, felt-tipped on fluorescent card, were one of the reasons they liked this shabby little caff. She'd spotted a new one. 'Look.' She pointed to the dog-eared little square over the till that warned, 'Remember – squeak takes longer.'

Two burly men were manhandling the new cooker into the kitchen. Evie leaned against a door jamb, arms folded, wondering how come she was spending a hefty portion of her TV fee on a *cooker*, of all things. Surely she should be buying high-heeled boots or sexy underwear or drugs or something.

The gleaming new cooker put the rest of the kitchen to shame. It looked even dingier than before. With revulsion Evie realised that she'd have to *clean* it. What was her life coming to? She snapped on a pair of Bing's rubber gloves.

The trouble with cleaning, Evie discovered, was that as soon as you washed one thing it made the thing next to it look filthy. So then you had to wash that thing. You were locked on to an endless merry-go-round of Vim and scouring-pads. And she had only another half-hour before Simeon would arrive to whisk her off to theatre hell – she hadn't even started on the skirting-boards.

Skirting-boards! It had come to this. 'I bet Kate Winslet doesn't scrub her own skirting-boards.'

The cavalry arrived, in the unexpected shape of Caroline. 'Just wondered if you'd like an 'and.'

'You any good at skirting-boards?'

Soon Caroline was crouched with a bucket of her own. Milly, who was of an age to find buckets of scuzzy water irresistible, stayed trussed up in her buggy.

It was quite restful, mused Evie, being around somebody who preferred not to talk. Particularly if you were used to Bing's surroundsound gossip. They toiled away companionably until interrupted by the phone.

Evie stiffened. She hated herself for the way her heart was suddenly fluttering under her tie-dye T-shirt like a caged bird.

'Aren't you going to get that?' Caroline was looking at her strangely.

'Of course!' Evie leapt up and dashed into her room where her mobile was immersed in the mess that lived happily undisturbed by her bed. She flung newspapers, knickers, takeaway menus and novelty slippers wildly into the air, snatched up the phone and stared at its tiny screen. *Number withheld*. Willing herself not to be so expectant she cleared her throat and punched the OK button. 'Hello,' she said, trying to cram sexiness, sophistication, intelligence, wit and firm breasts into the one small word.

'Evie? It's Beth. Is that you? You sound funny.'

'Oh.' The crushing, right-down-to-her-toes disappointment was swiftly replaced by panic. Beth *never* rang her. 'What's happened? Is somebody dead? Is everybody dead?'

'What? Of course not. Nothing's happened.'

'Right. Sorry. How are you?'

'Fine. You?'

There was no point in sharing the whole Dan débâcle with Beth: it was so far removed from her clean, tidy life in Henley. 'I'm great.' Sharply she remembered what had come out the last time she'd seen her sister. 'And how is Marcus?'

'Oh he's, you know . . . Marcus.'

The twinge of sadness didn't pass Evie by: she didn't have the monopoly on man trouble. She felt a rush of sympathy.

'I need a favour, actually.' This was yet more unusual behaviour. Beth had never needed anything from Evie before. 'I've got an appointment in London on Friday. Can I dump the twins with you for an hour or so? About ten?'

'What sort of appointment?' Evie's antennae were twitching.

'Does it matter?'

Now Evie's antennae were jangling like telegraph wires in a storm. 'Is it a solicitor?'

There was a shocked moment of silence, then Beth said tetchily, 'Look, can you watch them or not?'

Evie said of course she could and the conversation finished

abruptly. Evie felt uneasy. It had been a shot in the dark about the solicitor. She hadn't wanted to be right. Bloody Marcus! It would take a lot to push somebody as placid as Beth towards divorce. Part of Evie was desperate to ring her mother and spill the beans so that they could embark on an orgy of Marcus-abuse. The urge passed. This was Beth's business. Perhaps they'd talk about it on Friday. Shamefaced, she realised that this was a scary prospect. The Crumps weren't big on intimacy.

Tugging the outsize Marigolds back on she rejoined Caroline, who had graduated to worktops.

'That was my sister.' Evie had no reason to believe that the psychotically self-contained Caroline would have the remotest interest, but she prattled on anyway. 'She's coming over on Friday. She never visits me, so I know something's up. I think her marriage is in trouble, and I don't know what to do. Families! Sometimes they're more trouble than they're worth, aren't they?'

Caroline's sponge landed in the bucket with an angry splash. She banged the Vim down on the new cooker, turned the buggy on a dime and was out of the flat in a trice.

Evie was just about to call Caroline a very bad name indeed when she remembered: Caroline had no family to get impatient with. She was alone in the world. Evie slapped her face with a rubber glove smeared in soapy grease. She figured she deserved it.

The phone shrieked. Evie slammed it to her ear. 'Hello?' she said breathlessly, forgetting to be sexy or intelligent.

'Hasserung?'

She reckoned she deserved that too.

11

The supermarket was vast, and packed to the rafters with food, but still Evie couldn't decide what Bernard should be forced to cook. She was severely hampered by her own lack of kitchen skills. Just opening a Delia Smith volume brought on terminal yawning, and the only TV programmes she hated more than the gardening ones were on cookery. She was browsing the deli section, wondering what the hell *cornichons* were, when her mobile rang.

She dropped her wire basket and fumbled maniacally through her bag. Bing's warning words about Dan had not done the trick. 'Hello?'

'Where are you? I'm standing outside your front door. They both want a wee!' Beth was not her usual cool self.

'Ohmigod! I for– tunately am only round the corner.' Evie didn't want to offend her sister by admitting that she'd forgotten their arrangement. 'Be there in two shakes of a lamb's tail.' Make that a rather lumpen, slow lamb.

Evie looked about wildly. A row of fat, pale little birds caught her eye. Chicken! Of course. You couldn't go wrong with chicken. And they were cheap.

It was evidently a long time since Evie had priced chickens. The organic ones were ludicrously expensive, the corn-fed ones only slightly cheaper. She bunged a bog-standard one into the basket. A few E-numbers might perk Bernard up.

Starring in her own private *Supermarket Sweep* Evie raced round the vegetables, snatching up various green things. 'Stuffing!' she muttered, then, 'Gravy!' She was knackered by the time she screeched to a halt at the checkout. How did normal women manage this every day?

The twins were cross-legged and bulging-eyed by the time Evie reached them. 'Smart suit,' she said to Beth, as the three-year-olds careered towards the bathroom like Exocet missiles.

'Thanks.' Beth was distracted. 'I'll be a couple of hours at the most.'

'Good luck.' Evie was rather proud of herself for asking no questions. She had vowed to be silently supportive until Beth felt ready to share. Mature or what? she congratulated herself.

A tentative knock at the door announced Bernard. He was sporting a spotlessly clean, obviously brand-new stripy apron, done up rather too tightly. His strawberry hair was more manic than ever, evidently having been shampooed for the occasion.

Evie longed to sedate him and get some scissors to it. It wasn't just roast chicken on the menu tonight: there was love for dessert. Although it was just as well she'd bought ice-cream, as the current hairdo was unlikely to set Caroline's loins a-tingle.

First things first. 'Come into the kitchen and meet your victim.' The chicken crouched in the middle of the table, looking insolently naked out of its wrapping.

'Oh dear,' said Bernard, with feeling.

'I'm bored,' said Charles, pulling at Evie's jeans.

'Me too. Read us a story,' pleaded Julius.

Luckily a shambling figure, newly resurrected from his bed, was shuffling past the door in Calvin Klein knicks.

'Look!' trilled Evie gaily. 'It's Uncle Bing! Let's all go and play with him!' The twins dashed ahead. 'Not you, Bernard!' she hissed, as he began obediently to unknot his apron.

Uncle Bing hadn't shaved. Uncle Bing smelt of alcohol and cigarette smoke.

'Uncle Bing! Uncle Bing!' The twins leapt wildly up and down, much as Bing had the previous night before the E wore off.

'Yuk,' he said vehemently. 'Put them away.'

Evie gabbled her predicament. 'The future happiness of Caroline and Bernard could hang on your co-operation,' she concluded. 'Please. Just amuse them for an hour until Beth comes back.'

Bing couldn't refuse.

But he did.

He refused until Evie agreed to forget the twenty quid he owed her.

'Where were we?' Evie marched into the kitchen.

'We were staring at the chicken,' said Bernard.

'First we have to wash it.'

'Surely it's clean?'

'We wash it anyway. Pick it up and swish it under the tap.'

'I can't!' Bernard was aghast. 'I'd have to touch it.'

'How did you imagine you were going to cook a chicken without touching it?'

'No. I can't.' Bernard stuck his hands behind his back.

'Oh, for God's sake.' Evie picked up the bird and thrust it hard into Bernard's middle. His hands automatically grabbed for it.

'Uuuurgh!' His pale face was mottled with distress.

Evie switched on the cold tap and propelled Bernard towards it. He certainly brought out the schoolmarm in her. 'Rinse it!' she commanded, like a dominatrix.

Enjoying her new role just a little too much, she prodded and bullied Bernard through the rudiments of preparing a chicken for the oven. He took all this treatment mildly, presumably as a result of all those years with his mother. She was amazed at his perfect lack of knowledge. 'You're not serious!' He was outraged by her suggestion that he put a halved lemon into the cavity. 'You want me to . . . in its . . .'

'Bernard, don't be so shy. It's a chicken, not a date.' She grabbed his hand. 'Just pull up the flap—'

'Dear God!' mewled Bernard.

'And thrust the lemon in. There. All done.'

Bernard looked at his fingers in horror, as if they belonged to someone else.

Bing stuck his head round the door. 'They didn't like the story,' he reported. 'Maybe they're just too young for Jackie Collins. What shall I do with them now?'

'Errr . . . Run about the garden screaming. They're really into that.' Evie returned her attention to Bernard. 'Now, peel the potatoes with this peeler and cut them into smallish chunks.'

The mobile rang. Evie thrust the potatoes at him, then rushed from the room. She took a deep breath and said, 'Hello,' perfectly. She'd been practising.

A German voice asked for Geraldine.

Evie slunk back to the kitchen.

Bernard was looking agonised by the sink. There was blood on a potato. 'Can't quite get the hang of this peeler thingy. A tad medieval for me,' he said apologetically.

Evie gave him a crash course in peeling and he finished off all the potatoes, managing to cut them into quarters without severing any major arteries. Then she introduced him to a packet of sage and onion stuffing and guided him through the intricacies of kettle-boiling.

Bing appeared, balancing a twin on each shoulder. 'This is too tough,' he moaned. 'They don't do drugs. They probably don't care for porn.'

'How about hide and seek?'

Evie's suggestion was well received. While Bing counted slowly to ten Evie helped the boys into the larder. When he stopped counting she mouthed, 'They're in there,' and pointed helpfully. Bing gave her a thumbs-up and lay down on the sofa, shouting, 'Oh, where on earth can they be?' at intervals. This occasioned stifled giggles from behind the larder door.

'We'll make the gravy now and warm it up later.' Evie took a jar of own-brand economy granules from a cupboard. Nothing but the best for her lucky guests.

'I presumed gravy just . . . happened,' admitted Bernard, as he carefully refilled the kettle at arm's length.

*   *   *

Beth raised an eyebrow when her precious offspring were retrieved from a cupboard. Their blond crops smelt strongly of dust.

'Everything OK?' Evie saw signs of strain around her sister's eyes.

'Of course.' Beth smiled glassily and was gone. 'I owe you one,' she shouted, through the car window.

'Yeah. You can look after Bing next time I go out.'

The phone rang, ooh, twenty times that day, according to Evie. It actually rang five times but she could be forgiven the exaggeration: each time her heart thumped and her blood pressure lifted her fringe. But it was never Dan.

One call was from Meredith. 'Darling, the ad agency called to say you were fucking perfect and they will definitely cast you again. The commercial starts playing out on Saturday by the way.'

This small evidence of being in Meredith's good books emboldened Evie to ask, 'Anything else on the horizon? You know, a nice, proper acting job?'

'On the horizon, darling? How would I know? I threw away my fucking telescope years ago.'

Ask a silly question.

Bernard was intrigued to learn that the oven had to be warmed up before his little fowl went into it. He was moving more confidently about the kitchen now, toying fearlessly with the utensils. He had even allowed Evie to tame his hair and she had coerced him into a plain blue shirt of Bing's.

'It brings out the colour of your eyes, tones down your hair and complements your pale skin.'

'Does it?' Bernard peered uneasily at the man in the mirror.

'Yes, it does.' Evie was firm. If Bernard was to find true love he had to learn to brush his hair and brave pastels occasionally.

She supervised his dainty arrangement of tortilla crisps on

a platter with a tub of salsa. They had a dry run of nibble-proffering. 'Very good. It's not so hard, is it?'

Bernard didn't seem to agree wholeheartedly. 'Shouldn't we start boiling the peas? Mother always boiled vegetables for hours.'

'Oooh, no. They go on at the last minute.' It occurred to Evie that Caroline *and* Bernard were alone in the world. This was another reason why they should be encouraged to find each other. *Another* reason? She corrected herself. There was no other reason, except that she thought it was a good idea.

The front-door bell rang. 'Our first guest!' Evie hugged Bernard for luck. He felt like an ironing-board. 'Bernard! Hug me back!' she ordered.

Bernard mustered up a limp embrace, obviously suffering.

There was a lot of work still to do on this strange, solitary man.

It was only as Evie put her hand on the latch that she remembered their guest lived on the floor above and wouldn't arrive by the front door. She swung it open and there was Aden.

He held out a bottle of wine. 'I've come to say sorry,' he said, looking all boyish with his denim jacket and his shiny hair. He didn't look anything like a porter.

'What have you got to say sorry for?' Evie was puzzled by his sudden appearance on the doorstep. She hadn't thought of Aden since the shoot ended. 'Oh, and hello.' She took the bottle. 'Thank you.'

'Sorry for leaving you in the hotel on the last morning. It wasn't very gallant. And sorry for not warning you.'

'About what?'

Aden shifted from foot to foot, adding to the boyish vibe. 'About Dan.'

Evie felt cold. She hesitated, fighting the desire to slam the door and stick her fingers in her ears. 'Come in,' she said quietly.

Caroline, clutching Milly, was coming out of her flat. She had put on some makeup and tied up her glossy black hair.

What with that and the black peasanty top she was wearing she looked lovely.

Evie introduced Aden, then said to him, 'We're just about to have dinner. Do you want to join us?'

'Er, yeah, if that's OK.'

'Of course it is.' Evie led the way downstairs, hoping that the little chicken would feed another mouth.

'Did you get my message?' asked Aden. 'I spoke to your flatmate. He suggested that a bottle of wine always does the trick when he wants to apologise to you.'

'Believe me, he usually has plenty to apologise for. No, he didn't mention you called.' Maybe he had. The only phone message that would have penetrated the recent fug around Evie would have been one from Dan.

Bing had dragged the kitchen table into the sitting room, and laid it with his usual flair. A cloth had been procured, glasses had been polished and candles lit. It looked inviting, and he hastily moved everything to make another place. Nothing on the table matched, but he had made that part of its charm.

Bernard emerged from the kitchen with his salsa and crisps, grimly intent on them as if he was holding a tray of nuclear waste. He circulated as rehearsed.

Evie introduced Aden to the others. She really wanted to scream, 'Whaddyamean warn me about Dan?' at him but that would have to wait. The purpose of this evening was to ignite something between two of her tenants: nothing must get in the way of that.

Evie swept up Milly so Caroline was free of distraction. Aden shook Milly's hand gravely, which made her giggle, and encouraged Evie to hand Milly over to him. He looked nonplussed as he took her, but didn't complain.

Evie checked on the chicken. She leant against the kitchen wall, her head drooping. Why had Aden been impelled to turn up just now? She felt a hot wave of antipathy towards him, which, if she'd thought about it, she would have realised was down to dread of what he had to say rather than the man himself. But she was in no mood for self-analysis. She slammed the oven door so hard that the chicken trembled in its tin.

The doorbell rang again. Glad not to have to return to the sitting room just yet, Evie took the stairs two at a time. 'Sacha?'

'Hi, hi.' Sacha swooped in, kissing and fussing, handing over a bottle. She was wearing her favourite poppy-red lipstick, which had left an indelible mark on unsuspecting males the length and breadth of Camden. 'Am I late?'

'Are you late for what?'

'Dinner.'

'You're not invited to dinner.'

'As if I need to be invited.' Sacha swept down the stairs to the basement, to leave scarlet marks on the cheeks of all present.

Bing glared at Evie as he moved everything on the table yet again. 'We'll be squashed up like Japanese commuters,' he hissed at Evie. 'You didn't say your insane friend was coming.'

'My insane friend wasn't invited,' said Evie. 'Bernard – *peas*!' she ordered imperiously and he scuttled off, rubbing at the lipstick stain on his face.

Sacha was plainly oblivious to any resentment directed at her. As Evie knew, she believed her wonderful aura meant she was welcome everywhere. As she struggled to pop the cork on the bottle she'd brought, she explained, 'This isn't really champagne. It's just fizzy stuff. I can't afford champagne.' Like many people who have never known real money worries, Sacha banged on endlessly about how poor she was. The economies she was forced to make were generally in the area of presents: the latest wacky mystic paraphernalia and designer shoes could usually be funded.

Bernard, looking frazzled from the mental and physical exertions of putting the peas on, sidled over to Evie. 'I've burned the gravy,' he confessed.

Evie followed him back to the kitchen, pursued by Sacha. 'Your hair looks much nicer tonight,' she said, in a heavily seductive voice to Bernard.

'Does it?' Bernard ran a hand nervously through it.

'Shut up, Sacha, and get out of the way.' Evie was brisk: she had to save the gravy. 'Take the chicken out of the oven, Bernard, and put it on that big plate so we can carve.'

It almost goes without saying that the chicken ended up on the floor.

'He's nervous around me,' whispered Sacha, who had not got out of the way, to Evie as they dusted down the bird.

Evie stared blankly at her, silenced by such arrogance. 'Get out,' she advised eventually, 'and don't tell anyone what just happened.' Then she and Bernard tipped various overcooked and undercooked foodstuffs on to serving plates she had neglected to warm. 'What do you think of Caroline?' she asked him casually. 'Nice, isn't she?'

Bernard was focusing on the peas. 'Yes. She seems like a lovely girl.'

Evie smiled to herself. That was enough to be going on with. She picked up the dish of steaming, perfectly roasted chicken and carried it aloft into the dining room. 'Dinner is served!' she announced.

The huddled diners, knees touching under the table, grinned in anticipation.

'You'd never think that'd just been on the floor,' snorted Sacha, as the fizzy wine began to kick in.

The grins wavered.

'You're sitting in the wrong place.' Bing redirected Sacha to the chipped plate and the glass they used to catch the drips from the cistern.

The food was passed round. Milly lolled on the sofa with a little bowl of her own while the adults tucked in at the table. The chicken had sportingly managed to feed them all, even the gatecrashers.

Aden declared that his was 'Delicious!'

Bing thought it 'The best roast hen I've ever had!'

Caroline eked out, 'Hmm. It's fine.'

They all raised their glasses and chorused, 'To Bernard!'

'Oh, no. Nononono.' Bernard was blinking rapidly, sweating with self-consciousness. He was smiling, though. 'Thank you. Really. It's too much, too much. Thank you.'

Evie was glad of her training. She didn't feel like the life and soul of the evening so she acted it. Somehow she encouraged both Caroline and Bernard to join in with the conversation, slyly topping up their glasses. She made jokes and laughed at everyone else's. She listened to Bernard's halting anecdotes about the wacky world of statistics with rapt attention. She even swapped Sacha's glass for a more hygienic one.

All the time the rock of coldness inside her refused to melt. Nobody guessed at how she was feeling – if she'd brought half as much technical accomplishment to Kidz!OK! Simeon would have been a happy man. Evie looked at Aden, who was nodding at Caroline's tale of Milly's latest naughtiness. He looked so innocent, but he had come to shatter her dream. Evie didn't allow herself too many dreams and now she remembered why.

'Do you ever get the chance to go out? Who looks after Milly for you if you want to have an evening out?' Aden was asking, with real interest.

'There isn't anyone to baby-sit.' Caroline fiddled with the stem of her glass. 'There used to be, but . . .' She tailed off into one of her habitual glum silences.

'Bing and I can baby-sit!' Evie offered enthusiastically, and ignored a sharp kick beneath the table. She turned to Bernard. 'You could take Caroline out somewhere nice one evening, couldn't you?' she prodded.

Caroline saved him from answering: 'I can arrange me own social life, you know.' She didn't sound as if a night on the arm of a virginal statistician was lighting her fire.

Evie conceded that she had lost a battle, but couldn't accept that she had lost the war. She decided sensibly against stating that she would *only* look after Milly when Caroline went out with

Bernard, and said meekly, 'Of course you can. It was just a suggestion.'

'Time for afters.' Bing ended the silence that had cloaked the table.

Bernard looked panic-stricken.

'It's just ice-cream.' Evie rose. 'I'll get it.'

Bernard breathed a sigh of relief.

Sacha started clearing the table. Evie rolled her eyes. Sacha always helped ostentatiously in a way that was distinctly unhelpful. One drunken evening she'd put the plates in the cupboards without washing them.

As Evie wrestled with the soft-scoop, Sacha glugged the remains from her glass and whispered, 'Did you notice Bernard staring at me? God, it was so embarrassing.'

'Was it really?' Evie had been here before and knew better than to try to dissuade Sacha that Bernard was nuts about her.

'I kept catching his eye. I thought it best to act natural.'

'Yes. That's best. Act natural.'

'I'll have to be honest with him at some point, though. I just don't fancy him. How do you think he'll take it?'

'He'll cope.'

As they juggled plates and spoons Sacha nudged her dangerously. 'Aden's a bit of a dish.'

'Aden?' Evie had never spotted any dish-like tendencies in him. 'Bit bland, I thought.'

'No, he's nice.'

They went back into the sitting room just as Bing flung open the conservatory doors. 'Let's have pudding outside.'

It was a good idea. The night air was warm and sweet, heavy with the scent of next door's magnolia and the takeaways on the high street. Sacha switched on the fairy-lights. 'Don't you wish your whole life could be lit by fairy-lights?'

Bernard and Caroline, dragging their chairs outside, gave her a wide berth. At least they had something in common: they both considered Sacha worth avoiding.

Aden was investigating the flowers in a stone urn near the house. Evie strolled over to him with leaden feet. It was time to hear what he had to say. Her gut lurched. 'Heartsease,' he said.

'Eh?'

Aden pointed at the flowers. 'Heartsease. Lovely old English plant. Are you interested in gardening?'

'No.' Evie was emphatic. She would never, ever garden, not if Robbie Williams was out there naked with the lawnmower.

'I do. I love it.'

That didn't surprise her. 'You know what you said earlier about warning me?' She ushered in her own unhappiness. 'What did you mean?'

'Ah.' Aden sat down heavily on a large empty flowerpot. 'It's difficult. I mean, you're having a party. I don't want to spoil it.'

'I've news for you. You already have.'

Aden looked hurt. 'I thought very hard before I came round. I told myself it was none of my business, you didn't need to hear any of this, and I'm sure you can look after yourself. But . . .' He paused, apparently casting about for the best way to express himself. 'You didn't deserve it.' He looked directly at her. 'Am I a patronising sod? Shall I go away?'

'No, no, Aden. Spit it out.'

'OK. Dan and I have been mates for years. He's a top bloke, I love him, but he has one huge flaw: his attitude to women. Dan was every bit as handsome as he is now when he was seven. The playground was full of girls crying over him. It's been that way ever since.'

'I haven't cried over him,' lied Evie.

'Good.' Aden didn't look as though he believed her. 'Dan has never had a serious relationship. He thinks falling in love would get in the way of his career. He's deeply ambitious. I can relate to that – so am I. I *can't* relate to the way he treats the women in his life. He likes . . .' Aden faltered, unable to look at Evie

'. . . conquests. He likes numbers. He prides himself on being able to pick up a girl whatever the situation. Particularly at work. That's why I was so disapproving on the shoot, by the way. I knew it wasn't harmless flirting. I knew he was pulling out all the stops to get you into bed. But something about the way you looked at him told me it meant a bit more to you. Was I right?'

Evie swallowed. 'You couldn't be more wrong.' She even managed a smile.

'Really?' Aden looked taken aback and unconvinced. 'Well, anyway, knowing him as well as I do I asked him to lay off. Not to make you another notch on his bedpost. When you didn't show up on the last morning and Dan had dark circles under his eyes it was obvious what had happened. I really am sorry, you know, that I didn't wait for you. I had to get the whole crew on to the train and Dan reckoned you'd be unconscious for hours.'

''Sfine.' It was the least of her worries.

'On the way home Dan told me he'd promised to take you out for dinner.' Here Aden dried up.

'He didn't mean it, did he?' Evie helped to put herself out of her misery.

'No, Evie, he didn't. It's been on my mind ever since. I knew you'd be waiting for his call. I've seen all this before, all the pain the bloody idiot causes. I thought you should know, so you could just get on with things and not hang around for him.'

Evie felt as a if a large frying-pan had hit her smack in the face. The last smidgeon of hard-won hope was gurgling down the drain. But her acting muscles were still warm: 'You're very sweet to do this, but there was no need. It was just a bit of fun as far as I was concerned.'

'Good. Although I feel a fool.'

'Don't! It really was sweet, like I said.' And it was. She just wished she hadn't had to hear it.

*　　*　　*

The party was straggling to an end, and Caroline was the first to make a move. 'Thanks. I've had a lovely evening,' she said, without expression. She looked a little more relaxed than usual, less reined in. Evie had noticed her chatting to Aden and even floating the occasional smile his way. Then Bernard walked Sacha to the door. Or, to be precise, Sacha leapt up as Bernard was making his long-winded, stammering goodbyes and grabbed his arm.

'Do you think Bernard enjoyed the experience?' Evie asked Bing, as they tidied up with Aden's help.

'I hate to admit it, but I think you did him some good,' replied Bing. 'He was trying desperately not to look proud when we all complimented him on the chicken.'

'If we can lure him away from the chip shop his complexion might improve,' mused Evie. 'He might look less freshly dug up.'

'I don't think the matchmaking is going to be a success.' Bing was carrying a teetering pile of plates out to the sink.

'What matchmaking?' Aden was incredulous. 'Not Caroline and Bernard?'

'We'll see,' said Evie, in a mysterious manner. She wasn't about to give up. Caroline needed someone to take care of her and Milly, and Bernard needed somebody to blossom with. 'You off, then?'

Aden was pulling on his jacket. 'Think so. Early start tomorrow.'

'God, I haven't even asked what you're working on.'

'Just a little low-budget film. Arty crap. But I'm directing, so I have to get my beauty sleep.' Aden kissed Evie's cheek. His lips were soft. 'Don't see me out, I know my way. Sorry I was such a party-pooper. Can I come round again *without* tidings of doom and gloom?'

Evie nodded. Aden was a relaxing person to be with. 'Any time.'

'Night, then.' He pointed a directorly strict finger at her. 'No pining for Dan, now!'

'Dan who?' Just then her mobile buzzed into life. 'See? I didn't even jump.' She put the phone to her ear and said, 'Hello,' without a trace of intelligence or sexiness.

It was a bad line but through the crackle she heard, 'Hi, gorgeous, it's Dan.'

12

When Evie was unhappy she over-ate. When Evie was happy she *really* over-ate. 'More biscuits!' she yelled at Bing. 'Jammy ones this time, not those plain bastards!'

It was two a.m. and they were still up. Evie couldn't go to bed because she was too excited and Bing couldn't go to bed because Evie was too selfish to let him.

'Ask me again,' she ordered, as Bing joined her on the sofa with a topped-up biscuit barrel.

'Hasserung?'

'*Yes!*' She crammed a Jaffa cake into her mouth. 'And what were you?'

Bing rolled his eyes. 'I was wrong. And that's the last time I'm saying it,' he added grumpily.

'He rang, he rang, he rang, he rang,' sang Evie to an improvised tune, showering her companion with damp crumbs.

'I'm glad you hardly ever have sex if this is how it affects you.' Bing took a Club orange. 'If I went on like this every time some bloke fancied me I wouldn't hold down a job.'

'He's not "some bloke". He's Dan. Isn't that a lovely name? Manly. Strong. *Dan*.' Evie underlined its qualities by thrusting her fist in the air.

'Mmm. Very manly. Like Danny La Rue.'

'Wait till you see the way he dresses.'

'Is that anything like Danny La Rue?'

'He's really cool, really stylish, but kind of casual, you know?'

'I'm very happy for him.'

'And he's mine, all mine!'

Bing gave her what used to be called an old-fashioned look.

'Hang about, doll. He's taking you out for a bowl of pasta, he hasn't proposed.'

'I know. But it must mean something.'

She had been flabbergasted to hear his voice. Instead of answering his 'Hi, gorgeous,' she had mouthed, 'It's Dan,' at Aden, whose face had matched hers as an illustration of extreme shock. His jacket froze, half off half on, as they faced each other like waxworks.

'Are you there?' asked Dan.

'Yes, I'm here. Sorry. A – a thing just happened,' ad-libbed Evie ineptly. 'How are you?' God. Fascinating. Hopefully her personality would kick in soon.

'Knackered. I've been on another commercial shoot in Spain. It came up the day I got back to London. That's why I didn't ring before. Left your number in my flat.'

Evie was flooded with warmth. The explanation healed her sore heart. Waving away Aden, who was listening too intently for her liking, she retreated into her bedroom and closed the door. 'I thought you'd forgotten all about me,' she teased.

'As if. I've never had sex on a chest-of-drawers before. You're not an easy girl to forget.'

Evie didn't turn on the light. The world had shrunk to the darkness and Dan's deep voice. 'Really?'

'Really. Have you been thinking about me?'

'Occasionally. I lead the full life of a modern young woman, but you've crossed my mind.'

'Glad to hear it. I hope you haven't been inviting any other blokes on to hotel furniture.'

'No.' She laughed. 'Oh, I saw Aden tonight, though. He was here for dinner.'

'Aden?' Dan sounded surprised and not all that pleased. 'Didn't realise you two were so cosy.'

'It was only dinner.' Evie trembled at the sound of Dan's jealousy. She loved it, but didn't want him to back off. 'There were six of us. Aden turned up out of the blue.'

'Right.' Dan was back to his relaxed sexy self. 'Where are you right now?'

'In my bedroom.'

'I'm hoping you're on the bed.'

'Your hopes are fulfilled.' Evie nipped hastily on to the bed.

'Lie back, sweetheart.'

Sweetheart lay back. Her ear throbbed with the dark notes of his voice. Her body tingled and twitched. 'Are you lying down too?'

'Mm-hmm. I wish I was there with you. I can smell your hair. I wish I could lift it up and kiss you, just under your perfect little ear.'

'Oooh, I wish you were here too.' Evie's voice had dropped, become smoky with lust.

The door flew open. A hundred-watt bulb illuminated the room. 'I'm off,' squawked Sacha, swaying in the doorway. 'Who's that on the phone? Why were you in the dark?'

'*Fuck off!*' roared Evie, switching to a quite different persona.

Sacha was not an easy person to get rid of at the best of times. She made limpets look aloof. 'Who is it?' she persisted. A pillow hit her full in the face. 'No, really, who's on the phone?' Another pillow, harder this time. 'Who is it?'

Bing jerked Sacha out backwards by her scarf (a manoeuvre he'd been itching to try ever since they'd first been introduced) and closed the door firmly.

'Who was that?' Dan was laughing.

'My best friend.'

'I'd hate to hear you talk to your worst enemy.' The mood was broken.

Evie clenched her fist. She'd almost had her first ever phone sex. Damn.

'Anyway,' Dan continued, 'you know why I'm ringing. I owe you dinner. When are you free?'

Unless you counted her promise to do Bing's roots Evie was free every night from now until the end of the world. 'Let me think . . .' It was important to sound sought-after, a party girl rather than a sofa-and-soap-operas girl. 'I could do Monday if that's any good.'

'Nah. What about next Saturday?'

Next Saturday. But that was over a week away. Mind you, it *was* a Saturday. That's a special night, the night you save for your special bird. Part of her itched to say, 'I'll have to move something but I think I can make it,' but she censored that as going too far: he might tell her not to bother. 'That would be perfect.'

'Where would you like to go?'

Anywhere. A hole in the ground as long you're in it. 'Oh, God, I don't know. Why don't you call for me and we'll see what we feel like?'

'OK. As long as we eat as well.' Dan took down the address. He even managed to say, 'Kemp Street,' in an erotic way. 'That's a date. I'll pick you up at seven.'

The conversation was winding down. 'See you, then,' she said, using the sexy, intelligent voice she was thinking of patenting.

'You can get off the bed now.'

'I think I'll stay here for a while.'

'Night, gorgeous.'

'Night.'

He was gone and Evie was alone on Belle's overstuffed bed but it was floating high above the Camden chimney-pots. She was blissfully happy. Only one thing could improve her mood and that was where the biscuits came in.

'Please let me go to bed. I don't want to live here any more.' Bing was worn out. 'I can't talk about Dan any longer. I've never even met him. It's three in the morning! If you won't let me go to bed then at least have the decency to shoot me at point-blank range.'

Evie relented. As she brushed her teeth – oral hygiene was paramount between now and next Saturday – she remembered that she had an early start with Kidz!OK!. Even the thought of Simeon couldn't dampen her mood. Dan thought she was gorgeous and that was all that mattered.

It was debatable as to whether Dan would have thought gorgeous the dishevelled, unwashed creature with sleep in its half-closed eyes that dragged itself into Simeon's van the next morning.

'Jesus. Save your screams till you see its face,' sneered Simeon.

'And top of the morning to you, sir.'

'Have you been up all night? In a hedge?'

'Just drive, why dontcha?' Evie was too happy, despite her lack of sleep, to let this bargain-basement John Hurt get to her.

'Good morning, Crumpy.' The mole who had replaced the replacement mole stuck his head over the front seat. 'Want a bacon roll?'

'Do I?' Evie was suddenly awake as the best thing in the world, apart from Dan's penis, was put into her hands.

This newest mole was called Terry. He was short, squat and easy-going. You might have mistaken him for a plumber but he was a talented actor. Simeon had been delighted at first, but as it had dawned on him that Terry was twice as good as him with half the fuss, resentment had crept in. As a result he was more tyrannical and pretentious than ever.

'I wish you'd remember there's a vegetarian in your midst,' said Simeon loftily. 'The smell of slaughtered pig is unbearable.'

'I know,' sympathised Evie. 'Really makes you want one, doesn't it?'

'No!' snapped Simeon. 'It makes me feel sick. I won't put the flesh of another in my body.'

Bing wouldn't take that for an answer, mused Evie. 'Where are we headed today?'

'Is there any point in giving you a schedule? We're taking our politically corrected *Winnie-the-Pooh* to Hayward's Heath.' He swivelled nervously towards Evie. 'You did remember to bring your Piglet costume?'

'Of course.' She hadn't. And Simeon had spoiled her bacon roll. How she hated him.

There were traffic jams all the way. Simeon took them personally. 'Hello? *Hello?*' he would say to the road in front of him, exasperatedly. 'Theatre coming through. Or doesn't that mean anything to you people?'

Two subjects were jostling for space in Evie's already rather crowded head. One, obviously, was Dan. The other was her Piglet outfit, which was hanging in her wardrobe, miles back. 'I'll get in the back with Terry,' she said suddenly.

'Why?' Simeon was testy.

Not feeling up to the honest answer ('So I can beg him to help me botch together a Piglet costume from the odds and ends in the back of the van to stop you beating me to death with *The complete works of Shakespeare*'), Evie said simply, 'I just want to.'

'Oh, all right. Wait till I can pull over.'

'Pull over? We haven't moved in ten minutes.' Evie opened the door and dropped to the Tarmac. As she clambered into the back she whispered her dilemma to Terry, who went pale.

'We'll do it somehow,' he vowed bravely, throwing open the lid of the wicker basket that contained the oddments they used for improvisation. 'Look!' He put his hands on an ancient man's bathing suit, the Edwardian kind made of stripy material with a vest top and legs. 'Piglet has a stripy body, doesn't he?'

'But it's Johnny-Vegas-sized,' Evie pointed out.

'We've got belts.' Terry was evidently a good man in a crisis. A little more digging produced a swimming-cap and a rubber glove. He waggled them triumphantly.

'Sorry. Don't get it.' Evie frowned.

'We can cut the tops of two fingers off, stick them to the swimming-cap and that's Piglet's ears!' Terry was enjoying this.

Evie wasn't. She was beginning to wish she'd never involved

him. 'I don't think it'll work. It'll look stupid. Maybe I should just tell Simeon.'

Just then Simeon bellowed out of the window. 'Move, move, you soulless scum, and let the artists through. *You're murdering my soul!*'

Evie tugged on the swimming-cap.

'Obviously we'll have to paint you pink,' said Terry solemnly.

We all know that Pooh is small and round and we all know that Tigger is long and bendy. Despite this, six-foot-two Simeon had cast himself as Pooh and small, round Terry as Tigger. Pooh had more lines.

And what lines they were. Kidz!OK!'s dedication to being politically correct meant that there could be no teasing Pooh because he ate too much honey: that was sizeist. Pooh's home was no longer in the roots of a great oak, it was above a dry-cleaner's: Kidz!OK! had a horror of alienating urban children. Tigger had a long speech about mankind's slaughter of tigers and other endangered species. In order not to patronise their audience of six-year-olds this was illustrated by graphic pictures of dead animals. Tigger's subsequent song about bouncing was usually drowned by sounds of weeping.

Piglet, it goes without saying, was a feminist lesbian. Instead of dancing around the Hundred Acre Wood Piglet was much given to propagating female autonomy and insisting on the right to have a child. Being painted pink wasn't going to make any of this easier.

The traffic meant they had only minutes to spare when they got to the primary school. Simeon zipped himself into his yellow fur all-in-one and rushed on stage to give his first soliloquy.

Terry rammed on his latex mask. They had four minutes to transform Evie.

The paint got into her eyes. Her head itched: the swimming-cap was for a child and not a perfect fit.

'I'll paint your legs as well. For realism,' said Terry enthusiastically, squatting down.

'Realism?' marvelled Evie. The Edwardian swimsuit was tightly
belted but still hung in folds.

From the stage she heard her cue and ran on.

Meredith didn't often laugh. At first Evie wasn't sure what the
gurgling sound at the other end of the line was. 'Well, darling,'
gasped Meredith, 'you're fired but at least it sounds as if it was
fucking worth it.'

Bing couldn't stop laughing either. Admittedly, she was still
in costume when she told him. 'You went on stage like that?
What did the children do?'

'Most laughed, some screamed.' She didn't tell him about the
tiny boy who had wet the floor in case Bing did the same.

'But – you're *painted pink*! And that swimming-cap is all
bunched up on the top of your head!' Tears were sprouting
from his eyes.

Evie angrily snatched off the cap. 'The paint affected the glue.
One of the ears fell off.'

'They're *ears*?' Bing was off again.

'The audience had to be led out. They were all either laughing
or sobbing.'

Wiping his eyes Bing did his best to console her. 'At least you
got a reaction. That's what every actor wants.'

Evie sighed. 'I didn't want the sack.'

Bing had opened a bottle of wine while she was in the shower,
depinking. 'It's not quite – here's some plonk.' His landlady's
glowering face had warned him she did not need to be told
that the pink paint was not all gone. 'I've ordered a pizza.
Extra everything. Enough garlic bread to feed all my one-night
stands.'

'I can't afford it,' said Evie miserably.

'I can, so shut your trap.' Bing was holding an envelope. 'I don't suppose it's the right moment to show you this, but it has to be faced up to, sweetie.'

'What is it?' Evie stared at the piece of paper. 'I don't like it. It looks like a bill.'

'It's an estimate. For sorting out the damp.'

'What damp?' yelped Evie. 'Bloody hell. A grand! I don't have a grand! Where will I get a grand? A grand! A *grand*? How am I supposed to afford—'

'I know. A grand.' Bing held the glass to her lips. 'Drink. It's good for you. Trust Dr Bing.' She calmed down a little, enough to listen anyway. 'I got these guys in to give us a quote 'cos there's signs of damp all over the back of the house. I didn't want to worry you until I knew for sure. It could wait, of course, but it's worst in Caroline's flat.'

'Milly!' said Evie immediately.

'Exactly. It ain't good for a little one. So we've got to find the money somehow. But it *is* we – you and me. You don't have to do it on your own.' Bing spoke lightly, stuffing his gym clothes into a nylon bag.

Evie appreciated that. He was wrong, though. It was her house and her responsibility. She couldn't accept any money from him.

Bing paused on his way out to refine his toned body and his flirtation with his personal trainer. 'Anyway, who cares? You're having dinner with Dan next Saturday.'

That did the trick. She was grinning again.

Sacha and Evie stood in Caroline's bedroom. It was papered in a bright, manic floral pattern, which gave it a cosy, if dated air. They were both staring at an irregular, brownish patch on the wall where the wallpaper was peeling away and the plaster was moist to the touch.

'Yup. That's damp.' Sacha nodded vigorously.

'We know that,' said Caroline tonelessly.

'It's got to be dealt with.' Sacha was nodding again.

Evie said grimly, 'We know that too, Sacha.'

'It's getting worse,' said Caroline. 'Milly used to sleep in the corner there, but now I've got her bedded down on the sofa. She cries most nights.'

Evie's head throbbed. Just an hour ago she'd got the sack and now she was standing here listening to what sounded like an accusation from Caroline. There was something about the unvarnished way the girl expressed herself, and the way she stared at you impassively while she did it, that made it seem that way. Evie felt got at. She knew that damp was A Very Bad Thing, she didn't need to hear any more details, thank you very much.

Caroline wasn't finished, though. 'And Milly's developing a cough.'

Christ. It was Dickens.

Sacha was nodding again. 'Could be TB.'

Evie glared at her, daring her to go on.

But go on she did. 'The *chi* will be incredibly blocked in here. That's very dangerous.'

'*Chi*?' Caroline wrinkled her nose. 'What's that? You never said nothing about *chi*, Eve. It's bad enough with the damp, without this bloody *chi* as well.'

Evie realised that it had always bugged her that this moody, sullen, antisocial girl, this difficult girl she'd been trying to help ever since they'd met, called her Eve. 'It's Evie,' she snapped. 'Don't worry. I'll sort it. I'm the landlady, after all.' She shoved Sacha out, saying, 'And I'll take the *chi* and I'll stuff it down your interfering neck.'

'By the way,' Caroline called after her, 'you've got pink in your eyebrows.'

With her unerring timing, Bridgie called that evening. 'How's the job going? And the house?' asked the woman who normally showed less interest in her daughter's career and legacy than she did in the latest breakthroughs in molecular science.

'I was sacked, Mum, and the back of the house is covered with damp.' Evie held the phone at arm's length while she finished reading an article about *EastEnders*, but not for long enough to miss her mother's final 'Will you never learn?'

'No. I'm an abject failure,' Evie said flatly. She had almost had enough.

'Anyway, I didn't ring up to talk about you.'

'I didn't imagine for one moment that you had.'

'What's the matter with your voice? It's about your sister.'

'Why? What's the matter?' Evie dropped the resentment.

'She's been behaving oddly. I could just be imagining things.'

'What sort of things?' Evilly, Evie milked her mother with no intention of pooling information. She was sticking to her vow of non-intervention.

'She's out when I ring.'

Sensible girl, thought Evie.

'And when I ask her where she's been she never gives me a proper answer. And she's started making sarky comments about Marcus. That's not like her.'

'What sort of comments?' queried Detective Inspector Crump.

'Just pointed little ones, calling him "her perfect husband" in a funny voice. Things like that. Am I making a fuss over nothing?'

Bridgie Crump made a fuss over nothing to world-class stand-ards on a daily basis, but this time she was spot on. There *was* something going on in Beth's hitherto perfect life. However, Evie was a creature of habit and she had got to twenty-seven years of age without agreeing with her mother. There was no need to start now. Besides, if Bridgie got wind of the fact that Marcus was playing away she would be half-way to Henley before Evie put the phone down. 'Beth's fine, Mum. She came up the other day and we had a great time. Don't worry about her, worry about me.'

'You? Haven't I been worrying about you since the midwife slapped your arse?'

So, St Evie the Martyr selflessly deflected her mother's fire, like the loyal bodyguard who throws himself in front of the president and takes the assassin's bullet. Beth needed space to sort out her problems in her own way.

'There's still time to be an air-stewardess,' her mother was gabbling. 'Or an estate agent. Or maybe you could train to be a kennelmaid – you make enough fuss of Henry . . .'

Bullets would be so much easier to take.

13

The parcels in the hall had disappeared. P. Warnes had spirited them upstairs without revealing him/her/itself. 'This means war,' breathed Evie, peering up to the top floor. It was now a place of mystery, a weird eyrie at the top of the house. '*My* house,' she reminded herself, as she marched up the stairs. Her brisk step became markedly slower as she neared the top landing.

It was chilly up there, in sharp contrast to the baking ground floor. London's heatwave hadn't ventured as far as P. Warnes's door.

Evie hesitated, then found her courage and rapped on the door with her knuckles. 'Ow!' Only then did she notice that it was not the original wooden door, but a sheet metal one, studded with rivets. She knocked again. 'P. Warnes!' she shouted. 'I need to speak with you urgently.' She had decided to use the damp problem as a ticket over her tenant's threshold. 'Please let me in!' Evie pressed her ear to the cold metal. Fathomless silence. It might have been a door to the edge of the universe. She strained. A tiny noise far away, like the scraping of a chair leg on the floor of a distant cell. She concentrated hard, but only silence followed. Frustrated, she stepped back to knock again.

It was then that she noticed the scratches at the left-hand side of the door. They ran towards the edge, as if some razor-sharp claw had scrabbled to get out.

From behind the door a slow shuffling commenced, accompanied by an odd dragging sound.

It drew nearer. It was ominous, unsettling. Evie was finally to get her wish. Her eyes were mesmerised by the scratches. She shivered.

The shuffling stopped. The dragging stopped. The only sound was Evie's flip-flops racing down the stairs.

'You ran away?' Bing clutched the towel round his neck as Evie smothered his head with noxious peroxide paste. 'You could have found out what he, she, it was like.'

'I was freaked out. I mean, it was *cold* up there. The whole of London is collapsing with heat exhaustion and I was shivering. Isn't that a classic symptom of, you know . . . ?' Evie didn't want to use the word.

'Ghosts?' Bing filled in fearlessly.

'Yeah. What if my house is haunted?'

'Ghosts don't usually get post.'

'Maybe he lived here until he died so stuff still arrives for him.'

'Oh, no. You've been giving this serious thought.'

Evie shrugged, and tied a Waitrose carrier-bag round Bing's scalp. He was probably the only human she knew who looked good in such headgear. 'A bit. How do you explain the scratches? They were very . . . demon-like.'

Bing scoffed. 'Why can't they be Yorkshire terrier-like?'

'Maybe a demon Yorkshire terrier,' Evie compromised. 'They were *deep*. Something had tried to get out of that flat. What about the noises? Shuffling? Dragging? Moans?'

'You didn't mention moans before.'

'All right, I threw in the moans. Sue me. You've got to admit, moans or no moans, it's bloody spooky.'

'No, I've got to admit you watch too much *Buffy*. There's a simple explanation for all of it.' Bing was solid, literal. He had never seen a ghost and if he did he would work on the assumption that it fancied him. 'We do not have the undead on the top floor. We have a shy weirdo. Don't tell Sacha any of this shit. She'll take the ball and run right off the pitch with it.'

'Actually, I've already told her,' Evie confessed. 'She had lots of ideas.'

'I bet she did.' Bing eyeballed himself in the mirror and rearranged his Waitrose bag so that it was more aesthetically pleasing.

'She suggested an exorcism.'

Bing spun round. 'No! No way! You'd scare yourselves to death.'

'A proper one,' cajoled Evie. 'By a priest with all the proper qualifications.'

'Oh, a *proper* one.' Bing dipped into his considerable reserves of irony. 'I thought you meant one of those cut-price ones, own brand, from a kit.'

'Be serious, Bing. Do you think it might work?'

'You know what I think. You'll just give yourselves the willies. There's nothing other-worldly about P. Warnes just because he's keen on fluorescent lights, makes strange noises and keeps odd hours. He's a freak but he doesn't deserve an exorcism, you wazzock.'

'You're right.' Just as Evie had talked herself into believing P. Warnes was from the other side, now she was talking herself out of it.

'If you were going to start exorcising where would you stop? Every flat in this building has its fair share of strange occupants. Caroline's bad moods could well be from Satan himself.'

Nimbly Evie forgot how Caroline had depressed her earlier and defended her. 'Don't be horrible.'

'I'm not being horrible. I like the girl, but she can be bloody hard work.'

'She's all alone in the world,' said Evie dramatically, adding with less drama, 'Do you want me to do your nails?'

'Oooh, yes!' Bing could never resist a beauty treatment. 'What does that mean, all alone in the world? You make her sound like a heroine in a Victorian melodrama.'

'I can't help that. She *is* all alone in the world. All her family are dead. Wiped out. Every one of them.'

'Poor cow,' said Bing, with feeling.

'She's a lot softer than you think.' Evie lowered Bing's hand into a cereal bowl of warm milk and lanolin. 'Do you remember me telling you about my visit to Belle's grave?' Bing didn't and there followed a short, shrill digression.

EVIE: What's the point of talking if you never bother listening?
BING: You talk non-stop and it can't all be fasci-fucking-nating, can it?
EVIE: I won't say anything in future.
BING: If only.

After a short huff Evie carried on, getting her revenge via over-enthusiastic use of a cuticle stick. 'I visited Belle's grave the day we got the keys to the house. I was a bit nervous – cemeteries and all that – but it was really nice. It was peaceful and I felt close to Belle. I wasn't the only one there. Somebody, a girl, flitted off when I arrived. I disturbed her while she was putting a bouquet, just a simple one, on Belle's grave. There was a note on it: "You are missed."'

'Aw.' Bing melted.

'And that girl was Caroline.'

'How do you know?'

'The flowers were tied up with a ribbon with little smilys on it. Who wears ribbons like that?'

'Me, in some of the clubs.'

Evie ignored this. 'Milly. She's always got them round her bunches.'

'Hmm. Sherlock Crump. I'm not convinced. It's not Caroline's style. She's the least sentimental person I've ever met. She never mentions Belle, except to say that she's dead and we should all forget her.'

'Denial,' said Evie with all the confidence of someone who watched psychologists on breakfast telly. 'She mentioned Belle at dinner the other evening. She said somebody used to baby-sit Milly and I just know she meant Belle.'

'I presumed she meant the kid's father.'

'No, it was Belle, I'm sure of it. And Belle refurbished Caroline's kitchen.'

'And left herself with a wreck.'

'Exactly. I think Belle mothered Caroline. Her heart went out to her because she was a single mother with no relatives to rely on.'

'So, of course, Caroline misses her.' Bing admired his newly buffed fingers. 'Am I ready to rinse yet?'

'Oh, Gawd, yes. Hurry or you'll be like a billiard ball.'

Bing dashed off, saying over his shoulder, 'Belle knew what she was doing when she put you in charge.'

Evie hoped he was right.

On Monday morning there was great excitement in the basement. There had been a reliable sighting of Bernard with a carrier-bag from a man's clothes shop. True, it had been only a fleeting glimpse as he had let himself into his flat but Evie was prepared to swear that the bag had looked fairly full and was from Top Man.

'Hugo Boss would have been better.' Bing was in nit-picking mood.

'Top Man's a good start. All his current wardrobe seems to have been left to him by his great-grandfathers. Don't you see what this means? My gentle persuasion to improve himself is working.'

'Gentle persuasion? Oh, you mean the psychotic bullying. I saw what went on over that chicken carcass last week and that was not gentle persuasion.'

'No pain, no gain.' Evie snapped open a bag of Monster Munch.

'That's your third,' warned Bing, uncannily like Evie's old Mother Superior.

'Who's counting?'

'I am, or I wouldn't be able to inform you that it's your third.'

'If I don't care why should you?'

'Because I'm the one who'll have to listen to your ravings about the size of your backside as you try on every garment in your wardrobe before your date with Dan. After the tears will come the blame – something along the lines of "Why didn't you stop me eating all those Monster Munch, you heartless bastard?" – and then the physical attack. I still bear the scars of your trying-on session before your cousin's engagement party. A girl can do real damage with a pair of platforms.'

Bing's reasoning was sound but Evie answered serenely, 'I've got it all worked out. Dieting between now and Saturday won't make any difference to my shape, but denying myself the tiny but vital sensual pleasures of life—' she gestured at a newsagent's bag full of Monster Munch, Wotsits and Flakes '—will make me miserable, which will show in my face. I have a theory that men are attracted to happy women, not thin ones.'

'A woman with a big arse is not a happy woman.'

'Thank you, Confucius. Pass me the Quavers, please. These adorable little snacks will never get as far as my bum. I intend to work them off.'

'How?' Bing looked dubious. 'By watching a *This Morning* special on exercise?'

'No. By going for a run. Now that I don't have a job I have lots of time to get fit. That's why I'm in my workout clothes.' Evie did a little twirl in her grey leggings and sweatshirt. Like the trainers on her feet, they were pristine. She had bought them at the time of her last speech on getting fit, about a year ago. She had tried them on and run round her bedroom in them, walloping an imaginary punch-bag. Then she had rewarded herself with a nice KitKat and had never put them on again. She thought of them often, though – my workout clothes – and always felt vaguely Anthea Turner-like when she did. 'I'm running over to Sacha's shop in a mo.'

'Why don't you go now?'

'I've got to wait for the damp men.'

'That's all right. I'll look after them. Off you pop.'

Evie narrowed her eyes at her usually unhelpful flatmate. 'Look after them? Is that what they call it nowadays?'

'It's a fair cop. The guy who came to do the estimate was absolutely *stunning*,' gushed Bing. 'Looked straight as a die, but gave me a little smile when I mentioned he could get his hands on my moist sections whenever he liked.'

'So you're hoping love will blossom over the putty?'

'Not love.' Bing pulled a face. 'Plenty of time for that when my looks go. A bit of slap-and-tickle with a builder is definitely my idea of home improvement.'

Bing dashed out when the damp men's van pulled up. He returned sharpish, looking crestfallen. Evie peered up out of the basement window. Unless his tastes had changed dramatically the stunning workman was not among them. There was a very fat one, a very small one and a third with no front teeth.

'I'll leave you to it, then,' said Evie airily, jogging down the front steps. 'Try not to get over-excited. I know the no-teeth look is very in on Old Compton Street at the moment.'

Evie took to the pavements at a gentle pace. Even so, she was wilting by the corner of Kemp Street. When she reached Bernard's beloved chippy she was struggling to catch her breath. That was the bit she always forgot to factor in when she made her keep-fit resolutions: it takes effort. However, she arrived at Calmer Karma composed and breathing evenly. The thirty-six was a handy bus.

Sacha was pleased to see her. 'I found just the book!' she said, dumping an American tourist who was inspecting a crystal as big as his fist. She reached under the counter and dragged out a huge tome. As she slapped it down the draught blew out her joss-sticks.

'*Daemonology*?' Evie read. 'Why not *demonology*? With no A? When is a demon a daemon?'

Sacha ignored such a disrespectful question. 'If we can discover what kind of evil spirit is in flat D we can set about freeing it from its earthly bonds.'

Bing had been right. Sacha had taken the ball and run with it until she was just a dot on the horizon. Evie was shamefaced at the memory of how scared she had been the other morning. In the warm sunny light of day she could see that although P. Warnes was an unusual person it was unlikely that he was a visitor from Hell. 'Why don't you do the research and get back to me?'

'OK.' Sacha looked proud to be trusted with such an important task and didn't seem to realise that she was being royally fobbed off.

'Er, excuse me, ma'am, how much is this?' asked the American tourist meekly.

'Seventy pounds,' answered Sacha absentmindedly, not even looking his way.

'*Seventy pounds?*' mouthed Evie, in silent disbelief, shooing Sacha away to deal with the customer.

When seventy pounds had been transferred from the gullible tourist's wallet to the till, Evie got down to the real business of her visit. 'Shoes.'

'No.'

'You don't even know what I'm going to say.'

But Sacha did know. 'You're going to ask to borrow my red Prada shoes.' This knowledge wasn't due so much to Sacha's psychic abilities as to the fact that every time Evie saw Sacha's red Prada shoes she salivated and made a high-pitched mewling sound.

Sacha carried on: 'Your feet are bigger than mine, so no.'

This wasn't like Sacha. She was easy-going about lending her stuff. Shoes, however, were a different matter. Borrowing a boyfriend, maybe – borrowing shoes, never.

'My feet are a tiny bit bigger,' cajoled Evie, curling up her toes in the snow-white trainers.

'Remember when I let you wear my stilettos to that wedding? They came back like wellies.'

'That was years ago! We were still at drama school! Your feet have probably grown to catch up with mine by now.'

This pathetic line of reasoning was never going to get her anywhere. As Evie jogged to the bus stop she experienced the first pangs of panic about what she would wear on Saturday. It was four days away and she was proud that she had staved off the first twinges until now.

'You're on! You're on!' Bing was yelling, as she put her key into the lock.

Forgetting to feign breathlessness she dashed into the sitting room in time to see herself on the TV screen, strolling across the sand with Dan.

'Fuck me!' said Bing elegantly. 'I see what you mean. He's eleven out of ten.'

The voiceover was burbling on about pasta shapes over a pastiche of Elvis's 'Hound Dog'. Evie policed the images of herself on the screen with a severe eye. Did she look fat? 'Do I look fat?' she interrogated Bing.

'Oh, give it a rest.'

'That means yes, doesn't it?' There was no doubt that the cotton trousers they'd forced on her were not flattering. However, even with all her womanly *and* actressy paranoia combined, she had to admit she looked fine. 'Urrgh!' She pulled a face at the cheesy fireside scene. 'I don't look like that when I smile, do I?'

'They've lit your double chins with especial care. The dog looks sensational.'

Undoubtedly Tootsie was the star. Which was the way it was meant to be. 'Second billing to a West Highland white terrier. Great.' Evie kicked the door frame.

'Aw, diddums. Massage the cheque into the wound.'

Every item of clothing Evie possessed was on the bed. None of it, but none of it, was good enough. 'Why aren't you a girl?' she shouted at Bing, as he drifted past with some green tea.

'It's usually cab drivers who say that to me.' Bing cleared a space to sit in the midst of the jumble-sale pile. 'Why do *you* want me to be a girl?'

'Because then I could borrow something from you to wear on Saturday.'

'If I was a girl I doubt we'd be the same size, love. What's wrong with this?' He plucked a burgundy chiffon gipsy skirt from the tangle.

'Gipsy styles make me look like I burn tyres in the back garden and ask for change for the baby.'

'Hmm. How about this?' Bing held up a knitted dress.

'I look like a bag of cats in that. *Old* cats.'

'Fine. This?'

'Too old-fashioned for a nun.'

'This?'

'Too short. My knees aren't that fond of daylight.'

'This?'

'Too long. Makes me look like a spy.'

'This? *This?* For the love of God, this?'

'There's a period stain on the back.'

Bing threw down the denim skirt as if it had bitten him. 'You're right. We have proved it scientifically once and for all. You have nothing to wear.'

Evie took a break from the black hole that was her wardrobe and plodded upstairs to see how the ugly damp men were doing.

Most of flat B was submerged under dust sheets. The men were drilling and shouting in the bedroom. Caroline was seated glumly at her tiny kitchen table while Milly plastered herself with her dinner. 'How much longer will this take?'

No hello, but at least she didn't call me Eve, thought Evie. 'Shouldn't be too long.'

'Hope not. It's doing me bloody head in.'

'It'll be worth it.'

'S'pose so.'

Evie stomped back downstairs. The work was only taking place to protect little Milly. Each whir of the drill was costing her another chunk of her precious TV fees. Why had she bothered trying to defend Caroline to Bing? She was a sodding misery. Yes, it was a great shame that her family had all died but Evie was beginning to suspect they might have killed themselves to get away from her.

'Meet me for a glass of wine by the canal.' Sacha had made it sound so inviting: a summer evening, the sparkling water and a chilled glass of something nice.

This was Camden, however. A filthy duck floated past, balanced on a rusty crate. The dying sun illuminated the various carrier-bags snarled picturesquely in the weeds and glinted off the broken windows of the semi-derelict housing estate opposite. Almost everybody in the postcode had had the same romantic idea and the scraggy stretch of canalside outside the Weaver's Arms looked like Dunkirk late on D-Day.

'Plenty of blokes!' whispered Sacha excitedly, as one knocked her elbow and sent half her wine over another.

'I'm not interested in blokes. I'm interested in Dan and Saturday night.' Evie guided Sacha to a couple of miraculously free wrought-iron chairs. (They were free because of an impressively large blob of bird poo on one of the seats. This would not be discovered until Evie got home, when she would shriek, 'It's ruined my jeans,' and Bing would argue sagely, 'No, your bum ruined your jeans.')

'Don't be so pious. Not all of us have hot dates with sex machines to look forward to.'

'No, not all of us, but I do,' said Evie happily.

'Are you putting all your eggs in one doodah?' queried Sacha anxiously.

Pretending not to understand her friend's tortured way of

expressing herself was one of Evie's favourite hobbies. 'I don't have a doodah. And if I did, I wouldn't risk putting my eggs in it.'

'No, I mean, are you going out with Dan just for a bit of fun or do you want something to come of it?'

'I want something to come of it.' That was an easy one.

'Even after what Aden had to say about the way Dan treats women?' Sacha was looking intently at Evie over the rim of her grubby glass.

'But he hasn't treated *me* like that. What does that tell you? I must mean a lot to him, just like he said I did.' Evie had the sensation that a door was being opened into conversation territory that she didn't want to explore. Aden had been so certain that Dan wouldn't ring *but he had*. That meant something, right? Right?

'Aden didn't make him sound very nice,' said Sacha, choosing her words carefully for once. 'Not the sort of bloke I'd like to go out with.'

Just as well as he hasn't asked you, then, thought Evie bitchily. 'Aden was exaggerating. He made him out to be a monster so I wouldn't be too upset if he didn't call me.'

'Aden came across as a really straightforward person,' Sacha muttered. 'Dan's the one who likes playing games.'

'How can you say that about someone you've never even met?' Evie flared up.

'All right, all right!' Sacha sounded alarmed by the passion in Evie's response. 'I'm only trying to protect you.'

'I don't need protecting, thank you very much.' Evie checked herself: she was practically snarling. Sacha didn't deserve this. A change of subject was called for. 'How did your aura workshop go?'

'Brilliantly!' Sacha was as easily distracted as a kitten with a ball of wool. 'I could see the whole class's auras as clear as day. Mine was the nicest.'

Funny, that.

14

'Evie, can you do a nice York accent?' barked Meredith down the line.

'Can I do a what? I'm sorry, Meredith, I can hardly hear you over the terrible noise. What on earth is happening?' It sounded as if a demented sealion was loose in the office.

'It's only Barry. A shard of Viennetta went down the wrong way and we're getting the fucking dying-swan routine all over the place. *Cough it up, man!* He only does it to annoy. Well, the accent? Can you?'

'A York one? Yes.' Evie felt confident. She had toured in a production of *Kes* and the voice coach had been delighted with her Yorkshire accent.

'Good. You've got a voiceover, then.'

'I've never done one before. Are you sure that—' Evie was silenced by a loud crash. 'What was that?'

'That was Barry collapsing for effect.' Meredith sounded angry now. 'Get up, you superannuated office junior. I sanction petty-cash use for an individual Viennetta and this is my thanks.' She returned her attention to Evie. 'It's tomorrow. Midday. Get yourself along to Miracle Sound Studios, fourteen Little Row, Soho. Ask for Derek. It's an airlines ad, I think.' Meredith paused. 'Oh, shit. He's gone a queer colour. *Barry! Don't be dead, you cunt!*'

The phone went dead. Evie hoped the same couldn't be said of poor Barry. It wasn't right for him to go down in history as showbusiness's first Viennetta fatality.

Voiceovers were a thorny subject for Evie. She knew they should be easy – it was only talking into a microphone, after all. Many an actor, however, had been humiliated back to his drink problem after an hour of torture in the voiceover booth.

What disconcerted her was that there was so little to work with. Most commercial scripts contain only a couple of lines of dialogue, and Evie had become accustomed to developing a character over days of rehearsal in league with a director and found the abbreviated voiceover process bewildering. She had often heard that either you can do it or you can't and she'd soon find out which of these two camps she fell into.

For the ones who could do it, there was a mountain of money to be made. She'd met plenty of actors who were snobbish about voiceovers, but they tended to be the ones who didn't get any. The actors who did were usually too busy arranging the purchase of a second home in a hot climate to worry about their artistic street cred.

Evie was just glad of the work. She'd do her best and see what happened. With her usual attention to detail Meredith had neglected to say whether it was for TV or radio. TV usually meant more money but, whatever happened, Evie was guaranteed her studio-attendance fee of a hundred and eighty pounds. Not bad for an hour's work.

The date outfit was chosen and ready a whole two days ahead of time. Evie turned this way and that in front of the mirror, scrutinising herself with the kind of concentration usually found only at a post-mortem.

She was all in black, chosen partly for its slimming effect, partly for its glamour and partly because almost every garment she owned was black. Her tight-fitting jersey V-neck showed just enough cleavage: sexy without overtones of a butcher's shop window. It fitted neatly to the waistband of her longish black jersey skirt, and if you squinted they looked as if they matched. Her feet were nestling happily in a pair of pointed black suede boots, which she had pounced upon in a high-street sale. (Yes, all right, she shouldn't have spent money on suede boots when she was unemployed but she had.)

The detail that really made the outfit, that pulled it together and made it date quality, was the fitted black leather jacket that cinched in her waist and showcased her boobs. It was a triumph, and it was Sacha's.

Poor Sacha had been so overwhelmed by guilt for refusing to lend the red shoes (not so overwhelmed as to lend them, mind you) she had practically begged Evie to borrow her new jacket.

You have to realign a lot of *chakras* to afford stuff like this, thought Evie, as she ran her hands over it. As Sacha had successfully realigned a total of exactly nought *chakras* to date, it had obviously been a trust-fund buy. Evie thanked God for Sacha's rich posh forebears. 'I fancy *myself* in this lot.'

Bing had to see the outfit. It was almost ten and he hadn't emerged from his room yet. When Evie threw open his door she realised why. He had company. 'Oh, Gawd! Sorry!' Evie staggered backwards, blushing.

'Don't be silly.' Bing was propped up on pillows, like an Eastern potentate. 'Say hello to Georgie.'

'Hello, Georgie. Er . . . nice hat.'

Georgie, kneeling on the bed in a gold loincloth, sported a wide-brimmed straw hat laden with huge silk roses. 'Ta very much!' Georgie couldn't stop laughing. It was almost as if he was under the influence of drugs.

Evie backed out again. 'See you later, guys.'

'No, wait!' Georgie was laughing so hard at the invisible joke that his hat fell off, revealing a turquoise crop. 'You haven't met Mick yet.'

Another man popped up from under the covers at the foot of the bed, rather close to Evie. She jumped as his Chippendales torso rose from the duvet. 'Good morning,' he said politely.

'Good morning, Mick,' said Evie politely. 'Cup of tea, anyone?'

*   *   *

The laughing Georgie was folded into a minicab. 'Hope he doesn't give his old gran any trouble,' commented Bing.

'He lives with his gran? With turquoise hair?' Evie's remaining gran was still being shielded from the fact that Evie had pierced ears.

'His gran doesn't mind the hair, but she'll kill him for borrowing her hat,' said Mick, whose presence in the kitchen shrank it to the size of a lift. He was immense. His chest and arms were bronzed, gleaming and superbly muscled. It took Bing an age to assemble the bacon sandwiches as he kept pausing to slap or caress him.

When the sandwiches had been consumed and patently insincere promises exchanged to do this again sometime, Mick was ready to leave. 'Can't go out like this,' he said, rippling his pecs to good effect, and went to Bing's boudoir to finish dressing.

Bernard appeared, rent in hand. 'I'm terribly sorry that this is a few days late. I've been so busy at work I forgot all about it.'

'That's all right, Bernard.' Evie was good-natured for someone who had spent the previous evening calling him all the foul names she knew in alphabetical order. 'Better late than never. New clothes?'

Bernard squirmed. ''Fraid so.'

'Ver-ry nice,' said Bing encouragingly.

And so they were. True, Bernard had been drawn to his faithful cords, but they were of a trendy cut and didn't have the dust of many generations on them. The slate grey went well with the pale blue shirt, still in its shop creases. He'd evidently been listening when Evie had extolled the virtues of blue for his colouring.

'But you mustn't tuck yourself in like that,' chided Bing. He yanked Bernard's shirt out of his trousers and straightened it.

Bernard stiffened. His face wore the expression of a Chihuahua having its testicles felt by the vet: something hovering between consternation and terror. Human contact unsettled him.

'There. Much better.' Hands on hips, Bing surveyed his handiwork.

'Thank you.' Bernard's voice was as feeble as an old lady's.

Evie's heart went out to him in his struggle to fit in and be 'normal'.

Mick reappeared. Dressing to go out hadn't involved much effort. He had slipped on a minuscule singlet that stretched inadequately over his exaggerated torso.

Bernard looked at him sideways. 'Well, I must get off to the office,' he mumbled. But he went nowhere: he was transfixed by what Mick did next.

'Goodbye, tiger,' said Mick, wrapping his beefy arms round Bing. 'Something to remember me by.' He kissed Bing full and sensuously on the mouth, incongruously gentle for such a powerful man. They drew apart and he said cheerfully, 'Goodbye, all!' and left, tapping Bing on the behind for good measure.

''Bye!' sang Evie.

Bernard had turned into a statue. A crimson statue. He was blushing, so violently that it must have hurt, and staring at the space where Mick had been.

'Bernard? You OK?' asked Evie.

'Bernard, mate,' Bing slapped him on the back, 'you've got to get out more!'

There was something about being on the top deck of a bus – peering down at the unsuspecting heads of pedestrians below, nosily inspecting first-floor flats along the route, watching the drunken waddle of passengers making their way down the aisle – that always made Evie feel schoolgirlish. Possibly because much of her schooldays had been spent on buses. Or in the park. Or at the shopping centre. Or in the arcade. She had spent little time in local-education-authority property.

To add to the teenage vibe she was sucking a lolly. She was on her way to her voiceover and Bing was on *his* way to a *Joseph* matinée. They were discussing Bernard. Evie was saying, 'He reacted as if he'd never seen a pouf before.'

'He must have. We're everywhere,' Bing pointed out.

'Bernard hardly goes out. He might have seen gay men on television, but he's obviously never seen one in the wild before.'

'They don't come much wilder than Mick.'

'I hope he took our advice and went for a nice lie-down instead of to work.' A thought struck Evie as she sucked up the last chunk of orange-flavoured ice. 'Were you insulted by the way he reacted?'

'No.' Bing was too robust to be disturbed by that kind of thing. Besides, Evie couldn't guess at half of what he'd had to endure along the road to becoming the flamboyant character he presented to the world. 'Bernard didn't mean any harm. I know homophobia when I see it and Bernard was just being provincial. He'll get over it.'

'He'll have to, living two floors above you. It's kill or cure. Oi! You didn't say what you thought of the date outfit.'

'Very good. Perfect. Just enough bosom, and the sharp boots add a hint of sexual tension. Leave the jacket on for a while, then slowly remove it, unzipping seductively. No jewellery, and absolutely none of those wacky belts you're mad for.'

'Thank God for gay men.' Evie gave his arm a little squeeze. She had grown up hearing her father say, 'Very nice, dear. Are you sure you'll be warm enough?' in response to her mother's 'How do I look?' The torrent of input she always got from Bing was invaluable.

'Nervous?' he asked.

'About Saturday?' Evie considered the question. 'Not really. Just excited. *Really* excited. Knicker-wetting excited.'

Bing shifted away on the itchy red London Transport seat. 'What's your plan? Toy with him, then dump him? Lead him on, then cross your legs?'

Evie pulled a face. 'Why would I do any of that?'

Bing studied her. 'You're . . . serious about him?'

'Not *serious*,' corrected Evie. 'I'm not a complete twat. We hardly know each other. But, yes, I think I'd like to see him for a while, find out if anything develops. I don't just want a one-night stand.'

'You're a night in already.' Bing shook his head. 'I don't get this, doll. Aden – who seems like a regular guy – gave Dan the worst character reference a woman could hear, yet you're planning to go out on Saturday and sleep with him *again*?'

'Too bloody right I am.'

'But he didn't even ring to see if you were OK after he abandoned you in a west-country hotel.'

It sounded awful when he put it like that. 'He was in Spain,' she reminded him.

'And he didn't even have *one minute* to make a quick call before he went?'

'It was all very last-minute. You know how it is.' Evie's voice was becoming shrill. A woman in a headscarf two seats ahead was discreetly swivelling her head, trying to listen in without being rumbled. Evie lowered the volume. 'The main thing is, he kept his word. He's taking me out to dinner. If he meant that bit, why shouldn't he mean the bit about me meaning a lot to him?'

'It's 'cos he's good-looking, isn't it?' Bing accused her. 'You wouldn't take this treatment from Aden but you're so flattered that a sex god's coming back for seconds you're going to open your legs again.'

The headscarf woman jumped and risked a quick peek to see what they looked like.

'What is all this psychoanalysis shit?' asked Evie. 'You're watching too much *Trisha*. Why aren't I just allowed to have a bit of fun for once?' She couldn't help it. She was loud enough now for Headscarf Woman to listen in comfort. 'I'd like to get away from the fact that my career is going nowhere, that my house is falling apart and eating money as it goes, that my tenants are all sociopaths that I can't get rid of. But, oh no, my two so-called best friends want me to turn down the handsomest man I've ever met and live like a nun!' The bus had reached Oxford Street. She stood up and pushed roughly past Bing, even though she knew it was his stop too. 'I can't believe I'm getting all this puritanical gobshite from a man who spent last night in a threesome with a bodybuilder and the laughing gnome!' Evie stomped furiously down the stairs.

Before Bing made for the stairs he leant forward and whispered in the ear of Headscarf Woman, 'Episode two, same bus, same time, next week.'

Bing escorted Evie to the door of Miracle Sound. 'Just let me say this and then I'll shut up, promise.'

'Good,' snapped Evie, still fizzing. 'All I've got to look forward to is Saturday and you're ruining it.'

'I don't want to rain on your parade. I'm just looking out for you because I *care*, you rancid old bat. Dan sounds like a perfect one-night stand, but he's not boyfriend material. Any sensible woman would know that. Belle left her house to you 'cos she trusted you to be strong and to take care of all her misfits. What would she think of you falling for someone like Dan?'

'Maybe she'd understand. Maybe she would have fallen for him too.' Evie was in fighting mood. She reckoned Dan was worth fighting for.

'And she died alone, right?'

That was below the belt. Suddenly Evie felt tearful. 'What you and Sacha aren't taking into account is how I *feel*!' she spluttered. 'I'm mad about him! Being with him makes me happy! I can't wait to see him again! Why aren't I allowed to feel that?'

'Oh, baby!' Bing could be soft as butter. He enveloped Evie in a big warm hug that smelt of expensive aftershave. 'I'm sorry. You have a great time on Saturday and fuck the lot of us with our advice. I mean, if Sacha's agreeing with me I must be wrong. Right?'

Evie managed a giggle. 'Don't!' she commanded, as Bing tried to disengage himself. So they stood there, rocking gently, as Soho whirled around them.

*   *   *

'I'm Evie Crump and I'm here to meet Derek.'

'Derek . . .' The receptionist looked blank beneath her highlights. 'Take a seat!' she said brightly, pleased with this plan.

Evie walked across the blond-wood floor and sat down in a low, squashy black leather chair. Very low. Her knees were earrings. Getting up was going to be a challenge.

Two actresses she vaguely knew from the box and one drunk man, with an impressively veined red nose, were sitting much more comfortably on the other seats. The two telly names were middle-aged, familiar from sit-coms. They were conspicuously more glamorous than their television alter-egos. Both were impeccably made up, with glossy hair that had been carefully cut and coloured. One was stick thin, shoulder-blades jutting like cutlery. The other was mumsily plump and aware of it: she plucked constantly at her T-shirt, which was tight round her midriff.

They both looked at Evie when she shifted on the leather seat and it produced a spectacularly authentic fart. They returned to their animated conversation, leaving her condemned to trying to reproduce the noise to prove it had been the chair and not her.

'I only had four last week,' the thin one was complaining, gesticulating showily with manicured hands. 'A tampon, a Bovis Homes, a *Sunday Times* and a godawful Shreddies.'

'Not the one with all the puns? No! They got me in for that too! It took longer than the twins' birth. They don't have a bloody clue, do they?'

'No, darling, they don't. What are you in for today?'

'Female incontinence.' They both laughed.

'I'm yoghurt.'

'Haven't done a car for ages. They're the best payers.'

'The men get all the cars, have you noticed? I've been bogged down with sanitary towels for weeks on end.'

'I lost Toilet Duck to Richard Briers.'

'No! But you *are* Toilet Duck.'

Derek was towering over Evie, extending his hand. Except he was Eric. 'Your agent is a little hard of hearing,' he said.

'Well, she's hard,' agreed Evie, extricating herself from the chair and unleashing another fart across Reception.

She followed Eric downstairs to studio three. It was a small, dark room, rendered timeless and seasonless by the lack of windows and the hum of air-conditioning. A leather sofa lined one wall, and opposite was the mixing desk. The writer, a trendy cute guy wearing a Phat Farm T-shirt, and the client, a large man in a suit who owned a chunk of Southern Cross Airlines, were on the sofa. Evie was introduced to them, then said hello to the sound engineer, who was skinny and pale. Engineers are always skinny and pale (it's called a studio tan) because they spend their lives manacled to their mixing desks. This desk was superbly high-tech and futuristic. 'So many knobs,' Evie commented, and added, 'So little time!' with a little laugh that no one echoed.

Farts, knobs – shut up already! Evie instructed herself, as Eric shepherded her into the voiceover booth. It was a claustrophobic space, with carpeted walls, separated from the studio by a glass partition over the mixing desk. Evie sat down, put on her headphones, looked over the four lines of script and took a sip of water without making a tasteless joke or producing an offensive noise. Maybe things were looking up.

Eric flicked the talkback button, which relayed conversation in the studio through to Evie's headphones. His first words made it clear that things were looking down. Right down.

'OK, my love, if you're ready just give us a quick read-through in your best New York accent.'

Evie stared rabbit-like through the glass at Eric and the rest of the eager characters on the other side. Now that the talkback was off she couldn't hear what they were saying but they were content and relaxed and waiting for her to earn her hundred and eighty pounds.

With her best *New* York accent. Unfortunately her best New

York accent was the same as her worst New York accent. She couldn't do one. Full stop.

Evie would have liked to linger over the images that were flitting through her brain, images of Meredith being garotted, or beaten to death with a frozen Viennetta, but she had to concentrate.

'In your own time.' Eric was smiling encouragingly through the glass.

Confess! shrieked the voice of reason in Evie's head.

Bluff it! shrieked the voice of sheer stupidity, which was louder and more accustomed to getting its own way.

Evie, her mouth as dry as a Saharan sandal, looked down at the page headed 'Southern Cross Airlines 30" radio script'. The words were dancing like paralytic ants. *Concentrate!* she told herself, aware that she was sweating like a rapist despite the chill of the air-conditioning.

The talkback clicked. 'Can we get you anything?' There was a note of concern in Eric's words as they floated through her cans. 'Cup of tea? Quick massage?'

She heard the others' polite laughter before the button was pressed and she was back with her own silent terror.

Think. *Think.* What do New Yorkers sound like? She conjured up Robert de Niro, Woody Allen, the girls from *Sex and the City*, but they all mouthed mutely at her, like silent movie stars.

Right. There was nothing else for it. Evie had to open her mouth and *go.* With the all-purpose American accent that she and Bing used when they made up Oscar acceptance speeches, she read the script with all the energy, confidence and insight that her training could supply. She paid special attention to the pace of the piece. She teased out all the nuances of the gentle jokes in it. She sold Southern Cross Airlines faultlessly and to the best of her ability.

When she'd finished she looked up slowly through the glass, hoping that all the effort and skill she'd poured into her reading might impress them enough to eclipse the lack of a New York accent.

They looked confused. Eric seemed to be choosing his words carefully before he pressed the talkback. 'Can we have that again, just like that – it was a perfect read – but with your New York accent this time?'

Evie stared at him, a beseeching look in her eyes.

Eric was not a stupid man. 'That *was* your New York accent, wasn't it?'

Evie nodded. The click of the button banished her into silence again. The figures on the other side of the glass were standing up and talking all at once. She was grateful not to hear any of it, particularly whatever the burly man from the airline was saying. It didn't look as if he was commenting thoughtfully on her intelligent performance – if the vein on his forehead was anything to go by.

The engineer slipped into the booth beside her. 'It might be best if you go out this way,' he suggested, opening a concealed door.

Out in Reception he heard how Evie had turned up expecting to do a York accent. He shook her hand. 'You've made my day,' he told her, trying not to smile. 'They thought you were doing Welsh.'

Only intravenous chocolate can revive a spirit as battered as Evie's was after her voiceover. She parked herself at a window table in the nearest café and ordered a slice of chocolate cake with a large hot chocolate. 'Quickly!'

There would be no fee for that disaster. 'Bums,' she muttered dejectedly. She felt as if she should offer to pay them.

Having hoovered up a slice of cake the size of her overdraft, Evie spotted a face she knew in the narrow street. 'Aden!' She banged on the window.

Aden was distracted, worried-looking, but he smiled broadly when he saw her. 'You've got chocolate on the end of your nose,' he pointed out as he slid on to the plastic bench opposite her.

'Thought I'd missed a bit.' Evie noticed the circles under his eyes. 'You tired?'

'Shattered. I've been editing in a basement since . . . the dawn of time, I think. You look perky, though.'

'Thank you. Do you want some cake? I'm going to order another slice. I'm eating to forget.' Evie recounted the tale of her voiceover.

Aden laughed and sympathised, and let her eat half of his cake too. 'How's the children's theatre thing going?'

'Gone.' Evie told him what had happened, uncomfortably aware that her life sounded like a sit-com. 'How's your arty film going?'

'Just finishing it. That's what I've been editing. Next I'm AD on a big telly thing. Nice meaty drama, filming here and in the States.'

Evie was pierced with envy, and hated herself for it. 'You're lucky.' She corrected herself: 'No, you're not. You're good at what you do and you work hard.'

Aden wasn't too hot at accepting compliments. He ran a hand through his unwashed sandy hair. 'So, anyway, you and Dan, what's the score? Last time I saw you he was at the other end of the phone.'

'Haven't you spoken to him since then?'

'I've been tied up.'

'Well, we're having dinner on Saturday.' Evie smiled. 'Thanks for the warning but it doesn't look like it was necessary.'

Aden coughed. The tortured body language told Evie that he was uncomfortable with the subject. 'I'm sorry. I can be a sanctimonious schmuck sometimes.'

Evie couldn't disagree but she could say, with complete sincerity, 'You did it for the right reasons. You can tell the story in your speech at our wedding.'

Aden raised his eyebrows.

'Joke! It's a joke! Blimey! Why can't girls make jokes about weddings without blokes taking them seriously?' complained the girl who had already chosen the dress, her bridesmaids, and the children's names.

'Have a great time. Let me know how it goes.' Aden was making a visible effort to be nice about it, despite his reservations. 'I'd better get off.' He stood up and bent to kiss Evie's cheek with those soft lips of his.

'Happy editing!' trilled Evie.

Aden didn't walk away. He was toying anxiously with his mobile. 'Look,' he said, 'I was hard on Dan. Don't pay any attention to me. It was only because . . .' He tailed off. 'There were many reasons.'

Evie smiled. 'I know. You two have history. You were only trying to protect me. Although,' she wagged a finger at him in mock sternness, 'you could have told me he'd been in Spain since we got back from Lyme. It would have helped me feel less anxious.'

Aden said gravely, 'Yes. I should have told you.'

And then Aden was gone, leaving Evie with nothing to do but lick the plates and look forward to telling Sacha and Bing that the tales of Dan's dastardliness had been greatly exaggerated.

And order more cake.

15

'Of course Barry isn't dead. What a peculiar question.' Meredith brushed aside Evie's attempts at conversation. 'Why did you lie about being able to do a New York accent? That was foolish and wicked. You made me look like a complete imbecile. We only narrowly escaped being liable for the studio time. Don't you know that to exaggerate your abilities is a cardinal sin in this business?'

Evie took her telephone ticking-off like a man, even though she could have cited the occasion when Meredith sent her along to a panto audition having confirmed that she was a trained fire-eater. 'I'm sorry, Meredith, I misheard you.'

'Don't mishear this – *do that again and you're in fucking trouble!*' yelled Meredith, and added '*darling!*' as an afterthought.

'Is that all?' asked Evie hopefully.

'No. Amazingly you have an audition. For what you would call a proper job.'

'Eh?' This was out of the blue.

'Quite. I don't have the details, don't ask me, but it's a big telly, prestigious, costume drama, blah-blah-fucking-blah. The director is Hugh Thomas and he's interested in you.'

'Hugh Thomas?' squeaked Evie. The name was familiar to her from the credits of various big-budget productions but she'd never met him. 'How come he's interested in me?'

'Fuck knows.' Meredith coughed operatically. 'Darling.'

Fabulous new man – tick.

Potentially fabulous audition – tick.

Things were looking up at Kemp Street.

'Oi!' yelled Bing, from where he stood frozen, willing his fake tan to dry. 'Your mother rang.'

Refusal to ring witchlike parent – tick.

Sacha was there on the dot, clutching a reduced-for-quick-sale wine-box in one hand and the *Best Music in the World 107* in the other. She stationed herself on the bed. 'Shower! Chop-chop!'

Evie rinsed all her bits, both rude and not-so-rude. She anointed herself with Calvin Klein body lotion. This expensive product rarely saw the light of day, but tonight was worth it. Then she brushed her teeth vigorously, just as dentists suggest, and plucked her eyebrows, wincing as she yanked out the last stragglers.

'Hurry up!' Sacha yelled. 'I want to start your nails!'

Evie speeded up, teasing the tangles out of her wet hair. The magazine articles she read on *Getting Ready for a Big Night Out* always featured a model in a pristine fluffy white dressing-gown. Hers was in the wash after a traumatic hot-chocolate spillage. She pulled Bing's shortie robe off the hook on the bathroom door, then checked it for stains of a personal nature.

'You're behind,' chided Sacha, referring not to Evie's impressively upholstered sitting-down parts but to the schedule. 'French?' she queried.

'Yeah.' Evie stuck out a hand and let Sacha get cracking with the base coat. Holding a glass in her free hand, she sipped her wine. The plan was to be just tipsy enough to be confident, but not so tipsy that she pulled down Dan's trousers with her teeth when he walked in.

'Do you know,' began Sacha, trying and failing to keep the whinge out of her voice, 'the only man to ask me out since Christmas is the bloke with the pudding-bowl haircut from the newsagent's?'

'Yes.'

'And he's mental.'

'Evidently.'

'Don't! This is important. Why don't I get asked out?'

Bing was passing the open door. 'Do you want that alphabetically, in ascending order of importance, or just as it comes?'

Sacha attempted a dignified silence.

'Bing!' Evie scolded, trying not to laugh.

'Sor-ree. I have news!' He had just seen Bernard leave the house, resplendent in yet more new clothes.

'I told you. We're getting through to him!' Evie clapped her hands.

Sacha tutted and reached for the varnish remover.

Bing enlarged on the sighting. 'Nice chinos. Cute white tee. *But* he was headed in the direction of the chippy.'

'Aw, *no*,' Evie said despairingly. 'Right. Keep an eye out for him. If he comes back with chips, we'll jump him and confiscate them.'

'Hel-looo? Earth to Evie?' Bing sang. 'What gives you the right to confiscate Bernard's chips? He can eat his own weight in chips if he wants to.'

'Maybe I should just give in and go out with him,' Sacha remarked gloomily, as she repaired Evie's nails.

Evie and Bing exchanged an eloquent glance over her bowed head but wisely pretended not to have heard her. Evie said, 'I have every right. I'm his landlady.'

'And?' laughed Bing.

'And Belle wanted me to look after her tenants, so therefore I must protect Bernard from his own self-destructive addictions.'

'We're talking chips, not heroin,' Bing reminded her.

'Bernard will never find love and personal fulfilment if he doesn't change his ways. We're getting there with the clothes, we can't fall at the chips hurdle.'

'You're power-mad.'

'Shut your face and keep a lookout.'

'OK.' Bing withdrew.

'You should be on hair drying by now,' Sacha scolded.

Her hair co-operated, much to Evie's surprise. She positioned herself in front of Belle's chipped dressing-table mirror and opened her makeup bag – a Smurfs pencil case. She gazed at her bare face in the mirror. She wondered how many times Belle had looked at hers in it, watching herself age. She touched the cold surface of the glass – strange that all those reflections should leave no trace. No spots, thank God. A hint of puffiness under the eyes – which looked a little nervous. 'Kylie!' she snapped, and sipped her wine.

Sacha was a few glasses ahead, so dancing inevitably broke out. 'I *love* Kylie!' she declared euphorically, shimmying past Evie who was now patting translucent powder on to her cheeks.

'Mind the—' A slosh of Sacha's wine slopped over the rim of her glass. 'Carpet.'

Slowly, glamorous Evie emerged. Don't overdo it, she cautioned herself. She could be heavy-handed with the lip-liner at times like this.

'Ooooh, you look lovely!' cooed Sacha, leaning shakily over her shoulder.

'Do I?'

'Definitely.' Sacha got back into the groove with Atomic Kitten.

Is this right? Evie asked herself, watching Sacha whirl by in happy unco-ordination in the mirror. Shouldn't I have a more adult life by now? Some responsibility? She shied away from the thought, but wasn't it rather *sad* for two girls in their late twenties to be *still* getting excited about what to wear on a hot date?

There was no point in posing this question to Sacha. There she was, using a hairbrush as a microphone, giving it loads. Her answer would be a resounding, *Yes, of course this is right!*

Just because Sacha could moan spectacularly about her lack of a boyfriend, it didn't mean she disliked her life. She had Evie for chat and laughs and all the thousand little benefits of friendship. She had Calmer Karma to fill her days. She relished the lack of responsibility. She loved shopping in the 7–11 on the way home. She loved sitting in bed all day with the TV on and only a selection box for company. She loved painting the sitting room aubergine just because she felt like it. She loved getting drunk at the drop of a hat. Or even a headscarf. All that so-called adult stuff could wait.

Evie, clicking herself into a front-loading Wonderbra, wasn't so sure. It would be nice, wouldn't it, to go out just once without hoisting her boobs up? It might even be nice to stay in, sober, with a man she knew well, whose sentences she could finish.

Watching Sacha go-go dancing on the bed she felt vaguely guilty at such thoughts. She extracted a new pair of expensive, very sheer tights from their package. A piece of paper hidden beneath them slipped out and floated to the floor. It was the damp men's bill. 'Sheesh!' said Evie expressively. 'And there was me wishing I had more responsibilities. I was forgetting I have a houseful of them.'

'Oh, don't wear black,' pleaded Sacha, coming over to wrestle the skirt out of Evie's hands.

'We can't rethink my outfit when I'm practically out of the door!'

'Black brings bad vibes! It's the colour of darkness! *It's evil!*'

'It makes me look slimmer.'

'Oh, yeah.' Sacha relinquished her grasp.

A shout came from the hallway. 'I have a prisoner! Come and get him, girls!'

Bernard was standing with his hands behind his back, looking even more sheepish than usual. 'What's—' he began, but got no further.

'Silence.' Bing held up his hand. 'You may not know this, Bernard baby, but your landlady has certain rights over you. One of these is the right to rifle through your carrier-bags. If they contain tweed or chips she has the right to hang you by the neck until you are dead.'

Bernard gulped. 'Er . . .'

'Don't pay any attention to him,' Evie reassured Bernard, delving into the bag. He had been to Sainsbury's and there wasn't a chip in sight. 'Ooooh!' She pulled out a bag of apples, some broccoli. 'This is *good*!' She retrieved a packet of Rich Tea biscuits, a bag of rice, some fancy sausages and . . . an organic chicken. 'Oh, Bernard, I'm so proud of you!' She held it aloft like an Olympic medal.

Bernard left, clasping his shopping to his chest and looking bewildered.

'He's making real progress.' Evie sighed happily.

'Did you see how he was undressing me with his eyes?' asked Sacha.

'They'd have to be bloody big eyes,' muttered Bing.

'Oi, Date Mate!' Evie nudged Sacha. 'My glass is empty.'

'Sorry.' Sacha beetled off to find the wine-box.

'Don't worry. I'm pacing myself,' said Evie, in response to Bing's reproachful look. 'Please, spare me the Women's Institute speech on the evils of drink. It doesn't suit you.'

'And getting your heart broken doesn't suit *you*.' Bing ducked just in time and was saved from further violence by Evie's mobile ringing.

'That's Dan cancelling!' prophesied Sacha, reappearing with the wine.

'Don't say that!' Evie snatched up the phone. For perhaps the first time in her life she was glad to hear her mother's voice. 'Hi, Mum. Bing told me you rang. Sorry I didn't get back to you.'

'You've got a man, I hear,' said Bridgie, without preamble.

Evie scowled at Bing. 'I suppose a little bird told you. A little bird with a big beak. I wouldn't go that far, Mum.'

'Don't be coy. Not at your age. Bing told me all about it. You're seeing him tonight so I won't keep you. I'm sure it will take time to make yourself presentable. Daddy's bought a barbecue.'

'Oh . . . good.' Bridgie was always steering conversation round hairpin bends.

'So invite him tonight and we'll have a lovely barbie next Saturday. Just like in *Neighbours*.'

The thought of sexy, smouldering, virile Dan balancing a plate and a spork on her mother's scrap of lawn was all wrong. 'It's much too soon for that!'

'Soon? I've been waiting *years* for this.'

It was settled. 'I'm doomed,' pronounced Evie, switching off the phone and reaching for the larger glass, filled with wine, that Sacha had thoughtfully provided.

'If you want a relationship with him he'll have to meet your parents,' said Bing.

'Why? *I* don't even want to meet them. He'll never have sex with me again once he's got a load of my mother and her rock-hard perm.'

'He probably won't last that long anyway,' slurred Sacha. 'What? What did I say?' She was baffled by Evie's thunderous look. 'I'm only trying to be philosoph—'

Evie left Sacha to conclude the rest of what she was only trying to be and went to finish getting dressed.

Just as she applied the final slick of lipstick the doorbell rang. She resisted the urge to jump up and down and scream. Instead she inhaled deeply and pulled back her shoulders.

It had begun.

The trendy bar was packed. The glass tables were lit from underneath, casting an eerie glow on Dan and Evie's faces as they clinked glasses.

'Here's to keeping promises,' said Dan.

'Here's to a nice quiet drink,' shouted Evie, over the deafening din of funkily dressed people enjoying themselves.

'You look tip-fucking-top, by the way,' bellowed Dan, directly into her ear. 'I've wanted to say that since you opened the door.'

'Thank you.' Evie glowed like the Ready Brek kid. Even in this crowded, hectic place she could sense Dan's body keenly. Anticipation was making her giddy. She gestured at a glass and metal cabinet full of surgical instruments. 'Nice touch.'

'Yeah. So romantic.' Dan crinkled his eyes at her. That shared sense of humour was still intact.

There was a lot of conversational mileage to be got out of their fellow drinkers. The men made David Beckham look like Bernard. Dan outshone the lot of them, thought Evie proudly.

'That flatmate of yours,' Dan was saying, 'he plays for the other team, does he?'

'What other team?'

'You know. An uphill gardener?'

'Eh?'

'A fudge packer.'

'You mean, is he gay?'

Dan laughed indulgently. 'Well done. Took a while, though.'

'I've never thought of Bing as . . .' Evie couldn't bring herself to use Dan's phrases. They didn't seem to come anywhere close to describing the man with whom she shared her house. 'He *is* gay, yes.'

'I can always tell.'

'He doesn't hide it.' Bing had been wearing a fluorescent pink shower cap when introduced to Dan.

'No,' agreed Dan. 'Calling me sugar-arse as we left was a bit of a giveaway.'

A silence showed signs of taking hold between them. Some people are perfectly at home with the odd silence, but on dates Evie regarded silence as a farmer might regard potato blight. She warded it off at all costs. 'What are you working on next?' She used the old actors' standby.

Dan took a swig of his Becks. 'Corporate role play.' He grimaced. 'I think it's Resolution of Conflict in the Workplace. I can't wait.'

'It keeps the wolf from the door.'

'What about you? Are you working?'

'No. The wolf is not only at my door, he's climbing into bed with me.'

'Lucky old wolf.'

'It's a perk of his job.'

They exchanged a loaded glance. There was so much twinkling going on at their table they could have powered a provincial town.

Dan had moved his squat leather cube seat nearer to Evie's. Their thighs touched. A hand sneaked on to Evie's knee and squeezed it slowly. She smiled. 'I think the wolf may have followed me to town.'

'Yup. I knew this sheep's clothing wouldn't fool you for long.'

Evie was enjoying his nearness but another silence seemed to be poking its head round the door so she asked, 'Where do you live?' She knew so little about him.

'Chiswick.'

'Fancy!'

'Not the bit where I live. My flat's nice, though. Well, it's not mine, it belongs to Astrid.'

'Astrid?' Evie repeated, hoping she sounded more casual than she felt.

'Swedish bird. She owns the place and I pay her rent.'

'Is she a nice landlady?' Evie had conjured up a blonde Nordic goddess with endless legs and a bosom you could balance a tea-tray on.

'She drives me mad.'

Good old Astrid. Instantly her legs shrank and her boobs became Smarties. 'In what way?'

'It's nag, nag, nag. I might as well be in the army. Every time I put a coffee cup down I get sworn at in Swedish.' Dan warmed to his subject. 'There's always some investigation going on. Why didn't I wash the pan after I used it? Why didn't I take the washing out of the machine? When will I learn to put the toilet seat down? Living with women is bad for your health.'

Evie bridled. 'Not all women. I don't nag,' she said, with playful defensiveness.

'Really?' Dan cocked an eyebrow.

'Not every woman is on a mission to disinfect the known world. I've got more on my mind than making sure you can see your face in the kitchen floor.'

'I bet you any money you'd change if you lived with a guy. A *real* guy, not Bling, or whatever he's called.'

'Bing.' Evie couldn't let Dan get away with that, although she smiled as she corrected him.

'Sorry – Mr Bing.' Dan carried on. 'You'd be telling him to take his feet off the coffee table, not to leave a ring round the bath, not to drop his underpants on the floor. It's genetic.' He grinned at her combatively. 'Women are all the same.'

'Yeah. Me and Florence Nightingale and Jordan and Helen of Troy and the Queen – we're all the same.'

Dan giggled. 'Jordan worries about her whites wash, you can tell. Helen of Troy made everyone wipe their feet. You're all the same.'

'Then why are you so keen on us, then?'

'I think you know why.'

'There must be more to it than that.'

Dan regarded her coolly, quite serious for once. 'I think with you there might be.'

'That's good,' said Evie, keeping the excitement out of her voice. 'By the way, wipe that table. Your bottle's left a mark.'

Dan laughed and squeezed her knee again. 'Let's move on and grab something to eat.'

'Good idea.'

Evie's ears were ringing when they hit the street. She zipped up her killer jacket, angling herself so that Dan could slip his arm round her easily. No arm was forthcoming. Dan walked a few paces ahead, peering at text messages on his mobile. Evie caught up, keeping a small distance between them. 'Sorry!' He flicked his phone shut. They walked on, with the Black Death of silence trotting between them.

Evie panicked. It was only low level, subdued, but it was panic. First dates were such delicate creatures. Had she said something to turn him off? Suddenly she felt isolated, even though Dan was only a couple of feet away. His face looked closed.

As if she'd called his name, he turned to her and stopped dead. He thrust out his arms, took her by the shoulders and pushed her roughly into the dark doorway of a shoe shop. He crushed her to his chest and breathed huskily into her startled face, now only an inch away, 'You're beautiful. I'm glad I'm here.' He kissed her, harsh and gentle in equal measure.

Evie didn't feel isolated or ignored any more.

He hugged her tightly, then kissed the end of her nose. 'C'mon. Let's get to the restaurant. It's hungry work being a wolf.'

16

'Sushi?' Evie stared up from the pavement at the neon-lit chopsticks.

'It's my favourite food.' Dan dropped her hand. 'Oh, no. You hate it.'

'I don't. I love it. Mm-mmmm. Lovely, lovely sushi.' Evie picked up his hand. 'Just let me at all that raw fish.'

Evie had confidently expected to live and die without ever setting foot in a sushi joint. They were places where things she didn't like collided. Expensively.

The restaurant was busy and bright. Booths lined the walls and a long white oval counter stood in the centre of the room, surrounded by high stools.

Dan guided her to a stool, saying anxiously, 'Is this really OK? We can go somewhere else.'

Evie was touched. 'This is perfect,' she reassured him, hoisting herself on to the seat, legs dangling like a country-and-western singer. She was transfixed by the tiny conveyor-belt that ran round the counter at nose level, transporting plates of various odd foodstuffs. She was so engrossed at watching the journey of a combo of prawn and what looked like semen that she undid her jacket without remembering to be seductive.

None of what was trundling past under little plastic covers looked good. None of it looked *edible*.

'It's all so delicious I don't know where to start,' drooled Dan. 'Squid, I think.' He reached for a plate as it passed by. 'What about you?'

Still reeling at the mention of squid, Evie didn't know how to answer. 'Er, what's that?' She pointed at the nearest strange pale thing.

'Raw eel.'

'Aiee.' Evie emitted an unusual noise she'd never made before, and retracted her finger sharpish. Raw? Were the Japanese mad? Was there some terrible shortage of Nippon frying-pans?

'How about some rice and vegetables to break you in gently?' Dan was unsuccessful in covering his amusement.

'I'm not frightened or disgusted or anything like that, you know.' Evie accepted the bowls he'd selected for her.

'Of course not. That noise was an expression of pure joy, wasn't it?'

'What's happened to these vegetables?'

'They're pickled.'

'Pickled!' Evie glared resentfully at the grey, squidgy cubes, and sighed. What she wouldn't give for some shepherd's pie!

'I think you need a drink.' Dan pressed a red button on the table top. 'Some *sake* will get you in the mood.'

Evie watched him happily eat his squid with the kind of appalled fascination normally reserved for car crashes. 'Ow!' Something struck her ankle.

A tiny trolley had careered into her. 'The robot waiter,' Dan informed her, and leant down to pick up a pottery flask and two tiny beakers. 'Cool, isn't he?'

To somebody reared on cheap sci-fi it didn't look much like a robot.

'It's radio controlled,' he added.

'God. Boys *love* gadgets.'

'And girls are wimps about sushi.'

'Is that a challenge, Daniel?'

'I'm only saying that most girls I know come over all squeamish in a sushi bar.'

'That *is* a challenge. Get me down that lump of raw . . . whatever.' Evie gestured at a piece of flesh the colour of putty.

'Ah, I wouldn't recommend—'

'Get it before it escapes.'

Dan set the dish uneasily in front of her. 'It's a sea urchin. Even I don't eat those.'

'Then *you*'re a wimp.' Evie fumbled it into her mouth.

If Dan was watching her with interest it wasn't surprising: the expression that illustrates a mouthful of cold salty snot is rarely seen. 'Oh, God!' she grabbed her drink. She'd never tried *sake* before and this wasn't a great time to be introduced to it. 'Yaaargh!' She had invented a word to celebrate drinking nail-varnish remover. 'Dan,' she whispered.

His face, close to hers, was grinning widely. 'What, gorgeous?'

'I don't like sushi.'

Evie sighed with contentment at the sight of a big plate of spaghetti and the big hunk of bloke on the dog-eared banquette opposite her. They were in Pepito's, where the waiters were fat, the prices were lean, and the food-poisoning was free of charge.

'I'm sorry,' said Evie.

'What for? I don't care what I'm doing as long as it's with you.' Dan looked down at his meatballs in murky sauce. 'Besides, I've never been rushed to Casualty before. It might be fun.'

Evie sniggered. 'When everywhere else is full you can always get a table at Pepito's.'

'I wonder why?'

A waiter coughed unself-consciously over a basket of rolls. Dan and Evie pulled a face at each other and pushed aside their bread plates.

'Something's on my mind.' Dan's abruptness halted a forkful of spaghetti on its way to Evie's mouth.

'What?'

'I need the answer to a question or I won't be able to relax. It's very important to me. At this moment it's the most important thing in the world.'

Evie didn't know what was coming but the hairs on the

back of her neck were standing on end. She half smiled. 'Ask me.'

'Are you coming home with me tonight?'

There it was, the unbearable electric stillness that Dan could throw over them like a cloak. Damn being wary. Damn playing hard to get. This man thrilled her to the core. 'You try and stop me.'

'Ooooh, goody.' Dan spun the words out in his deep, dreamy voice, like a cat stretching. Evie felt like a box of chocolates that he would linger over. 'I have plans for you and me.'

Plans? Sexual ones − or relationship ones? Somehow Evie suspected them to be more concerned with tying her up and covering her with cream than with opening a joint bank account. That was fine by her. She would have liked to throw him across the table and straddle him there and then. If the tablecloth hadn't been so grubby.

'I'd love to see you act,' said Dan. 'That commercial didn't stretch either of us. I bet you're good.'

'I bet you are too.'

'No, no, I didn't say it so you'd repay the compliment. I suspect you're a good actress. I can see it in your face. It's got soul.'

'You're making me blush.'

'Good. I like to see your face go pink. Women's faces flush when they orgasm, you know.'

'Really?'

'Yours certainly did.'

'*Dan!*' Evie looked round to see if any of the portly waiters were eavesdropping.

'And will again in about . . .' Dan looked at his watch '. . . an hour and a half. Unless you want dessert.'

Evie laughed, embarrassed but loving it. 'I meant it, you know, when I said you're a good actor.'

'Well, you're wrong, gorgeous.'

'What?'

'You're wrong. I can't act. I'm shite. I try, but I just can't do it.'

'But . . .' Evie was confused. She'd met countless actors who couldn't act, but not one who admitted it.

'Don't get me wrong. I'm going to have a fucking great career. I'm going to be famous. I'm doing OK already. I know what I am and I know what I can do. I sell myself. I use the way I look. But I definitely can't act.'

'You're very frank. What if I don't believe you?'

'It's still true. There are arthritic old ladies in amateur dramatics companies all over the south coast who can act me off the stage, but I have confidence and self-belief.'

'And a great bod.'

'Thanks. Yours isn't so bad either, as it goes.'

Evie smirked and felt her bottom purr. 'Here's to success, whether we can act or not.' She held up her glass for Dan to clink.

'Here's to being famous and rich!' Dan threw back his wine in one gulp. 'Let's have one for the road, then go back to mine.'

'There's nothing wrong with that plan, as far as I can see.' Evie was becoming long-winded, a sure sign that she had drunk too much. 'Make mine a coffee for the road, though.'

Dan pulled a face, but Evie stood firm. She wanted to remember this encounter, not have to look for clues on her body like last time.

As a sweating waiter put the coffee and a sambuca before her Evie said, 'I bumped into Aden yesterday.'

Dan cracked a knuckle. 'Oh, yeah? You bump into him a lot.'

Evie thought it was funny that Dan should become instantly uneasy when she mentioned Aden. How could a specimen like him be envious of her friendship with somebody as unremarkable as Aden? She liked being the girl in the middle, though. 'We had coffee and a chat. It was nice.'

Dan was tracing a shape on the table. 'Chat about me, did you?'

This was irresistible. Evie assumed a serious expression. 'Oh, yes, we chatted about you, all right.'

Dan continued to stare moodily at the tablecloth.

Evie bit her lip. She'd only meant to tease him, not ruin the atmosphere. The relaxed, intimate, sexy atmosphere.

Dan was darkly silent, glaring at his sambuca as if it had insulted his mother. Frantically Evie rifled her ragbag of a mind for something innocuous to lighten the mood, something that was nothing to do with Aden.

Ah! She had it. 'How was Spain?'

Dan's reaction was as extreme as it was unexpected. 'I knew it!' he roared, and thumped the table so hard that Evie's coffee cup bounced. 'That little shit had to, didn't he? He just *had* to,' Dan ranted, leaning towards her. 'St Aden. That's what we called him at school. It's about time he fucking grew up. I'll kill him for this.'

Evie drew back. Dan's face, contorted with anger, scared her. He was snarling like a dog, but why?

His next outburst made it clear. 'Why couldn't he keep his mouth shut? So I didn't go to Spain. It was none of his business. It was between me and you.'

Evie felt as though a bucket of cold water had been chucked over her. Everything changed. As if she was looking at a photograph, she saw herself and Dan: the Seducer and the Victim; the Liar and the Idiot. She swallowed hard. The Arrogant Bastard Who'd Say Anything To Get A Shag and the Desperate Bird Who Believed Him.

Evie couldn't think of anything to say. She stood up, picked up her borrowed jacket and her handbag, and made for the door at an even, almost relaxed pace. She was numb, but she knew that tears were on the way. She had to be far away from Dan when they arrived.

Dan scrambled after her, fumbling for notes in his pockets and flinging them at the waiters. 'Wait! Hang on, gorgeous!'

Evie, now marching like a stormtrooper, was at the corner

before he caught up with her. She still did not intend to waste a word on him. The stone in her throat made it impossible to talk anyway.

Dan was dancing sideways awkwardly, gabbling, 'Will you let me explain? I made up the story about Spain because I– *ouch*!' A lamp-post stopped him painfully in his tracks. He recovered and ran after Evie, who was on the kerb, peering up and down the street for a taxi. 'Listen, I lied about Spain because I didn't want to hurt your feelings. I'd been busy, I'd had loads of, er, stuff to do and I kept meaning to ring you but suddenly three weeks had gone by. I knew you'd be upset that I'd left it so long so I made up a little white lie. A harmless lie. It was for *you*! I did it for you!'

Evie kept scanning the road, willing the tears to stay back.

'Oh, come on, give me a break,' Dan cajoled. 'You're behaving like a girl.'

That did it. Evie found her tongue. 'How dare you? I'm behaving like *me*. You lied to me and this is how I behave when people lie to me,' she shouted. 'And now you're trying to tell me you did it for my sake! You're just trying to make sure your target for the evening doesn't get away.' A memory from Lyme Regis popped into her head. She muttered, 'Melody was right about you.'

'Brilliant.' Dan threw his arms up into the air. 'Aden told you about her as well.'

Evie's mouth fell open.

'She meant nothing to me.' Dan was carrying on, unaware that he was hanging himself. 'She was drunk. She was a slapper. You weren't playing ball. It was just a bit of fun.'

More than anything, more than world peace, Evie wanted a taxi to appear. And one did. As she tugged open the door, evading Dan's restraining lunge, she said, 'Aden didn't tell me a thing.' She got into the cab and said, 'Kemp Street, Camden, please,' to the driver just as the first tears fell.

The taxi pulled away, leaving a shell-shocked Dan on the

pavement. Evie wrenched the window down and leant out, her conker-coloured hair streaming as the taxi speeded away. 'And my name isn't *gorgeous*, it's *Evie*!'

17

Would you prescribe an open-air handicrafts fair for a bruised heart? Well, neither would Evie but that was where she found herself on Sunday afternoon, strolling in Sacha's wake.

Note that Evie only considered her heart bruised. She was realistic enough to admit that it was nowhere near broken. A long night without either Bing or a bottle of red to lean on had led to some unusually clear-sighted introspection. An uncomfortable question or two had come up. The biggie was, why had she been so blind to the obvious, twelve-foot-high, neon-lit defects in Dan's character? Was she really so easily blinded by a pert buttock and a saucy smile?

The answer was an uncomfortable yes. When she replayed the time she had spent with Dan it was apparent that his louse-like tendencies had always been there. From the beginning, he had come on to her like a runaway train. He had doled out sultry looks, tickles and pinches with gay abandon. What, in the name of Dale Winton, had made her imagine that this treatment was exclusive to her? Of course Melody had been getting the benefit of it too – for all she knew, he might have been rogering the runners in the lunch-break.

Shame had crept over Evie, huddled in bed with only a giant Snickers for comfort, as she remembered sneering at Melody's drunkenness. She'd thought she'd been in cahoots with Dan as they took the mickey out of the sozzled Welsh girl, when actually he'd been busy making a fool of them both.

Worse, much worse, was the knowledge that brainless Melody was much more clued up than she was. She hadn't entertained any virginal notions of a 'relationship'. She had guessed that

Evie was the next target, the next notch on Dan's pretty rickety bedpost.

'I'm desperate,' concluded Evie miserably. It was an ugly word, and she shied away from it. 'Maybe I'm not desperate.' She'd rallied after a second Snickers. 'Just gullible.'

'No, you're desperate,' Bing had confirmed, when she'd shared her thoughts with him in the morning.

'No, you're not desperate.' Sacha had pooh-poohed *that* idea when they'd met at the handicrafts fair.

Evie's shoulders had relaxed in relief, until she reminded herself that she considered *Sacha* desperate. Definitely. One-hundred-per-cent, top-quality, no-doubt-about-it desperate. So, could she trust the opinion of a certified desperate person on her own status as desperate?

What was abundantly clear was that it was truly desperate to be asking people if she was desperate.

At this point, mercifully, she was distracted by a stall selling jumpers knitted from dog hair. 'How do you find these places?' she asked Sacha.

Sacha, who had no concept of a rhetorical question, said coquettishly, 'I have my sources.'

'Can we please have a drink?'

'Sure. There's a mung-juice bar somewhere around here.' Sacha consulted her pamphlet. 'Ooh, and a soya milk-shake stall.'

'Since when have I meant soya milk when I use the word "drink"? Where's the bar?'

'There's no bar, silly!' Sacha looked shocked. 'This is an alternative-lifestyle event. There are other ways to alter your consciousness, you know. You might try meditating for once, instead of reaching for the bottle.'

Evie peered closely into Sacha's eyes. 'Sorry. I mistook you for my friend Sacha.'

'I understand. You must mock what frightens you.'

'No, Sash, soya milk doesn't *frighten* me. It *bores* me.'

'You *understand* alcohol, so you reach for it.'

'But you normally beat me to it.'

They were by a Past Lives T-shirt stall. 'Oh, look!' Sacha said excitedly. 'Let's get one!'

'What are they?' asked Evie tetchily, guessing that she'd have even more need for a drink after Sacha explained.

'The woman regresses you to a past life and then she prints you a T-shirt about it. Go on. It's only a tenner.'

They were in a tarted-up gastropub near the craft fair, full of smart young professionals picking over sea bass in herbs. 'Why isn't there a nice roast on the menu?' complained Evie, as she nursed a glass of wine.

'Should I have got a size bigger?' Sacha tugged at her sky-blue T-shirt, which read '*I cared for orphans in medieval Norway*.'

'No. It accentuates your boobs,' said Evie, who considered boob accentuation a good thing. Her own navy T-shirt bore the legend '*I was a Victorian miscarriage*'. 'Can we go somewhere else to eat? It's all too fancy here. I need to stuff my face with carbohydrates and calories.'

'I'm considering going vegetarian,' announced Sacha, with a touch of hauteur. 'It's a much more holistic way of life. I mean, if I really love this planet why am I eating some of the beautiful animals that share it with me?'

'I really don't know,' replied Evie, standing up and hoisting her bag on to her shoulder. 'I'm off to the Wimpy. Coming?'

'Sometimes you just don't listen to me,' said Sacha, as the Wimpy waitress placed their order on the tiny plastic table.

'I always listen. It's just that sometimes I ignore you.' Evie thought this sounded perfectly reasonable.

Apparently so did Sacha. 'I'm sorry, beautiful cow,' she said solemnly.

For an instant Evie presumed her friend was talking to her, but she was apologising to the half-pounder before she wrapped her gums round it. Truly having your burger and eating it.

Later they walked home, taking it slowly in the sunshine. The tall white Camden terraces stood like elderly ladies longing to loosen their corsets in the heat. Londoners were out everywhere, quitting their homes to catch some rays, pale arms and legs bared in front yards by the bins.

'I've been doing my research, as you asked,' said Sacha.

'What research?' Evie's mind cranked slowly in this weather. 'Oh – you mean the exorcism?'

'I've found just the guy.'

'Hmm. Maybe it's not such a good idea.'

'But P. Warnes is evil! You said you wanted to do something about it!'

'When I told Bing he said I was overreacting. And I agree with him. He said we were daft.'

'He would!' Sacha snorted. 'Bing is very unspiritual. If he's had any past life at all, which I doubt, it was probably as a . . . a . . . horrid man.' Sacha was no good at insults. 'I've booked Smoking Eagle now, so we have to go through with it,' she said, with an air of finality.

'Smoking Eagle?'

'He's part Native American.'

'Red Indian?'

'*Native American*. He's dealt with this kind of demon many times.'

'What kind of demon?'

'I described the chilly spot, the scratches on the door, the spooky noises and all that. The exorcism's a doddle apparently. He can fit us in on Wednesday at three.'

Evie was feeling railroaded. The energy Sacha poured into this kind of project was difficult to resist. She tried to wriggle out of it. 'How much is it? If it's expensive you'll have to cancel 'cos I'm not working and there's no money coming in.'

'He simply asks that you make a donation to his Red – Native American charity.'

'Oh. Suppose we'd better do it, then.'

A juggernaut thundered by as Sacha mumbled, 'A donation of about three hundred pounds.'

Sunday-night telly as undemanding and comforting as a favourite aunt was just what the doctor would order, if he was around. Evie snuggled down on the couch to let a brainless costume drama wash over her, and turned up the sound to cover the yelps of what she presumed was pleasure emanating from the small Puerto Rican in Bing's room.

The television was so loud that at first she didn't hear the knocking. Caroline looked as if she had been standing on the step for some time. 'You deaf?'

Evie was used to these greetings by now. 'Evening, Caroline.'

'I want to talk to you about my flat.'

'Right. Come in.'

At that moment the Puerto Rican shrieked, '*I love you, you monster!*'

'No, I'm fine here,' said Caroline. 'It's about the damp you sorted out.'

'There's no need to thank me. I'm your landlady, I was just doing my duty. Honestly,' said Evie magnanimously.

'I know that. I was going to say that now my bedroom needs redecorating where they stripped off all the wallpaper and I don't see why I should do it.'

Evie was gobsmacked. She hadn't meant it, of course, when she'd said there was no need for thanks. 'Fine,' she said, through gritted teeth. 'Fine. Finefinefine. I'll redecorate. Why should you pick up a paintbrush after all? You already pay a whopping fifty per cent of what the rent should be. Don't worry. Leave it all to me. I'll gold-leaf the dado rail while I'm at it. G'night.'

Evie stomped back to her nest on the sofa. '*Oh, shut up!*' she yelled, as she passed Bing's room.

It was impossible to concentrate on the telly. Damn Caroline. Damn her ingratitude, damn her surliness, damn her . . . loneliness. Damn her poverty. Damn her vulnerability from being all alone in the world. Above all, damn her for bringing out the very worst in me and making me feel unbelievably guilty. Evie pounded on Caroline's door.

'Yeah?'

'I think the whole flat needs redecorating.'

'OK.'

Evie backed away. There would be no whoops of delight from this tenant. 'Good. Right. That's settled, then. See you.'

As Evie reached the bottom stair Caroline's voice drifted down to her. 'Oi! I don't want gold leaf on my whatsit rail.'

Sacha believed that Evie's audition had gone well because earlier she'd cast the runes at Calmer Karma and they'd prophesied it would be a good day for creativity. Evie knew that her audition had gone well because she'd been given well-written material to read and a sensitive, inspiring director to guide her. Hugh James was a small, round, bearded bear who showed lots of teeth when he giggled, which was often. He had spent plenty of time with her. There had been no long-winded hot air about motivation, they had simply discussed the character in depth. By the time she performed, the lines felt like a comfortable cardigan. Hugh's reaction made her dare to hope that he'd liked her.

Bing was impressed that she'd got as far as an audition with Hugh James, and insisted on calling her Judi Dench for the rest of the day. 'Oh, your mum rang while you were out, Judi.'

'What did she want?'

'She was keen to know how things had gone with Dan on Saturday.'

'*Noooooooooo.*' Bridgie's I-told-you-sos could take off the top layer of skin.

'Don't worry. I didn't tell her the awful truth. I bought you a bit of time by saying that it went brilliantly and you were very happy and he's lovely blah-blah-bleedin'-blah.'

'Thanks. You're a hero.'

'She said, "Don't forget Saturday", whatever that means.'

'Knickers.' Then Evie corrected herself: '*Giant* knickers. She's expecting me to bring my lovely new boyfriend to her barbecue. Bing, you stupid craphead.'

'*Craphead?*'

'I'm upset. It's all I could come up with. Anyway, you are a craphead.'

'I was a hero a moment ago.'

'That's life, isn't it? What shall I do?'

Bing picked up the phone and held it out to her. 'Call her now. Get it over with. Say you've just found out he's a serial killer. Or a goat-fucker. Or he likes marzipan. Whatever. Come on, Judi! They didn't make you a dame for nothing.'

Evie took the phone grimly and dialled. 'Mum, it's me.'

'I've heard all about him! Bing sang his praises.' There was only one topic Bridgie was interested in.

'Not quite all.' Evie took a deep breath.

It was a mistake to take a breath around Bridgie. She leapt in, like the SAS. 'I was just saying to Daddy, I'm so proud of you, getting your life together and finding a decent young man. We can't wait to meet him at the barbie. I've sent Daddy's long shorts to the cleaners already. We're going to . . .'

Bridgie wittered on with the boundless energy of the empty-headed. Evie had stopped listening after 'I'm so proud of you'. She had never heard those words from her mother's mouth before. 'I'm so ashamed of you' was a favourite combo, but this was new.

And it was nice. She felt taller: her mother was proud of her. So what if she was proud of her for something she hadn't done? Evie wanted to prolong the feeling. For a little while, anyway.

Bridgie was approaching a natural break. 'So, do you think he likes potato salad? Will I do a big bowl?'

Bridgie's potato salad somehow incorporated curry powder and liquorice in its long list of ingredients, but Evie was feeling indulgent. 'I'm sure he'll love it. He's looking forward to meeting you,' she added recklessly.

As she hung up she said anxiously to Bing, 'Find me a man by Saturday.'

'Darling, I could find you a hundred but not one of them would be suitable for your mother's barbecue.'

The day before the exorcism was notable for two things: first, the panic that assailed Evie in anticipation of Bing's reaction and, second, the extraordinary increase in strange goings-on at the top of the house.

Bernard timidly reported hearing the growl of wild animals while he was brushing his teeth. 'Which is fine,' he added hastily. 'I'm not complaining.'

In the late afternoon an incredible light display shimmered out through P. Warnes's windows. 'It looks like he's letting off fireworks in there,' said Bing unhappily, standing in the garden with the hose in one hand and the other on his hip.

Evie saw an opportunity to introduce the exorcism in a positive light. 'That's very dangerous.' She tutted from the deckchair. 'He could burn the house down.'

Right on cue Bing said, 'We've got to do something about it.'

'I agree. That's why I've booked a – person for tomorrow.'

'A person?'

'Yup.'

'What kind of person, Evie?'

'A . . . helpful person.'

'A helpful exorcist, perhaps.'

Evie nodded and returned to *Marie Claire*.

Bing promptly turned the hose on her.

Smoking Eagle was outside the door at three sharp. As Evie went to let him in she hissed at Bing, 'Don't you have a matinée to go to?'

'I threw a sickie. D'you honestly think *anything* could keep me away from this?'

Sacha frowned. 'An unbeliever may block Smoking Eagle's energies.'

'I'm not an unbeliever,' Bing assured her. 'I'm a believer. I believe this is all a pile of cock.'

Smoking Eagle was tall, thin and, surprisingly, wearing a dark suit, subtly flecked with dandruff. His gaunt, serious face wore a tired expression.

'Welcome, Smoking Eagle,' declared Sacha solemnly, obviously relishing her role. 'We are honoured.'

'It is I who am honoured,' Smoking Eagle answered in a jaded voice.

Bing stuck out his hand. 'Hello, Mr Eagle. Or may I call you by your real name?'

'I do not divulge the appellation of my present incarnation,' replied Smoking Eagle haughtily. He turned to Evie. 'I will need somewhere to prepare myself.'

Evie led him to the bathroom.

'He's having a laugh,' was Bing's succinct opinion.

'Bing, *please*, enough of the smart remarks,' begged Evie. 'It's embarrassing. Let's just make the best of it now that he's here.'

'Sorreeeee,' sang Bing, without the faintest trace of repentance.

Sacha was fuming at him. 'He deserves a little respect. He's a direct descendant of a famous Native American chief.'

'Which one?' asked Evie.

'He doesn't like to say.'

Bing couldn't keep quiet. 'I bet. Funny that. Perhaps it was Dribbling Owl. Or Big Chief Wanking Postman.'

'Bing!' snapped Sacha, then 'Evie!' The wanking postman had set Evie off. 'Please act your age. You're paying this man three hundred pounds so you might as well let him get on with the job.'

The laughter stopped abruptly. 'Did you say three hundred pounds?' asked Evie.

Sacha nodded, wincing.

There was no time to strangle her because the bathroom door creaked slowly open, framing Smoking Eagle in all his glory.

As they all agreed later, he looked different in his finery. He was wearing the tiniest of suede loincloths, a turquoise necklet and flat suede boots trimmed with multicoloured feathers. He stood impassive and magnificent, his arms folded at nipple height, staring fixedly ahead. The crowning glory was his headdress: a stunning confection of white and black eagle feathers, it sprang up from a band round his head and trailed down to his ankles. It was oddly familiar from countless cowboy films.

Smoking Eagle strode out manfully, his eyes still fixed on some mysterious distant point. 'Take me to the place of evil.' His voice had changed: it had acquired a gruff accent.

It was a sure sign that his ancient spirit guide had taken control of his body, Sacha whispered to the others as they led him up the stairs. It was a slow business, partly because his preferred gait was plodding and heavy-footed, *à la* Frankenstein, and partly because he paused on each landing to perform a short song.

The words were simple enough, just *haiee haiee*, sung in a kind of rhythmic chant. A loud rhythmic chant. Amber smoke trailed behind him.

As they waited uneasily on the second landing Bing whispered to Evie, 'You've got to hand it to him – hiding dry ice in that loincloth can't be easy.'

Evie slapped him. Sacha flashed them a stern look. Smoking Eagle was unperturbed: he was in a world of his own, a world that was noisy and slow-moving,

Caroline threw open her door, got as far as snapping, 'Could you keep it down I'm—' before she spotted the Red Indian in full regalia, surrounded by smoke, lumbering up the stairs. Wisely she slammed her door.

Eventually they reached the top floor. There wasn't much room up there. Evie, Bing and Sacha flattened themselves against the wall. Smoking Eagle needed space. He was concentrating deeply, inhaling and exhaling fiercely.

Evie was regretting the whole thing. What if P. Warnes turned nasty? Whether or not he was a demon he could probably take her to court for letting an exorcist try to cast him out. What if he suddenly opened the door?

'What if P. Warnes suddenly opens the door?' Evie tugged at Sacha's sleeve.

Sacha, sardined against her, said, 'He wouldn't dare.'

Smoking Eagle was humming now.

Evie coughed as unobtrusively as she could. That eerie smoke certainly got up your tubes. 'I'm scared,' she whispered.

'Why?' whispered Bing. 'It's better than panto.'

'I don't like it up here,' she whined. 'Can't you feel the drop in temperature?'

'Don't be st— oh, yeah! Fuck me.' Bing was startled, which spooked Evie even more.

'*Silence!*' roared Smoking Eagle, with his new accent. His audience jumped. From somewhere (where?) he had produced a large rattle, covered in beads.

'*Hooooooahhhh! Hooooooahhhhh!*' he chanted. Then he began to dance in a shuffle that worked itself up into a prance. All the while he shook his rattle in strict time. The rise and fall of his yodelling song droned on mesmerically.

Sacha was transfixed. At such close quarters Evie, too, was falling under Smoking Eagle's hypnotic spell.

Bing put his mouth to her ear. 'It's a surprisingly nice bod.'

'*Haaaaah!*' roared Smoking Eagle. He threw his arms into the air. Nostrils flaring, eyes blazing, he stood, legs apart, feet planted firmly on the ground, facing P. Warnes's door. '*P. Warnes!*' he bellowed. 'Begone! Leave us in peace, foul creature!'

Just as Evie was thinking, I'll never get the rent out of him after all this, a flash blinded her and the tiny landing exploded in white light. When her eyes adjusted, Smoking Eagle was standing limply, head bowed and shoulders drooping. He said, in an undertone, 'It is done.'

Then he collapsed.

'Let's get him downstairs and try to revive him,' said Evie.

'Let's rifle his loincloth and find out how he fits all those props in,' said Bing.

Smoking Eagle recovered quickly, slipped back into his civvies and his everyday personality. 'Slippery little chap,' he commented. 'You won't have any more trouble.'

Shakily Evie signed a cheque and he was gone. She peered up the stairs. It was certainly very quiet up there.

And it stayed very quiet. The house seemed to be holding its breath. There was not a peep from P. Warnes.

'It's worked!' declared Sacha, with the confidence of someone who had been an idiot in at least a dozen past lives.

'It looks like it *might* have worked.' Evie was more cautious, although she was mentally totting up how much she could charge a new tenant. Belle's rules would no longer apply: she could bump up the asking price *and* do her level best not to get involved in the newcomer's life.

As ever, Bing sounded a sour but realistic note. 'If Smoking Eagle really has despatched P. Warnes down below I'll eat my hat, your hats and the hats of any passers-by.'

'You have a closed mind,' announced Sacha sadly.

'But he has a very open—'

'*Evie!*'

There's nothing like a good Red Indian exorcism to take your mind off man troubles, and Evie was surprised to find that she hadn't thought of Dan for almost a day. She wasn't surprised by how the thought pierced her.

It wasn't that she wanted to see him. He had proved himself to be a shit of the highest calibre – she couldn't *possibly* miss him. Worse than that was the knowledge that she was morphing into the sort of woman she'd always despised. She was becoming a statistic, a stereotype, a single girl who mistook sex for intimacy, a 'singleton' who, condemned to stay that way, cried into her wine with her single pals.

Yuk. Evie didn't want to be the girl that Dan had exposed. Perhaps a glass of wine would help her chase the thought away. She picked up the phone to see if Sacha fancied making a night of it.

Just as she went to dial the phone rang.

'Yikes!' she squeaked.

'Yikes? Am I through to the Famous Five?' asked Aden.

'Aden. Hello. This is a surprise.'

'I wanted to know how things went with Dan.'

'Ah.'

'Actually, I'm fibbing. I *know* how things went. I just wanted to hear your side of it.'

'It was poo,' sighed Evie. 'He's a . . . Sorry, Aden, I don't really know you well enough to swear in front of you, but if I did, I'd say he was a cunt.'

Aden took a sharp breath.

'Don't tell me you're going to defend him?' said Evie, with spirit.

'No, no, I think that's a pretty good character assessment. It's just that . . . he's my friend, you know.'

'Well, he's not mine. He hadn't been to Spain at all! Imagine how I felt when I found that out.'

'I should have told you, but I reckoned I'd interfered enough by then.'

'I wouldn't have listened anyway. I just didn't want to see the truth about Dan,' admitted Evie, in a small voice. 'I've made a right twat of myself, haven't I?'

'Yes,' answered Aden.

'Oh.' Evie had expected a little more sympathy from him.

'But it doesn't matter,' he went on. 'Only your friends know about it. And me,' he added, with a short laugh. 'Dan's an expert. He's done this before and he knew which buttons to push. He's never had a victim who reacted quite like you, though.'

'Eh?'

'He rang me just after you took off. He was incoherent.'

'Really?' Evie couldn't help feeling pleased.

'Women don't walk out on Dan, it's always the other way round. He was in a right state. So maybe you're not quite the twat you think you are.'

'Maybe.'

'Dan's not a *complete* bastard. I know you'll find it hard to believe but he's been a good mate to me over the years.'

When she recalled how Dan had badmouthed Aden, Evie reckoned there was only one good mate in that relationship. 'Whatever,' she said, borrowing a perennially useful expression from *The Jerry Springer Show*.

'Enough Dan-talk,' said Aden decisively. 'How are *you*? Got another job yet?'

'Nah. Had a *fantastic* audition, though, for a dream job.'

'Do you think you got it?'

'Er, dunno.' Evie was distracted by a flash of inspiration. Experience had not taught her that it was safest to ignore these flashes. 'Aden, do you fancy being my boyfriend next Saturday?'

There was a short silence. 'You're going to have to explain that.'

Evie hated explaining herself so she trotted through the salient points rapidly. 'My mother mad. She think me have boyfriend. She invite boyfriend to barbecue Saturday. Dan exposed as C dot dot T. Me need fake presentable boyfriend for barbecue. Yes or no?'

'So I'm presentable. That's something.'

'Please, Aden, there'll be free sausages and you can play with my dog.'

'You know how to tempt a guy. I don't know, Evie. Wouldn't it be awkward?'

Evie wanted to growl. Typical Aden: cautious, wary, no damned fun. 'It'll be a giggle. You can laugh at my family. In their faces if you like. They're used to it.'

'It's not really me.'

'You'd be getting me out of a huge hole. My mother will just go on and on and on and on and on.'

'I don't think I could pull it off.'

'And on and on and on and on and on and on—'

'OK, OK. I'll be your boyfriend on Saturday.'

Phew. Good old Aden. Evie always liked a man she could manipulate.

There was an envelope on the mat. On opening it, Evie found a wad of twenty-pound notes and a neatly typed message. 'HUMBLE APOLOGIES FOR LATENESS OF RENT. HAVE BEEN IN COUNTRY FOR SHORT BREAK. REGARDS, P. WARNES.'

Evie crumpled the piece of paper. The noise of foghorns drifted down the stairs.

18

'Magnolia is cheaper than off-white,' Evie had argued, in one of the endless aisles of B&Q.

Bing had been adamant. 'You can't do Caroline's flat in magnolia. It's too drab. It's too . . . rented accommodation.'

'But it *is* rented accommodation.'

'Now now. What would Belle say if she knew you were scrimping on her tenant's paint?'

Which was how Evie had come to be dipping her brush into off-white bright and early on Saturday morning. 'Is this colour OK?' She took the risky course of consulting Caroline.

''S fine.'

Slap went the brush satisfyingly on the wall. Evie did not want to be here. She did not like decorating. She would rather move house than retouch a cornice. Her behind looked enormous in the old dungarees Bing had dug out for her to wear. And all she had to look forward to later was parading her pretend lover to her family. *Slap*.

Bing came up with a tray of coffee. 'More Bernard news!' he said gleefully. 'He was spotted going into a hairdresser's on the high street.'

'No!' Evie almost dropped her mug. 'Which one? Toni and Guy?'

''Fraid not. Sizzerz or Snipz or whatever the other one's called.'

'Hmm. Toni and Guy would have been better but I'm sure the other place is fine.' This was very good news. They were really making progress with Bernard. Perhaps it was time to try to make headway with another project. 'When was the last time you had a really good night out?' Evie asked Caroline, who was half-way up a ladder.

'Can't remember. I told you, there's nobody to look after Milly. I can't dole out money to baby-sitters.'

'Sure. You need somebody you can trust. My offer still stands. Bing and I will look after Milly. In fact, I insist. You need to have some fun.'

'Fun.' Caroline repeated the word like a caveman who had never come across it before.

'Why don't you let us have her one night next week?'

'Maybe.'

Evie put down her brush and stood at the foot of the ladder. 'Not good enough. Name a night. Go on.'

Caroline stared down at her. Evie stared back. Eventually Caroline muttered, 'Friday.'

'Brilliant. Where will you go?' Evie asked, with sly intent.

'Dunno.'

'*I* know. Go out with Bernard. Don't look at me like that. He's got a new wardrobe and he's gone to the hairdresser's for a groovy new look. He's intelligent, he's kind, he's good with children.' Evie had no evidence to support that last virtue, but Caroline's look of mingled horror and anger was making her gabble. 'If I'm going to look after Milly for a whole evening the least you can do is give Bernard a chance.'

The horror disappeared, leaving pure anger on Caroline's face. She climbed down the ladder and stood nose to nose with Evie. 'Strings attached, eh? You look after Milly as long as I go where you want me to go with who you want me to go with? Who do you think you are?'

Just then Evie thought she was a very frightened woman. 'I'm only asking that you give him a whirl. It can't hurt. I'm not trying to boss you about, honest, it's just that Bernard might be the man for you and you're not giving him a chance.'

'Ladies!' Bing thrust open the door. Both girls swivelled towards him. 'I present to you Mr Bernard Briggs, modelling his new haircut.'

Bernard shuffled in shyly.

There was no way to describe Bernard's hair: it would have been impossible to do it justice. Suffice to say it had a fringe, a very short one, and most of the back was sticking up. It wasn't a look Evie had seen before, and it wasn't one that was likely to be copied. It was extraordinary. She broke out in a torrent of praise. If she kept talking she reckoned she'd stave off the hysterical laughter that was threatening to overwhelm her.

'Thank you. I'm not sure about it, actually,' Bernard said faintly.

'No, no, no, no, no, no, it's gorgeous,' gushed Evie.

'Come along, Bernard, stop distracting the ladies.' Bing shepherded him out, raising a telling eyebrow behind his back.

As the footsteps receded down the stairs Evie took Caroline's hands in her own and said earnestly, 'I am truly, truly sorry.'

'Why were you so surprised that I have a car?' asked Aden, as they hurtled Surbitonwards.

'I wasn't. I was surprised you have such a *funky* car.'

'That's worse.'

'I didn't mean it in a bad way.' Evie was enjoying the drive, her hair swirling crazily as they bombed along in the little red open-top.

'Is it funky?' queried Aden innocently. 'It offers excellent fuel consumption and air-bags come as standard.'

'Aden, don't spoil it. Next on the left.'

'Pretty road.'

'You're joking, right?' The tidy houses with their tended front lawns and newly painted carports gave Evie the dry heaves.

'No, it's nice. I love the suburbs. They're so tranquil.'

'They make me want to scream. That's the house, with the roses at the front.'

'Who's that woman jumping up and down on the pavement?'

'That's my mother.' Evie's heart sank. 'She doesn't normally hop from foot to foot like that but I don't normally bring boyfriends over.'

'Oh, God,' said Aden as he parked and Bridgie Crump broke into a run towards them. 'How did we meet? How long have we been seeing each other? Is it serious? We should have gone through all this.'

'Your name is Dan,' said Evie, as her mother screeched to a halt by her door.

'He knows his own name!' Bridgie leant rudely over her daughter and shook Aden's hand. 'You can call me Bridgie. Or Mum!' She laughed loudly.

'Hello, Mummy,' said Aden, with the boyish smile that came in so handy at times like this.

Bridgie whispered, 'Thank God he talks nicely,' in her daughter's ear as Evie got out of the car.

'What did you expect?'

'He might be one of those DJ fellas, all rap and what-have-you.'

Evie shook her head. Her mother's take on popular culture, based on information gleaned from *This Morning*, *Bella* and the woman next door, was always baffling.

'In you come, you two!' Bridgie slipped her arms through Evie's and Aden's and propelled them up to the front door.

Evie realised with horror that there was a crowd on the doorstep. She felt insulted: was it really so unusual and interesting for her to bring a man home?

'Hello!' they all chorused, raising glasses of Buck's Fizz as if they were welcoming sailors home from a war.

'Hello,' muttered Evie.

'Hello, everyone,' said Aden brightly, with a wink in Evie's direction.

Evie could see her father, her sister, Auntie Bea – her parents' oldest friend – the swinish Marcus, her cousin Pippa with the lazy eye, Bob from the garage and the woman next door. It was a warped version of *This Is Your Life*. 'Hello, Dan!' They were all grinning as Evie and Aden passed through them into the house.

'Come on into the back garden, everyone!' trilled Bridgie, in the sing-song voice that was only heard when the Crumps had company. 'Let's get our teeth into Daddy's sausages!'

'Yes,' whispered Evie to Aden. 'Before you ask, she always says things like that.'

There were more people in the garden, some of whom Evie didn't recognise. Bridgie steered them towards the new barbecue. 'It's built-in!' She beamed.

'It's the most magnificent built-in barbecue I've ever seen!' Aden proclaimed.

Evie was impressed. Maybe Aden was good at this sort of thing.

'Do you prefer a speciality sausage, Dan?' enquired Bridgie, waving a hand over the array of bangers.

'Which do *you* like?' asked Aden.

'I get very excited about a good old pork,' declared Bridgie.

'Amazing. That's my favourite too.'

'Ooooh!' Bridgie trembled at such wonderful news. Evie edged away, as her mother guided Aden animatedly through the salads.

There was a tap on her shoulder and Beth's voice in her ear: 'He's cute.'

'I know.' And Aden did look cute, listening patiently to the litany of 'potato salad, bean salad, chickpea salad, chicken and pea salad, chickpea chicken and pea salad . . .'

'Well done.'

'Shucks, it was nothing,' said Evie, with some accuracy.

'Is he as nice as he looks, or is he a bastard like the rest of his gender?' asked Beth evenly.

'There you go again. Behaving in an unBethlike way.'

'I *am* Beth, so I can't behave in an unBethlike way.'

Evie pulled a face, to admit defeat, and changed the subject. 'Where's the booze?'

'I got you one.'

'Mmm. Buck's Fizz.'

'Taste it.'

'Ah. Bucks Fizz made with . . .'

'Marmalade. You get used to it.'

Evie looked around at the sausage-waving throng. 'I wasn't expecting so many people. Nice to see Auntie Bea, though.' A fixture of their childhood, Bea had moved to Scotland and wasn't around much any more. 'She hasn't changed a bit. Apart from the odd stone or two.' Bea had always been the sort of woman who was described as 'larger than life'. Always laughing, usually sporting a boa, she'd let Evie smoke in her house and provided a respectable alibi when she'd been snogging sixth-formers in the park.

'I think she looks great,' said Beth fondly.

'So do I. She always does. I hadn't realised how much I miss her.'

Beth lowered her voice. 'Can I leave the twins with you again this week?'

'Sure.' Evie toyed with her champagne and marmalade. 'How are things?'

Beth's eyes were troubled. 'Things are . . .' She ran a hand through her hair. 'Things are fucking awful, Evie.'

Evie decided to plunge in. 'You've seen a solicitor about a divorce, haven't you?'

Beth crumpled slightly. 'Yes,' she said wearily. 'It's not what I planned, but I don't have any choice.'

Evie dragged Beth to the side of the shed – or the gazebo, as Bridgie styled it. 'It's adultery, isn't it?'

Beth was startled. 'How much do you know?'

'I knew something was going on. I just didn't know who with. There's another woman, right?'

'Yes. Yes.' Beth drained the glass, and wiped a sticky chunk of orange peel off her lips. 'Are you shocked?'

'I'm furious!'

'Please don't be angry. Can't you try to understand? Some people shouldn't get married.'

'That's hardly an excuse,' said Evie pompously. Honestly, nice people could be so bloody wimpish at times. 'It makes me *sick*.'

'It kills me to hear you talk like that,' said Beth sadly.

'How else do you expect me to react to something like this in our family?'

'Keep your voice down,' said Beth urgently. 'She's here!'

Who? The other woman? The adulteress responsible for her sister's unhappiness was lurking somewhere in the garden! Evie started to splutter but Beth shushed her, looking about in a hunted manner. 'For God's sake, Evie, keep cool. We're at Mum and Dad's. We don't want a scene!' Beth gasped. 'Christ. Act normal. Here comes Marcus and his . . . girl.'

Evie wheeled round. Marcus, in one of his endless supply of suits, was heading their way with a petite, slim, dazzlingly pretty girl at his side. So that's the bitch, thought Evie, feeling her fingernails grow.

Beth gripped her arm. 'Just act normally. I won't have my dirty washing aired in public. *Evie*.'

Marcus was upon them, smiling broadly. 'Greetings, sibling-in-law,' he burbled. Marcus was always laughing, yet never made a successful joke.

As a reply Evie stared at him insolently. It was a trick she'd picked up from Caroline.

Marcus was either too dense to notice, or too pleased with himself for managing to flaunt his mistress in public. 'This is Tamsin, my dental nurse.'

'Hello there!' Tamsin was as bright as a button, fresh as a daisy.

'Hello there, yourself.' Evie spoke – she hoped – witheringly.

Tamsin did not appear in the least withered. 'Gosh, I'm so thrilled to meet you. You're an actress, aren't you? How exciting!' The accent was pure Sloane. Evidently Marcus was returning to his roots.

'Yes, I am. But surely things can get pretty hot in the dental surgery too.'

Tamsin was blind to any subtext. 'Ooh, yes. Specially with Marcus around.' She shot him a glance of collusion. Evie gripped her glass while Tamsin giggled like an electrocuted schoolgirl.

Evie looked at her sister. Beth was gazing determinedly over everyone's heads, dignified as ever. Evie's own instinct was to punch Marcus first, then Tamsin. No, Tamsin first, then Marcus. Whatever. She had to get away from the gruesome pair before the urge got the better of her. 'I'm just going to find my boyfriend,' she muttered, and slid away.

Aden was still firmly under Bridgie's wing. She was introducing him to her 'lovely girlfriends' or, as John Crump alluded to them, the coven. Aden was smiling and nodding. Judging by the gales of post-menopausal hilarity he was going down a storm.

'Mum, are you trying to steal my bloke?' Evie was relishing the fiction she'd started. She took Aden's other arm in a lock every bit as strong as her mother's.

Between them, Aden winced.

'If I was twenty years younger!' simpered Bridgie.

You'd still be a nutter, mused Evie. 'I want to introduce A – er, Dan to Dad.'

'He hasn't even put his lips to a sausage yet.' Bridgie did not give in easily.

'There's plenty of time for that. I want him to meet Dad.'

Reluctantly Bridgie relinquished her prize. The shoulders of the coven slumped beneath their M&S summer co-ordinates. 'Make sure you bring him back for the salsa!'

'Salsa?' gaped Evie.

'Oh, yes. We've all been having lessons, haven't we, girls?'

They nodded furiously.

The notion of her mother, the most physically uptight person in the known world, the woman who could have given uptight lessons to Queen Victoria, salsa-ing was extraordinary. The marmalade must have gone to her head, Evie reasoned.

John was standing a little aloof from the crowd, one foot in a flowerbed and a bemused look on his face. 'Wasn't this meant to be a family do?' he asked Evie. 'I should have known something was afoot when Mum forced me into my good shorts.'

'And damn fine shorts they are too, Dad.' Evie stretched to kiss his whiskery cheek. 'This is Dan.' Suddenly she felt uncomfortable. She didn't like pulling the wool over her father's eyes.

'Ah!' John stuck out his hand. 'I suspect you're the reason we're pushing the boat out. My wife gets a little overheated about Evie's admirers. She's always had plenty but she never brings them home,' he said, loyally and incorrectly. 'How are you, son? You're very welcome.'

'I'm glad to be here.' Aden sounded so sincere that Evie was impressed.

'What do you do?' John asked, then added, 'Don't worry, I'm not asking about your prospects. I'm just interested.'

'Right now I'm an assistant director on commercials and TV drama, but I've just directed my first independent film and one day I hope to direct full time.'

'Good for you. Yes. Good for you.' John was obviously unable to conjure up a pertinent question to ask, perhaps because Aden's career was so far removed from his own life at the bank. 'Got any hobbies?' he asked lamely.

Evie smiled. People her age didn't have hobbies. They didn't kill time like the oldies did, unless you counted getting pissed and watching soaps. She eyed Aden with interest. He'd done so well up to now. Could he come up with a hobby to chat to her dad about?

'Just bird-watching.'

John and Evie both gasped, John because bird-watching was one of his main reasons for living, Evie because, unless Aden was a better actor than she was, it was *true*.

'Where do you twitch?' asked John breathlessly, like a débutante at her first ball.

'Suffolk. Best birds in the British Isles.'

If John had been Italian he would have thrown his arms round Aden and claimed him as his own. Instead he limited himself to 'There's nowhere like Suffolk for spotting a colourful migrant.'

'Saw a hoopoe last week,' Aden said smugly.

'No!' John seemed amazed.

Evie was amazed too. Amazed that she'd introduced a closet bird-watcher to her family as her boyfriend. 'What the hell is a hoopoe?'

It was, she discovered, as Aden and her father fell over themselves trying to describe it, a large black and white bird who visits our shores each summer and sounds like this – *hoopoooo, hoopoooo*.

That was plenty of information – in fact, far too much. Evie spotted Auntie Bea draped over the garden bench and left the men to their feathery impressions.

'Evie, Evie, Evie!' boomed Auntie Bea fondly, in her theatrical voice.

'Auntie Bea, Auntie Bea, Auntie Bea!' Evie hugged her. 'It's been years! How come you're back from Scotland?'

'Fancied a change, love. You know me, I like to be where the action is.'

'So how come you're here?'

'Now now, madam. Your mother's gone to a lot of trouble.'

'I know.' Evie looked sheepish. Auntie Bea had always been able to get through to her. Many times during her childhood Evie had blasphemously wished that Auntie Bea was her real mother. 'When did I start calling you Auntie?' asked Evie, in the mood to be nostalgic.

'You didn't. It was Beth. She was only toddling and because I lived a few doors away and was always in and out of your house she must have presumed I was an auntie. I loved it.' She tilted her head, as if looking back down the years. 'Who'd have thought . . .' She turned to Evie with a grin. 'Do you remember when you came sobbing to me convinced you were pregnant? How old were you?'

'Twelve. How was I to know you couldn't get pregnant from holding a boy's hand during Irish-dancing class?'

'Quite. Perfectly feasible.'

'If you'd grown up in my mother's house you would have imagined you could catch pregnancy from Tupperware. Or posters of Duran Duran. Or television programmes with swearing in them.'

'You came to me again a few years later.'

Evie grimaced. 'That scare was real, though. I was so frightened I didn't know what to do or who to turn to. You were the only adult I could dream of telling.' She looked into Bea's wide, lined face, framed by a bird's nest of pure white hair. 'Thank God you were there. I might have done something stupid otherwise. Sex was a hanging offence in our house.'

'It only took a quick trip to Boots and a pregnancy test to sort you out, thank God.'

'And a good ticking-off! I remember you giving me a good ten minutes on how sex is a beautiful thing to be enjoyed by two mature people who had real feelings for each other. My mother never mentioned sex and if anyone else did she had the house fumigated.'

Auntie Bea swerved the conversation. 'Beth tells me you're aware of the changes in her life,' she said, with her trademark compassionate directness.

'Oh.' Evie was surprised that Auntie Bea should already be up to speed but, then, Beth had also relied heavily on her for advice when they were younger. It made sense that she should turn to her now. 'Yes. She has. I've been trying to keep out of it but it's not easy.'

'No.'

'I'm not happy about it. Obviously.'

Bea studied Evie's face. 'Do you remember what I said when we were worried that you might be pregnant?'

'Which bit? There was an awful lot of it.'

'I said that whatever happened you'd have to make the decision on your own, for yourself, based on your own feelings and reasoning. That you mustn't let anybody influence you because in the final analysis the only way to be content is to be true to yourself. That you shouldn't waste time worrying what others think of you.'

'I remember now.' Evie frowned. 'Why are you bringing that up?'

'I'm just suggesting that when you look at Beth's situation remember that people, however much you love them, won't always behave the way you want them to. Everyone must follow their own guiding light.'

'I know that,' said Evie earnestly. 'Don't get me wrong. I think she's dead right to leave him.'

'Good for you!' Bea enfolded Evie in another hug that smelt of vanilla and musk. 'How did I manage to brainwash you into a little hippie right in the middle of Surbiton?'

'Dunno, but I'm glad you did. Otherwise I'd be going through something similar to Beth right now.' Evie's ears were assailed by a burst of Latin-American music. 'Oh, my God! She's come good on her threat – Mum's starting the salsa!'

A horde of whooping ladies swarmed on to the patio, dragging men ruthlessly after them. One of the men, Evie noted, was Aden. Arthritic hips were soon grinding enthusiastically and arms were thrown in the air, accompanied by wild shrieks of middle-aged delight.

'I reckon this is a kind of acceptable wife-swapping,' Bea said conspiratorially. 'Just look at them, all pumping their genitals into their neighbours'.'

'Yeah,' laughed Evie. 'Post-menopausal women getting their kicks in the only way left to them.'

'Oi!' Bea delivered a vehement dig to Evie's ribs. 'We post-menopausal gals have no need for your pity, young lady.'

'I don't suppose *you* do.' Evie was fairly certain that Bea's sex life was spicier than her own. But, then, a dead person's sex life was probably spicier than hers. 'Crikey, look at them go!'

Reg from number thirty was Ricky Martining with far too

much gusto for a man with a hip replacement. The woman next door was shaking her booty like one possessed. The undoubted star of the show, however, was Bridgie, who was gyrating wildly and shouting, 'Hi, caramba!' at regular intervals.

'Your young man doesn't look *entirely* at home,' said Bea, with a twinkle.

'He's not really . . .' Evie quelled an urge to confess. 'He's not much of a dancer.'

Poor Aden was almost invisible in the sea of flailing limbs. Bridgie was twirling him like a top.

'I'd better rescue him.' Evie strode over and purposefully entered the scrum. 'You're nicked.' She grabbed Aden's hand and spirited him away while her mother was engrossed in a complicated manoeuvre involving Reg and some maracas. 'Trust me. You'll be safe here.' She bundled him into the garden shed and banged the door behind them. 'Sorry, I should have rescued you sooner but I was enjoying it too much.'

'Jesus, that was scary.' Aden was trembling. 'One minute they were all chatting about gardening, the next they were leaping about like a voodoo cult.'

Evie laughed. 'Sit down and make yourself comfortable. When you've recovered we can plan our escape.'

'Blimey. An armchair.' Aden sank into it.

'This is where Dad escapes the long arm of my mother. It's his refuge.'

'I like your mum.' He said it as if it was the most reasonable thing in the world. 'I do!' he insisted, in answer to Evie's disbelieving look. 'She's lively. She's got spirit. She's friendly.'

'Friendly. Hmm. In the same way Hitler was friendly when he annexed Poland.'

'Give her a break,' said Aden, maddeningly and characteristically reasonable. 'She's being very nice to me.'

'Only 'cos she thinks you're my boyfriend. Don't get too used to it. You're living a lie,' she ended dramatically, perching on the wonky arm of the chair.

'It's not so funny now we're here, is it?'

Evie sighed. 'I know. I feel a bit . . .'

'Mean?'

Evie nodded. 'Dad really liked you, and Auntie Bea approves too.'

'We could always confess.'

'Oh, shut your face.' Evie was horrified. 'I'd never live it down. No, you and I can have a huge row next week and vow never to speak to each other again. Perhaps I can discover you in bed with Sacha.'

'That's not fair,' remonstrated Aden. 'They'll all hate me.'

'What do you suggest to break us up, then?'

Aden looked distinctly uncomfortable with the whole idea.

'You could die,' Evie said.

'Bit drastic, isn't it? What if I bump into one of them somewhere?'

'A twin? An *evil* twin?'

Aden shook his head. 'This isn't a made-for-TV movie. No, we'll just have to split up 'cos . . . 'cos . . . Pressure of work keeps us apart.'

'It'll have to be pressure of *your* work. I don't have any.'

'So that's our story?'

'Yup. Your career takes off and we never get to see each other so our relationship just dwindles and dies.'

There was silence.

'It feels quite sad,' Aden said.

'Don't be daft.'

'I want you to know that of all the fake relationships I've ever had this has been the best. I'll never forget you and all the things we didn't really do together.'

'And all the lovely things you didn't say to me aren't engraved on my heart.'

'And now that our fake love affair is over, let's be fake friends for ever.'

Evie laughed. 'For ever.'

Aden smiled ruefully. 'Let's be real friends, Evie. This joke's giving me the creeps. We *are* friends, aren't we?'

'Of course we are.' Evie was brisk. She hadn't expected sincere emotion here in the shed. 'What's that pong?'

'Smells like dog to me.'

'Henry!' Evie kissed the black snout sticking out from under the workbench. 'Out you come, boy!'

With a great deal of waddling, straining, huffing and puffing, Henry emerged and a flurry of licks and tail-wagging commenced. 'Ooooh, I love you, Henry.'

'Hello, Henry.' Aden offered a hand, which was politely slobbered over. 'Lovely boy. What a beauty.'

'He likes you too.' Evie was like a stage mother about Henry, absurdly pleased when somebody took to him. 'Sorry about the smell, though. I've never noticed it before. For the first time I can see what Mum goes on about.'

'Who minds doggy smell?' said Aden, playing with Henry's floppy ears.

Suddenly there was a loud crash. The salsa music stopped abruptly and was replaced by muted screams. Aden and Evie looked at each other, then raced out of the door.

There was chaos on the patio. Several prone Surbiton bodies wiggled among the upturned garden furniture. Potato salad was splattered across the capacious bottom of the woman next door. Sausages were rolling on to the grass. The survivors were staggering to their knees and dusting themselves off gingerly. The yelps and shrieks were fading.

'I never thought I'd get to witness a real-life salsa accident,' said Aden with awe.

Bridgie, hair askew and a pitta bread attached to her left breast, yelled hysterically at Evie, 'Don't just stand there! *Help!*'

Evie righted a couple of chairs, while Aden coaxed a rotund lady to her feet.

'Where's John? Where does that man get to when I need him?' shrieked Bridgie, her hysteria rising a notch.

Evie could see her father: he was lurking on the far side of the shed, his shoulders shaking helplessly. It was obvious where Evie's tendency to uncontrollable giggling fits had come from. Tears streamed down his face.

Beth, miraculously untouched by flying finger food, put an arm around her mother and led her into the house. A moment or two later she emerged. 'Mum's gone for a little lie-down. Why don't we all have a good stiff drink?'

There was a murmur of approval and soon normality had been restored to the good people of Surbiton.

John returned to the patio and asked innocently, 'What happened? What did I miss?'

Evie was impressed by her sister's presence of mind. So impressed that she actually helped to hand robust gin-and-tonics to the flushed ladies. Beth was so cool and gracious, making sure that all the rumpled, twittering guests were looked after. I'm proud of her, thought Evie unexpectedly. She knew that inside Beth was in turmoil, but it didn't show. That's where we're different, she mused, as she spied Tamsin giggling animatedly at Marcus's side by the compost heap.

Aden saw the glint in her eye. 'Er, what are you planning?' he asked.

'It's time I sorted out some garden pests.' Evie strode away too fast to hear his groan.

'All right, are we?' The chilling sarcasm was lost on Marcus and Tamsin.

'Yes, thank you very much,' chirped Tamsin brightly. 'Are the ladies recovered now?'

Ignoring her, Evie asked Marcus, 'Do you have anything to say for yourself, Marcus?'

Marcus looked wary. 'On what subject?'

'I think there's only one at the moment, don't you?' Evie spluttered.

Aden came up behind Evie and laid a hand on her arm.

'Gerroff.' She turned to Tamsin. 'I know all about you, love.

I know your sordid little secret. How can you show your face here, of all places, with him?' She jabbed a finger so hard in Marcus's direction that he had to step back to avoid it.

'Now look here—' began Marcus. He was silenced by the wail that arose from Tamsin.

'She knows! She knows! I'm so humiliated.' Tamsin's perfect little face was scrunched up like a used tissue. 'I'm sorry, everyone,' she blathered, in a fury of tears and snot. Then she darted, sobbing, into the house and right through it.

The slam of the front door galvanised Marcus into action. His bland features contorted with anger and he hissed, 'You always have to interfere, don't you?' into Evie's face. Then he raced after Tamsin.

Evie was shocked by the effect of her words. She might have expected to feel triumphant, but she didn't: she felt rather nervous, as if she had let a tiger out of its cage.

On the far side of the silent, staring guests, she caught Beth's eye. Her sister was standing with an empty tray. Bea approached her to place a comforting arm round her, and Beth turned away from Evie's gaze.

But the look in her eyes lingered in Evie's mind. It was a look of pain – and panic. 'Aden, we have to go,' she muttered, her throat dry.

With no farewells they went out to his car and drove away.

19

The open-top was parked by the river, surrounded by ducks squawking in their daft insistent way.

'They're hoping for a chip,' remarked Evie.

'They'll be lucky.' Aden was making strange shapes with his mouth to cool the fat, hot, delicious chip he'd just popped into it.

'As chips go, these are the *crème de la crème*.'

'It is truly a chip among chips.'

'It is King Chip.'

'It's the chip of my dreams.'

There was a pause, punctured by the quacking of water-fowl and the mastication of fried potato.

'Thank you for today,' said Evie.

'I had a great time.'

'Now, don't spoil it all by telling porky-pies.'

'I'm not.'

'God, Aden, you do that sincerity thing so well.'

'That's because I *am* sincere. I don't *do* a sincere thing.'

'You mean you enjoyed being squeezed half to death by my mother, talking about bird-watching, witnessing a mass salsa collapse, and being part of a family disaster?'

'*Yes,*' Aden said patiently. 'I enjoyed being squeezed. She meant well. Yes, I enjoyed talking about bird-watching – it might be naff but that's never bothered me. Yes, I enjoyed the salsa incident. Very few people are privileged to see such a thing. And I don't think that was a family disaster.'

'Beth was devastated.'

'You're exaggerating.' Aden had a way of saying stuff like

this in a non-confrontational way that didn't make Evie flare up. If Bing had uttered those words Evie would have defended herself.

She only said, 'I wish I was.'

'You did it for the right reasons even if it was a bit . . . reckless.'

'I did it because I can't keep my nose out of other people's business,' confessed Evie, in a rare moment of candour. 'Beth made it clear she just wanted to get through the day without any trouble. But I had to go in like Annie Oakley.'

'More Lara Croft.'

'Oh, God.' Evie covered her face with hands that smelt of salt and vinegar.

'Beth's your sister. She'll understand. Just talk to her about it.'

'That's what we don't do.' Evie sighed through her fingers. 'Crumps don't talk. We skirt, we avoid, sometimes we'll go mad and *allude*, but we never talk.'

'It's time you started, then. God knows, you talk to everybody else.'

Evie popped a chip miserably into her mouth. (Never too miserable to eat, you'll note.) 'I'm sorry to drag you through all this shit, Aden. It's not your problem.'

'Haven't you been listening? I enjoyed myself. My family don't get together much.'

'Why not?'

'Oh, Dad lives in Florida, and Mum married again. My stepfather isn't such a great guy. My brother's kind of difficult. Works in the City. Thinks film-making is a gay-boy job. There aren't many dos – nobody bothers to arrange them.' He slapped the steering-wheel.

Evie was moved. Who would have imagined that organised, sensible Aden was so lonely at heart? 'So that's why you liked being at my parents'. Even though it was dull and surreal in equal parts, it was family life.'

'Something like that.'

'Well, you're welcome to take my place at all future birthdays and Christmases,' smiled Evie, 'and divorces.' She gulped.

'Let's get you home.' The revving of the engine sent the ducks, much affronted, skedaddling back to the water.

'Right to my door. That's what I call service. Do you want to come in for a coffee, or something to eat? There was nothing remotely edible at the barbecue.'

'I'd better get back.'

'Okey-dokey. Oh, Christ, how do I . . .' Evie had been born without the gene that enables humans to understand car doors.

Aden rolled his eyes and leant over to let her out.

'Thank you,' she said, 'for pretending to be my bloke.'

'No problem. It was easy.'

There was a stillness between them that Evie recognised. It was the stillness between two people who are about to kiss. The invisible elastic that draws one to another at times like this was attached to their chests. She felt herself lean a millimetre towards him.

'Let me know when you hear how the audition went!' said Aden jauntily, turning the ignition key.

'Yes! Ooh, yes!' Evie, just as jauntily, nipped out and slammed the door. ''Bye!'

What came over me? she wondered, as she dashed up the steps. Usually she had to be sozzled before she kissed men she didn't fancy. It might have been very embarrassing *indeed*.

'You did promise,' insisted Evie.

'I didn't,' Bing insisted right back.

'You bloody did.'

'Nice language.'

'Oh, fuck off. You promised.' Evie didn't relish baby-sitting on her own and was determined to rope in Bing.

'I have plans.'

'You said you were staying in.'

'I have plans to stay in. I'm busy tonight. You're the big mouth who offered, not me. I don't do kids.'

So Evie went upstairs to flat B on her own, trying to ignore the harpsichord music drifting down from behind P. Warnes's scratched door.

Caroline's door was open. 'Hello?' Evie edged inside. She could hear Milly crying – maybe Caroline was having trouble settling her. She tiptoed towards the kitchen and the sound of the sobs.

When she put her head round the door she saw Caroline at the table. There was a crumpled piece of paper in her fist.

'Caroline, what's wrong?' Evie moved round to face her. 'Is that bad news?'

'It's nothing,' said Caroline, throwing the paper across the room. She sniffled and wiped her eyes with an almost shredded tissue. 'I'm fine.'

'Are you sure?' Evie reached out gingerly to place a hand over Caroline's – she knew Caroline didn't much like personal contact but she was determined to offer some comfort.

Caroline looked at Evie's hand quizzically as if it was an animal, but she didn't shrug it away. 'I'm sure,' she said, in a clear, strong voice. 'Milly's asleep. I won't be long.' She stood up.

'You look lovely,' said Evie admiringly. She had never seen Caroline dressed up before and she certainly scrubbed up well.

'Hmm.' Caroline treated the compliment with suspicion. 'See you.'

'Where are you going?' Evie trotted behind her like a little dog greedy for titbits.

'Cinema.'

God, Caroline was excruciatingly stingy with detail. 'What are you going to see?'

Caroline tutted. 'I'm going on my own. That's what you really want to know.'

Evie shrugged unconvincingly. 'No, no, it's not. Just interested. You go and enjoy yourself and don't worry about a thing.'

Evie settled herself on the sagging couch while Caroline checked on Milly, then left.

A minute later she was off the sofa like a greyhound and into the kitchen. 'Damn!' The screwed-up letter was gone. Caroline was a fine judge of character. Hating herself, Evie placed a toe on the pedal of the bin.

Nothing.

Evie settled down in the newly painted sitting room to watch the news. She was only ever interested in the wacky item at the end, so her gaze was soon drifting around the room. There was a small bookcase, filled with a mixture of baby-care manuals and blockbusters. Framed photos of Milly stood on every surface. No pictures of her family, noticed Evie, and felt sorry for her. There was something poignant about seeing her go out on her own to the cinema, but Caroline was the sort to square her shoulders and just get on with it. Evie admired her for that. But something had managed to pierce her tough veneer.

The wacky item was about a cat who could answer the phone but Evie barely noticed it. She was too busy thinking of what might have brought tears to Caroline's eyes. Money, she guessed. Debt.

There wasn't much Evie could do about that.

Bing's plans for the evening became clear when Evie returned to the basement rather earlier than she'd expected. They involved a bath, lots of bubbles and the six-footer from Asda's checkout.

'Darling,' rasped Meredith, 'Hugh James has got back to me about that little audition you did for him.'

Evie crossed her fingers, her legs, her eyes. 'And?'

'He said – *Barry!*' Meredith erupted into a shriek. 'Not the

Tippex! You've had enough already!' She came back to Evie. 'Anyway, darling, we'll speak soon. Goodbye!'

'*No, Meredith, no!*'

'Fuck me, you're a trained actress not a strangled pig. Don't make noises like that.'

'You haven't told me what Hugh James said.'

'Oh. So I didn't. Well, you've got the job, darling.'

Evie was stunned. She had prepared herself assiduously for disappointment but she wasn't sure how to cope with success.

Meredith was typically vague with the nitty-gritty. Shooting would start in a few weeks. A script would arrive in a few days. The fee was in negotiation. What Meredith *could* confirm was that the series was called *The Setting of the Sun* and Evie's character was called Hepsibah.

'Hepsibah!' cooed Evie, waltzing around her bedroom. 'What a lovely name!' She stopped when she caught sight of herself in the mirror. She looked different. She traced her features with her fingers, trembling with emotion. 'Oh, Belle,' she whispered. 'I'm on my way. I'm a real actress at last!'

There was nobody around to share her news. Bing had left for his evening performance. Sacha was having a two-for-one massage evening at Calmer Karma. Evie didn't dare call her mother or her sister after the scenes in Surbiton a couple of days earlier. Aden! He'd asked her to let him know.

'I got it! I got it! I got it!'

'Great! Calm down!' laughed Aden who, right on cue, suggested a drink to celebrate.

'Good idea! Let's go somewhere special.'

The Hand and Flower was a pub, nothing more, nothing less. Beer slops on the tables. Crisps trodden into the carpet. Australian barman who was actually a New Zealander.

'I don't go to special places much. Will this do?' Aden was apologetic.

'This is perfect.' Evie was so elated she would have been happy in an abattoir. She was bouncing in her seat like Tigger when Aden brought their drinks to the table.

'Here's to you.' Aden raised his lager with ceremony.

'Here's to Hepsibah!' Evie raised her vodka and tonic. 'Do you mind if I burble on for a bit? Maybe quite a long bit?'

'Be my guest.' Aden sat back and folded his arms behind his head, a sneaky little smile on his face.

'I don't have all the details yet but I do know it's a series based on a Victorian novel called *The Setting of the Sun*. I *think* it's six episodes. It's the story of a young woman who is married against her will to this grumpy older guy. He obligingly dies, and leaves her alone with two young children. She moves out to the country and has to manage all on her own. Victorian society expects her to be all wimpish and faint all over the place but she discovers that she likes hard work and she relishes making difficult decisions. So we watch her blossom into a mature independent woman. It's quite weepy, apparently.' Evie leant back with a sigh. 'It sounds so good I'd watch it if I wasn't in it.' She jumped forward again, elbows in the slick of beer that adorned their table. 'I'm not playing the heroine – God, if only! – I'm her maid, Hepsibah. I'm very loyal and our friendship grows as we struggle together. Oh, Aden, all that and I get paid too!'

'I should hope so.'

'I'd do it for nothing!' squeaked Evie. 'I'd pay them! It might be a lot of money if Meredith can concentrate while she's negotiating.'

'I'm sure they'll make it worth your while.'

'I'm a real proper actress! A proper one! A real, real one!'

'Yes. You are.'

'Right. That's enough burbling. It's not fair. What have you done today, Aden?'

'Let's see. I spent part of the time looking at pictures of locations for my next job, then I got back to the editing suite to put the final touches to my film.'

'Sorry, Aden, there's too much burbling still in me. It has to come out or I might need to be hospitalised.'

'OK. Go on. It's quite relaxing, actually. You don't seem to need any input.'

Evie opened a packet of crisps. 'I wonder if there'll be any famous names in it.' She sat bolt upright. 'I never thought of that. Ralph Fiennes might be in it. Or, erm, Ewan McGregor!'

Aden put his head to one side. 'And if he is?'

'He might fall madly in love with me!' said Evie, through a mouthful of crisps.

'Thought you were off actors,' said Aden, finding something of interest deep in his glass.

'I'm off unknown actors,' confirmed Evie. 'Nobody in their right mind is off famous actors. Might be Sean Bean!'

'A famous actor is the same as an unknown actor except he's more . . . well, famous,' persevered Aden.

'I could get my wedding in *Hello!*.'

Aden winced.

'I'm only joking.' Evie was perfectly serious. 'Don't pull faces. I'm allowed to fall in love with the star now that my fake boyfriend is leaving me through pressure of work.'

'There's a man with odd hair gesticulating at you,' Aden informed her.

'That'll be Bernard.'

And it was. He was at the bar in one of his less successful new outfits. He wasn't designed to wear leather trousers, particularly not cheap ones. Aden beckoned him over and he creaked and squeaked his way towards them. Heads swivelled as drinkers tried to locate the source of the strange noises.

'Hello there,' said Bernard, head bobbing in self-deprecation. 'You said it would be OK to join you?' He looked liked a puppy fearing a kick.

'Of course. Lovely to see you. Sit down.'

Bernard pulled up a stool, which lifted him much higher than Evie and Aden. Looking down at them from his perch, he said quietly, 'I'll find a chair – oh, and I'll get a round in.' He pronounced the last bit in inverted commas, evidently proud to be talking like one of the lads now that he was in a public house.

After he'd creaked away Aden whispered, 'I didn't recognise him. What happened to his hair? Was he attacked?'

'No. I'm afraid it's a haircut. Poor thing. He's doing his best – and he's come a long way. He's wearing new clothes and eating properly.' She stared at Bernard's back. 'And the hair will grow,' she added wistfully.

Bernard inserted himself between them at a more comfortable height. 'I ordered myself a Guinness,' he confided.

'Right.' Aden seemed unsure how to take Bernard. He was leaning away from him with puzzlement in his eyes. 'Good.'

Bernard lowered his voice. 'It's my first ever beer.'

'Sip it and see what you think!' encouraged Evie.

'I feel terribly guilty.' Bernard had his hand round the glass but didn't raise it. 'Mother abhorred beer. Well, she was violently against all alcohol but she singled out beer because she felt it was only drunk by a certain sort of low man.'

Evie guessed that Mother hadn't often been invited out clubbing. 'How's it feel to be a certain sort of low man?' she teased Aden.

'Oh, gosh, no, I didn't mean, dear me, oh, my goodness—'

'Enough, Bernard.' Evie held up a hand, like a traffic cop. She was getting the hang of Bernard. It was best to treat him the way she treated Henry. Firmly, kindly, but with no doubt about who was boss. 'We know you didn't mean to give offence. Now, try your Guinness.'

With trepidation Bernard brought the glass to his lips. He took a sip. He swallowed. He smiled.

Four Guinnesses later Bernard was talkative. 'Of course I want a relationship,' he said, much more loudly than was his habit. 'I want a relationship more than anything in the world. But I can never have one.'

Aden was slumped, chin on chest.

Unlike Evie, who was electrified and alert. 'Why can't you have one? You're as good as the next man,' she urged.

Aden, who was the next man, raised an eyebrow.

Evie was ranting like a motivational guru. 'You can change, Bernard. Don't say, "Why?" say, "Why not?" You can fall in love and be happy ever after. You deserve it. *If that's what you want.*'

'It is! It is what I want!'

'Then you and I are going out tomorrow night.'

Bernard shrank back in understandable fear.

Aden straightened up and looked questioningly at her.

'Not on a date, for God's sake.' Both men relaxed and Evie tutted. *Of course* Bernard deserved a relationship but not with *her*. 'We're going out and I'm going to coach you while you approach girls and chat them up.'

All the Guinness left Bernard's system instantaneously and he said timorously, 'Oh, I couldn't.'

'So you want to be alone for ever?'

'Evie, don't be too hard on him,' Aden muttered.

'It's a fair question.' Evie was adamant. 'Bernard, do you want to die alone or do you want to come out with me and possibly meet someone special?'

Bernard hung his head. He didn't have the weapons to fight Evie in this mood. 'I want to come out with you and possibly meet someone special,' he said, his voice very small.

Last orders were called by the Antipodean barman. Aden stood up. 'I'd better get off. Bernard will see you home.'

'There's time for one more,' cajoled Evie.

'Nah. Don't fancy it.'

'At least wait until Bernard gets back from the loo.'

'I'll go now. I feel a bit uncomfortable around Bernard, to be honest.'

'Why? He's harmless.' Evie defended her *protégé*.

'That's true. Actually, it's you who makes me feel uncomfortable.' Aden threw his satchel over his shoulder.

Evie blinked. 'What do you mean by that?' she asked.

'You're picking up where his dragon of a mother left off.'

Evie was stung. 'I'm trying to *help* him.'

'Really? Or are you enjoying the power you have over him to make him do what you think is best for him?'

Evie repeated herself. 'I'm trying to help.' It came out as a whine.

'Why do you treat him like Henry, then?'

Startled, Evie wondered if the down-to-earth Aden was a mind-reader.

Aden shrugged. 'Look, ignore me. It's not my business. I always seem to spoil your fun, don't I?' And, with that, he left.

Evie stared after him. Where on earth had all that come from? She wasn't enjoying her power over Henry, erm, Bernard. Well, all right she *was*, but she was using it for his own good. Evie felt misunderstood.

She had never imagined that Aden had such teeth. Nor that he'd bare them at her. Part of her wanted to rush after him and beg, 'Oh, please, like me again,' while the rest wanted to shout, 'Fuck off, you pompous earwig!'

Evie couldn't do both so she did neither. Instead she had one for the road and another packet of crisps with Bernard.

The stroll home cleared their heads. They were quiet, sunk in their own thoughts. Bernard's trousers provided a musical backdrop to the whirrings of Evie's mind.

'There's that car again,' commented Bernard, as they turned into Kemp Street.

'What car?'

'The white one across the road. It's been there on and off for a week.'

Evie peered through the yellowy fog under the street-lamp. 'There's someone in it.'

'There usually is. I don't know if it's a lady or a gentleman.' Bernard sent a barb of fear through Evie when he added, 'Who-ever it is, they seem to be watching our house.'

'Come on, let's get inside.' Evie picked up the pace. The knowledge that the stranger's eyes were on her made her fumble with her keys.

'Allow me,' said Bernard gallantly. He took the keys and dropped them. 'Oh dear. A little too much Guinness.'

He had managed to drop the keys right over the side of the steps, deep into the holly bush. 'Oh, Bernard!' Evie was exasperated and frightened. What if the figure in the white car decided to step across the road and introduce themselves? With a knife. The darkness was helping Evie's fear grow, like a mushroom. 'Use *your* keys. QUICKLY!'

'Ah. Yes. Now.' Bernard patted his pockets elaborately.

Evie bit her lip. It probably wouldn't help if she tore all his clothes off but that was what she wanted to do. She darted an anxious glance across the road.

'Here we are!' Bernard flourished a key-ring. It looked like something a pantomime jailer might carry. 'I inherited Mother's,' he explained.

'JUST OPEN THE DOOR!'

The laborious task of trying every key began. Evie was jogging on the spot with fear.

Footsteps sounded on the path, and she yelped as a figure strode purposefully into the circle of porch light. 'Bing! Thank God!'

'That's better than your usual oh-it's-you. What's going on?'

'He's full of Guinness, I've lost my keys and there's a stalker watching us so *open the door*!'

'You're not staying in here all night,' said Bing firmly. Evie was at the end of his bed, cradling a mug of hot chocolate. 'You'll get me a bad reputation. I don't want accusations of heterosexuality levelled at me.'

'I'm worried about the stalker.'

'Give me strength,' Bing beseeched the ceiling. 'Why have you decided it's a stalker? At the moment it's just someone sitting in a car. We've only got Bernard's word for it that they were here before. Frankly, with that hair and those trousers, he's got enough troubles.'

Evie wasn't listening. 'Do you think it could be someone who saw the Toby ad? Someone who's now obsessed with me?'

Bing groaned. 'Why does it have to be about *you*? Why can't it be someone else's stalker?'

'It was only a theory,' Evie said huffily.

'How's this for a theory? *You're deranged.* Now get off my bed. If the stalker jumps you just scream and I'll write to the police straight away. Goodnight.'

'Goodnight,' said Evie, but she didn't move.

Bing burrowed under the covers and squirmed like a maggot in an effort to evict Evie.

'Aden's not very happy with me,' said Evie abruptly.

'Oh?' Bing stopped squirming. 'How come?'

'He had a right go at me. Some rubbish about the way I treat Bernard, saying I manipulate him and that I only try to help him 'cos I'm power-crazed.' She cast a sideways glance in Bing's direction to gauge his reaction. 'That's not fair, is it?'

'No comment, doll.'

'It's *not* fair. I'm not horrible.' Evie yawned. 'Can't I sleep with you?'

'*Never* say that again.' Bing shuddered. 'How do you feel about Aden having a go at you?'

The question was unexpected. 'I feel . . . strange.'

'More detail, young lady.'

'OK. Let's see. I feel . . . If I'm honest I feel a bit – a *little* bit – upset because Aden's opinion of me has gone down and he's such a nice, decent person.' Evie nodded. 'Yup, that's how I feel. Aden's a bit of a Goody-two-shoes and he can be a party-pooper, but I like him. And now he thinks I'm a bitch.' Evie did one of her sudden about-turns. 'Sod him.'

'If I tell you something that will surprise you about Aden will you go to bed like a good girl?'

'No.'

'Then you'll never know.' Bing nestled under the covers again.

'Fine by me.' Evie slurped the last of the chocolate, then said tetchily, 'All right, I promise.'

Bing sat up, plumped his pillows and began. 'This revelation is in two parts,' he began, thoroughly enjoying himself. 'The first part is, Aden put you up for *The Setting of the Sun*.'

Evie puckered her brow. 'No, he didn't.'

'Ho ho, yes, he did. One of the chorus in *Joseph* works part-time in Hugh James's office. Apparently Hugh James always employs Aden for his projects. Aden came in one day and suggested you as Hepsibah. Said you were a star in the making.'

'Sheesh.' Evie was knocked out. 'Why didn't he tell me?' Vague feelings of guilt swirled in her. 'I went on and on about it. Shit, Bing, he went to all that trouble for me and now he thinks I'm a cow! I feel awful.'

'Stop bleating. We're coming to the second part of the revelation.'

'I'm still trying to absorb the first part. Why on earth did he keep it a secret?'

'Because, and this is the second part of my revelation, *he's mad about you*.'

Now, Evie was as vain as the next girl, and occasionally had fits of self-delusion worthy of Sacha, but she laughed at this. 'No, he isn't! You're crazy!'

'I've always known it. It's in the way he looks at you.'

'He looks at everyone like that. He's got a sweet face.'

'Nope. I'm telling you, doll. Aden is nuts about you.'

Evie had plenty of evidence to shore up her case for the defence. 'But he encouraged me to go out with Dan. He even covered up for him about going to Spain.'

'That's Aden all over. He was doing his duty as a mate, even though it hurt.'

'Bollocks,' said Evie plainly. 'If he fancied me surely he'd have made sure I knew that he suggested me for Hepsibah.'

'How come you spend so much time talking about men and

yet understand them only a *little* better than you understand quantum physics? Let me explain. Aden is a decent, modest guy. You have never given him the tiniest scrap of encouragement. In fact, you've made it quite plain that you consider him to be an also-ran: nice, reliable, safe, *unsexy*. Aden doesn't think he has a hope in hell with you. He didn't tell Hugh James about you to curry favour with you, he did it to help you, because he cares about you. Because he's one of those rare things, a genuinely nice guy.'

Cowed by this speech, Evie stared at Bing. Had she really been so blind? If Aden had feelings for her the whole texture of their friendship changed. 'But why hasn't he ever made a move if he's so crazy about me? We've spent a lot of time together and he never ever—' She stopped short. The almost-kiss in his car. She was silent.

'I like you like this,' said Bing. 'So, the sixty-four-million-dollar question is, how do you feel about Aden now?'

'Why should this change anything?' said Evie, with a hint of her old defiance. 'He's still dull and pompous and a killjoy.'

'Oh, grow up,' said Bing vehemently. 'I have a low boredom threshold and I don't find him dull. He's thoughtful, intelligent and makes you laugh. He doesn't twitter on like an imbecile or bury you under a mountain of compliments, but that doesn't mean he's boring. As for being a killjoy – wasn't he dead right when he warned you about Dan? If you're frank with yourself, isn't he dead right about the way you treat Bernard?'

There was no answer from the end of the bed.

20

Early morning wasn't a time of day with which Evie was too familiar. 'Go back to bed,' said Bing, in place of the more traditional 'Good morning'. The flat was his domain until ten a.m., he informed her brusquely. He liked reading the paper and partaking of a dippy egg in solitude.

'I'm discombobulated,' Evie said, shuffling about, filling the kettle and putting the last slice of bread in the toaster. 'I don't know what to think.'

'Why don't you think about going back to bed and leaving me in peace?'

'But the discombobulation is all your fault. If you hadn't told me that Aden likes me I'd be fine. I'd be snoring happily instead of showing you how crap I look in the morning.'

'You don't look crap, you look beautiful. Mind you, I have an awful lot of sleep in my eyes.'

'Where's the teapot?'

'In the sink.'

'Oh, God, don't we ever wash up?'

'No, we never do.'

Evie turned and leant against the sink, arms folded. 'Do you want to know what my real problem is?'

'Apart from all the very obvious ones? No.'

Evie took this as encouragement to go on. 'Now I don't know how I really feel about Aden. I didn't fancy him before last night so how come I have a kind of sneaky little twinkle for him today? Is it only because you said he fancies *me*?'

Bing shut the newspaper with a gesture of resignation. 'Maybe you have a twinkle for him because you've finally realised he's very fanciable. Aden's a nice-looking guy. I should know, I'm an expert.'

'So *you* fancy him?'

'No, you fool. I'm a real pouf, not a stereotype. I don't just fancy any man. Aden's much too heterosexual for me to bother my devastatingly handsome head about. Everybody who meets him thinks he's an absolute cutie except you.'

'That's true,' replied Evie wonderingly. Both Beth and Sacha had made noises about his looks.

'If you'd had any sense at all you'd have gone for him right from the start, instead of dastardly Dan.'

'Him!' sneered Evie, nimbly forgetting the hours she'd spent swooning over him.

'You've got no taste.'

'You might be right.' Evie drifted back to her room.

Bing returned to his egg.

The car was there again. Sacha had given the driver a surreptitious once-over as she arrived. 'It's definitely a person. It's wearing dark glasses and I couldn't tell whether it was a man or a woman. Or a big child,' she added, as an afterthought.

Bing tutted scornfully. 'How could a *big child* drive itself here? Dear God.'

'All right, sorry,' said Sacha, affronted. 'I'm only trying to help.'

'He didn't mean to be horrible.' Evie pinched Bing's bum hard before he could insist that, yes, he did. 'Our nerves are on edge. It's an eerie sensation, knowing a stranger's watching you. If only we could work out who it is. Think!'

'I hope it's not some ex-lover with a grudge,' said Bing anxiously.

'Jesus, we'd never narrow down a list like that,' groaned Evie.

'Please God it's nothing to do with me,' said Sacha, looking distressed. 'I'd feel so guilty if I'd brought a stalker to your home.'

Bing closed his eyes and said, with strained patience, 'And why, pray, would *your* stalker be watching *our* house?'

'Who can tell what goes on in their crazy minds?' mused Sacha philosophically.

'Whoever it is, it just has to be *bad*, doesn't it?' reasoned Evie. 'I mean, nobody sits outside your house wearing dark glasses for days on end to give you good news, do they?'

'Maybe,' suggested Bing, 'he's something to do with P. Warnes.' The girls made no reply but stayed very still. 'You remember P. Warnes, don't you, ladies? The tenant you exorcised so efficiently a little while ago?'

The faint sounds of a threshing-machine could be heard from the top floor.

'I don't think it's anything to do with P. Warnes,' said Evie decisively.

'Neither do I,' agreed Sacha. 'I must get back to Calmer Karma. I've reduced all the tarot cards by an eighth so I'm expecting a rush.'

'Hang on. I'll put on my flip-flops and see you out. Just in case.' Evie slipped into her bedroom, annoyed that their mystery voyeur was unsettling them all. 'An Englishwoman's home is her castle,' she muttered, poking about with her toes in the accumulated debris strewn under her bed. Two flip-flops were retrieved, both lefts but they would do to escort Sacha off the premises.

Suddenly a dusty smell, sweet yet old, swamped Evie's senses. She closed her eyes and inhaled deeply. It was a nostalgic scent, provoking a vague memory just round the corner of her mind . . . She opened her eyes wide. It was the smell of Belle's big black leather handbag that Evie had played with as a child.

The aroma was fading, ebbing like a wave sliding down the shore. Evie strained after it, but it dissolved.

Oh, Belle, she thought, thank you. Everything was going to be OK. This was Belle's house and Belle was still watching over them all.

*   *   *

Rehearsals would start on 1 September, Meredith informed Evie. Shooting would take eight weeks. The stars were Anna Friel and Toby Stephens. The fee was, well, wonderful.

After hopping about, screaming and burping for some time after this call, Evie realised she'd be able to get the front of the house painted.

'Beth!' Evie hadn't expected to see her sister on the doorstep. 'Get inside. Quickly!' She tugged her sister over the threshold and slammed the front door. 'We've got a stalker.'

'You really are the girl with everything.'

When she was sitting beside Beth on the sofa, Evie said in a rush, 'I'm sorry. I'm so sorry. And I'm sorry I didn't ring to say sorry. I shouldn't have made a scene at Mum's.'

'It's all right.' Beth smiled sadly. 'And that really is the least of my troubles. To be honest, I don't even know what you said.'

'Oh.' Evie was relieved to be off the hook. 'Why are you here, then, if not to duff me up?'

'To see if you can help me.'

This was obviously about more than twin-sitting. 'I hope I can.' Evie was aware that she didn't have much to offer someone as mature and organised as her sister, but she'd do her best.

'The you-know-what has really hit the fan in Henley,' said Beth. Her interlocked fingers writhed in her lap. 'I've told Marcus I want a divorce. He's rather . . . unhappy about it.'

'Serves him right.'

'*Please* don't talk like that. He won't get out of the house so I have to. I can't live a lie any longer. That's where you come in. Is there any chance of a flat here for me and the twins?'

Why couldn't Beth have asked her a question she could say 'yes' to? Evie wondered. She wanted to help, but she couldn't.

'It wouldn't be for long, just until we work out the financial settlement. Please, Evie?'

Evie spread her hands. 'The flats are all occupied.' She shook her head. 'I can't help.'

Beth nodded. 'I just . . . Well, it was worth a try.'

'But you can stay with Bing and me,' exclaimed Evie. 'The twins are small, we can tuck them in on the sofa. You and I can share my bed. We'll be fine!'

Beth was laughing and shaking her head. 'That's so sweet,' she said, 'but I have to give the twins some stability. That means beds of their own in a room of their own. Thanks for the offer, though.'

Evie was warmed by her sister's gratitude and relieved by her refusal. It would have been a bit of a squeeze.

Beth sat back and wiped her eyes. 'I'd better get out there and start flat-hunting. Bea's helping me. She can work miracles when she puts her mind to it.'

'When did Bea lose the "auntie"?' asked Evie.

'I can't call her "auntie" now, can I?' said Beth, and laughed.

'I'll always call her Auntie Bea,' said Evie stubbornly.

'That's different,' smiled Beth. 'I'm planning to live in London, so as soon as I'm settled you must bring the delicious Dan round. You can baby-sit and snog on the sofa all night.'

'Eh? Oh. Yes!' Evie remembered, with a start, that Beth thought Aden was Dan. She also thought he was Evie's boyfriend. And, apparently, she thought he was delicious.

Two days earlier Evie had called Aden without thinking twice about it. She'd simply picked up the phone and dialled. Now she stared at her mobile as if it held the secret of the universe. She didn't know what to say and she didn't know how to say it.

Would Aden be pleased to hear from her? Bing was lobbying hard for her to ask him over for a drink. 'You can take it from there,' he advised. But Bing's analysis might have been wrong. It had happened before: he'd once slept with a bus conductor in the belief that he was Sting. She hadn't heard from Aden since he'd made his feelings clear about her treatment of Bernard. Maybe he'd gone off her.

As for how Evie felt about Aden – that had become a complex brew indeed.

'Oh, for God's sake!' expostulated Bing. He reached over and snatched the phone. He looked up the number in Evie's address book and jabbed at the digits. 'It's ringing. Here.' He thrust the phone back at her.

Heart pounding, Evie heard the answer-phone click on. Thank goodness. Now she had time to calm herself and compose an elegant, witty message. The beep sounded. 'Ooh. Hello. Yes. It's me. By me I mean Evie. Hello! Erm, just ringing to say, well, hello, really. And how are you? And that's . . . about . . . it, really. Give me a ring. 'Bye! But only if you want to. Ring me I mean. Good—' The second beep sounded. Evie beat her head on the worktop. Why was it all so awkward now?

Taking Bernard out and showing him to the lay-deez was a two-woman job and Sacha was glad to help out. She felt it would be instrumental in helping him to get over his feelings for her. And, besides, 'I've got this fantastic book, a dating self-help manual. We'll follow it to the letter.'

'How do you know it's fantastic?' asked Evie, as she tapped her slingbacks in the hall, waiting impatiently for Bernard to appear.

'It's by those people on that television show about finding a perfect partner.'

'Right. Must be fantastic, then. BERNARD! COME ON!'

There was a clamour on the next landing. Bernard bustled down like the White Rabbit, scattering sorrys and forgive-mes as he came.

'Turn round.' Evie sighed.

'Pardon?' Bernard stopped, one pale hand on the banister.

'Look down at your legs.'

'Oh dear. That's right. You said no leather trousers.'

'Quite. They won't be able to hear the chat-up lines above the creaking.'

A few minutes later, suitably trousered in dark denim, Bernard followed his guides out into the warm evening. 'Where are you taking me?' he asked, evidently terrified of the reply.

'A drink or two round the corner, then on to Manhattan Dreams,' Evie informed him.

'*Manhattan* Dreams? In Camden?' queried Bernard.

'Yup. Don't worry. It's better than it sounds.' This was a lie. Manhattan Dreams was even worse than it sounded. Evie and Sacha had plumped for it on the grounds that it guaranteed a plentiful supply of young women, many of them drunk enough to be impressed by Bernard.

'How are you feeling?' Evie was giving Bernard a motherly once-over by the glow of the flickering sign that spelt out Manhattan Dreams.

'I'm feeling . . . determined.' Bernard balled his slender hands into fists.

'That's my boy.' Evie flicked some fluff off his collar.

'But I want to go home.'

'Not an option, Bernard.' Evie was touched by his timidity. 'We're here to look after you. It'll be *fun*.'

'Yes.' Bernard smiled unconvincingly, like a condemned man attempting to enjoy his last meal.

Sacha kissed his cheek, and a tidal wave of crimson engulfed his face. 'Forget me,' she whispered huskily. 'There are plenty of other fish in the nightclub.'

So, puzzled as well as scared witless, Bernard stumbled into the world of Manhattan Dreams.

Seated on an itchy red banquette, sipping from drinks bristling with tiny umbrellas, Evie, Sacha and Bernard peered down at the book on their laps, which was lit by the beams from the flickering multicoloured lightshow.

They don't make clubs like Manhattan Dreams any more. Untouched since it sprang to life in the eighties, it had a tiny dance-floor lit from beneath. The glossy bar was long and sticky, manned by pimply boys resplendent in red waistcoats and limp silver bow-ties. Sickly palms sprouted from dark corners, bending over the heads of local girls dressed to the nines. Now punters were outnumbered by the prowling simian bouncers, barely contained by their dinner jackets and barking self-importantly into their walkie-talkies. By midnight the place would be packed.

'What a dump,' said Sacha, under her breath.

'It's perfect.' Evie adored nightclubs. She liked their tackiness and the opportunity they offered to watch swarms of humans behaving badly. For her, the kitscher the better. 'I couldn't stand it if we took him somewhere cool. This is going to be a scream.'

'You're right. It's perfect.' Sometimes Sacha was just too easy to persuade. She struggled to make out the text of the book: '"The three vital ingredients in any attempt at chatting up,"' she read, '"are as follows."'

'Are you listening, Bernard?' chided Evie.

'Yes. Just, please, can we stop calling it chatting up?'

'Why?'

'It's so . . . It doesn't sound like something I'd do.' Bernard put down his Long Slow Screw Up Against A Wall. 'I spoke to Mother every day but, really, you two are my only female friends. I'm not sure I could engage another lady in deep conversation, especially not *chat her up*.'

'Aaah, Bernard.' Evie squeezed his arm, but gently so she didn't alarm him. 'It's so nice to know that you think of us as friends. And if we are your friends, trust us. You don't have to find a girlfriend tonight, think of it as dipping your toe in the water.'

'Yes. Toe. Water.' Bernard rocked, his hands jammed between his knees. 'All right.'

Sacha cleared her throat and carried on, rather louder than

before. The club was filling up and the shaven-headed DJ had turned up the volume. '"The three vital ingredients are, one, confidence."'

Evie and Sacha exchanged a glance over Bernard's head. 'Have another sip of your drink,' Evie counselled him. 'At least that'll be Dutch courage.'

'"Two, ask your chosen target about themselves."'

'Now that *is* good advice. Everyone loves to talk about themselves,' said Evie.

'What kind of questions?' Bernard was panic-stricken. 'I can't ask a lady personal questions.'

'You don't start off with her bra size,' Evie told him. 'Use your imagination. Where does she work? Where does she live? Does she like this music?'

'Does she come here often?' Sacha suggested.

'Oh dear.' Having heard about the second vital ingredient Bernard was even more lacking in the first.

Sacha ploughed on: '"Three, be aware of your body language."'

'My body language?' yelped Bernard, looking down at his legs as if they were about to betray him. 'What's that?'

'Hang on. I'm just finding the relevant chapter.'

Evie noticed a dark-haired guy staring at them. She dropped her eyes, then cast a surreptitious glance his way. He was still looking.

'Here we are.' Sacha scanned the page, then précised the advice for Bernard. 'Apparently you must lick or touch your lips a lot. That's a clear sexual signal.'

'A sexual signal?' spluttered Bernard. 'I'm not altogether sure I want to send a clear sexual signal.'

'It's subtle, Bernard. Just a little lick. Like this. You try it,' encouraged Evie.

Bernard darted his tongue out like a lizard.

'Hmm. Well, we can work on that.' Evie peeked slyly at the dark-haired guy. His eyes were still on them.

'Try to put your hands on your hips,' said Sacha, 'and thrust your genital area at the girl.'

'I'm going home.'

Evie and Sacha dragged Bernard back into his seat.

'What Sacha meant was just lean *that bit* of you ever so gently in the girl's direction.'

'She makes it sound like pornography!' Bernard was almost in tears.

'Not at all. I meant like this.' Sacha stood up, put her hands on her hips and inclined her own *that bit* at him. This did little to ease Bernard's distress as it was roughly level with his face.

'Move on, move on,' ordered Evie. The dark-haired boy raised his glass to her and she covered her face with her hair.

'Mirroring is another important thing, apparently. That means copying what the girl is doing. If she leans to the right, so do you. If she crosses her legs, so do you,' Sacha explained.

'But why?' asked Bernard, bemused.

'Don't question the manual!' Sacha slapped the cover of the cheap paperback, which had somehow achieved the status of the Bible. 'Just mirror!'

Evie was keen to get started. 'Look around you, Bernard. See anybody nice?'

'I think I need another drink.'

'Good idea.' Sacha leapt up. 'I'll get us three more cocktails. Different ones this time.'

Evie studied Bernard. She'd seen that look before: Henry on Bonfire Night. Aden's accusations, buried in the excitement, clamoured to be heard again. He hadn't called her back. The thought stung. Where was Sacha with those drinks? She whispered to Bernard, 'If you want to go home, just say the word.'

Bernard looked at her as if he couldn't believe his ears. 'Really?'

'Of course!' She laughed.

His shoulders sank again. 'No. You're right to make me do

this. I've got to start somewhere. And you've gone to so much trouble. I'm staying.'

'Attaboy.'

It was eleven o'clock. Sprawled on the banquette in a posture of hopelessness, Evie was saying, with synthetic calm, 'There must be *somebody* you like the look of, Bernard.'

Sacha, who had more energy than Evie and had downed several strange blue concoctions, pointed at a girl gyrating on the dance-floor in a fringed skirt. 'Her. What about her?'

'She's too . . . thoughtful.' Bernard had almost exhausted the wealth of adjectives the dictionary had to offer. The girl with a blonde crop was 'too careless'. The one in the sparkly slash neck was 'too cunning'. Another, in denim shorts, was 'too haughty', and a fourth with a Piña Colada in both hands was 'too winsome'. Anyone would have thought that Bernard was trying to wriggle out of the whole thing.

The dark-haired guy was still looking over. He and his gaggle of mates had migrated nearer. They were two banquettes away, growing braver with each pint.

Evie decided to take matters into her own hands. 'Bernard, *she* is perfect.'

A girl was sitting alone, awkwardly, on a low pouffe a few feet away, scanning the dance-floor shyly. She seemed a little removed from the action, which was what made her 'perfect' for Bernard's first foray into the realm of chatting up.

Bernard surveyed her with trepidation. She was pretty but with none of the sparkly makeup favoured by the other girls. He took a deep breath. 'How shall I begin?' he murmured.

'Introduce yourself and ask if you can sit down,' instructed Evie.

'Right. Right.' Bernard nodded.

Sacha butted in: 'Remember, be confident, ask her about herself, and body language.' She was slurring slightly.

'Right.' Bernard put his hands on his hips.

'Not yet!' Evie batted them away. 'When you're standing up. Now, no more thinking. *Do it!*'

Bernard stood up, smoothed back the various lengths of his alarming hair and walked over to the girl on the pouffe.

Evie and Sacha propelled themselves to the end of their banquette and leaned in to eavesdrop on Bernard's endeavours.

The dark-haired guy and one of his mates broke away from their gang to alight on the far end of Evie's seat. She noticed this out of the corner of her eye and smirked inwardly.

Bernard bent over the pouffe girl, who jolted backwards. 'Hello, I'm Bernard Briggs,' he shouted, sticking out his hand.

'I'm Cathy.' The girl went pink as she shook it.

'Body language,' hissed Sacha, in a discreet aside that could have been heard in the toilets.

Bernard attached his hands to his hips and poked his groin rather close to Cathy's nose. 'What do you do for a living?' he barked, with all the charm of a Nazi interrogator.

A voice from behind Evie interrupted her surveillance: 'All right, ladies? Mind if we join you?'

Evie turned and looked into the really rather brown eyes of the dark-haired bloke. 'It's a free country,' she said sassily.

'Ssssh!' Sacha pulled at Evie to get her back to watching Bernard.

Evie rolled her eyes at the dark-haired guy, and turned to see the girl looking uncertainly at Bernard, who was saying brusquely, 'May I sit down?'

'I'm Gareth, by the way.' The boy had shuffled closer to Evie. He cocked his head on one side. 'Do I get to know your name?'

'Guess,' said Evie, feeling coquettish.

'Liz, as in Hurley? Pamela, as in Anderson?'

'Look, look! Shit!' Sacha was murmuring urgently.

Evie dragged her attention back to Bernard. Cathy, who was apparently as shy and awkward as he was, had agreed to let him sit down. Bernard, alarmed by his own success, had looked round wildly for another chair but there was none to be seen, so he was attempting to make Cathy budge up so that he could join her on the pouffe, which had definitely been built for one.

'Dear God,' marvelled Evie.

'Marilyn, as in Monroe?' persisted Gareth.

The only way to fit two bums on the pouffe was to sit back to back. Folded up like a stick insect, Bernard was shouting over his shoulder, 'What's your favourite food?'

'What?' yelled Cathy in reply.

'What?' roared Bernard.

'I can go if you'd rather,' said Gareth good-humouredly. 'It's not much fun talking to the back of someone's head.'

'Sorry.' Evie smiled her best, widest smile. She wanted Gareth to stay. It was a long time since she had been eyed up in a nightclub. He fitted her bad-boy template far more accurately than Aden did. For some reason Evie felt the need to blot Aden out. She had done nothing but think about him for the last twenty-four hours. Did he fancy her? Did she fancy him? Whenever she attempted to analyse her feelings she felt as if she was unravelling damp knitting. 'I'm Evie and this is Sacha.'

At the mention of her name Sacha swivelled round and yapped, 'Where did you spring from?'

Gareth's friend, evidently earmarked for her in some secret guy-arrangement, asked, 'You girls fancy a bevvy?'

They did, of course, and while Gareth and his friend battled to the bar, Evie said firmly, 'We've got to put Cathy and Bernard out of their misery.'

Still facing away from Cathy, Bernard was now bawling, 'No, sorry, I said *what's your favourite food*?'

Evie stalked over to them and said brightly, 'There you are, Bernard! Come back and join us, you naughty boy!' She grasped him firmly by the hand, yanked him up and mouthed, 'Sorry!' at Cathy, who looked relieved.

'Hmm. Not too good, was it?' Bernard mopped his sweating brow.

'It was a start,' Evie encouraged him. 'Next time just try to make sure you're facing the girl you're talking to.'

'It will help,' said Sacha sagely.

'Does there have to be a next time?'

'Courage, Bernard Briggs!' Sacha gripped him by the shoulders. 'There's a sexy piece all on her own over there with a whole free seat beside her. Go!'

Bernard set off like a shaky Exocet.

'Way to go, Sash,' said Evie admiringly.

'I have to help him.' Sacha's face clouded. 'I'll never forgive myself if he pines for me for the rest of his life.'

Evie was tipsy enough to put her right on this, but Gareth and his mate swooped in with luminous cocktails.

'Cheers!' All four clinked glasses, but as Evie and Sacha knocked theirs back they were watching the seat opposite.

'He's sitting down,' whispered Evie, out of the side of her mouth.

'She's chattering to him!' Sacha said softly. 'Bingo!' They high-fived each other.

'Why aren't you two dancing?' asked Gareth. His arm was arranged casually along the back of the banquette. He was in no need of a manual.

'Not in the mood. We're just . . . chilling out.' The flirtatious eye-contact was doing Evie the world of good.

Sacha wasn't too good at flirting. She preferred the more direct approach. 'You needn't think you're going to get a snog,' she informed Gareth's mate. 'We're here on a mission. We don't have time.'

Evie's insides contracted. Why did Sacha have to wear conversational hobnail boots all the time?

'Didn't want a snog,' mumbled Gareth's mate, affronted.

'I do,' said Gareth, close to Evie's ear.

'Like I said, we're chilling out.' Evie smiled, hopefully in a way that was encouraging but not *too* encouraging. Gareth wasn't quite blotting out Aden.

Yet.

Opposite, Bernard was gazing intently at the pretty brunette while she nattered happily, gesticulating freely.

'He's not saying much.' Sacha frowned.

'He's fascinated by her!' Evie was delighted. 'He's pulled! They've clicked!'

Gareth's mate muttered, 'Lucky bastard.' He was now facing away from Sacha, staring moodily at the dance-floor.

'You smell nice.' Gareth sniffed the air close to Evie's neck. 'What is it?'

The truthful answer was Sainsbury's own-label bath gel, but in a bid to appear mysterious, Evie said, 'Chanel No. 5.'

'Classy.' Gareth raised his cocktail to his lips.

The brunette opposite jumped up, gesturing at Bernard to stay put. She tripped off in the direction of the ladies'.

Evie and Sacha beckoned to Bernard excitedly.

'Well?' said Evie.

'Well?' said Sacha.

Bernard seemed afraid to speak. Eventually he said, 'I can't understand a word she's saying. She's foreign.'

Evie groaned. 'Why are you sitting there if you can't understand her?' Bernard's meekness knew no bounds.

'It would be impolite to leave.'

Sacha tutted. 'She'll understand. It's the cut-and-thrust of the dating game. All's fair in love and nightclubs.'

Evie was in complete accord. 'Cut your losses. She left you to go to the loo. Don't be there when she gets back. Be *there*.' She pointed at a red-haired girl standing by a pillar, looking bored.

'She's got nice hair,' conceded Bernard.

'Off you go.'

And off he went. Henry-like, thought Evie ruefully.

The girl seemed grateful for the distraction. She shook Bernard's hand warmly. As far as Evie and Sacha could ascertain, she was speaking English.

Evie sat back. 'What's a nice boy like you doing in a place like this?' she asked Gareth.

'Hoping to meet a nice girl like you.'

'She's not nice, mate,' said a voice so close behind them that they jumped and spilt their drinks.

'Bing!' He was kneeling behind them, his perfect teeth gleaming like a wolf's.

'Sorry, mate. Sorry.' Gareth removed his arm at warp speed and scooted off down the cushions.

'Oh, get yourself back here,' said Bing impatiently. 'I'm her lodger, not her boyfriend.'

Gareth scurried back, but not as close as before.

'What are you doing here?' asked Evie, as Bing perched his iron-hard buns on the low table in front of her. 'Come to help with Bernard?'

'Looks like he's getting on just fine.'

'We're pleased with his progress,' said Evie, headmistress-like.

Bing obscured her view of the little foreigner who had returned not from the ladies' but from the bar. She was standing, puzzled, looking about her with a drink in each hand.

Bernard had his hands on his hips, as instructed. His groin was tilted delicately. He was the perfect pupil.

Sacha wasn't satisfied, though. She leaned on Gareth's mate's shoulders and screeched, 'Mirror! Mirror!' at Bernard.

'Leave him alone. He's fine.' Evie was glad to note that Gareth had recovered enough to put his arm back.

'He *must* mirror! The book says so!'

Gareth's mate was frantically trying to catch Gareth's eye, but Gareth steadfastly ignored him.

Bernard looked puzzled over the redhead's shoulder, but then the penny dropped and he gave Evie and Sacha a sneaky thumbs-up.

Bing appraised Manhattan Dreams. 'Nothing much here for me,' he complained. 'It's a temple to heterosexuality. I feel like an alcoholic in a dairy.'

Behind him, the brunette had spotted Bernard. He had not guessed that she was Spanish, but he might have done if she'd been pawing the ground and huffing angrily as she was now. However, he was oblivious to her, busy mirroring the redhead's actions. Sacha smiled benevolently but Evie cringed; he was mirroring a little too slavishly. The girl touched her hair: so did Bernard. The girl put her head on one side: so did Bernard. The girl sneezed: so did Bernard.

'He's trying too hard,' Evie whispered to Sacha.

'It's working!' Sacha had great confidence in the book.

The Spanish girl downed her drink in one gulp. She shot Bernard a murderous look, and knocked back the one she'd bought for him. Then she wrapped her arms round herself and tapped her foot ominously, never taking her small black eyes off him.

Gareth's mate was reduced to semaphore. He was desperate to leave: Sacha was ignoring him in favour of monitoring Bernard.

Over by the pillar, Bernard was working overtime. He had folded his arms now because the redhead had. One foot was pointed awkwardly, just like one of hers.

A noise caught the attention of Gareth, Evie, Bing, Sacha and even Gareth's increasingly morose mate. It came from behind Bing and was a loud snort, denoting final loss of rag by a small Spaniard.

She hurtled towards Bernard. In front of the five shocked faces on the banquette she slapped him hard across his face.

They all held their breath.

Bernard slapped her back.

All hell broke loose. Security men lumbered in from all directions. The redhead screamed. The Spaniard *really* screamed. Drunken guys were circling Bernard menacingly, while he spluttered, 'I'm so sorry! I was mirroring. *I was mirroring!*'

Bing was on his feet. 'Look after the bird,' he ordered Evie. 'I have to get Bernard out of here or he'll be torn to pieces.'

Evie rushed over to put her arms round the sobbing Spanish girl and lead her back to their table. She watched Bing, tall and commanding, stride into the middle of what looked like a mob. She couldn't hear what he said but the crowd parted and he escorted Bernard smartly to the exit.

Evie and Sacha petted and soothed the Spaniard, who sat between them, gradually recovering. Gareth's mate had taken the opportunity to disappear. Gareth showed what a good bloke he was by fetching a glass of water and looking concerned.

This is all my fault, was the one thought buzzing in Evie's head.

As soon as they had deposited Sacha at the door of Calmer Karma. Gareth took Evie's hand. 'Let's get you home.' He smiled.

His hand wasn't welcome. Evie would have preferred to be alone. She had checked her mobile, but Aden hadn't got back to her. She felt vaguely shifty, as if he would know somehow about all the trouble she had caused tonight. And, she thought sadly, he would have even less respect for her.

Perhaps the hand wasn't entirely unwelcome.

They strolled along, ears still ringing from the pounding music of Manhattan Dreams.

Gareth was growing braver. He relinquished his hand to snake an arm round Evie's waist.

That felt OK. Or did it? Why am I constantly questioning myself? Evie wondered. Damn Bing and his revelations. She focused on Gareth. He was here and now, and he was uncomplicated. 'What do you do?' She hadn't even asked the basic question with which she'd armed Bernard.

'Maths, chemistry, history.'

'You're a teacher?' Evie was impressed.

'No.' He gave a puzzled laugh. They stopped under a street-lamp.

In the fuzzy glow Evie discerned a couple of spots clustering on Gareth's chin. She saw a tuft of bumfluff on his jawline.

Gareth said, 'I'm doing my—'

'DON'T SAY IT!'

Evie had spent all night flirting with someone who should have been at home revising for his A-levels. She was being held round the waist by a schoolboy. 'I'm old enough to be your . . . big sister.'

'I love older women.' His teenage grasp tightened.

'Older women? I'm twenty-sodding-seven!' Evie struggled.

'Almost thirty! Wow!'

'Surely this is illegal? Does your mother know you're out? Stop that!' Evie tussled with her underage suitor. He was very strong. 'What do they put in school dinners these days?'

21

'And how is the seductress of *Grange Hill* this morning?' asked Bing, as Evie shuffled, scowling, into the kitchen.

'That's not funny.'

'Oh, but it is.' Bing was warming up for his run by cocking his leg on the kitchen table. 'It's very funny.'

'You're forgotten to put your shorts on.' Evie sat heavily at the table. 'Oh, no. They *are* on.'

Bing's running shorts were legendary. They were a supremely economically cut item of clothing. 'They are a bit brief, aren't they?' he said. 'I'll get changed.'

'What?' Evie was flabbergasted. Soon Bing returned in a proper pair of full-sized running shorts. She hadn't known he owned such a thing.

While he stretched and warmed his muscles Evie asked about Bernard. 'How was he?'

'It took a while to calm him down.' Bing was touching his toes with elastic ease. 'He couldn't believe he'd struck a woman. You know what a gent he is.'

'He was mirroring what she'd done to him. We'd wound him up about it so much he was doing it automatically. It was my fault,' muttered Evie.

'Yup.' Bing did a couple of jumping jacks, rattling the crockery in Belle's old cupboards.

'How did you manage to get him out of Manhattan Dreams? What did you say? There was a lot of steaming testosterone in that club.'

'I said he was on medication and shouldn't be drinking. If you say anything loudly and confidently enough, people believe you.'

'You were very brave,' said Evie, almost shyly. 'Thank God you were there.'

'The difficult bit was getting him to stop crying.'

Evie looked stricken. 'Bernard was crying? That's awful.'

'He hated himself. I'll save you the trouble of saying it – that was your fault too.'

Evie laid her head on the table. It was cool, but it did nothing to help.

Bing kissed the back of her bed hair. 'Don't worry. For some strange reason I still love you, and I'm sure Bernard does too.' He bounded away for his run.

I don't love me, thought Evie miserably. *Look after my tenants*, Belle had said, and Evie had contrived to make one weep with self-loathing *and* almost get thrashed by a drunken mob.

'Postie has something for you!' yelled Bing, from the front door.

Oh, thought Evie dully. She dragged herself up the stairs.

On the mat, holding a large envelope, stood Aden.

'You're not Postie.' Evie sucked in her tummy and put one hand up to the matted fright wig that was her hair. She wished she'd bothered to check herself in the mirror – she was almost certain she had mascara tracks down to her knees.

'That's true. I did meet him on the steps, though, and he had this for you.' He handed over the envelope at arm's length. 'Looks like your script.'

'Ooh.' Despite the recent memory of tussling with a minor and being the worst landlady ever, a spark of excitement ignited inside her. 'Brilliant.' She paused. 'Did you get my message?'

'Yeah. That's why I'm here.'

'Right.' It was hard to act normal when Evie knew she looked like an unmade bed. 'Look, do you want to come downstairs and have some coffee while I tidy myself up?'

'Can't. Don't have time. Really just, you know, popped round.'

'Oh.' So he wanted to get away. But why, Evie asked herself, had he come round if he wanted to get away? Perhaps her dressing-gown had scared him. Bing often said that an eyeful of Evie in the mornings would turn Casanova gay. 'Are we friends again?' she asked impulsively.

Aden's face crinkled. 'Of course we are.'

'I might as well tell you that the whole Bernard night out ended in disaster. You were right. I do treat him like Henry.'

'I don't need to hear that,' said Aden. 'Let's forget it. I was too hard on you anyway.'

'No, you were right. You weren't hard enough on me.' Evie was up to her hips in self-recrimination.

'It doesn't matter. Friends again.'

They grinned at each other.

'I know you got me the part,' Evie plunged in.

Aden peered down at the floor. 'Ah.'

'So . . . thank you.'

'You're welcome.' Aden met her eye sheepishly. 'You deserve it. Enough said.'

Enough had certainly not been said. 'Why didn't you tell me?'

'I felt awkward.' Aden shrugged. 'I don't know, really. I just wanted you to get it.'

'It's the nicest thing anybody's ever done for me,' said Evie simply.

Aden smiled, then turned away.

''Bye,' said Evie, in a soft voice she didn't often use.

Caroline, like a Goth genie, appeared in the hall. 'Me boiler's giving me gyp,' she complained flatly.

Evie would have loved to answer, 'So?' but she heard herself say wearily, 'I'll call a man in.'

'Caroline!' Aden said, with a broad smile. 'Do you want me to take a look at it? I'm good with boilers.' He zipped through the open door.

Just why Evie's lips were so thin is hard to say but it might have had something to do with how beautiful Caroline looked and how keen Aden was to help her out, even though he couldn't stay for coffee with her.

* * *

There was much more mascara smudged over Evie's face than she could recall putting on her lashes. She cleaned it off, pulled a brush through her hair and ran up to flat B.

'He's just gone,' Caroline informed her. 'He fixed it.'

'Good.' Evie noticed how great Caroline's figure looked in her black jeans and black T-shirt. Now she came to think of it, Aden had always admired her, saying she was too good for Bernard. 'Did he say anything?' she asked stupidly.

Caroline gave her an odd look. 'Like what?'

Like he fancies you and not me? With difficulty Evie restrained herself. 'The car isn't there today,' she said instead.

'I don't know anything about a car.' The finality of Caroline's delivery told Evie the conversation was over. So did the shutting of the door.

Reverently Evie slipped the script out of the envelope and placed it on her knee. She laid her hands on it and shut her eyes. Shivering, she savoured the feel of it. Her first television script. She raised a glass of wine. 'Here's to you, Belle. You know how special this is for me.'

As she opened the first page, she chased away all thoughts of Aden and how they might or might not feel about each other. She must focus on the script. She was a professional and this was an important job.

Evie took a deep yogic breath through her nose, then exhaled deeply through her mouth, releasing all her tensions and feeling spiritual calm seep through her. She almost jumped out of her skin when her mobile rang.

'Yes?'

'Evie, my heart is broken.'

'Hello, Mum.' Evie was accustomed to melodramatic openers from her mother, but this promised to be a biggie. 'What's happened?'

'Your sister has gone berserk.'

Aha. 'I know about this, Mum. Try to stay calm.'

'You knew?' Bridgie took a moment off from being heartbroken to be affronted. 'I'm the last to know? Isn't that nice? My own children are keeping secrets from me.'

Evie didn't bother to defend herself.

Bridgie picked up obligingly where she had left off. 'Berserk. That's what she is. Mad. Crazy. Off her bonkers.'

'She does have her reasons.'

'Oh, does she?' spat Bridgie venomously. 'Is it because of her beautiful home? Or her two adorable children? Or her devoted husband?'

So Bridgie didn't know everything. Evie trod carefully, which, for her, was not easy. 'Beth knows what she's doing.'

'Does she know she's breaking poor Marcus's heart? I had that poor man crying all over my conservatory last night. He's wretched, absolutely wretched at losing his marriage.'

'Perhaps if he'd valued it more he might not have lost it.'

'So it's his fault now?' Bridgie screeched.

She was not taking the traditionally partisan approach of the average mother-in-law. She seemed to be entirely on Marcus's side. Evie reckoned she understood why. 'I know you think it's sinful even to consider divorce, Mum, but Beth has to do what's right for her. When you feel really strongly about something you must do it, however other people react.' Consciously or not, Evie was echoing Bea's little homily.

'I'm so *ashamed*.' Bridgie's voice trembled. 'We all saw her get married in church. What am I going to tell the family?'

'Don't tell them anything. It's nobody's business.'

'Do you know how she explained the whole thing to me?' Bridgie's pendulum swung back to fury. 'She said she has to find herself. *Find herself!* She'll find herself in the gutter if she's not careful.'

Evie found her mother unbearable in wrathful-suburban-matron mode. She stayed schtum while a lot more ordure poured over her, until her mother amazed her by saying, 'Thank God we have you. At least we can hold our heads up over you.'

'Eh?' Until now Evie had been more of a family burden than a serial-killing grandma would have represented. 'What do you mean?'

'You're doing so well. You're going to be in a nice thing on the telly and you've found yourself a presentable young man. I always knew you'd make something of yourself.'

This was too much. Since Evie had been old enough to decipher language she had listened to Bridgie prophesy various bad ends for her. It was even worse hearing her heap unmerited praise on her head. 'Look, Mum, I have to tell you something. I'm not seeing Dan any more.'

'Holy Mother of Jesus, this family is cursed. Why not?'

'Pressure of work.'

'And what does that mean?'

'It means work, and its, er, pressures. It's complicated. I really have to go now, Mum.'

'Hold on!' ordered Bridgie. 'Your father wants a word.'

As the phone was handed over she heard her mother say, 'Don't breathe too heavily in the mouthpiece, dear. It makes it greasy.'

With the tiniest long-suffering sigh, John was on the line. 'Hello, sweetheart.'

'Dad.'

'This is a sad business, kid. A very sad business.' He sounded tired. 'I didn't see it coming.'

'That's 'cos Beth was so careful to hide it, Dad. None of us realised. Don't be hard on yourself. She has to do this on her own.'

'I have to reproach myself. All I want is for you girls to be happy . . .' John seemed to pick himself up. 'Listen to me, mithering on. It's done now and we must make the best of it. I asked her to come here for a while but she was having none of it. Such an independent lady, our Beth.'

Evie could hear pride in her father's voice, mingled with worry. He sounded so much older than usual.

He carried on: 'And so are you.'

'S'pose I am.' Evie had never thought about it before.

'You see what you want and you go for it. I admire that, pet. The only trouble is, life offers so many choices, these days, it's working out what you want that's the real problem.'

'You've just hit so many nails right on their heads, Dad.'

John raised his voice: 'What's that you say, Evie? A nude scene in *The Setting of the Sun*?'

Amid the screams and wails this provoked, Evie giggled. 'See you, Dad,' she said, and put the phone down.

Too many choices. How true. Evie was strung up like a cat's cradle trying to dissect her feelings about Aden.

It's more than friendship. She was sure of that.

I think about him all the time. She couldn't even get through the washing-up without his face flitting across her mind. Had she given as much brain space to him before Bing's revelation? She had to admit that she hadn't. She'd thought he wasn't her type – too fair, not enough muscle.

Now, though, things were different. Standing in the hall he had seemed changed, transformed, supercharged. His fair hair was silky, inviting her touch. His greenish eyes weren't pale any more: they sparkled.

I fancy Aden. Evie wasn't confused any more. *Not because I've been told he fancies me but because I've realised he's a damn fine man*.

Most importantly, he was not a bad boy. *That* cycle was broken.

'I hate Sundays,' mewled Evie, bundled up in a duvet on the sofa. 'It's ten years since I left school but I still get the nagging feeling that I haven't done my homework.'

'Know just what you mean.' Bing was under a duvet on the armchair.

Outside the sky glowered and cast a pall of gloom over London. After weeks of scorching heat it was a shock.

'I feel all premenstrual,' she muttered.

'Me too,' said Bing companionably.

'I really should be reading my script.'

'I wish you'd stop saying that. Why don't you just bloody read it instead of talking about it?'

'I don't feel well.'

'Bollocks.'

'Thank you, Doctor.' Evie kicked listlessly at the duvet.

'Stop sighing,' ordered Bing. 'I can't concentrate on my reading.'

'It's only a tabloid.'

'A very important publication.' Bing shook out the inky pages importantly. 'How else could I find out which newsreaders like to be whipped and which footballers like fake boobs?'

'What is it with footballers and false tits?' pondered Evie. 'Every single one will risk everything for half an hour in a hotel room with somebody named Cheryl with 42GGs and duck lips.'

'Not my Becks.' Bing smiled serenely. 'He's a one-woman man.'

'We all know the next bit – *until he meets you*.'

'Becks's legs . . . I could write poetry about them.'

'Read me the problems.'

'Can't be bothered. They're not much cop. One should-I-have-a-threesome, one I'm-in-love-with-my-boss and one my-penis-is-so-small-girls-mistake-it-for-a-grape.'

'Rubbish. What's the photo casebook?'

'It's about a girl who's having sex with her brother-in-law every time her husband goes away. Terrible green bra and panties, cellulite like porridge oats.'

'Let's see!' said Evie avidly. She was always happy to examine other women's cellulite.

Bing tossed over the appropriate page.

'Make us a cup of tea,' wheedled Evie.

'*You* make us a cup of tea.' Bing was firm.

'I made the last one.'

'That is such a fucking lie. You don't even know where we keep the tea, you sow.' Bing rearranged himself beneath the duvet. 'Is this what marriage is like after about twenty-five years?'

'I hope so,' said Evie.

'My God!' yelped Bing. 'Look at the time! It's started!'

'Quick. Quick.' Evie was panicking.

'I can't find the bloody remote.' Bing plunged under the duvet. 'Here it is.' He sat back, pointed it at the TV screen and soon the trumpets of *The Antiques Roadshow* signature tune filled the air.

'I hate this bit,' moaned Evie. 'Who wants to hear about some mouldy old stately home and what civil-war battles were fought nearby? Let's get on to the greedy old bats and the heirlooms their revolting forebears left them.'

A hideous hat-stand carved with cross-eyed bears turned out to be worth three hundred pounds. 'I'd chop that up for firewood,' said Bing tartly.

'That's got to be worth loads,' gasped Evie, as an opal and gold necklace filled the screen. She was almost as disappointed as the owner when the valuation was a hundred and fifty pounds.

'This is the biggie,' decreed Bing knowledgeably, as a tiny white-haired woman sat by a dreary landscape featuring a handful of sullen long-haired cattle. 'Her grandfather bought it for a tenner,' he repeated excitedly. 'It's going to be thousands.'

Bing and Evie were on the edge of their seats as the paintings expert said, 'Would you believe me if I told you that you should insure it for between sixty and eighty thousand pounds?'

'Wa-hey!' whooped Bing.

The old lady appeared overcome, but she rallied and whispered, 'Oh, but I could never part with it.'

'Yeah, right!' shouted Bing at her innocent old pink and white face on the screen. 'You'll be off down Sotheby's as fast as your walking-frame can take you.'

Evie laughed. 'She'll take up with a toyboy of about my dad's age, and drink herself to death on sweet sherry.'

'Haven't *we* got anything we could take along?' Bing looked hopefully around the room.

'No. We always have this conversation. All these old biddies have inherited knick-knacks and furniture worth a fortune and we've got *nada*. I don't know what our great-grandparents thought they were up to. They didn't leave us a sodding thing.'

'It's about time they did an *Antiques Roadshow* from an inner-city council estate instead of Woburn, isn't it?' said Bing. 'Then we could go along with all our tat.'

'Ah, Ms Crump,' Evie adopted a stuffy voice and a superior manner. 'That's a most interesting hatbox full of odd buttons. There's a big market for these. I've seen a similar battered old bastard held together with Sellotape fetch up to two pounds at auction.'

'I'm glad you brought these along,' said Bing, in his doddery-old-man voice. 'It's so rare we have an opportunity to peruse the correspondence of an important historic personage such as your nana Bessie. I've taken the liberty of having a peek at one of the letters and it's a mesmerising account of a trip to the Isle of Sheppey. Such marvellous detail – apparently young Bert's glands is playing him up awful. I can hardly believe you have a huge smelly old handbag full of these documents. A London dealer would give you at least eighteen pence.'

'Talking of handbags . . .' Evie recounted how she had smelt the distinctive aroma of Belle's when she was fretting about the mysterious car. 'I felt calm, as if she was watching over us.' She eyed him worriedly. 'Am I going mad? Is whatever Sacha has catching?'

'I don't think you're mad, doll,' Bing reassured her. 'Why shouldn't Belle be looking out for us? I'm not so arrogant as to imagine I know everything about the universe and how it works. If the thought that Belle is out there somewhere keeps you happy then keep thinking it.'

'So young and yet so wise.' Evie hesitated. There was something she wanted desperately to share with Bing but it was so personal and so precious she was wary of mentioning it. If he laughed at her it would ruin everything.

'I know that face.' As usual Bing was a yard ahead. 'What have you done?'

'I haven't done anything. Yet.'

'Tell your Uncle Bing.'

It was probably best to say it quickly. 'I'm going to ask Aden out on a date.' Evie flinched, waiting for the shrieks of laughter.

Bing didn't laugh. 'About time,' he said, and returned to the *News of the World*.

'How about a Chinese?'

'Are we talking food? Or your next sexual conquest?' queried Evie. 'Just so I know.'

'Food. My treat, as long as you come with me to get it.'

'Bing, *my script*.' Evie waggled the sheaf of papers at him. She had crept, maggot-like, to the other end of the sofa. Only her head and one arm were out from under the duvet.

'Don't come that with me. You're not reading it. You haven't got past the title page. You've been rolling it into a tube and dropping Revels into your mouth through it.'

'We all have our own ways of getting acquainted with the text.'

'Come on. Think pork balls. Think spring rolls. Think sweet and sour.'

'Actually, that sounds brilliant. I've only had Revels and stuffing on toast all day.' Evie bolted off to change her fun-fur slippers for something more pavement-friendly. 'Hey,' she shouted from her room, 'how come you're in tonight? Sunday's normally a big one for you, isn't it?'

'Didn't fancy it.'

But Bing *always* fancied it. Nonplussed, Evie followed him out into the night. The sky was brooding and yellow, pregnant with the promise of a storm. Evie shivered, then stopped dead at the gate.

'What is it?' Bing scuttled to her side.

'The car's back.'

22

It seemed that their days were ruled by that car. 'It's there!' one of them would shout first thing. Or 'No car today!'

Wednesday was a no-car day. This was a good start. Evie was sorting the post – or, rather, the selection of unsolicited and unwanted special offers and cut-rate credit-card applications – when Bernard let himself in through the front door.

The sun, which was back to its ebullient former self, streamed in behind him, lighting up his worrying haircut like a forest fire. 'Good morning!' he said, with the brightness of a children's TV presenter.

'Bernard. I'm glad we bumped into each other.' Evie hung her head, an estate agent's flyer in one hand and a fifty-pence voucher for Pizza Hut in the other. 'I'm really sorry about the other night.'

'What other night was that?' Bernard seemed to have forgotten the chaos, tears and slapped Spaniard of Manhattan Dreams. 'Oh, that. You have nothing to apologise for. That night really opened my eyes.'

'Do you mean that?' Evie was taken aback.

'Gosh, yes. Changed my life.' He grinned maniacally at her, so full of energy he was practically hopping from one leg to another.

'We must do it again, then!' Evie was bowled over by the unsuspected success of her plotting.

Bernard laughed in a new, unself-conscious way. 'I'd rather not. I don't need you any more, if you know what I mean.'

Crushed, Evie said, 'Good. That's good. If I've given you confidence then that's my reward.'

The old Bernard emerged to take Evie's hand, shake it earnestly and say, 'I can never thank you enough,' before the new one bounded upstairs like a kangaroo.

Stacking shelves at Calmer Karma, Evie couldn't resist crowing about her triumph. 'He has a real spring in his step. Raring to go. I think he may turn out to be a lady-killer – if he has his hair fixed.'

'I don't get it.' Sacha handed up curly-toed slippers that smelt of yeast to Evie high on a ladder. 'It's not as if the evening was a success. He was almost lynched.'

'Oh, be fair. He was getting on like a house on fire with the last girl and the Spanish bird hit him 'cos she was jealous. That's success compared to sitting at home thinking about your dead mother.'

'When you put it like that . . .'

A workshop on Opening Your Third Eye had claimed Sacha that afternoon, so Evie had agreed to look after the shop. It would give her an opportunity to read her script. She had it open in front of her and she'd marked her lines with a magenta felt-tip, but she was thinking about Aden. Specifically, she was thinking about ringing him. Which was as far as she'd got with her plan.

Evie hadn't told Sacha. She didn't want it discussed endlessly. Her feelings for Aden were private, and she hugged them to her. Bing hadn't mentioned her plan since she'd blurted it out to him and she was grateful to him for that. (It was also possible that he'd forgotten about it, of course.)

Evie stared at the big red fifties phone on the counter. *I couldn't bear it if he said no . . .* She was immobilised by terror.

The bell over the shop door clanged, jolting Evie out of her reverie, and a hundred screaming children stormed in. No, it was only two. And she knew them.

'Charles! Julius!' Evie looked past them to the harassed figure trailing after them. 'So, you must be Beth.'

'I'm what's left of Beth.' She sank into a chair.

'What are you doing here?' asked Evie, and doled out an organic raisin candy bar to each twin.

'I'm supposed to be flat-hunting. The baby-sitter let me down so I had to drag this pair with me. I thought it would be OK but . . .'

'PSHAH!' Charles spat out his bar. 'Tastes like poo-poo!'

Julius screamed, 'I'm eating poo-poo!'

Beth looked at Evie with an expression of pure weariness. 'Imagine dealing with that *and* an estate agent.'

Evie did the decent thing. 'Let me have them. Don't touch those crystals, Julius!'

'Oh, God, you're an angel.' Beth's shoulders drooped with relief. 'When I went to your house Bing told me you were here. I would have asked him to mind them but he was just off to the Palladium. I know it's an awful cheek but I didn't know what else to do.'

'Don't worry about it. Things have changed. We all have to rally around. The quicker you get a flat the quicker we can get you away from that A-D-D-U-L-T-E-R.' Evie spelled it out to save the twins' innocent ears.

'Addulter?' Beth was puzzled.

'Oops. No. *Adulterer*.' Evie whispered it.

'It's only got one D.' Beth was studying her sister's face. 'What do you mean, Evie?'

'What do you mean what do I mean?' Evie laughed, then mouthed, 'Marcus,' while pointing elaborately at the children. 'He's an A-D, et cetera.'

Beth gazed at her.

'What?' said Evie, when she could stand it no longer.

'Marcus isn't the adulterer,' said Beth simply. 'I am.'

Forgetting about Charles and Julius, Evie squawked, '*You*'ve been shagging around?'

'Hardly. I've found someone else. I thought you knew.'

Quicksand squelched beneath Evie's feet. 'You said you couldn't live with him any more!'

'Not because he was unfaithful. Marcus would never do anything so interesting.' Beth exhaled slowly. She spoke with the air of one who had said this many times at great length: 'I married Marcus because he seemed like perfect husband material. I was young enough to imagine I was in love with him. I had everything a woman is presumed to want but I've been going quietly bonkers for years because I had nobody to talk to. Marcus and I have never had a real conversation. Then I met someone I can't stop talking to. It was as if I'd been shut in a tomb for years, then suddenly exposed to sunlight. The decision to end the marriage made itself. It wasn't brought on by Marcus being an adulterer.'

'I'm such a—'

'Sssh. There's been enough naughty words in front of the children. Now I realise why you were so down on Marcus. I couldn't fathom it before. I mean, Marcus isn't always the suave gentleman he seems to be but he's certainly no B-A-S-T-A-R-D.'

'I thought he was,' said Evie sadly. 'I thought he'd been unfaithful.'

'No.' Beth seemed suddenly fearful. '*I* am. Sis, do you feel the same way about things? If you don't want to get involved I'll understand.'

'Oh, shut up!' Not for the first time Evie wished that Crumps hugged. Then she put her hand to her mouth. 'Tamsin!' she said, reddening. 'I made her cry. I told her I knew all about her.'

'That's beyond me.' Beth heaved herself up. 'I haven't got time to dwell on Tamsin now. I've got to find a roof to put over these boys' heads. Can you keep them until about seven?'

'Sure. We'll be at home by then.'

Beth went off to look at flats, leaving Evie with the uneasy knowledge that, once again, she hadn't known what was going on right under her nose.

* * *

A string of worry-beads round his podgy neck, Julius was playing his own symphony on the wind chimes. Charles had overcome his distaste for poo-poo and was munching his way through a carton of organic raisin candy bars, well past its sell-by date.

Not one customer had arrived to perturb Evie, and she had long ago put her script into her bag to protect it from grubby little fingers. Her sole occupation was thinking about Aden.

One minute she was just thinking, the next she was *doing*. Speedily, with no time for scaredy-cat second thoughts, she dialled his number.

'Hello.'

Eek. It was him. Evie reminded herself she was twenty-seven. 'Hi, Aden, it's me.'

'Evie?'

Bad start. If he was mad about her, surely he would know her voice straight away. 'Yes.'

'Sorry, it's a shit line.'

She leant perilously to her right. 'Is this better?'

'Much. Have you been reading your script?'

'Oooh, yes, I gobbled it up.'

'So you've read episode three?'

'Hmm.' Evie didn't like the way this was going. Specific knowledge might be called for.

'Are you pleased? I don't think you knew about that, did you?'

'No, I didn't and I'm . . . pleased,' said Evie slowly. She had to change the subject. Indeed, she had to launch herself straight at *the* subject or she would lose her courage and die an old maid and leave all the money she didn't have to her cats. Or to somebody else's cats as she never intended to own any. 'Look, Aden, it's like this. Will you go out with me on Saturday?' It came out rather aggressively.

'Er, yeah. Sure. What do you have in mind?'

'Oh.' She wasn't certain that he had understood. 'No, Aden,

you're not getting it. I mean *come out with me* as in . . .' she gulped '. . . a date.'

Just then the wind chimes fell on Julius. Charles, startled by the noise, ran to his brother's aid and vomited twenty-three organic raisin candy bars over him.

'Oh, my God!' wailed Evie. Still clamping the receiver to her ear she bent down and tried to extricate Julius from the tangle of wind chimes and sick.

'What's happening?' pleaded Aden. 'Have aliens landed?'

'It's complicated,' puffed Evie, dragging the screaming Charles towards her by his foot. 'There's wind chimes and quite a lot of sick and – *no*!' Charles wasn't quite done. Sobbing, he vomited explosively over a stack of cut-price tofu cookery cards. 'Aden, this is a both-hands job. I have to go,' she gabbled. 'Do you want to come on a date with me on Saturday or not?'

'I do.'

'Good. Goodbye.'

Evie screamed even louder than the twins, when Sacha walked through the door. Sacha was tired and her forehead was sore due to the effort involved in opening her third eye. She vowed there and then never to ask Evie to watch the shop again.

'I'm all icky,' complained Charles. His previously brilliant white T-shirt now sported a brown and yellow tie-dye effect down the front.

'He pongs.' Julius was right.

Their aunt tried to make it into a game as they stood waiting for the lights to change. 'Let's sing a song about it. A pong song.' She started gustily. '"Poo! Somebody pongs. Who? You! Charles pongs of poo!"'

Now Charles was icky, pongy *and* sobbing.

'I didn't mean it, darling. You don't pong, honest.' A small hand in each of hers, Evie turned into Kemp Street.

She stopped stock still, yanking two tiny arms almost out of their sockets.

The car was back.

Evie's heart started to pound. She held the children's hands even tighter. If the watcher in the car was dangerous he might turn his aggression on the twins. He might even snatch them. Although, looking down at them, she reckoned that no one in their right mind would want them, the state they were in.

Anger simmered beneath the fear. She was walking down her own street and she felt threatened. It was intolerable that she couldn't guarantee her nephews' safety.

Like the cavalry, Bernard hove into view. He spotted Evie, statue-like at the corner, waved cheerfully and walked towards her.

'Bernard, I'm so pleased to see you.'

'Gosh.'

'Take these.' Evie transferred Charles and Julius to his charge. 'Don't ask questions. Get them indoors as quickly as you can. There's someone I need to talk to.'

Bernard obeyed Evie unquestioningly, partly as a result of his ingrained obedience, partly because no one could have mistaken her tone.

Evie took off across the road at speed. She was incensed and had almost forgotten to be afraid. As she marched up to the white car she could see that their mysterious watcher was a woman. A plump woman of, maybe, sixty.

Evie tapped sharply on the window. 'I want to talk to you!'

The window rolled down. The woman's face was creased with anxiety. She didn't seem to be armed, although there was a tartan flask in her lap. 'Hello.' It was said in the style of a comfortable aunt, not at all like a lunatic stalker.

'What do you think you're playing at?' Evie eyeballed her tormentor.

'Oh dear.' Once again the stranger had strayed from the accepted behaviour of deranged perverts.

'Oh dear?' mimicked Evie. She was even angrier now that she realised she'd been stalked by Thora Hird. 'Aren't you going to explain yourself? You're frightening us all to death, just sitting and staring at our house. Who are you?'

The woman fingered the Thermos awkwardly. 'I'm Caroline's mum.'

23

'But Caroline's mum is dead,' Bing insisted, a twin on each arm.

'She's not dead. She's on our sofa, crying,' whispered Evie, shutting the kitchen door.

'Caroline thinks she's dead.'

'Does she fu-lip.' Evie modified her language out of respect for the malodorous, snivelling boys. 'Caroline has more family than the von Trapps. She's got a mum, a dad, brothers, nanas and grandpas coming out of her ears. She refuses point-blank to see them.'

'This is good,' said Bing approvingly. 'Look, can you wash this one?' He thrust Charles in her direction.

'You'll have to do it.' Evie dodged the proffered child. 'I'm making a pot of tea for Mrs Millbank. Her flask has a crack in it and she's only had a bap since she left Bury this morning.'

'Why don't you bake her a cake? Have you forgotten that this woman's been terrorising us?'

'When you've spoken to her you'll understand.'

Bing did understand. He kept Mrs Millbank ('Call me Deirdre') supplied with tissues as, tearfully, she told them her story on their threadbare sofa.

The children had been gone over with a damp flannel and were watching *The Tweenies* with the sound down in the corner. Charles had been decanted into a 'Take That!' T-shirt of Bing's.

'Another bite, Deirdre?' Evie waved a plate of lumpen oversized sandwiches under their visitor's nose.

'Thank you, no.' Deirdre had struggled with the first. 'I'm so sorry I scared you all.' She began to cry again.

'Now, now, stop saying sorry.' Bing patted her on her arm and proffered the Kleenex again. 'No harm's been done. You gave us something to talk about.'

'You're very kind.'

'We just want to help,' said Evie.

'There's nothing anyone can do.' Deirdre shook her head sorrowfully. 'Caroline has cut herself off from us completely. I've lost my daughter.' This detonated some energetic nose-blowing.

When it had subsided Bing prompted her gently: 'Take us back to the beginning. How did things get to this?'

Deirdre sighed. Her accent was as juicy as Caroline's, but her voice was softer and more hesitant. She seemed embarrassed to be laying bare her troubles to two young people she'd only just met. 'Well, now, let's see. Caroline was always rebellious when she was growing up. All those black clothes and makeup – what is it? Gothic? She'd be late home. Only twenty minutes or so, but always late. Her dad is strict, you see. Perhaps he's been too hard on the kids but he's a good man. Caroline fought him all the way.'

Bing and Evie glanced at each other. That was their Caroline, all right.

'We're Catholics, you see,' said Deirdre.

'Me too!' chirped Evie.

'Really? Then you'll know that Catholic parents expect high standards from their children.'

Bing coughed discreetly.

'We're not terribly strict Catholics,' Evie conceded.

'Caroline's dad is. He didn't approve of her makeup and her staying out late. One night he smelt alcohol on her breath and hit the roof. It's not that I think my husband's wrong, it's just that he can be very . . .' she groped for a word and came up with a small sad one '. . . *hard*.'

'Did Caroline run away?' asked Evie.

'Not then. She started to live her own life. She didn't speak to us much. I didn't like that but at least there were fewer rows. Then one day she didn't come home from work. I found a note on her pillow. It didn't say much, just that she was leaving and wouldn't be coming back.'

'How long ago was that?' asked Evie tenderly, after some more nose-blowing.

'Over a year.' Deirdre almost wailed. 'We've been out of our minds. She's our precious daughter and for all we knew she could be . . .' She couldn't say it. 'Then about a month ago an old friend of hers came to see me. She'd heard how distraught we all were and took pity on me. She gave me an address. I wrote to Caroline. It was hard to know what to say.'

Caroline had wept over the letter, Evie knew. It was the paper she'd crumpled up when Evie had gone in to baby-sit.

'There was no reply,' Deirdre continued. 'Something in me just snapped. I jumped into the car and drove and drove until I was at her door.' She paused self-consciously. 'I don't know what I thought I was doing. I had no plan, nothing. I just needed to see her with my own eyes.'

A twin burped and was ignored.

'That was when I got the biggest shock of all.' Deirdre's eyes widened at the memory. 'The little girl.'

'You mean Milly?' asked Evie.

'Is that her name?' Deirdre asked. 'So sweet.'

'You mean you didn't know about Milly?' Evie was amazed.

'I had no idea. Now it all makes sense. Caroline ran away because she was expecting. She was too scared to come to us, her own parents.'

'Have you told your husband?' Bing wanted to know.

'Yes. He was shocked at first but now he wants to see his granddaughter more than anything else on earth.'

A hasty pow-wow was held in Evie's room under the pretext of preparing more tea for Deirdre.

'Can you believe Caroline?' hissed Evie. 'Fancy doing that to her poor mother.'

'Whoa! Consider how bad her life must have been at home for her to skedaddle to London on her own when she was pregnant. "Hard" was the word Deirdre used to describe Caroline's dad. Something tells me that's mild.'

'S'pose,' Evie agreed. 'What will we do with Deirdre?'

'I don't want to interfere.' Bing was adamant.

'So, what do you suggest? We send her back out to the car and wave at her every now and then?'

Bing looked uneasy. Then he punched the mattress. 'Dammit, you're going to interfere, aren't you?'

'No, *we* are,' Evie corrected him. 'We'll have a chat with Caroline. Try to persuade her to see her mum, just for a few moments, yeah?'

'All right. We have to do something, I suppose.' Bing was unenthusiastic.

Evie sniffed vigorously.

'Not me!' Bing was an infamous blower-off.

'No, no, it's Belle's handbag!' Evie beamed. 'Can't you smell it?'

Bing paled. 'Christ, I really can.'

'She approves. Everything's going to be all right.'

Thunderous. That was the best way to describe Caroline's expression as she barred their way into her flat with grimly folded arms. 'My family is dead,' she repeated.

'Caroline, why don't you give your mother a break?' Bing could be persuasive when he tried – if he'd got a Tory father of four out of his underpants, surely he could cajole a bolshy Goth down a flight of stairs. 'She's come all this way.'

'I never invited her.'

'It can't hurt,' said Evie.

'Oh, can't it?' snapped Caroline. 'What would you know?'

'Well,' said Evie, carefully, 'I can see that your mother's in a lot of pain and perhaps deserves a hearing.'

'You don't know what me dad used to say to me.' Caroline was looking over their heads. 'The words he used. He thinks single mothers are whores. He wouldn't spit on me if I was on fire. I don't ever want to hear him call Milly a bastard.' Her gaze clicked back to meet Evie's eyes. 'And he would, you know. He's . . .'

'Hard,' finished Evie.

'Tell her to sod off and leave me alone. Tell her me family are dead.'

Evie didn't put it in quite those words. 'She's adamant, Deirdre. She won't see you.'

'We're so sorry.' Bing sat down beside Mrs Millbank and laid a hand on hers.

The expected tears didn't come. Deirdre was passively accepting. 'She's a stubborn girl. I wish with all my heart I could change her mind, but I know her better than I know myself.'

Evie had to add, 'She seems frightened of her dad's reaction to Milly.'

Deirdre pursed her lips. 'I daresay. My husband always had a lot to say about *unmarried mothers*, as he calls them. I think he was trying to scare Caroline, sort of subconsciously, you know. He didn't want her to get into trouble. The sad thing is he's dying to see his granddaughter. Once he'd got over the shock and we talked it over he got used to the idea. Milly . . .' Deirdre stumbled over the unfamiliar name '. . . is his flesh and blood. All we wanted to do was give them a home and make up for the time we've lost. I've dreamt about bringing them both back with me.' She patted Bing's hand affectionately and stood up, brushing crumbs off her lap. 'It wasn't to be.' She stopped, transfixed by the figures at the door: Caroline, with Milly on one hip. Milly held out her arms and babbled a strange baby word.

'Mum,' said Caroline, chewing the word as if it was a mouthful of iron filings, 'do you want to come upstairs for a minute?'

Deirdre nodded mutely, and followed her daughter out of the

room. Bing and Evie were stunned. Bing's eyes glistened. A tear travelled down Evie's cheek. They hugged each other.

'It's boring here,' said Julius loudly, from behind the sofa.

'I am in *so* much trouble.' Bing was tugging on a clean pair of jeans. 'I'm going to miss the first number. They'll shoot me.'

'I'll ring and say you've been injured in a freak snogging accident.'

'Please don't bother.' Bing was fumbling with the laces of his trainers.

'Did you see Beth's face when she was stuffing the twins into the car and I told her I'd have a flat for her, after all?'

'Yes.' Bing was curt. He was packing his wallet and keys into his pockets.

'Although I'll miss Caroline . . .' Evie said.

'Shit.' Bing held up his denim jacket. A large chocolate splodge disfigured the back.

'Ah.' Evie looked chastened. 'Yes. Perhaps I shouldn't have given Julius that jar of Nutella.'

Bing was too late to waste time criticising Evie's childcare skills. 'Can I borrow your baggy white cotton jumper?'

'Course.' Evie followed Bing to her room and watched him rifle her wardrobe. 'What have you got planned for after the show?' she asked nosily. 'Some delicious little stage-hand? An usher or two?'

'I'll be straight home,' he muttered distractedly.

'Again? Are you feeling all right, Bing?'

'Yes.'

'But you've been home every night this week. I haven't even spotted any fresh lovebites. You're not ill, are you?'

'I am as fit as the proverbial flea,' Bing informed her. 'I can't see that fucking jumper. Your cupboards are like a jumble sale in Hell. WHERE IS IT?'

'Try under the bed.'

Bing tutted eloquently and dived beneath it.

'Why are you living the life of a monk all of a sudden?'

'Monks do not perform nightly at the Palladium.'

'I don't like it,' complained Evie. 'It makes me uneasy when you're not disgustingly promiscuous.'

'Found it.' Triumphant, Bing emerged with the jumper. 'Want to know what else I found?'

'Yeah.'

'You're not going to like it.'

Evie flattened herself against the wall in an untypically swift movement. 'Is it alive?'

'No, nothing like that. I'm shattering one of your illusions.' Bing plonked a heavy old-fashioned black leather handbag on the dishevelled duvet. 'The smell wasn't ghostly encouragement. Belle's handbag was open under your bed.'

'Oh.' Evie bit her lip and Belle took a step backwards into misty shadow.

24

It had been planned as a celebration. 'Meet me in Black's and I'll buy you a very big glass of champagne,' Beth had said, bubbling like Moët herself. 'I'm *so* excited at the thought of moving into Kemp Street.'

'Where's Black's? *What*'s Black's?' Evie had asked. 'The only Black's I know of is a snazzy drinking club in Soho.'

'That's the one. I've just become a member.'

'Bloody hell! You don't hang about. You've only been single for an afternoon and you're already joining fancy members-only gaffs.' Evie was impressed. She was also envious. She was above thinking, *I've been a single woman living in London for centuries but I'm not a member of Black's. I'm not even a member of Blockbuster.* But only just.

Right now, as Evie paced the chewing-gum mosaic on the platform at Mornington Crescent she was too preoccupied for jealous pangs. She was about to let Beth down to earth with quite a bump. She rehearsed her speech furiously as the platform filled up around her. 'It's like this,' she improvised. 'Unforeseen circumstances have compelled me to retract my previous offer.' Too formal. 'You can't have the flat.' Too abrupt. 'Please, please, please, forgive me. Don't hate me and give me an Oil of Olay gift set every Christmas from now on.' Too abject.

The tunnel growled and a train thundered in. Evie wasn't too distracted to nab a seat. All Londoners have the ability to barge, push and prod on automatic pilot. The tube would be such a convenient way to travel were it not for the other passengers.

Beth would understand. She was the understanding type. Mind you, Evie's perceptions of her big sister had shifted profoundly of late. She wasn't the content country housewife any more, she was a free woman with a secret lover prone to glugging champagne in Soho. Maybe she wasn't understanding any more either.

'But what can I do?' Evie whined in imaginary self-defence. The bottom line was that Caroline didn't want to move out. Evie winced as she recalled that morning's conversation. Caroline had been humming as she bumped Milly down the stairs in the pushchair.

'Hiya. Somebody sounds cheerful,' Evie had smiled.

'Oh.' Caroline had gone pink, as if she'd been caught masturbating.

Evie gave her a hand down the last couple of steps. 'I saw your mum leave quite late. She looked like a different woman.'

'Yeah. Well.' Some smiles can't be suppressed, although Caroline did her damnedest.

'I'm so pleased for you.' Evie was sincere though she itched to add, 'Even though you've been lying your head off for months.'

'Thanks,' muttered Caroline, looking bashfully down at her Doc Martens. 'I . . .' she faltered.

'Yes?' encouraged Evie.

Caroline was squirming with the effort of pushing out whatever she was trying to say. 'I'm sorry about the lies and that.'

Evie nodded and left a space in the hope that Caroline might fill it. She wasn't disappointed.

'There was so much, well, hurt, I suppose,' said Caroline awkwardly. 'Everything that happened at home, with me dad, was so painful I didn't want to think, never mind talk, about it. The easiest thing was just to say the whole past was dead.'

'You wanted to wipe it out and start again?'

'Exactly.' Caroline nodded earnestly. 'As far as I was concerned it was just me and Milly against the world.'

'Not any more, though. You've got a family again.'

'Yeah.' Caroline looked pensive. 'It was fantastic seeing my mum, seeing her hold Milly.' Caroline shook her head as if to shrug off the debilitating soppiness. 'But we'll take it slow. Some of the wounds are still raw.'

'God, you're so sensible,' Evie said admiringly. 'I'll be sorry to see you go, you know, even though it's for such happy reasons.'

'Go? Where am I going?' Caroline said sharply, with a flash of the old sourness.

'Home. Aren't you? I presumed . . .'

'Is this about the rent? Me mum's lent me enough to pay up to date.'

'Of course it's not about the rent.' Evie was getting quite sharp herself. 'I just thought you'd move nearer to your parents.'

'I'm not ready for that.' A shudder ran through Caroline. 'Some of the stuff me dad said to me . . . We'll have to take it steady.'

It made sense. Without doubt, it was the best way to proceed. It just wasn't what Evie had expected or wanted to hear.

'Is that a problem?' There was fear in Caroline's question.

'No, nononono,' replied Evie, much too hastily. 'God, no, not at all.'

Caroline studied her face. 'You sure?'

'That flat is yours for as long as you want it.' Evie was emphatic. Caroline was one of Belle's tenants, after all.

'Good, 'cos I don't know what I would have done without this place. Thanks . . .' Caroline was faltering again. 'Thanks for putting up with me.'

That really was the moment for a hug, but Caroline hadn't changed quite that much and ran over Evie's toes with the pushchair instead.

The metal stairs down to Black's basement entrance were slick with rain. Evie concentrated on not falling over as she went down them. She and stairs were a bad match at the best of times: she and wet stairs might result in injury to innocent bystanders.

'I'm here to meet Beth Lawrenson. She's a member,' Evie

announced to the statuesque and terrifyingly gorgeous black Valkyrie on the door.

'OK.' The goddess barely looked up but drew in her airstrip-length legs for Evie to get by.

The interior was not the sleek vision of elegance Evie had expected. The uneven wooden floors and the rough grey walls looked as if they hadn't been touched since the Georgian house was built. A real fire roared in a massive grate, and all around private drinkers lounged on wooden benches. If it wasn't for the diamanté tummy rings and combat pants of the clientele Evie might have imagined herself back in the days of Hogarth.

'Forgotten to pay the electricity bill?' she quipped, to the sullen-faced supermodel looming behind the bar.

'Eh?'

'I mean, all the candles everywhere, it's so dark, as if you'd forgotten to . . . Oh, forget it. A white wine, please.' Hopefully the girl was a better barmaid than audience.

Fingerprinted glass in hand, Evie delved into the gloom. Narrow but cavernous, the club was a warren of small candle-lit rooms full of battered baroque furniture. It was strangely thrilling, thought Evie, as if all the spirits who'd ever lived there might join you for a glass of indifferent house white.

Actually, it wasn't so much thrilling as scary. Where was Beth? Evie scowled in the darkness.

'Lost?' asked an unfeasibly handsome boy, just the wrong side of gay, from a tattered banquette. 'Try the Divan Room. There's always something going on in there.'

'Thank you,' simpered Evie, stumbling off in the direction he pointed. She came to a heavy, tasselled curtain across a crumbling archway and poked her nose round it. 'Beth!' she squealed, relieved.

The Divan Room was almost all divan with a touch of room at its foot. A wall-to-wall mattress was piled with opulent cushions of velvet and silk. Beth was lounging among the decadent haphazardness. She was laughing, her hair all tousled as she stretched full length. She looked ten years younger and a thousand times happier.

'This place is amazing!' Evie squealed, leaping on to the divan and drenching them both in wine.

A voice came from the depth of the cushions. 'I like my wine in me, not on me.'

Evie drew back on her knees, startled. Beth was not alone in this Arabian Nights fantasy.

A plumpish figure righted itself and knocked a bolster into shape. Bea grinned at Evie as she straightened her hair, with just the slightest, well-disguised hint of apprehension in her eyes.

'Auntie Bea.' That was a statement. 'Auntie Bea?' That was a question. Evie saw her sister's pale hand snake across the velvet and take Bea's. 'Auntie Bea . . .' That was realisation.

If a picture really can paint a thousand words, then the vision of Beth and Bea holding hands as they lolled, pink-cheeked and shiny-eyed, on the divan was particularly telling. Although only six words were needed: Beth and Bea were in love.

The two women stared intently at Evie, trying to read her. She looked from one to the other, took a deep gulp of the wine left in her glass and said, 'Now I get it.'

'And?' prompted Beth nervously.

'Ssssh,' said Bea quietly, soothingly. 'Let it sink in. The poor girl's only just arrived. Let her get comfortable first.' Bea lobbed a cushion at Evie. 'Put that behind you. Get comfortable, lovey.'

Automatically Evie did as she was told. *My sister the lesbian*, she thought. It sounded like a porn film.

'Champagne?' Bea had evidently decided to take charge now that both Crump girls had been struck dumb. 'Chuck that hideous wine in the yucca plant and take this.'

Evie complied and gazed meditatively at the champagne flute.

Bea leaned forward conspiratorially. 'The idea is that you drink it. Apparently the bubbles help you cope with shock.'

Evie managed a giggle, then downed the whole glass in one. This startled them all into laughter, which intensified with the impressive, rolling burp that escaped her immediately after. 'You're . . . together!' she yelped. 'You're a couple! She's *your* girlfriend and she's *your* girlfriend!'

Beth was nodding furiously.

'But you're Auntie Bea . . . You've always been my Auntie Bea.'

'She's a woman too,' Beth butted in.

Bea laid an appeasing arm on Beth's arm. 'I'm still your Auntie Bea, Evie,' her tone wafted Evie right back to chaotic teenagerdom, 'but I'm lots of other people too. I'm not auntie to Beth any more, I'm very special to her. She's very special to me. We want you to know because you're very special to both of us.'

Evie smiled a small gormless smile.

'It is all right, isn't it?' Beth asked timidly; the flash of defiance had sputtered out.

Evie looked at her sister. Really looked at her. She had never seen Beth tipsy before and it suited her. Being in love suited her. But, then, being in love suits everyone.

'Of course it's all right. It's wonderful!' Evie bounced up and down creating ripples that almost shipwrecked Bea and Beth.

There was no champagne left. Bea clambered awkwardly off the bed and scurried away to find more. Now Beth could shoot over to Evie's side and nudge her with a bony elbow. (This was about as physical as one Crump could get with another and not develop hives.) 'So. Is it really OK?'

Wagging a finger, Evie scolded, 'That's the second time you've asked me and it had better be the last. You look so happy I'm jealous. It's just that I've never thought of Bea in a . . .'

'Sexual way?'

A blush heated Evie's face. 'Shuddup!' she heard herself say, like a first-former.

'Bea has a saying. "Love is where it falls." That's beautiful, isn't it?' said Beth. 'We don't choose who we fall for. We can't design the perfect match. I mean, on paper Marcus was my ideal partner but eventually even the way he ate crisps made me want to scream. But Bea . . . She just amazes me every day and shows me such kindness and understanding and *respect*. Love is where it falls, and it fell on an old family friend.'

'Of the same sex,' Evie couldn't resist saying. She even added, 'And thirty years older.'

'Yes, the same sex and thirty years older. Love is where it falls.'

Evie nudged Beth. They smiled. They understood each other. 'Does Marcus know?' she asked.

A long, expressive sigh. 'Oh, yes, he knows. He said he'd rather I'd become a prostitute.'

'You could always do that as well.'

'He was livid. I've never seen him so angry. He's threatened to fight me for custody. Said he'd rather have a nanny looking after the twins than me.'

'Bastard!' Evie exploded. 'Well, let him fight you. He'll soon find out he's got all the Crumps to deal with.' She paused. 'Actually, that doesn't sound frightening at all, does it?'

'Not really,' laughed Beth. 'It's not like tangling with the Kennedys or the Borgias.'

'He wouldn't win, would he?'

'I promise I won't let him. Those boys stay with me. He can have as much access as he wants, but I've looked after them since I conceived them and I'm not going to give them up now.'

Evie quivered. There was a thread of steel running right down Beth's spine. 'If he makes you go to court you can bring up his adultery and make him sound like an unfit father.'

'Keep up, Evie. He didn't commit adultery, remember? *I* did. Marcus's illicit sex life with his dental nurse was all in your overheated head.'

'Oh, yes. Sorry. Champagne always makes me stupid.'

'Here's some more stupidity for you, then.' Bea was back with a shapely and expensive bottle. She struggled over the cushions like a spaniel, snuggling one foot cosily under Beth's thigh.

The Reluctant Landlady

Evie hurriedly knocked back some champagne. That kind of thing was going to take some getting used to. 'What I don't understand is—'

'This could be a long list,' hissed Beth.

'Why did Tamsin burst into tears and run off like that when I accused her of knobbing Marcus?'

'Ah. Yes. We got to the bottom of that,' said Bea.

'If you remember,' explained Beth, 'you didn't accuse her of . . . let's call it *making love* with my husband.'

'I did.'

'You didn't. You told her you knew all about her. That's a much wider statement.'

'But I *meant* I knew she was knobbing – and if you don't mind I'll continue to call it knobbing – Marcus.'

Beth was patient. She had had plenty of experience. 'Poor Tamsin wasn't to know that. She's not a mind-reader. She presumed you knew her deep dark secret.'

'Tamsin? That little budgie in high heels has a deep dark secret?' Evie was incredulous.

'Of sorts. She'd faked her dental assistant CV.'

Disappointed, Evie said, 'That's all? She's not a Satanist or a lap-dancer or the love child of Des O'Connor? I'd hardly call that a terrible secret.'

'In the cut-throat world of dental assisting it is,' explained Beth. 'The poor thing thought you'd stumbled on the fact that she wasn't as experienced with the saliva Hoover as she made out.'

'I'd have to have an awful lot of time on my hands to stumble on that.'

The mystery was solved. The women clinked glasses and shouted, 'To Tamsin!' Bea added, 'May her starched uniform never crease!'

A question occurred to Evie. 'Have you two told Mum about, well, you two?'

The lovebirds exchanged a look. 'What do you think?' asked Bea.

'I think you haven't.' Evie had to smirk at the thought of her ultra-conservative, ultra-Catholic, ultra-stick-up-her-arse mother coping with that particular news item.

'I don't know how to.' Even though Beth was worried about how to tell her parents, she was having trouble keeping a straight face. 'Every time I imagine it I get this mental image of Mum spontaneously combusting.'

'Dad will be fine, though.'

'I hope so.' Beth frowned. She wasn't about to take anything for granted.

'Of course he will. He's liberal through and through.'

'But his own daughter . . .' Beth's lips trembled.

'He loves you. Don't forget that.' Bea always put a positive spin on events. 'As for Bridgie, she'll come round. We've been friends for a long time.'

But that makes it worse, thought Evie. She didn't envy them the task of initiating Bridgie Crump into the joys of lesbian domestic harmony. 'I've just realised,' she said brightly, 'that in one fell swoop Beth has reinvented herself as the bad girl of the family. I'm off the hook for ever!'

Tipsily, Evie got off the tube at the wrong stop. As she traipsed through the darkened streets she marvelled at how easily Bea had extracted a confession from her about the Great Dan/Aden Deception.

After Beth's scandalised exclamations had died away, Bea had commented shrewdly that it would be ironic indeed if Evie was to fall for Aden after all that.

'Hmm. I suppose it would,' Evie had replied evasively, and not particularly convincingly, before she fell prey to Bea's cunning questions and confessed all. This would never have happened if she and Beth had been alone together, but Bea had a way of getting to the heart of things. Crumps tended to paddle at the edge of serious subjects.

It was surprising, therefore, that the most challenging angle on Evie's forthcoming date came from Beth. Perhaps she was taking lessons from Bea.

'If Aden really, really likes you,' said Beth, leaning back on a ripped cushion, 'you mustn't go out with him unless you really like him too. It wouldn't be fair.'

'Fair schmair,' Evie had replied blithely.

It was food for thought as she took another wrong turning off Camden High Street. She *did* really like Aden, and these feelings had crept up on her unexpectedly. All the relationships that littered the highways of Evie's heart had been with bad boys. Make that Bad Boys, all of whom had been pretty obviously Bad. And their Badness had not been a bolt from the blue: their failings were neon-lit and helpfully marked by arrows. Bea would probably claim something like *fear of intimacy*: Evie had chosen men whose Badness had inevitably caused a dramatic break-up before she could get too close to them.

Aden wasn't remotely Bad. In fact, he was good. Or Good. Not perfect, of course, or he would be unbearable and fit only for nuns to hang around with. Good, though.

Good is OK. Good is fine, thought the girl who had previously considered only card-carrying bastards as snog-fodder. Good might be fun for a change. After all, love is where it falls.

A drunk person has an unerring nose for the next drink. Evie didn't need to get down to the kitchen and read the scribbled note anchored to the table by a chipped sugar-bowl. She drifted up the stairs, following the sounds of inane chatter and giggling to Caroline's door.

A glass of something acrid and cheap was thrust into her hands by Bing, who was wearing deely-boppers. This was hardly unusual, but it was a surprise to see Bernard sporting a pair too. The loosening-up process was evidently continuing.

'No P. Warnes, then?' asked Evie.

'Nah,' said Caroline. 'He's in, though. There have been monkey screeches from upstairs all day.'

To a sober landlady this would have been unsettling news, but Evie simply sniggered and a morsel of quiche went down the wrong way.

'I've always wanted to perform the Hendrich manoeuvre!' shrieked Bing, whipping his muscly arms round her waist.

Evie fended him off, spluttering. 'It's the Heimlich manoeuvre.' If Bing didn't know what it was called it was unlikely that he knew how to perform it. After a minute's coughing, during which the others gathered around her, and watched as if she was a performing seal, the offending crumb reappeared.

'Thank God,' said Bernard gravely. 'I could never live with myself if my quiche choked you to death.'

Bing turned the Pet Shop Boys up to eardrum-spinning levels so Evie had to shout, 'What do you mean *your* quiche? You didn't make it, did you?'

Bernard nodded.

'That's wonderful!' Evie felt like a proud headmistress on Speech Day. Bernard was coming on in leaps and bounds. If only they could do something about his hair . . .

'Gosh.' Bernard was watching Bing dance. 'He's awfully, er, groovy, isn't he?'

'Oh, yes.' Evie laughed. 'And double-jointed. As most of the chorus in *Joseph* can testify.'

Bing was, he often claimed, born to dance. He relished the spotlight, losing himself in the music. He looked damn good and he knew it.

Milly, snuggled sleepily on her mum's lap, woke up and clapped. Evie sidled over to plant a kiss on her cheek. Milly wrinkled her nose. Two-year-olds smell of talc, and alcohol is a grim surprise.

'I didn't suggest all this,' said Caroline hastily, as if about to be accused of something. 'Bing thought it would be nice to celebrate.'

'He always does. He's been known to throw a party because his verruca's cleared up. This time he's quite right. We should celebrate you being reconciled with your family.'

'Yeah. Maybe.' Caroline seemed wary of happiness.

'I see you've got a couple of photos up.' Evie had spotted a picture of Caroline's parents in a frame on the mantelpiece. 'Who's that girl with them?'

'Me.'

'Never!' The grinning young teenager standing between her parents in the porch of an unremarkable semi was scrubbed clean and glowing. A velvet hairband held back newly shampooed auburn hair. What a difference family discord, an unplanned pregnancy and plenty of eyeliner can make.

'I was normal back then,' said Caroline ruefully.

'You're normal now,' asserted Evie gently, taking in Caroline's black layers and stripy black and white tights ending in clumpy men's lace-ups. She glanced at Bing, who had stripped to silver pants and was gyrating suggestively around Bernard. The latter was rooted to the spot like an embarrassed maypole. 'We all are.'

Bing's dancing wore out the onlookers long before it slowed him down. Wedged on to the small sofa, Caroline, Evie, Bernard and Milly all slumped in silence, watching him swerve and leap about. He was dancing very fast to hard-core clubby music but still had the breath to say, 'I've had an idea.'

'What is it?' Evie felt approximately eighty as she watched Bing's thighs, mesmerised.

'Bernard's flat needs decorating. It's the flat of a very old lady, not a young gun.'

Evie checked Bernard to see if he looked insulted. He was as hypnotised by Bing's performance as she was and didn't seem to be registering anything except disbelief that the human form could move so fast. 'So, what's your idea?'

'I'm going to decorate it. Funk it up a bit. The sexy new Bernard needs a sexy new pad.'

From where Evie was sitting the new Bernard needed a stiff drink, but she nodded. If he succeeded in pulling a gorgeous, pouting member of the opposite sex he couldn't bring her home to a sitting room that had been frozen in the mid-seventies and a bedroom that boasted a display of stuffed voles. 'One of your better ideas,' she congratulated Bing. 'I'll let you off a month's rent.'

'No need.' Bing wiggled his arse at warp speed inches from her nose. 'It'll be fun.'

25

It was imperative to keep Sacha away from the house on the day of the date. Sacha would analyse, hypothesise, cast runes, prophesy and ultimately scupper the whole thing. People who have never had a successful relationship, or even a relationship long enough to take in the run of a mini-series, are often the most vocal on the subject. Evie, usually so open, didn't want to share on this occasion.

It was important.

A picnic was the chosen activity. Lots of food and drink in the still-blazing end-of-summer sun in the park. Evie had a favoured tree, near a summer-house, where she and Bing had lounged on many an afternoon drinking beer from the bottle and playing Fuck or Die, a particularly cruel and grisly game. One player suggests two equally distasteful candidates for the other player to sleep with. They must choose one, giving solid reasons for their choice. The only alternative to congress is death. Evie had triumphantly killed off Bing by offering him Sacha or her dad.

With her unerring talent for being awkward Sacha rang at about eleven a.m. from her mobile. 'Just on my way round,' she squeaked. 'It's too sunny to work so I've shut the shop.'

'You'll never make any money like that!' scolded Evie, panicking. 'What if some desperate person badly in need of an, er, phrenology bust turns up? You could damage their *chakra* irreparably.'

'That won't happen.' Sacha didn't sound too certain. 'Will it?'

'You never know. You're doing a public service with that shop. You're a tiny beacon of spirituality in a materialistic world.

You're the only outlet for lunar calendars for fifty miles. You can't let your customers down, Sacha.' Evie injected a smidgeon of the wartime Churchill into her delivery. '*Camden needs you.*'

'You're right!' Sacha's head was successfully turned and she strode zealously back to Calmer Karma where she spent the rest of the day reading old *Psychic Weekly*s, disturbed only by an elderly lady who needed directions to the nearest post office.

Evie had the flat to herself. Bing had disappeared upstairs long ago in his decorating garb of pink-towelling hotpants and a medallion. Several large tins of white paint and a stack of hardwood flooring went with him. 'You can't see it till it's finished,' he instructed. 'Think of it as your very own episode of *Changing Rooms*.'

Hair washed and dried, armpits shaved and sprayed, lacy thong and matching bra on, fake tan applied to milky legs, Evie took a deep breath and opened her wardrobe door.

It wasn't inspiring. Aden had seen her in all manner of outfits, some of them remarkably unflattering, so she couldn't go all glam on him, it would seem incongruous. But Evie always went glam on a date – it was what she understood. But this isn't about making him fancy me, Evie thought, it's about getting to know each other.

What do you wear to get to know a man? What does it mean vis-à-vis cleavage? There was probably some official ratio of boob visibility to relationship viability of which she was entirely ignorant. In Evie's cupboards there seemed to be no sartorial middle ground between lying-on-the-sofa-watching-*EastEnders* and here-I-am-boys-come-and-get-me.

What was that sky-blue fabric peeking out at one end of the wardrobe? Evie pushed the crowded hangers out of the way and extracted a dress she didn't recognise. It was pale blue cotton with a neat, fitted bodice and a knee-length straight skirt. The thin straps were gingham. It was both sexy and wholesome, and she had no recollection of buying it. She had gone through a phase of buying period clothes, but they'd all been dusty granny coats and wacky hats, not a perfect fifties gem like this. It had to have been

Belle's. She had stuffed a selection of Belle's things into various drawers and cupboards, meaning to go through them later.

Excitedly she pulled it on, praying it would fit. The zip whispered up her backbone like a kiss. They certainly knew how to build dresses in those days, thought Evie, as she rotated happily in front of the mirror. Her bosom, though mostly concealed, was perked up no end. The seams on the bodice carved inches off her junk-food midriff. The tulip shape of the skirt transformed her child-bearing hips into hour-glass ones. She felt light and bright and ready to skip. It brought out her inner Doris Day.

Unfortunately for Aden's stomach, nothing could bring out Evie's inner Delia Smith. The beautiful wicker picnic basket (picked up at a car boot for a quid) was not filled with homemade delicacies to tempt the palate. Evie had dashed madly around the supermarket, swooping on Scotch eggs, pork pies, just-on-the-sell-by-date sandwiches, ham pinwheels and two bottles of own-brand champagne. A litre of the finest chocolate milk completed the sophisticated menu.

Evie crammed it all in and lifted it. Blimey, it was heavy. As she hoisted the hamper inelegantly on to her arm, she saw that it had been sitting on her script. Despite its ragged appearance – it had travelled everywhere with her, from bus to bath to bed and back again – it was still unread. 'Two weeks is plenty of time,' she consoled herself, turning it over so the title page could reproach her no longer. The back of it, she noticed, was covered with noughts and crosses and a small Biro portrait of Robbie Williams. She would read it from cover to cover when she got home, she promised herself.

Honest.

Packed buses and antique hampers don't mix. As Evie sweated and battled to push her way off the bus her inner Doris Day receded and her inner Charles Manson came to the fore. 'Excuse *me*,' she snarled, in serial-killer tones to a little boy before she stepped off at the park.

She tottered through the gate. She loved the feeling she got when she entered the park. It was as if a heavy invisible curtain had fallen between her and the swarming London streets only a footstep behind her. Suddenly birds were singing, flowers were showing off and the faint sound of a distant brass band could be heard on the breeze.

Butterflies, as if self-consciously completing the rural theme, skittered by. There seemed to be some trapped in Evie's chest too. Big buggers, they were beating their wings so hard it was difficult for her to catch her breath. The first time I saw him I thought he was the porter, she reminded herself, unwilling to admit that the prospect of meeting Aden was giving her palpitations.

A criss-cross pattern disfigured the flesh on her forearm. Evie swung the hamper on to her other arm and almost toppled over. The dress might be elegant but its new owner was not.

Having reached the designated tree, she spread a sheet on the grass. Carefully, in the manner of a serving suggestion, she arranged the cut-price goodies. 'Bloody Scotch eggs,' she muttered. 'They look as if they've been raped.' She rotated a paper plate of pork pies and stirred the coleslaw in its tub. 'Stop it,' she whispered to herself. 'It's only Aden. He doesn't care whether or not your sausage rolls are perky. *It's only Aden.*'

'What was that?' It was only Aden, standing over her, blocking out the sun.

'Oh!' Evie was on her feet as if the grass had electrocuted her behind. 'You!'

'Yes. Me!' Aden made a wry face. 'Your date.'

Those butterflies had slipped on some hobnail boots. 'Oooh, sounds funny, doesn't it? *Date?*' Unable to control herself, Evie found she was pulling a wry face.

'It is a date, isn't it? Jesus, have I got this wrong?'

'No! You didn't! You're right! It's a date!' Evie's volume switch had careered out of control. 'Sit!'

Obediently Aden sank on to the sheet. 'Wow. Look at all this grub. I *love* pork pies!'

Concentrating on taking nice deep breaths, Evie endeavoured to conquer her nerves.

Aden was reassuringly just like he always was. The fluffy hair, the faraway green eyes, the warm smile were all the same. Nothing to get nervous about. She'd seen those dark jeans and that khaki T-shirt before. Aden hadn't transformed into some superhunk overnight just because they were on a date.

The champagne bottle lolled suggestively in the basket. 'Here. Open this.' Evie handed it to Aden.

'The perfect accompaniment to cocktail sausages.' Aden took the bottle. 'I'm crap at this.' A minute later the sheet was doused with fizz. 'I did manage to get some into the plastic cups.' Apologetically, Aden leant across and handed one to Evie.

Gratefully she gulped down some champagne. It warmed the pit of her empty stomach and sent tingling waves of energy to her extremities. 'Open the other one.' A touch of tipsiness might help.

'Oh, no, you don't. We're not getting pissed, young lady. If we're going to have a real date it would be nice to remember at least part of it.'

Evie frowned.

Aden laughed. 'Looking at me like that won't make any difference. Now, how much of this stuff is safe to eat?'

'Hardly any of it. It's worth the risk, though, don't you think?'

'Absolutely. The only thing missing is Spam.'

'I had to draw the line somewhere.'

'We always had Spam on picnics when I was a kid. Nothing wrong with Spam.'

'We never had picnics,' admitted Evie. 'My mother could never fit all her neuroses into a hamper.'

'I've met your mother. Won't hear a word against her. Damn fine woman.'

'She speaks very well of you.' Evie raised an eyebrow. 'Even though she thinks your name is Dan.' She popped a Scotch egg with practised ease.

'I like the way you handle a snack item,' said Aden admiringly. 'You didn't drop a crumb. Think I'll try some of this salmonella on a stick.'

It's hard to stay upright on grass. It seems to beckon the body downwards. Soon they were on their sides. Evie was relaxing nerve by nerve, cell by cell. Aden was relaxing to be near and perhaps it helped that they had a sheet covered in crumbs between them. They hadn't touched each other yet.

'I feel we need to ask some date questions,' said Evie.

'Shoot.' Aden lay back with his arms behind his head. 'I'm an open book.'

'Most recent relationship?'

'Tamara Denskowitz. Complicated name for a complicated girl. She was a scientist.'

'Oh.' This wasn't what Evie wanted to hear.

'Very beautiful.'

'Right.'

Evidently Aden had caught her tone. 'Wore too much makeup, though.'

'That's awful. I *hate* that.'

'And her bum looked big in everything.'

Evie scowled at him. 'Honesty only, please. Why did you break up?'

'Because it wasn't going anywhere. We'd said everything we had to say to each other. Does that sound harsh?'

'It sounds very grown-up compared to the reasons I break up with guys.'

'For example?'

'If we don't count Dan . . .'

'Let's never count Dan again.'

'OK. Well, the bloke before him . . . we split up because he wouldn't stop talking about Liz Hurley so I threw his Simpsons mug at him and it broke.'

'Perfectly understandable.'

'And the one before *him*, we split up because he thought it was funny when my skirt fell off on Oxford Street.'

'But surely it *was* funny?' queried Aden.

'I'll ignore that.'

'OK. My go. Have you ever kissed a girl?'

That was a tricky one. To buy herself time Evie slowly masticated a mini quiche. The truth was she *had* kissed a girl. But was it wise to admit it? Aden would be either titillated or repelled. 'Well . . .'

'That sounds like a yes.'

'Yes. I have.' Evie raced through the story. 'I was at a party at drama school. I was as drunk as a monkey and this older girl dared me and I can never say no to a dare. So I kissed her.'

'Did you enjoy it?'

Oh, Christ. She shut her eyes. 'Yes.' She opened her eyes to check his reaction.

Aden was smirking. Funnily enough, he seemed to be relishing her discomfort.

'But,' she concluded truthfully, 'I've never wanted to do it again. I missed the stubble.' Evie started to gather up the crumpled sheet. 'Fancy a walk?' That was the kind of romantic thing couples did in films.

'Sure. Let me take that.' Aden stood and reached out for the hamper, staggering as he took it. 'Whoooah. Is it made of lead?'

'Sorry!'

They ambled off across the grass. Their bodies weren't touching. Aden was rendered lopsided by his wicker burden.

'Great dress, by the way.' Aden said it abruptly, without looking at her. 'Suits you,' he added curtly, with a brief nod in her direction.

How unlike his friend. Dan would have paid her a flowery compliment and rammed his tongue down her throat. Evie smiled. She believed Aden; she had never quite believed Dan. 'I think I should put my arm through yours,' she declared, in a schoolmarmy way.

Aden looked surprised.

'That's what people do on dates.' Evie slipped her hand through the crook of Aden's elbow. She felt him tense, then draw in his arm, trapping hers.

'How are your plans to matchmake your tenants going?' asked Aden.

'You mean Bernard and . . . Caroline?' At the mention of Caroline's name Evie's old suspicions flared up. 'Why?' she asked, with an edge to her voice. 'Why are you so interested?'

'Who said I was *so* interested?' Aden sounded puzzled. 'I'm just making conversation.'

'They'll never get together, but they're both a lot happier. Caroline has patched up a feud with her family and Bernard has been seen wearing clothes from this century. He's on the lookout for a woman and his flat's being redecorated.'

'When you interfere you really go for it, don't you?'

There was a smile in Aden's delivery but Evie found it necessary to get huffy. 'I don't mean to *interfere*. You make me sound bossy and I'm not.' She glimpsed the shimmering lake. 'We *must* go on a boat! That is *the* perfect date thing to do!' She speeded up, dragging Aden in her wake.

'Bossy? *Bossy?* Of course not,' he muttered, as Evie rifled his pockets for loose change to give the attendant.

It was peaceful in the middle of the lake. 'We could be a million miles away from London,' said Evie dreamily. She slipped a fine white cardigan over her shoulders and tipped her head back, enjoying the warmth of the sun on her face.

'Alone at last.' Aden rested the oars. Their knees met.

Evie gazed into Aden's greeny-grey eyes. 'Hey, you,' she said quietly. 'I think it's time we held hands. Get over here.'

'Yes, Miss.' Aden got to his feet unsteadily and stumbled to her side. He plonked himself down on the plank seat and the tiny boat rocked alarmingly.

Evie gripped the side. 'It's like *Titanic*!'

'A very low-budget *Titanic*,' corrected Aden, offering his palm.

Evie slid hers into it.

'How's it feel?' asked Aden.

'Good.'

'Good.' He grinned at her. Those crinkly bits at the side of his eyes were sexy close up.

Their noses almost touched. 'Now it's definitely time we kissed.' Evie's voice was so quiet it was almost under her breath.

'No.' Aden pulled away.

'No?' Evie yelped. She dropped his hand. 'What do you mean? What's the matter? I thought—'

Aden put a finger to his lips. When she was quiet he said evenly, 'Don't mistake easy-going for easy to manipulate, Evie. I'll kiss you when I'm ready.' He stood up and sat down heavily on the opposite seat.

Evie was silent but her expression was eloquent. Wide-eyed, she stared at her so-called date, a lump clogging her throat.

Aden sighed. Once more he got up and parked himself beside Evie. 'I'm ready,' he said, and took her chin in his hand. His lips pressed down on hers. No rockets went off and no celestial choir warbled. But she wanted him never to let go of her.

Aden's arms crept round her back as he increased the pressure on her parted lips. Evie's breath was becoming shorter and ragged as he kissed her. Eventually they pulled apart, but only a little. Eye to eye, nose to nose, they grinned manically. There were those sexy crinkles again.

When they handed the boat back to the attendant they owed him double the fee and Evie's cardi was buttoned up wrongly.

Despite the weight of the hamper neither of them wanted to go home. The sun was sinking as they strolled hand in hand through the streets. The day was special: they were loath to let it go. Their embrace in the boat had transformed it, as if a black and white film had suddenly blazed into colour. Their date was now a glistening, delicate thing and they were afraid to break it with a loud noise or a sudden movement.

'Fancy a pizza?' Aden nodded at the window of a Pizza Express they were snailing past.

'Mmm, yeah!' Evie realised she was ravenous. Her vow never to eat again, taken hours earlier after the speedy ingesting of three vol-au-vents, was forgotten.

'I always have a Four Seasons,' said Aden, as they sat at a minuscule marble table.

'And I always have an American Hot.' Evie smiled at him. This relationship was moving forwards in leaps and bounds: only a few hours in and they knew each other's pizza of choice. Surely there could be no secrets between them now.

'So, you like the script?' asked Aden.

Damn. A secret already. Evie was obliged to perpetuate the pretence she'd started. 'Umm. Hmm.'

'You're perfect casting for Hepsibah. You'll steal the show.'

'Oh, Gawd. Shush,' said Evie awkwardly, praying he'd go on.

'Hepsibah was just a background character in the original draft. The shooting script is much, much better. She's really fleshed out and believable.'

'You saw the original draft?' Evie hadn't realised that Aden was *that* friendly with Hugh James.

'Yeah. We discussed it before. Blimey, Crump, don't you ever listen?'

The question was playful but if Evie had answered it honestly she would have said, 'Not if you're talking about work, no, not really.' It was more tactful just to advise him to tell her important things in triplicate. If possible he should shout them too.

'Fair enough. I'll do that from now on.' Aden squeezed her knee as a waiter hove into view.

So, they were already planning how they'd do things 'from now on'. Evie liked that so much that she was polite to the waiter, which was by no means guaranteed. She laid a hand over Aden's on the marble without thinking about it. She felt comfortable and ever so slightly floaty sitting beside him. Tonight London belonged to the pair of them.

'I keep wanting to kiss you.' Aden looked grave.

'Is that wrong?'

'It is very not wrong.'

They kissed for so long that when they stopped the garlic bread had arrived and was sitting accusingly between them.

'I just can't wait to get to LA.' Aden tore off a lump of bread.

It had just begun to rain on Evie's parade. Rather hard. When, why and for how long was her new boyfriend (for that was surely what he was) going to L bloody A?

'I went once before,' Aden enlarged, oblivious to the thundercloud hanging over his new girlfriend (for that was surely what she was). 'It was just a flying visit. This time I'll be able to have a good look round, really get a feel of the place. Eight weeks is practically living there!'

The pizzas arrived. As Aden thanked the waiter and endured the performance with the giant pepper mill, Evie's mind raced. Eight weeks! How could he be so jaunty at the prospect of not seeing her for eight weeks when they'd only just got together? She glared at him as he carefully cut his Four Seasons into quarters, imagining him in Ray-Bans, surrounded by bikini-clad girls with breasts as big as their hair.

'Obviously,' he continued, waving a forkful of dough and anchovy, 'the best bit is that you'll be there.'

'*I'll* be there?' This made no sense. 'I don't think I will,' said Evie angrily. 'I'm just about to shoot a TV series. Or had you forgotten?'

Aden was staring at her as if she was mad. God knows, she was used to that but it was unwelcome from him.

'Yes,' he agreed, in a voice he had used only once before when trying to dissuade his doo-lally grandma from singing in John Lewis. 'You're shooting a TV series. In LA. With me.'

Evie stuck out her chin and frowned. The effect was unattractively ape-like but she couldn't help it. Finally she said quietly, 'You mean *The Setting of the Sun* is being shot in LA and you're working on it?'

Aden was very obviously doing his utmost not to laugh. 'You really do need it loud and in triplicate, don't you? Yes, darling, I'm second AD on the show and we're going off to La La Land for eight whole weeks together. Doesn't that agent of yours ever read the contract?'

With Aden's arms wrapped round her Evie felt the thundercloud dissolve. She was off to one of the most glam places on earth, getting paid for it, with her lovely, sweet, kind, funny, fantastic kisser of a new boyfriend.

And he had called her 'darling'.

You can't stroll indefinitely, even when you're in lurve. Midnight found Aden and Evie attempting to open the front door while kissing each other as if it was what they had been born to do.

As they stumbled in, Bing was lugging a ladder down to the basement. His hair, arms and legs were streaked with off-white. Miraculously his tiny pink hotpants were unscathed. 'How was the date?' he asked archly, when they were all assembled in the kitchen and the kettle was on.

'Oh, you know. A date's a date.' Evie's expression didn't match her words.

'The pizza was all right,' offered Aden.

'The boat ride was OK.'

'The picnic was quite tasty, I suppose.' Aden smiled.

'How was the *snogging*?' bellowed Bing.

'It was like this.' Aden yanked Evie to him and kissed her hard. 'Well, you asked,' he said, and nipped off to the loo.

'I thought you said he was shy,' Bing whispered.

'He's *quiet*. And they're the ones you have to watch,' said

Evie contentedly. She went into her room to ease off her shoes, followed by Bing, who was wearing a dazed look.

'This feels really weird,' he was saying. 'I mean, there's no problem is there? No hurdle. No deep dark secret. No inbuilt obsolescence. I know it's early days yet but you look . . .' He studied her. 'You look happy, doll.'

'I think I am.' Evie prodded herself all over. 'I bloody am. I'm happy!'

'About fucking time.' Bing bearhugged her, almost cracking her spine. 'Don't screw it up.'

'Such touching faith in me.' Evie froze, sucking in a giant breath through her nose. 'Can you smell that? Belle's handbag! If this was a couple of days ago,' she giggled, 'I'd be claiming that Belle was signalling her approval of Aden from beyond the grave.' She slapped Bing's hotpants as she passed him on her way out. 'I know better now.'

'Ow,' said Bing.

Sitting very close, like two kittens on a calendar, Evie and Aden ignored their tea and explored each other's bumpy bits instead.

The sitting-room door creaked open and Bing, freshly showered and with a tiny towel doing its best to cover his own bumpy bits, poked his head in and said, 'I know I'm not welcome but I just have to share something with you 'cos I'm so spooked. Evie, I threw Belle's handbag out yesterday. That's all. Goodnight.' Bing withdrew.

'What does he mean?' asked Aden.

Evie, who wasn't at all spooked, said, 'He means you've been approved by the top brass.'

26

There were certain things Bridgie was useful for, baby-sitting, advice on matters Catholic, narrow-minded abuse and suitcases among them. Evie had got to the age of twenty-seven without doing the decent thing and buying a proper suitcase. On the rare occasions that she left the country she always made a pilgrimage to Surbiton first to filch one of her mother's impressive collection of matching travel goods.

At Evie's side, supplying moral support and parent-pleasing manners, was Sacha. Bridgie approved of Sacha, who always wore good shoes and was posh. These particular assets guaranteed Bridgie's high opinion. In her universe posh people were wise, brave, talented, witty and probably related to the Royal Family. If *Evie* had dared advocate the use of crystals to cure haemorrhoids or suggest that Jesus was an astronaut, she would have been laughed at, told off and prayed for in that order. However, Sacha's colourful ramblings received rapt attention from *la mère* Crump.

On this occasion the three women were seated round Bridgie's clinically sterile kitchen table as Sacha explained the intricacies of aromatherapy.

'Who would have thought,' Bridgie was exclaiming, in carefully modulated tones of awe, 'that the smell of lavender could ease the pain of childbirth?'

'Oh, yes.' Sacha was certain. 'It's been proved time and time again.'

Evie, who knew that her mother had kicked a nurse through a plate-glass door while she was delivering Beth, was tired of listening to this barrage of nonsense factoids. 'Why don't we test it?' she suggested testily. 'There's lavender in a pot on the windowsill. How about I tie a sprig under Sacha's nose and you hack her leg off with the electric carving knife, Mum? We can see if she yells.'

'Your problem is you have to turn everything into a joke,' said Bridgie tartly, as she cut Sacha another hefty wedge of (shop-bought) Victoria sponge.

'It's *one* of my problems,' agreed Evie darkly.

'We can't all be blessed with an open mind, Mrs Crump,' said Sacha serenely, and accepted the cake with a queenly nod.

Keenly aware that her mother was as open-minded as the Ku Klux Klan, Evie buttoned her lip.

'Where is it you're going again?' Bridgie's question carried a whiff of exasperation, as if it was somehow Evie's fault that she had been unable to retain this information, despite being told a dozen times.

'LA, Mum. It stands for Los Angeles. Hollywood.'

'Hollywood!' squawked Bridgie. She jumped, setting the tea-things rattling.

Henry rolled over in his basket and broke wind noisily.

Evie flapped an arm against the tidal wave of noxious elderly-dog fumes. 'Wave a crystal in the direction of Henry's bumhole, will you, Sash?'

'Sorry. I don't have the appropriate one on me.'

'You didn't let on it was Hollywood before, young lady.' Bridgie was puce, a colour that had never suited her.

'But Hollywood is in Los Angeles, I presumed you'd know that.' Evie was bemused by her mother's tone, both of voice and skin.

'How am I supposed to know where Hollywood is?' snapped Bridgie. A reasonable enough question from a woman who rarely ventured past Waitrose. 'I thought LA was in New York.'

There was no answer to this, so Evie nibbled her cake, waiting for her mother to go on.

'Promise me, Evie, that you won't take your top off.'

'What are you on about, Mum?'

'You hear all sorts of horror stories about young actresses in Hollywood. It's a den of iniqui-whatsit. You think you're in a respectable family film and the next thing you know everything's turned kinky.'

'Doesn't sound so bad.' Evie turned to Sacha with a snigger.

'*Doesn't sound so bad?*' echoed Bridgie, far too much white showing in her eyes. 'That's the kind of flippant attitude that gets you into their clutches! How do you think your father will feel at seeing your chest ten feet high on posters all over Surbiton?'

'Calm down, for God's sake.' Evie was alarmed at the pitch of her mother's lurid fantasy. 'It's a British co-production of a quality TV series. It's not a porn film and it won't suddenly turn into one either. They're not remotely interested in my chest.'

'But you might get sucked into drink and drugs and everybody doing *it*.'

Evidently it had never occurred to Bridgie that drink, drugs and *it* were readily available, sometimes mandatory, in London. Now was not the time to enlighten her. 'I'll be working all day every day for the whole eight weeks. I won't have time to get dragged into any debauchery. Besides, I'll have my boyfriend there to protect me from the, er, pornsters.'

'Dan? I thought that was all over. Pressure of work, you told me,' said Bridgie, proving irritatingly that she did listen sometimes. Her colour was mellowing.

'I did tell you that, didn't I?' Evie was thinking on her feet. Unfortunately they were two left ones. 'I was just pretending. For a laugh. We're still together, really.'

'For a laugh? What's remotely funny about telling me you'd broken up with a lovely young man like that?' The young really were beyond Bridgie's understanding.

'I was practising acting,' said Evie, with the air of one who does not expect to be believed. 'If you believed me it would prove I was a good actress,' she finished lamely.

'Then you *are* a good actress. Too good. I was only saying

to Daddy last night we'll be too infirm to attend your wedding at this rate, and all along you were still with that lovely Dan.'

'There's one other little thing,' said Evie brightly, hoping to play down the absurdity of what she was about to say. 'Dan's changing his name. From now on he wants us all to call him Aden.'

'Whatever for?' Bridgie was high-pitched and seriously puzzled now.

'He just . . . feels it suits him.'

'But Dan suits him. It was the name he was given by his parents.' Bridgie was impatient with her daughter's generation and their self-indulgent ways. 'It's downright silly, if you ask me. You should stick with the names you're christened with. If we all picked names we thought *suited* us where would it all end? You don't catch me insisting everybody calls me Marilyn,' she ended modestly.

'As in Monroe?' queried Evie sweetly. 'Or Manson?'

'Who's she?' Bridgie stood up and began to clear the table. 'Get out from under my feet, girls. This kitchen is like a pig-sty and it has to be shipshape for three o'clock. I'm hosting this week's meeting of Surbiton Mothers Against Comedians Who Swear.' Bridgie ushered them out to the back garden with the promise of smoothies.

Prone on a lounger, Evie squinted up into the sun. 'Not as hot as it was,' she commented. 'The season's starting to turn. Can you feel it, Sash?'

'Yes. Everything's changing. For *you* anyway.'

'How do you mean?' Evie shielded her eyes with her arm and looked over at her friend, prostrate on the adjacent lounger.

'Oh, you know,' said Sacha reluctantly, as she lay with her eyes tight shut and the straps of her top rolled down. 'A new job. A new boyfriend. And here I am, going in and out of Calmer Karma every day, just like always.'

'I haven't had a worthwhile job or a worthwhile boyfriend for ages. Aren't you pleased for me?' Evie asked.

'Of course I am,' said Sacha passionately. 'You know I am. I just feel a bit . . . Oh, I don't know. Forget I spoke. Here are our smoothies. Yum!'

Beaming proudly, Bridgie set a tray down between them. 'You didn't know your old mum was so with it, did you, Evie? These are all the rage, apparently. You can take your pick, girls. That one's lemon and bacon. This one's a bit special – orange, banana, honey and onion.'

Silence fell until the back door swung shut behind Bridgie. 'It's OK,' said Evie. 'There's a drain just over there.'

'Do you want to come in for a bit?'

Sacha wrinkled her nose. 'Nah. I'd better get back to the shop.'

The two girls were at the corner of Kemp Street, a monolithic tweed-effect suitcase on wheels standing between them. 'OK. Why don't you come over later? Bring a video,' suggested Evie.

'Oh, right,' Sacha said, brightening up. 'I thought Aden would be around.'

'Well, he is. Or he might be,' faltered Evie. 'Does that matter?'

'No. No, no.' It obviously did. 'I'll see what I'm doing.'

This was difficult. Evie knew Sacha well enough to intuit that she was feeling marginalised, left behind. She wanted to shout, '*You're my best friend, you wazzock. I'm never going to leave you behind, you're too important to me,*' but instead she just nudged her and wheedled, 'Aw, c'mon. We can get a blanket out and sit under it if you like.'

'Won't Aden mind?'

'Why should he? He'll be getting two gorgeous gals instead of one.'

'OK. About eight.' Sacha started to walk away, then turned with a minxy look on her face. 'Perhaps I'll give Bernard a go, after all.'

*   *   *

Mercifully unaware of this development, Bernard was just leaving the house as Evie reached home. Gallant as ever, he took the suitcase from her and insisted on carrying it to her bedroom. With his usual White Rabbit distracted shyness he was about to dart off but Evie barred his way. She surveyed him from top to toe, then summed him up approvingly: 'Very nice. Linen trousers. Linen shirt. Open-toed but not offensive sandals. I approve, Bernard, and I'm sure all the young ladies of Camden agree with me.'

Of course, Bernard was instantaneously engulfed by a full body-blush. 'Oh, now now,' he managed.

'How's the redecorating going?'

'It's all finished. Bing has been marvellous.'

'Can I see it?' Vaguely aware that the flat was, after all, her property, Evie was motivated more by idle curiosity than anything else. She wondered if Bernard had managed to tone down the imprint of his mother's presence. Mrs Briggs had smothered him with chintz, lace, ornaments, antimacassars and standard lamps. A few coats of brilliant white weren't necessarily enough to silence the old dame.

Bernard threw open the door to flat C and said, 'Tadaah!'

'Bloody hell.' Evie stepped over the threshold, gawking unashamedly. 'It's beautiful!' Every wall was smooth and neutral. All the swirly carpets had been banished and varnished boards ran the length of the flat. More importantly, every knick-knack had been eradicated. The large sitting room was bare, except for a long, cream sofa of modern design and a sheepskin rug. Bernard's books lined one wall. 'It's so clean and fresh and *trendy*!' Evie was envious. If the rest of the flat lived up to this room, she'd have to put his rent up.

'Wasn't this your mother's room?' asked Evie, as she stood in a bright Japanese-inspired one, straight from the pages of an interiors magazine.

Bernard nodded. 'I think it's time I had a double bed.'

'Absolutely.' Evie smiled down at the futon covered with a crisp white cotton duvet. 'But where's all your mum's stuff?'

'It was time to move on.' This was a subject Bernard evidently found hard to discuss. 'I gave most of it to a charity shop.' He squared his shoulders and said, 'I'm a bachelor now. This is *my* home.'

'Besides,' said Evie gently, 'you don't need a load of dusty old furniture to remember her. She'll always be your mum, Bernard.' He's come so far, she marvelled. Bernard looked *right*, standing in his chic flat in his well-cut clothes.

Apart from the hair.

'Why, why, why, *why* did I agree to have a party the night before I go away?' There was no answer. Evie carried on throwing damp, unironed clothes into her borrowed suitcase.

'Let me help.' Sacha made a move to get off the bed.

'*No!*' Evie adopted a karate stance. 'I'm sorry, Sash, but I'm stressed enough. If you try to help me I'll have to hurt you.'

'Do you need a crystal?' asked Sacha infuriatingly.

'I need another pair of hands, I need an extra twenty-four hours and I need nicer knickers than this sad collection of grey bastards, but no, I do not need a crystal, thank you very much.'

The last thing to go in the hand luggage was the tatty, dog-eared script. Covered in coffee spills, obscenely thumbed but still unread. 'I'll read it on the plane,' Evie promised herself.

The case zipped up, which was surprising. Evie's packing philosophy was 'You never know . . .' So eight weeks in Los Angeles' high summer necessitated snow-boots. After the physical exertion needed to persuade the zip to close round the case's bulging girth, she lay full length on the floor, gasping, 'I'd better get dressed. People will be arriving any minute.'

'I thought you were going to wear that red dress tonight,' said Sacha casually, adjusting her knicker line in the mirror.

'I am.'

'But you packed it. Right at the bottom.'

Evie stared at her friend. 'Why didn't you stop me?'

Sacha shrugged.

'Instead of telling me in forensic detail about the bloke who might, just might, have been looking at your arse in the gym this morning why couldn't you have said, "No, best friend, do not pack the one decent dress you own because you must wear it tonight and actually look nice for once?"'

'You're in a bad mood.'

'*Aaaaargh!*' replied Evie.

'Why not wear this?'

'Because it's . . .' Actually there was no reason not to wear Belle's pretty blue sundress. Ungraciously Evie dragged it on.

'You look lovely,' said Sacha.

'Huh.'

The doorbell rang. The party had started.

'Are we the first? Fuck.'

'Hello, Meredith. May I take your . . .' Was it a wrap? A serape? A cape? A pashmina? A shroud? Meredith was swathed in her customary expensive layers. 'Mmmwah.' She kissed the air eight inches from Evie's cheek. 'Put on a few pounds, have we, darling?' She was wearing every bangle she owned, clanging like a one-man band as she picked her way out to the garden on stilt heels. 'Barry!' she brayed over her shoulder. 'Do keep up, you insufferable little cunt.'

Meredith was not designed to be viewed in daylight. The waning sun lit up the lines on her face as if it were a relief map of Ben Nevis. Her scarlet helmet of hair slipped over one eyebrow. 'Quaint,' she decreed damningly, looking about her.

In Evie's opinion the garden looked delightful. The grass was mown. The ubiquitous fairy-lights were scattered through the trees. A table draped in a floral cloth offered platters of mostly edible food. Chairs were placed in friendly groups. She ignored her agent and asked sweetly, 'How are you, Barry?'

'I've been better.' Barry sneezed and an avalanche of dandruff hurtled from his sloping shoulders. 'We're very busy at the office and I've been unlucky in love.'

'Do change the fucking record.' Meredith waggled her cigarette-holder recklessly. Barry was accustomed to such manoeuvres but Evie's reflexes were slow and her nose was almost singed.

'Let me get you a drink, Meredith.' Evie was keen to move out of cigarette range. 'Gin, isn't it? What do you take with it?'

'More gin,' rasped Meredith. 'Barry will have a lemonade.'

'Vodka,' mouthed Barry beseechingly.

Bing was barman. He had set up the bottles, glasses and ice bucket in the conservatory. 'I'm just trying to talk Bernard into a Sex on the Beach,' he said equably.

'It's a cocktail,' interjected Bernard nervously.

'Yes. That too.'

'Don't get him overheated,' ordered Evie. Can I have one gin and one vodka for my insane agent and her slave?'

All together, like a herd of cows, Beth, Bea, Caroline, Milly, Deirdre, Julius and Charles arrived. There was an outburst of introductions, hellos and you-look-lovelys as Bing speedily plonked a glass of something in everybody's hand.

'And for Mademoiselle Milly, I believe we have a very special vintage.' Bing reached beneath the table and reverently held up a bottle of Ribena Toothkind.

'What do you say to the nice man, Milly?' asked Deirdre indulgently.

'Bluuurgh!'

'Aaah!' cooed her indulgent grandmother. 'Just like Caroline at her age.'

Bing and Evie exchanged a look. It wasn't that different from Caroline at her present age.

A creaking voice, unmistakably Meredith's, was heard to comment misanthropically, 'Nobody said there'd be children here.'

'Is that a witch?' asked Julius innocently, peering out through a dusty pane.

'Yes,' answered Bing simply, sending a shudder of excitement through the twins.

'Let's take Milly to see the witch!' Charles, who had fallen in love with the little girl at first sight, grasped her hand.

'Oooh, I'm not sure. Better ask Milly's mummy first.' Beth shot a questioning glance at Caroline.

'They can't come to any harm,' said the new, improved, not-quite-so-grumpy Caroline.

Bing said, 'Obviously you've never met Meredith before.'

As the newcomers drifted out into the pinkish twilight Bernard sidled over to Evie. 'I've got to go, I'm afraid.'

'No!' Evie's deep-seated fear of throwing crap parties surfaced violently. 'It's only just started! You can't go! *No!*'

'Have you ever considered a career as a diplomat?' enquired Bing, detaching Evie's fingernails from Bernard's shoulders. 'He'll be back.'

'Yes, I'll be back.' Bernard took a pace backward, clearly rattled. 'Honestly. There's something I have to do.'

'Of course. I'm sorry. Take as long as you like.' Evie remembered something and caught Bernard by the elbow as he passed her, causing him to leap a foot in the air. 'I wrote a note inviting P. Warnes. It's on the hall table. Would you drop it through his door? It would be so nice to get the whole house together for once.'

'Of course.'

The devoted but clumsy attentions of the twins were too much for Milly. She burst into tears and was scooped up by Bea. In those capacious arms she was soon giggling again. From the other side of the gnarled apple tree Deirdre sweated gently in an uncomfortable new dress with a covetous look on her face. One minute was all she could take. She approached Bea and pleaded, 'Could I have her? She needs her granny.'

Bea was ignorant of Deirdre's recent history but she was an expert reader of faces. 'She certainly does,' she said kindly, handing over the infant.

'Doggie!'

It was a new and sophisticated word for Milly. 'There are no doggies here, darling,' said Evie erroneously, for Henry had just emerged into the garden, attended by her parents.

'What are you doing here, Bea?' Bridgie was surprised but pleased to encounter her old friend. 'I'm sure I don't know what you see in the company of these young people.'

'Oh, some of them are old souls, Bridgie.' Bea's sly wink at Beth made her choke on her drink.

'Ah, here's Sacha. How are you, love?' Bridgie beamed terrifyingly at her.

Swaying slightly, Sacha informed Bridgie that she was very well, thank you very mush.

'That's a nasty hiccup,' said Bridgie, concerned. 'Did something go down the wrong way?'

A litre of vodka had gone down the right way, but Sacha nodded.

The whirlwind of bangles that was Meredith swept past, headed for the bar at optimum speed. Her glass was empty.

'Oh, Meredith,' Bridgie waved, 'how are you? We're Evie's parents – do you remember us?'

'Of course. Howdyoudo. You must be very proud, et cetera, et cetera.' Meredith didn't break step. She slammed her glass on the bar. 'Fill that up with the same ghastly rot I had before,' she ordered, and added, 'Please,' as Bing was handsome.

'Shame for me,' requested Sacha, who had been caught up in Meredith's tailwind and was now draped over the bar.

'My pleasure, ladies.'

'Oh, and a pint for fucking Barry.'

'Will Stella Artois be all right?'

Meredith looked blank, then irritated. 'A pint of *vodka*.'

'He'sh gone mishing. Where ish he? I have to talk to him.' Sacha leant conspiratorially over the bar. There were peanuts in her hair.

'Who?' Bing was watering down Barry's vodka surreptitiously.

'Who? Who do you think?' Sacha was incensed that Bing

didn't instantly understand. 'Bernard, of course. I'm going to offer myself to him.'

'Hmm.' Bing took her by her shoulders. 'Don't,' he said loudly and clearly. 'Do not.'

'I want to.' Sacha was in the petulant phase of her drunkenness. 'Why shouldn't I? Doesn't me and Bernard deserve love jush like everybody else?'

'You deserve a lot of things but something tells me that Bernard is not the man for you.' Bing poured her a lemonade with a teardrop of vodka in it. 'Get that down you.'

'What would you know?' Sacha had progressed speedily to the mean phase. 'You're gay.'

'You noticed?' Bing was unperturbed.

Suddenly the smooth oozings of Burt Bacharach were swamped by a cacophony of noise from the top flat. P. Warnes appeared to have a funfair up there, staffed entirely by seals.

A host of shocked faces turned upwards. Evie shrugged. 'I suppose she/he/it's here in spirit if not in person.' Flashing lights pierced the dusk. An occasional feather floated down to the party. Bing turned up Burt.

Out of the conservatory, glass with cocktail umbrella in hand, stepped Aden. He looked all clean and new. But, as Evie noted approvingly, sexy, gorgeous and eminently fanciable too.

'Now you can stop watching the door,' Beth whispered in her ear.

'I wasn't!' Evie defended herself. She wasn't that sort of girl.

Beth rolled her eyes. 'Just go and get him.'

Was I watching the door? Evie wondered, as she sidestepped Deirdre, who was jiggling Milly at a dangerous level for a child full of chicken nuggets. Balancing an important relationship with trusty old friendships was evidently an acrobatic feat. Just because she'd acquired a Porsche didn't mean she should leave her old Reliant Robin to rust. Or something.

'Hello.'

'Hello, yourself.'

Aden kissed her and his mouth was like a warm feather bed on a frosty morning: she never wanted to leave it.

'You all right?' he asked.

'Me all right. You all right?'

This fascinating exchange was interrupted by Bridgie. 'Dan!' she screeched. Then, for good measure as she pumped his hand, 'Dan Dan Dan Dan Dan.' She let go of his hand with a final dramatic 'Dan!'

Her husband, distracted from mopping coleslaw off Barry's sleeve, said loudly and distinctly, '*Aden*. Nice to meet you again, son.'

Nursing his hand, Aden smiled and was polite. Perhaps he hoped Bridgie would move on but she took him by the arm and led him purposefully away from Evie. 'Now, Dan – *Aden*,' she stammered, 'now that you and Evie are – what do they call it these days? – *going out*, I think we should have a little chat.'

'I see. Are you going to ask me about my prospects?'

'No. I want you to help me persuade my daughter into some nice clothes. If she's going to be in a telly series she might get her picture in the paper. We can't have her in the national press looking like a bag of spanners. A smart skirt suit and a pair of good walking shoes would do wonders for her.'

Bernard was back. Evie noticed him out of the corner of her eye while she was attempting to stem Barry's tears and turned, incredulous. 'Bernard? Your hair!'

'Is it OK?' Bernard grimaced.

'OK? It's amazing. You look completely different.' And completely handsome. The alarming layers and inexplicable sticky-out bits had all disappeared. A simple short cut with a few spikes on top brought out the lean angles of Bernard's pale face. It also accentuated the deep beauty of his coppery hair. 'My God, Bernard, you've gone auburn,' said Evie wonderingly.

'Bing gave me strict instructions for the barber. I hope I got it right.'

'You did. The ladies are going to be flying at you from all

directions. You'd better arm yourself with a big broom to swat them away.' Bernard had such blue eyes, she noticed for the first time. And such a well-defined torso under that Ted Baker shirt. 'Have you been working out?' she asked disbelievingly.

'I'm afraid so.' Bernard chewed his lip as if he had admitted to some grubby peccadillo.

'That's wonderful!' Evie laughed and slapped her newly attractive tenant on the back. Bernard had made an astonishing journey over the past few weeks. His makeover was every bit as satisfying as those of the women who lost eight stone in a year and amazed their husbands by looking acceptable in a halter-neck whom Evie was always reading about in her mother's slimming magazines. 'I could fancy you myself, Bernard.' She added, 'Almost,' as he began to shrink with embarrassment.

The haircut – or 'smashing hairdo', as Bridgie described it – was the talk of the party. A tidal wave of compliments washed over the cringing Bernard, and Meredith was witnessed hastily reapplying her bloodcurdlingly red lipstick. The change in Bernard's appearance even pierced the membrane of Sacha's squiffiness. 'He'sh good enough for me now!' she informed Bing.

Bing remained Sphinx-like, saying nothing as he watched Sacha trot unsteadily in a meandering route Bernardwards, then fall into a bush.

'We should help her.' Bea was uneasy about leaving her to lie there.

'Let somebody else help her.' Beth stopped her getting up from where they sat on scattered cushions on the grass.

'You're a very selfish woman.'

'About you I am.'

Beth and Bea held each other's gaze for a long moment. Any onlooker might have wondered why the younger woman seemed about to burst with happiness and why the older one seemed so serene and satisfied. Any onlooker would have had to conclude they were in love.

Unless that onlooker was Bridgie. 'What's that face for? Is your stomach giving you gyp again?' she asked Beth, managing to present concern as a scolding. 'Oooh. Ouch.' She winced as she bent her stiff knees to join them at floor level. 'You'd think they'd supply proper seats for us OAPs, wouldn't you, Bea?'

'Yes. Us poor old crocks need looking after. Past it, we are. Over the hill.'

'*Bea*.' Evidently Beth couldn't bear to hear her talk like that, even in jest.

'I wouldn't go quite that far,' reproved Bridgie. 'I like to think there's some life left in me. Only this morning I signed up for an Esperanto class.' She frowned over at the bush. 'What *is* Bernard doing over there? He seems to be struggling with that shrub. Oh dear!' Bridgie was surprised to witness Sacha emerging. 'They must be practising a magic trick. Sacha's pretending to have no strength in her legs.' Posh people, according to Bridgie, did not get drunk. 'It's nice to see them getting on. She could do a lot worse than that Bernard.'

It was exactly this sentiment that Sacha was attempting to convey to Bernard as he manhandled her across the lawn. 'I always thought you were a geek,' she confided, as she drooled on to his chest, 'but now I am reconshidering,' she added generously.

'Good. Good.' It took so much energy to support Sacha's drooping frame that Bernard had none left over to be alarmed. 'That's jolly nice of you. Thanks ever so,' he wheezed, as he folded her into a deckchair.

'Don't leave me!' pleaded Sacha, dramatically.

'Um . . . OK.'

Bernard wasn't ardent enough for Sacha's requirements but he'd do. She could work on him, her sozzled brain decided. 'Oh, Bernard.' She sighed, gazing up at him, her air of erotic mystery slightly marred by the mascara smudged down one side of her face and the grass stains on the other.

*   *   *

Aden and Henry were looking for Evie and discovered her in the kitchen. 'This old fella needs a drink,' Aden pointed at Henry, 'and this one needs a kiss.' He didn't have time to point at himself before he was engulfed by his lady love.

'Let's send everyone home,' Evie suggested, close to his ear, 'and snog recklessly until the sun comes up.'

'That's a lovely idea, beautifully put, but I don't think we can.'

'Never mind. I'll just have to wait until they all sod off, then rip your kecks off.'

They kissed again, bodies entwined like ivy on a stone column. A loud whine from the kitchen floor reminded them that they were not alone.

'Henreeeee!' Evie smothered his grizzled old snout with kisses then gave him a bowl of water.

'Hey.' Aden pulled her to her feet. He looked serious. Cute, but serious. He held her by the shoulders at arm's length. 'Just so you know, I'll say it again. I'm not like Henry.'

'Of course you're not. You're a completely different colour. Your ears aren't floppy, I've never seen you in a leather collar and your breath doesn't smell of Pedigree Chum.' Evie tried to put her arms round him again but Aden held her away.

'What I mean is, you're not going to get away with treating me like Henry. You're not going to get away with your usual tricks, the games, the scheming. *This* is what intimacy is – two people just being together, being honest, being a partnership.' Aden shook her slightly to stop her squirming. 'Got that? No agony-aunt theorising. No self-help shit. Just you and me. Neither of us is the boss. OK?'

'OK.'

'Good. Oh, and another thing,' Aden said gravely, 'it'll be fun.' He surrounded her with his arms and squeezed her with life-threatening intensity.

Even while she was relishing the pressure of his arms Evie was promising herself, No games. No strategies. Definitely no games or strategies ... Although I *will* get him to chuck out that revolting leather blouson. She jerked her head back. 'Can you smell that?' she asked urgently. 'Can you?'

'No. What? Is it Henry?' Aden sniffed the air questioningly and Henry hung his head.

'No. No. A nice smell, sweet. Sort of roses and talcum powder. It's faint but ...'

'Nope. Sorry. Hang on! Yes, I can. Just. What *is* it?'

'Just a message from a friend.' Evie snuggled contentedly into Aden's shirt.

John Crump was at the kitchen door. 'Come on, you lovebirds. Young Bing's rounding everyone up for a speech.' The woody aroma of his pipe chased away the delicate floral notes.

Out in the garden the unmistakable sound of a steam engine at full throttle spilled from the top windows.

In an atypical burst of helpfulness Caroline was topping everyone up with £3.99 sparkling stuff that tasted fine until it reached your throat.

Gathered in a little semi-circle they all looked well, thanks to the thoughtful lighting provided by the pink, pearly setting sun. The slightest of breezes tickled bare shoulders. Summer was saying goodbye.

Evie unfurled herself from Aden to look up at the back of number eighteen. She'd overseen a lot of alterations to the distinguished but elderly building since Belle had passed it on to her. A lot of paint, paper and elbow grease had been applied. And not only the fabric of the house had changed: Evie looked at Bernard with his new haircut and confidence, she watched Caroline tut at the way her mother had combed Milly's hair. She reached out and took Aden's hand. So much had changed, so much had stayed the same. She recalled a fragment of the letter from Belle that Mr Snile Jr had given her: 'Only the folk who were really meant to live here have approached me.' 'Belle approves of what I've done,' she whispered to herself. 'I know it.'

The Reluctant Landlady

Bing tapped his glass for hush, and stepped up on to a crate. 'We're here today to say *au revoir*, not goodbye, to someone who is very special to all of us.'

'Who?' screeched Meredith, the sharpness of her tone causing Barry to burst into tears again.

Ignoring her, Bing continued, 'We'll miss her. Well, *I* won't but some of you might.' Bing glanced over at his victim, who stuck her tongue out at him. 'Well, all right, I admit it. She's like the sister I never had.'

'You've got four,' Evie corrected him.

'Who's making this speech?' Bing hissed at her, before resuming. 'This is a big step for Evie's career. She's going to be brilliant in *The Setting of the Sun* and I have a hunch she's going to be a famous actress one day soon. We'd better make the most of her 'cos she certainly won't call us when she's made it.'

The partygoers laughed, confident this wasn't true. (Although in Meredith's case it most definitely was.)

'She's been a good friend to me,' Bing said, with feeling, 'so it's wonderful to know that not only is her career looking up but she's found herself a decent bloke.' He gestured at Aden. 'It's a tough job, mate, but somebody's got to do it.' While the guests giggled and Aden circled Evie's waist with one arm, Bing raised his glass. 'To Evie,' he said, with drama-school diction. 'Have a fantastic eight weeks away but don't forget to come back.'

'To Evie!'

Hearing her name on the lips of the mismatched crowd was unexpectedly moving. Evie found she had little voice to squeak, 'To you!' in reply. Embarrassed, she wiped her eyes as Aden cuddled her and everyone *aaah*ed with the exceptions of Caroline and Meredith, who yawned and requested gin respectively.

Still up on his crate Bing appeared unwilling to step down. After everyone had raised their glasses and sipped, he carried on. His voice was so unusually charged with emotion that Evie found herself forgetting to gaze at Aden and stared hard instead at her flatmate. 'Every so often, folks, Evie says something memorable to me and I can't take the mickey out of her. She was the one who told me that love is where it falls. I think we all know that's true. *To love!*' he shouted, with that actorly projection he could always dig up when he needed to.

Evie didn't echo, 'To love!' and raise her glass with the others. She watched Bing's line of sight. She followed it to Bernard. Who winked at him.

Evie stood with her mouth open as Bing stepped down and made his way towards Bernard. He held out his hand. Bernard took it and held it to his heart. Together they pushed through the throng to stand in front of her.

Bing looked sheepish for perhaps the only time in his larger-than-life life.

'Why didn't you tell me?' It wasn't fair to sound quite as whingey as Evie did but she couldn't help it.

'Some things you can't share. Not until the time is right.' Bing put his head on one side. 'Maybe you can understand that these days, doll.'

'Well, of course I can, you idiot.' Evie stood on tiptoe to throw her arms round Bing's neck. She hugged him tight to suffocate her own ungracious feelings of being left out. 'Of course I can.' She pulled away. 'Bernard, you sly old dog.'

'Oh, gosh, hardly,' Bernard stammered.

'When did all this start? Hang on, I know.' Evie narrowed her eyes, sleuth-style. 'It was the night of the Manhattan Dreams fiasco, wasn't it?'

Bernard and Bing nodded manically, infected with the over-enthusiasm of the newly besotted. Bing said, 'Poor B was in a bad way. I sat with him until he calmed down and then we talked. For hours. I'd never taken much notice of him before that night. I wasn't looking for a partner, I was on the lookout for fun, but then we talked. Hours went by in a flash and I discovered that he was fascinating and deep and caring and . . .'

'Do shush.' Bernard was writhing.

Evie was marvelling that Bing was describing a man without reference to his arse.

'And he has a *fantastic* arse.'

Reassured, Evie said, 'So that's why you've been coming straight home from the show every night. I thought you were ill when you were just faithful.'

'Yup. That's a new one for me and I like it. Every time you closed your bedroom door I was off up the stairs like a guided missile.'

'I still can't get my head round this.' Evie stared at the pair, hip to hip and shoulder to shoulder. 'I mean, Bernard, if you knew you were gay why did you let us drag you into that terrible nightclub and aim you at all those girls?'

'I didn't know what I was.' Bernard struggled to overcome his natural reticence in order to express himself. 'I was just . . . me until Bing came along. When we sat down and talked I thought, Ah, here you are at last.' He gestured despairingly with his pale hands. 'I can't describe it any better than that.'

'You don't have to.' Evie pulled Aden to her. There *he* was at last.

'There's one more thing and you're not to shout,' Bing said. 'I'm moving out.'

'You can't. I won't let you.' It was unreasonable and selfish, but that had never stopped Evie before.

'I'm only moving upstairs. Bernard and I are going to suck it and see. Oh, don't you love it when he blushes?'

'Oh.' Evie felt as if the ground was shifting beneath her flip-flops. 'But you'll still come down for *The Antiques Roadshow*?'

'Yes.'

'And you'll still be on call for spider-removal duty?'

'Yes.'

'And you'll still laugh in my face and make sarcastic remarks about me and tell me I dress as if there are no lightbulbs in my bedroom?'

'Trust me, that will never change.'

'Then you can go.'

'Thanks, ma'am.'

Aden pointed out that if Bing was leaving, the flat would be empty for eight weeks.

'And?' asked Evie stupidly.

'Maybe Beth could use it.'

'Beth! Beth!' Evie waved her sister over. 'Have you found somewhere to live yet?'

Beth hadn't and was thrilled with the offer of the basement for eight weeks. 'It'll get me away from Henley and give me some breathing space,' she said excitedly. 'Thank you, sis.'

'Shucks. It's nothing. Hey,' said Evie, 'now that Bernard's turned this into a coming-out party maybe you and Bea should follow his lead?'

They both turned to seek their mother's face. She was lecturing Deirdre on the peril posed to modern society by allowing *Blue Peter* presenters to drink alcohol. 'Perhaps not,' they concluded in unison.

Then Aden pulled Evie back into their own private bubble. 'All change for Evie, eh? You OK?'

Evie assured him that she was. *And I am*, she told herself firmly, unwilling to accept that she was slightly overcome. She felt a sharp pang of empathy for what Sacha had been experiencing. 'Where's Sacha?'

The deckchair was empty. The shrub had proved irresistible. Sacha was once more in its leafy embrace, only her feet visible to the observer.

Bridgie, hurrying out of range of Barry's breath and Meredith's ill humour, noted the size fives protruding out of the bush. She beckoned Evie over.

Whoops, thought Evie. My mother is just about to discover, at this late stage in her life, that posh people get drunk too.

Bridgie, however, was a dab hand at denial. Bending down to take a closer look at Sacha's feet she was saying dictatorially, '*Those* are exactly the sort of shoes I want to see you in.'

'All right, Mum. I'll buy a pair tomorrow.' Evie distracted her mother with talk of toning separates while Aden and Bing hauled Sacha back to her deckchair.

'S'cuse me, Mum.' Evie cut her off in mid-flow about the unbelievable benefits a well-cut raincoat would bring her in LA. She wanted to make sure that Sacha was all right.

As she tucked a moth-eaten blanket of dubious provenance around the snoring figure, Evie experienced a rush of tenderness for her confused, confusing friend.

'She'll be fine,' said Bing airily. 'Tough as old boots. It's the blanket you should be worrying about.'

'She won't be pleased when she wakes up and hears about you and Bernard.' Evie stroked a tendril of damp hair back from Sacha's forehead. 'You're greedy, you know that? Can't you leave any men for us poor heterosexual women?'

'Can I help it if I'm sexual catnip?' Bing flexed his biceps.

'All around me people are turning out to be gay at a rate well above the national average.' Evie frowned. 'Why don't I notice? I didn't cotton on that my own sister was a lesbian, or Bea. And now Bernard . . . I just don't listen to my friends, I suppose,' she concluded sadly.

'Or maybe everybody in the world is gay except you,' suggested Bing.

'I'm not.' Aden was at the conservatory door.

'That sounds like a challenge.' Bing loved a dare.

'Oi! You're monogamous now. And, besides, he's mine,' warned Evie.

'Oh, yeah.' Bing sighed. 'I forgot.'

'There's something else we forgot.' Evie scrambled over to the crate and clambered up on to it. 'Ladies and gentlemen. And Bing,' she said loudly. Expectant faces turned towards her in the purplish night. 'There's one more toast. To Belle!'

'To Belle.' They all drank to the absent old lady while the trees whispered to one another above their heads.

Evie could almost, *almost* smell it—

'*Hey!*'

The solemn moment was shattered by a shout from a short fat man with negligible hair striding down the garden at a furious pace.

'P. Warnes?' Evie leapt down from the crate. 'Are you really P. Warnes?'

'I certainly am.' P. Warnes, clad in a stained boiler-suit, was walking so fast that he almost toppled over when he halted abruptly in front of his landlady.

'I am *so* glad to meet you at last,' gushed Evie, and held out her hand.

Ignoring it, P. Warnes snapped, 'Will you please keep the bloody noise down out here?' He wheeled round and, with a curt 'I thank you', bombed back into the house.

After a shocked pause the giggling began, ripening into hearty laughter. Somewhere in the mix, along with Bing's guffaw, Meredith's phlegmy cackle and Evie's freeform yelping, was the wry, delicate, knowing laugh of Belle O'Brien.